AN UNEXPECTED JUNE

A NOVEL

L. B. JOYCE

An Unexpected June
PRINT ISBN: 9780960031184

ALSO BY L. B. JOYCE

Twelve Months, Twelve Love Stories

A Million Decembers

For the Love of July

February's Angel

Promise Me November

An Unexpected June

A January to Remember

September's Moonlight Serenade

Goodbye Heartbreak, Hello May

March, a Song and a Dance

~

Holidays in White Oaks Valley

A Grand Slam Kind of Christmas

Book 5... can you believe it?

Who would have thought, what started as a simple attempt to write just a single book would turn into a series about such a remarkable and lovable cast of characters? My biggest hope is you enjoy reading about them as much as I love writing their stories. I know sometimes they might seem a little mixed up and do crazy things, but all's well that ends well. As it's been said so many times, love always prevails. Enjoy!

One day, someone will come into your life and
you'll realize why it never worked with anyone else.
~ Unknown

CHAPTER 1

George cleared his throat.

Quite loudly, he did this.

"Livy, as Director of Human Resources, I'm afraid I have some unexpected news in regard to your position here at the company."

What?

This certainly was *not* what Livy had expected to hear. When George called, asking her to stop by his office, she thought it was about the latest book series she'd recently finished editing.

She was very proud of that job. The chief editor had been happy, the author had been happy and Livy had been happy. Three out of three. All happy. You can't get any better than that.

But now this?

You know that feeling you get when your intuition is telling you something is wrong? Your heart starts thumping really hard in your chest, so much so, it becomes a loud echo in your ears. Then your throat suddenly becomes so dry, you can't swallow. If it's really bad, your hands start to sweat, too.

Well... Livy was feeling all this.

And, yes... this would include the sweaty hands.

Because what exactly did he mean by unexpected news?

She peered more closely at George, her mind frantically trying to get a clue as to what he was going to say. He, in turn, ducked his head and began shuffling through the papers in front of him.

This wasn't a good sign. No, this was bad.

In the silence that followed, she stared at the name plate on his desk.

George Eddlebaum, Director of Human Resources.

Yes, George... the same George she considered as one of her more reliable friends.

At least when it came to work, he was. She'd gone to company picnics at George's house. Gone to the movies a couple of times with his wife Sandy. She'd even babysat for his two kids, filling in for a no-show babysitter.

She watched as, the papers now stacked in a neat pile, he finally glanced up to look her in the eyes. The expression on his face was a clear indication of how uncomfortable he was with what was coming next.

He cleared his throat.

Twice, he did this.

"Livy, let me start out by telling you, what I'm about to say is in no way a reflection of your ability to do your job. And certainly, not of you as a person. If anything, the past six years you've been with the company, the dedication you've put into your work and your loyalty to the company, has more than surpassed our expectations. It's only because of major changes being made within the company, we've come to the decision certain cuts were needed to bring about a better flow within the new proposed work structure. Unfortunately, one of these cuts was the elimination of your current position."

When she remained silent, he again cleared his throat.

"You will be given six month's severance pay, along with any bonuses or vacation time you've accrued during your time with us. Please know we will be more than happy to answer any concerns you may have, and you're also more than welcome to use us as a reference in your future job search."

He cleared his throat again and for what she was hoping, would be a final time. "So… do you have any questions?"

Did she have any questions? Well? Yes and no.

First of all, he's wrong. You've been with the J. L. Bagley Publishing Company for at least seven years. Almost seven and a half, to be specific. Shouldn't this count for something?

She looked over at him, shaking her head. "I don't know what to say. I thought… well, I thought everything was good."

He shook his head, his expression almost as distressed as she was feeling at the moment. "And it was. But the company feels this is the time to move in a new direction."

He frowned. "It's these damn indie publishers… they're changing the world of publishing as we know it."

Running his hand through his hair, he gave a long, drawn out sigh. "Livy, I'm so sorry. You know if it was up to me, this wouldn't be happening. I'm only following orders."

He gave her a bright smile. "But hey, I'm not worried. Why, this might be the best thing that could ever happen to you. I'll be willing to bet you find a job in no time… a better job. This could even be the perfect time for you to lay low for a while and start writing that book you've been talking about. In fact, this is what I'd highly recommend you do."

She could only nod, the thought popping in her head she now completely understood what people meant when they said they were absolutely speechless.

Because honestly? She couldn't have uttered a single word even if she'd tried.

Besides that, there really wasn't anything else she could think of to say.

She shook her head.

Nope, she had nothing.

Livy vaguely remembered shaking George's hand and nodding to his request she keep in touch.

He and Sandy would be calling her about dinner soon, he told her. And once again, he reminded her to call him if she needed references. All this came at her as she reluctantly began to back out into the hallway, the severance package he gave her clutched to her chest. The knowledge, that once she left the safety of his office everything would become final, was something she was still finding too hard to comprehend.

Her head held high and George's words repeating like a chant in her mind, she began making her way through the maze of cubicles that took over the entire fifteenth floor of the Manhattan office building.

She had only one goal in mind and this was to escape to the solitude of her office.

What used to be your office, you mean.

This promptly sent a spark of anger shooting through her. What bout all the extra time and effort she'd put into the last seven-plus years she'd been with the company—reaching another deadline, or dealing with yet another hysterical romance writer over editing changes. Never once had she complained about the late nights, or long deadline driven holidays and weekends.

In fact, she was tempted to march right over to the office of the president of the company, Mr. J. L. Bagley himself, and demand he listen to what she thought about this latest development.

Yeah… by the time she got done pleading her case, he'd realize how much she'd contributed to the success of the company, and what a mistake it had been to let her go.

And did company loyalty mean nothing? Because how many of the other employees had been named Employee of the Year? Four times, she'd be sure to remind him.

An amazing achievement in itself.

But then, just like that, the spark petered out.

Because none of this mattered anymore, did it? Like George had told her, almost as though he'd been reciting the words by heart, the decision had been made and there was nothing more to be done.

The pained expression on his face was what had finally got through to her.

There was no bargaining here. No going back.

Simply said, Livy had now joined the ranks of the unemployed.

She'd walked this same path at least three or four times a day since she'd been with the company. But on this Monday morning, never had her destination seemed so far away, the path so long.

Blinking rapidly, to avoid the possibility of tears, and avoiding eye contact with anyone she passed, she made it to her office and closed the door. She leaned back against it and let out a long, shaky breath.

The cardboard box setting on her desk caught her eye right away. Her initial thought was someone had left her more books to work on.

Then it hit her.

The box had been discreetly left for her to fill with her possessions. She knew the sooner she did this, and left the building, the better it would be for everyone.

Employee layoffs were not good for the morale of the company. She should know, she'd witnessed her share of these while working here.

Remember? Seven-plus-years worth?

Oh God... what are you going to do?

She slowly dragged her hands back through her hair, the thought of having to search for a new job enough to make her suddenly feel very, very weary. But then, as of lately, it felt like she was always tired. No matter what she did. Or how much she slept.

Even Zack had commented on this. He kept dropping little hints. Not subtle hints, mind you. No, he had begun to bug her until it was now beginning to be annoying. Throwing out hints she should start eating more healthy foods. Get more exercise. Join some new clubs or groups. Expand her interests. Get out more. Meet new people.

Blah, blah, blah...

Ever since he'd signed up for a gym membership, he'd been after her about this, every one of his lectures ending with his earnest assurance this was only because he was concerned about her.

Look at me, he'd say as he practically strutted around the apartment in front of her. He couldn't believe how much better he felt since he'd started working out. Why, he even had to go out and buy all new clothes.

He'd also brought home one of those fancy, expensive drink blenders. She was constantly finding him in the kitchen, whipping up yet another combination of fruits and vegetables, most of these he'd probably never ate before in his life, let alone even knew what they were. In the beginning, he'd tried to get her to taste these concoctions of his. It was only after his latest, with her almost gagging at the taste before spitting it into the sink, he'd become extremely annoyed with her.

At least this had put an end to him asking her to try any more.

Her gaze going back to the box, she slowly shook her head. Now he'd have even more of a reason to be annoyed with her.

In a relationship with him, for almost the same amount of time she worked at the J. L. Bagley Publishing Company, she knew him well enough to predict he wasn't going to be happy when he found out she no longer had a job.

She sank down into her chair and gazed around at what was almost more of a closet than an office. Besides the desk and the filing cabinet, there was hardly enough room to move around. Add to this the piles of books stacked against the one wall and it was definitely a tight space. To top it off, there wasn't even a window.

Not very inspiring.

But it was hers.

At least, up until about ten minutes ago, it was yours.

The knock on her door proceeded its opening, a face peeking around at her. It was Julie. She was the head editor of children's books. She was also Livy's friend and confident here in the office. The smile on her face rapidly disappeared as soon as she saw the box, all in its glorious display and like an omen, on the desk.

An omen of the worst kind.

Quickly slipping into the office and closing the door, she stared openmouthed at Livy. She pointed at the box.

"Oh my God, please don't tell me that is what I think it is?"

Livy merely nodded.

Julie shook her head. "But why? If they're letting you go, this means none of us are safe. I don't get it. What did they tell you?"

The expression on Julie's face was so tragic, Livy wanted to laugh. Something that saved her from bursting into tears instead. She repeated to Julie, everything George had told her.

Julie kept shaking her head. Over and over she did this. "I'm so, so, sorry. But I know you'll have no trouble finding another job. You have so much experience and everyone respects your work. You're the top requested editor here for romance novels. Why, I've heard there's even a shortage on editors for the genre, since it's the most popular one out there. I bet once all the major publishers find out you"re available, they'll be fighting over you."

Then she closed her eyes, shaking her head. "But this is just awful. I can't think of anyone else in this company I'd rather work with than you." She took a moment to think about this before she frowned. "I don't know how I'm going to be able to come in to work every day if you're not here. I swear, I'll go crazy."

Suddenly, Livy wanted to be anywhere else. She didn't want to talk about this. She didn't want to talk about anything. Or anyone.

She just wanted to be alone. So, she could grieve in private about this newest loss in her life.

Quickly coming to her feet, she had to stop and take a deep breath at the dizziness that overtook her. This was another thing that kept happening to her lately. She wondered, was this a sign of depression? Stress? If so, this latest crisis certainly wasn't going to help matters. One of these times, she was going to pass out completely.

She closed her eyes while she waited for the dizziness to subside, Julie's voice coming at her, as if through a dense fog.

"Are you okay? Maybe the shock is too much for you. Sit down and take some deep breaths." Her brow furrowed in thought, she suddenly started for the door. "A paper bag... isn't that what you're supposed to do when this happens? Breathe into a paper bag? Since everyone in the office brings their own lunch, too cheap to go out, I'm sure I can find one. Let me go check."

Livy waved her hand at her, shaking her head. "No, no... I'm fine. I think it's because I haven't been sleeping well lately." She gave Julie a wan smile. "Even though I've been so tired. But hey, now it looks like I'll be able to sleep as much as I want. I'm also going back home this weekend. Remember? For Carrie's wedding. My flight is booked for Thursday. Carrie wanted me to come earlier, but I didn't want to take off work."

Her laugh was harsh. "Now I don't have to worry about taking time off from work, do I? I can go home whenever I want."

After the long silence that followed her comment, she glanced over to see Julie was watching her, a pained expression on her face.

She gave her a bright smile. "You should go back to work. It might not be a good idea to be hanging out with me. I might be considered a bad influence. And I need to pack up my stuff." She gave a quick glance around her office. "Not that there's much to pack. It's sort of sad this is all I have to show for how long I've been here." As she gazed back at Julie, she felt her bottom lip start to tremble. "Now, get out of here. Before I start blubbering like a baby and embarrass the both of us."

She shrugged. "I'll be all right."

Yeah, she might as well tell herself this.

Because she really didn't have a choice, did she?

CHAPTER 2

*L*ivy trudged up the final flight of steps to her third-floor apartment, thankful her landlord wasn't cruising the halls on her usual search for, as she put it, any unusual shenanigans. The fact Livy was carrying her now almost empty cardboard box would definitely be a tip-off she was no longer employed, something every landlord in the city frowned upon.

After she entered her apartment, she set the box on the kitchen counter, wondering why she hadn't thrown it in the trash container downstairs. Because there wasn't all that much left inside. She'd handed out most of the items to people sharing the subway car with her.

Surprisingly, everyone had been extremely nice to her on her ride home. It probably had a lot to do with the box and what it represented. And no doubt, they were all thankful they weren't in her shoes.

Yes, the evidence you were no longer a part of the work force, put you right there at the top of the loser category didn't it?

One man had quickly jumped up from his seat, dragging his teenaged son with him. Livy was pretty sure the son wasn't even aware of this, simply leaning against one of the poles, while never taking a break from his texting. The father had given her a sympathetic smile as he nodded towards the now unoccupied seat. "I think you need this seat more than we do, so please, sit."

This comment brought a lot of interest her way.

The elderly lady sitting next to her kept shooting nervous glances over at the cardboard box. Finally, and very hesitantly, she had leaned over to peer inside, immediately giving a loud gasp. "Lordy, what in the world did you do to that poor plant, honey? It looks like it's been through the war."

Livy had taken the plant out of the box and handed it to her. "Unfortunately, I think this needed more sunlight than my shoebox of an office provided. So, here... if you want it, it's yours. I'm sure you'll have a better chance of bringing it back to life than I'll ever have. If nothing else, the pot is a nice one. I got it in a gift exchange this past Christmas. I think it's from West Elm?"

The woman had been absolutely thrilled and kept thanking Livy over and over, holding on to the pot and studying it as though it was made of solid gold.

This brought a big smile from the man who'd given up his seat. Along with an actual grin from the mad-texting son. Granted it was a fleeting grin, but hey, it was a start.

A little girl, across the aisle and seated on her mother's lap, frantically kept hopping up and down in order to get a better look at what was going on. Noting this, Livy searched through the box to pull out a set of colored markers and a small dry erase memo pad.

She held it out to the little girl. "Here, this is for you. This is what I used to keep track of all the books I was editing." She frowned down at the pad and pens. "But now I won't be needing them. Do you think you can put them to good use?"

The big smile on her face had almost been enough to make Livy feel better.

Well... almost. Maybe a little.

A balding and middle-aged man, who looked like he'd worn and slept in the same clothing for who-knows-how-long, had sidled over to hand her his card. This was in case she needed representation, he'd told her. At her questioning look, he'd nodded, telling her this was for anything. He was one of the best in the business and could even give her a list of references. His fees were also, by far, the most reasonable in the city.

Taking the card, she had tried to act as polite as possible. Because, hey... who was she to judge?

When it came time to get off at her stop, the box was almost empty. Only two items remained. A framed photograph, taken of her and Zack when they spent the weekend in Vermont over two years ago. And a smaller framed photo of her and Carrie, taken when Carrie came to New York last November. In the photo, they were standing in the showroom of the Gallery East, where they had attended an artist preview show.

As usual, Carrie looked like a model.

And how did she look? She'd never come out and admit this to anyone, but she'd have to describe her appearance as that of a shaggy sheep dog wearing glasses. Even though, from the neck down, she didn't look that bad. She had Carrie to thank for this, since she was the one who'd insisted she buy the dress she was wearing.

Studying the photo now, Livy had to admit, the dress really was quite flattering.

Sam had taken the photo. A friend and business associate of Carrie's, it was the first time Livy had ever met him.

Sam...

She sighed. What was it he'd said? Ah, yes... nothing could take away from how good the dress looked on her.

Come on, you remember exactly what he said. You also remember the way he'd looked at you when he said it. He had you so flustered, you couldn't even respond to his compliment. Not even with a simple thank you.

But she didn't want to think about that night. And she certainly shouldn't be thinking about Sam.

You're with Zack now, remember? You made your choice. And after all the time you've invested in the relationship, you should be happy with the way things are.

True to his word, Zack had remained faithful to her since the little affair he had. Granted, he still hadn't come through on all of the promises he'd made, with setting up a plan up for their future, heading the top of the list.

Which meant they really hadn't talked about getting married, or set any kind of date.

But, everything was comfortable. This is what she liked. And it was exactly what she wanted. It was almost as though they were already married.

She stared off into space. Unfortunately, there was none of the flip-flopping, heart racing eagerness coming at her like she'd experienced with Sam.

If you remember correctly, it wasn't like you and Sam hit it off, at least not in the beginning. If anything, you despised him, finding fault with just about everything he did. Or criticizing almost every word that came out of his mouth.

Suddenly feeling anxious, she ran her hand through her hair as she gazed around the apartment. She wasn't used to being home at this time of day. Since she wasn't quite sure how Zack was going to react to her losing her job, it might be a good idea to make something special for dinner.

She also needed to answer the text Carrie sent earlier. She wanted to know when she'd be arriving in Cleveland. Wednesday or Thursday? And what time?

Thursday. She'd booked her flight for Thursday. This was the only thing Livy could remember for sure.

She would call Carrie later. She briefly considered sending her a text, but Livy wasn't fond of this method of communication. She thought of it as not only impersonal, but very iffy. One of the biggest 'disagreements' ever between her and Zack had started out with a text he sent. To then claim she'd taken what he said entirely out of context. Thinking back on how heated the situation had become, she shook her head.

She looked at her watch. If she started on dinner now, she might even have time to make a cake. Not that there was anything to celebrate.

But then again, this wasn't true. For her, this could be a whole new start in life. A celebration of a new beginning.

Sort of like the start she'd wistfully told Sam she wanted to happen. If she remembered correctly, he'd told her to go for it.

Whereas Zack told her she was too much of a dreamer.

But again, she shouldn't be thinking about Sam.

She only got all worked up when she did.

CHAPTER 3

When I first met her... I knew in a moment
I'd have to spend the next few days re-arranging
my mind so there'd be room for her to stay.
~ Anonymous

Sam Bridges pulled his car into a parking space right outside of Carrie's office.

After he got out of the car, he opened his trunk and pulled out the box holding the printed programs and place cards for Carrie and Chris's wedding. Since he knew he'd be in the same neighborhood as the printer, he told Carrie he would pick them up for her.

It was a beautiful day. A perfect start for not only a Monday, but also for the first day of June. Especially for Cleveland. The sky was a brilliant blue, with not a cloud in sight, the temperature a perfect seventy-two degrees.

He hoped there would be a repeat of this come Saturday. He knew Carrie was starting to second guess her choice of having an outdoor wedding. And this would be taking place on the shores of Lake Erie, no less. It also didn't help it had rained the last five days straight.

When he walked into Carrie's office, she was on her phone. He set the box down on her desk and plopped down in one of the chairs.

Carrie smiled over at him, rolling her eyes. He could tell by her conversation, she was talking to one of the contractors they'd hired for their latest collaboration, a house Chris had purchased in Shaker Heights. In dire need of a total renovation, it seemed like every time they turned around, something else had decided to go wrong. But since unexpected problems were something to be expected when dealing with older houses, Sam wasn't quite ready to panic yet. It also helped they already had a sure buyer for the property.

While he waited for Carrie to end her call, he pulled out his phone to check his messages. Scrolling down through the long line of texts, he groaned.

He shut off his phone. The calls could wait. According to his watch it was already pushing six o'clock. Time to call it a day.

He watched, smiling, as Carrie set her phone down on the desk and eagerly opened the box to check out the contents.

She began chattering a mile a minute. "I hope these don't have any mistakes. After the day I've been having, I don't need any more problems to deal with." She looked up to smile at Sam. "Thanks again for picking these up. I really appreciate it." She paused, looking almost apologetic. "Chris or I could have easily gone to get them."

Sam gave a dismissive wave of his hand. "No big deal. Like I told you, I was right there in the neighborhood. I had to stop at Charlie's to pick out the fixtures for the bathrooms. Which, I was informed, won't be delivered until the fifteenth."

He shook his head. "Thank God, the people that want this house have pretty much given us carte blanc on everything and they're not in a hurry to move in. Because, with all of the delays and extra problems that keep cropping up, who knows when we'll get the job finished."

He smiled at her. "But, forget about that. Right now, you should be concentrating on only one thing and this would be your wedding." He grinned. "You only get married once, you know."

Carrie gave him a brilliant smile. "I know. I can't wait." She suddenly looked anxious. "Even though it's all finally starting to feel real, I'm still finding it so hard to believe."

Sam shook his head. "Carrie, Carrie, Carrie… when are you going to start believing in yourself? And in Chris?"

A laugh came from behind him. He turned to see Chris come striding into the room and right over to Carrie. He took her into his arms and gave her a big kiss before he turned to Sam. "I keep telling her the same thing. The only way I can shut her up, is with a kiss." He grinned. "Not that I'm complaining."

His arm around Carrie, he peered into the box on Carrie's desk. "*Ah… more wedding stuff?*"

Carrie smiled up at him. "I think this is the last of it. Everything else is done."

A worried look came over her face. "There's only one thing I'm not sure about and this is Livy. The last time I heard from her, she wasn't sure if she'd be arriving on Wednesday or Thursday. I sent her another text only a short while ago to see if she even booked her flight. But she hasn't responded."

She sent Sam a sly look. "It would be nice if someone met her at the airport, don't you think?"

Sam shifted in his chair, his discomfort at this suggestion obvious. "*Uh, geeez…* Carrie. I don't know if that's a good idea."

He was confused. "Won't she be bringing, what's-his-name, Zack?"

Carrie made a face, waving her hand at him. "Zack… don't even start me on him. When she came home for my bridal shower, I asked if I should mark him down as a guest for the wedding. She never answered. Almost as though she was avoiding the subject. So, I assumed the answer was a no."

Sam frowned. He was still kicking himself for scheduling a trip to Chicago the weekend of Carrie's shower. If he'd been here, he might have been able to see Livy—get the chance to talk to her. Spend some time together. If only to find out if she still affected him in the same way she had when they were together that November night in New York. What was even more of a bummer, the Chicago lead had been a bust.

It would have been nice if you could've been here. If only for the sake of your sanity.

But, in typical Sam fashion, he'd decided there was no use dwelling on this. What was done, was done. Time to move on.

Even so, he let out a resigned sigh as he slowly came to his feet and smiled over at Carrie and Chris. "Whatever you guys want me to do, I'll do it. Hell, I'll pick up the both of them if need be. What day? Wednesday? Thursday? Let me know as soon as possible so I can plan out the time."

He nodded to Chris. "Remember we have a meeting with your favorite realtor tomorrow morning at nine to check out that new listing."

Carrie groaned. "Valerie?" She shuddered. "I don't like that woman at all. It's good to be aggressive and all, but not the way she goes about it. I don't even want to know how she's managed to close some of her deals."

Chris laughed. "You better be careful about what you say. She's got her eye on Sam... big time. Since she specifically asked that Sam be at this meeting, I'm sure she won't be happy when I tag along. No doubt she's already got some kind of plan in place to seduce him.'

He laughed. "If only to make the sale."

Sam was shaking his head. "I believe you're exaggerating as bit. But I will admit, she can be a little pushy. She definitely doesn't have the traits I find attractive in a woman. Or in a man, for that matter."

He could see the calculating look on Carrie's face. Before she could say more, he began making his way to the door, directing his comment to Chris. "Okay then, I'll be off. I'll see you tomorrow at nine. Then we have the meeting at two with the contractors at the Shaker site."

At Chris's nod, he gave both him and Carrie a mock salute before he left. "Again, if you need anything, let me know."

Chris pulled Carrie against him, dropping a kiss to the top of her head.

At her sigh, he smiled down at her. "Not too much longer, princess." He pressed another kiss to her forehead "It seems like only yesterday, I was still in New York, thinking the only thing I wanted, was to be able to come see you any time of the day. Like this."

She nodded against him. "I know. Me, too."

He started to chuckle.

Suspicious, she pulled away. "What's so funny?"

He pulled her back. "Don't think I didn't notice what you were doing with Sam, asking him to pick Livy up at the airport. Carrie, for all you know, Livy might show up with Zack. You're setting Sam up for a letdown, if not a total disaster."

She shook her head. Vigorously, she did this. "No, I know I'm right about this. I trust my intuition and it's telling me that isn't going to happen." She sent him an anxious look. "But this Valerie... she worries me. You don't think..."

And now it was Chris shaking his head. "Nope, I can't see that happening. Whenever she's around, the only reaction I see from Sam, is complete indifference. And the harder she tries, the more he backs off. If she wasn't so blatantly aggressive with her moves, I'd probably feel sorry for her."

"This is what I'm afraid of, with Sam being such a sweetheart. She might get her claws in him and not let go. I'm certainly not going to stand by and let that happen. Sam is way too good for her." Her sigh was irritated. "She's not fooling me. She'll try to reel him in with all of these promises. I should know."

Chris stepped back, a look of surprise coming over his face before he burst out laughing. "Oh really? Is this what you did to me?"

She groaned.

Oh, geeeez... that wasn't what you meant to say.

"No... yes. What I meant, women are good at finagling to get the man they want."

She closed her eyes, shaking her head.

Where are you getting all of this from?

Evidently, he was thinking the same, an amused expression on his face as he pulled her back into his arms. "Finagling. Now, there's a word you don't hear too much of these days." He gave her one of those crooked smiles she loved so much. "So you finagled me, huh?"

She started to laugh. "I give up. Yes, I finagled you. And I'd do it again in a heartbeat. But seriously, I'm worried about what Valerie might do."

"Ah, baby… I can hear those wheels turning in your head, cooking up some kind of plan. You need to leave it alone. If Sam and Livy are meant to be together, it will happen."

He glanced around the office. "Come on, why don't you close up here and let me take you out to dinner."

He grinned. "Maybe we'll be able to finagle a table outside so we can enjoy this great weather."

The last thing on Sam's mind as he made his drive home was Valerie. No… believe it or not, his thoughts were occupied with Livy.

Yes, Livy.

He still wasn't quite sure how he felt about how she'd somehow settled in his mind, popping out at him during the most unusual times. This happening more often than he wanted to admit, and even more so in the last couple of weeks.

Especially when he was alone.

He sighed. Had it really been almost seven months since they spent such an explosive, yet memorable evening together in New York? Because you'd think, over that substantial period of time, he would've forgotten all about her.

But he hadn't. In fact, she'd become more embedded in his mind than she was those seven months ago.

Since then, nothing seemed right. He felt empty, incomplete, this bringing on a sense of urgency. If he had to describe his life, he'd say he was teetering on the edge, waiting for who knows what the hell was going to happen.

You're pushing thirty-five.

You want to be settled.

He'd even considered buying a house of his own, something he'd already decided he wasn't ready for. But now? He was having second thoughts. Maybe he was ready after all? Or was he at the point in his life he needed something he could call his own? Be it a house, or whatever?

You want a wife... kids... a family

But, as far as relationships go? He was still batting zero. None of the women he'd met over the past few months interested him. Nothing clicked.

Certainly not with Valerie. Just the thought of her had him thinking a solitary life might be the better way to go. She made him so nervous, it was to the point he wanted to turn around and run whenever he saw her.

No, he wanted something more. He wanted that connection. That I've-found-exactly-what-I-want-and-all-is-right-in-the-world kind of feeling. He wanted a relationship like Carrie and Chris had, but even better.

He had the feeling what he was looking for was right under his nose. And believe it or not, this would be Livy.

Call him crazy. No, call him completely out of his mind. But for some reason, and completely beyond his control, he couldn't shake the feeling something was about to change. With Livy being a big part of this change.

He'd tried... believe him, he'd tried really hard to convince himself this restlessness wasn't because of her. After all, they'd only spent a few hours together, so how could she have made such an impression on him?

A smile came over his face.

He'd really be interested to know what her opinion would be about this. No doubt, she'd have plenty to say.

He chuckled. He could almost picture the expression on her face.

He pulled into the parking space in front of his condo and turned off the engine. He studied the row of identical units, the address plaques the only way to differentiate between them.

Yeah, he was ready for more than this.

So much more.

CHAPTER 4

$\mathcal{L}$ivy was spreading the last of the frosting on the cake when she heard Zack open the door to the apartment.

As usual, he was talking on his phone.

She set the bowl in the sink and walked out of the kitchen, nearly colliding with him in the process.

"Whoa… this is a surprise. I didn't expect you to be home already." As he ran his hand through his hair, the expression on his face was almost more irritated than surprised.

Taken aback, Livy gave him a tentative smile. "I've been home for a while. So, I thought I'd make a nice dinner for a change."

She could see he wasn't really listening.

His gaze darting around the kitchen, he zeroed in on the cake. "A cake? Are we celebrating something? You know I don't believe in all of those first date, first this and first that kind of anniversary type celebrations."

Studying him, she was silent. She wondered… when had they stopped greeting each other with a kiss? Or even a hug?

If she had done this same exact thing earlier in their relationship he would have probably whisked her off to bed, telling her the food could wait. All he needed was her.

A sliver of uncertainty went running through her.

Something wasn't right.

Pressing her lips together, she turned and walked back into the kitchen to take the pasta dish she'd prepared out of the oven. Only after she set it on the counter, did she answer him.

"Nope. No celebration. No anniversary. I just felt like doing something nice for a change. I hope you're hungry."

He watched as she took a bowl filled with salad out of the refrigerator before he finally spoke. "Let me go change first."

After he'd gone into the bedroom, firmly closing the door behind him, she went about setting the table. As she added the dressing to the salad and heated the rolls in the microwave, she couldn't shake the feeling there was something he was hiding from her.

Maybe it also wasn't the best time to tell him she no longer had a job? The timing certainly didn't seem right.

Suddenly irritated, she threw the salad tongs into the bowl.

Why don't you just come out and admit it... nothing feels right anymore.

It was only after everything was ready and he still hadn't come out of the bedroom, she went over to knock on the closed door. Her hand raised in midair, she slowly lowered it to her side. He was still talking to someone. But it was the tone of his voice that bothered her. It was different. It was softer, more relaxed.

She felt another sliver of unease. But this time it was laced with an unknown fear. She closed her eyes at almost the exact moment he opened the door.

He jerked back, his voice coming out all sharp. "What the hell? Geeez... you scared me."

And suddenly Livy was mad.

Almost about to cry mad.

She practically spat out the words. "Everything is ready. Can you take the time away from your precious phone to at least pretend you appreciate the trouble I've gone through to make this dinner?"

She turned to storm into the kitchen. She suddenly didn't care if he followed her or not.

But he did.

She didn't know whether to be glad.

Or resigned.

They ate their meal in almost total silence. Two times Zack's phone rang. And both times he reached for it before pulling his hand back, a pained look on his face.

It was almost a relief to finally began clearing the dishes off the table. When Livy picked up the cake and turned around to bring it to the table, she had no idea he was right behind her.

And this is when everything hit rock bottom... literally. Abruptly coming to a halt, she lost her grip on the plate. This sent the cake sliding off the plate and right into Zack, where it then proceeded to slide down the front of his shirt and his jeans. They both looked down to watch as it settled on the floor in a pile of cake crumbs and frosting.

For a few short seconds, they remained silent.

Then Zack stepped back and looking down at the mess he'd become, his voice vibrated with anger. *"Dammit*, Livy... how can you be so clumsy?"

Without a word, she handed him the cake plate, and slipping past him, she walked out of the kitchen. Once she was in their bedroom, she closed the door.

She threw herself down on the bed and closed her eyes.

She was done.

No...

They were done.

Zack scooped up as much of the ruined cake as he could and threw it in the trash can. After he cleaned up the rest of the kitchen and wiped as much of the cake and frosting from his jeans and sweater as he could, he glanced over at the bedroom door. Briefly closing his eyes, he gave an exasperated sigh before he went over and put his hand on the door knob.

He shook his head.

He wasn't in the mood for this right now.

He grabbed his jacket and was out the door, closing it hard behind him.

When he reached the stairs, he paused to send a quick text.

> I'm leaving now, babe. I'll be there in about twenty minutes. Save some of that wine for me.

Livy heard the door to the apartment slam. Pulling the comforter up over her, she cried herself to sleep.

CHAPTER 5

*L*ivy opened her eyes to complete darkness, the silence surrounding her letting her know she was alone in the apartment.

She squinted over at the clock to see it was 3:36 am So, she closed her eyes, her intention to go back to sleep.

But this didn't happen. Instead, she was suddenly very wide awake.

She stumbled her way to the bathroom and turned on the shower.

Her hope was a hot shower would wash away everything that happened.

Or at least clear her mind.

It was obvious she had a lot of thinking to do.

It was only after she'd dried her hair, she ventured out of the bathroom to see if Zack had left a note.

There was nothing.

She was relieved to see he'd cleaned up the mess in the kitchen. But when she saw the ruined cake into the trash, she had to blink back tears.

Wrapping her arms around herself and peering down at the gooey mess, she slowly shook her head.

It's sort of like your relationship... ruined beyond repair, your only option to throw it away.

She gazed around the room, filled with this sudden urge to run. Anywhere. As long as it was far enough away from this mess that had become her life.

And she'd never come back. Because, honestly? What was there to stay for? She had no job. And it now appeared she didn't have Zack.

The keys hanging on a hook by the refrigerator caught her eye. They belonged to the car she'd bought when she first graduated from college. Rarely did it leave its parking space here on the street.

Used only about a half dozen times a year at the most, it was the cause of an ongoing argument between her and Zack. He wanted her to sell the car. But she told him, no, she wasn't ready to do that. She didn't know if this was because she was trying to hang on to when she first moved to New York? A time in her life when she was filled with the excitement of living in a big city and embarking on what was to be a promising career? Or maybe she merely wanted to keep the car as a back-up, in case of an emergency.

Yes, she knew it was on its last legs... or should she say, last wheels... but it gave her a sense of security, knowing it was there if she needed to get away. Or, if she needed to escape.

Like now...

She removed the keys from the hook and for a few moments, she stared down at them in her hand.

This was an emergency, right? And let's face it, if she ever needed to get away, this would be now.

She wanted to go home.

. . .

Three hours later, Livy had packed most of her things in the two large suitcases she'd dragged out of the storage room at the end of the hall. Everything else she threw in the same type of large, black garbage bags Zack had used when he left her back in November.

Since the apartment had come furnished, she really didn't have all that much to pack. As she stuffed the last of her things into the trunk, the realization that seven years of her life had now been reduced to a backseat and trunk full of her belongings, was almost too depressing to even think about. And that most of it was stuffed in garbage bags? This made it seem even worse.

The landlord had grudgingly let her use the service elevator to take everything down to the first floor. This was only after Livy had assured her they wouldn't be backing out of their lease because Zack would still be using the apartment. It also helped it was only the second day of June and the rent was paid up until the end of the month.

She'd sat at the kitchen table for the longest time, thinking about what she wanted to write to Zack. Finally to decide, at this point, it really didn't matter. Evidently, for Zack, nothing had changed, and nothing ever would. Quickly scribbling out her message, she set the note on the table and with one last look around the apartment, she closed the door.

Without another glance, she ran down the stairs.

She started up her car, pulled out onto the street and never once looked back.

Almost another nine hours had passed before a bleary-eyed Livy passed the Cuyahoga Falls exit. This meant in about an hour, she would finally be home.

Thank God...

When she'd left Manhattan, the sun had just begun to rise. So, ideally, she should be home by now. But a major traffic accident and road work had added over two hours to her drive.

So, she was beyond exhausted. She'd stopped for coffee at least three different times during the drive, but the caffeine was no longer doing the job of keeping her awake.

She pulled the visor down against the late afternoon sun and opened her window, hoping the fresh air would revive her. It was then she glanced down to see the gas gage was hovering just above empty.

As she slowed down to pull off at the exit, a loud rattling began to vibrate throughout the entire car. She'd barely pulled into the service station before there was a loud pop, followed by a long hissing sound. Quickly putting the car in park and turning off the ignition, she watched as a huge cloud of steam rose from under the hood of the car.

No, no, no... please, no...

She closed her eyes and dropped her forehead to rest on the steering wheel.

Now what are you going to do?

It took the joint effort of four men—grouped around the front of her car and peering down at the engine—almost twenty minutes to determine there was a major problem with her car. There had been a lot of head shaking going on when they found out she'd attempted such a long journey in a vehicle at such an advanced age.

The final consensus from the group was the car definitely wasn't fit to drive.

After she convinced them she could get someone to come pick her up, her new friends pushed the car to the far corner of the lot. She thanked them for their help, got back in the car and picked up her phone.

She hoped this wasn't an omen of some kind. Because this was not the way she'd envisioned her homecoming would go.

Carrie's phone rang.

When she saw the call was from Livy, she grabbed it and jumped right in with her greeting. "So, you finally decided to call me back, huh? As the maid-of-honor, don't you know you're supposed to return the bride's calls ASAP? There could be a major catastrophe of sorts brewing."

She laughed. "Seriously, let me at least have this one time to be the center of attention."

There was only silence.

Uh, oh...

Just as she opened her mouth to speak, Livy beat her to it. "Carrie, I'm so sorry. This is the last thing I wanted to have happen, but I'm sort of in a bind here. I'm parked in a gas station in Cuyahoga Falls. I had stopped to get gas, but when I pulled off the exit, my car began making all these funny sounds before it died."

After another short silence, she followed with a long, weary sigh. "And now it won't start at all."

Carrie was confused. "But why are you driving? I thought you had a flight booked for tomorrow?"

After another short silence, there was a long sigh from Livy. "I did. It's a long story. And now I don't know what to do. I thought of calling for a taxi, but I can't just leave my car, since I have about everything I own packed in here with me."

Carrie was even more confused. "Is Zack with you?"

"No." This was delivered rather sharply.

Carrie began searching through the papers strewn across her desk for a pen and paper. "Okay, let me see what I can do. Tell me exactly what exit and gas station you're at. Then I want you to stay right where you are and we'll get you home. I'll call Aunt Evelyn, too. Since she was expecting you tomorrow. She'd never forgive either of us if you just showed up and she didn't have enough food for an army, in case you hadn't eaten."

Carrie wrote down the information Livy gave her. "Okay... I'll call you as soon as I figure out what to do. Just hang in there, okay?"

"Thanks, Carrie. And again? I'm really sorry. I guess this was a bad idea on my part."

Carrie could hear the shakiness in her voice. "Livy, it's okay. I'm just glad you're okay and almost home."

As soon as she ended the call, she immediately called Chris. This was because she knew he was with Sam. And even though she knew she had no reason to smile, she was… big time.

This was perfect. She couldn't have planned this better herself.

Yes, this was a job for Sam.

Chris and Sam were just finishing up the meeting they'd scheduled with the contractors for the Shaker site, when Chris's phone rang. He excused himself to answer the call when he saw it was from Carrie.

She wouldn't be calling unless it was important.

The contractors gone by the time her returned, he found Sam going over the blueprints of the kitchen, making notes on his laptop. After he finished typing, he looked up at Chris.

"*Uh,oh…is everything all right?*"

A resigned smile on his face, Chris shook his head. "Well, I'm not quite sure. It is and it isn't. It seems Carrie has finally heard from Livy. The down side is Livy has gotten herself in somewhat of a predicament."

He then told Sam what happened.

Sam immediately shut his laptop and shoved it into his briefcase. "Send me her location and I'll go get her." He gave Chris a puzzled look. "I take it she's alone? No Zack?"

Chris shook his head, no.

Sam frowned. "I only met the guy briefly, but I have to say, I wasn't too impressed. Now, I'm beginning to find even more of a reason to dislike him."

Chris shrugged. "Yeah, I don't know what's going on with that. I only know when Carrie starts talking about him, she gets all riled up. Chester, the same."

He shrugged again. "So, I try to stay out of it."

Sam was almost out the door when he suddenly turned back to Chris. Running his hand through his hair, he exhaled a huge breath. "Wish me luck. From my past experience with Livy—as brief as it was —I learned very quickly how much she hates to accept help from anyone. With me at the top of the list." He shook his head. "In fact, she seems to have an aversion to almost everything about me."

The corner of his mouth lifting in a slight smile, he shook his head at Chris's inquiring look.

"Nope, that's between Livy and me."

He was out the door and gone.

Chris called Carrie to let her know Sam was on his way to pick up Livy.

Carrie was relieved. She was also very happy.

In fact, to Chris, she seemed almost too happy. "Oh good… I'll call her right away. I'm sure she's pretty anxious, wondering how much longer she'll be stuck there. Was Sam put out about having to go to her rescue?"

Carrie heard Chris start to chuckle.

Uh oh…

But she was already smiling. "What's so funny?"

Even though he knew Carrie couldn't see this, Chris was shaking his head. "I've gotta hand it to you, princess. You just might be right about them. Or at least, about Sam. Since I've known him, I've never seen him move so fast. He was out the door like a rocket. Any other person might have been annoyed, but not Sam. If anything, he looked like he'd just won the lottery!"

Carrie laughed. "*Ah ha…* I told you. Remember what I said… fireworks. Lots and lots of fireworks. I think it's going to take some time for the two of them to get it, but once they both finally give in… BAM!"

He heard the frown creeping into her voice. "But we have to persuade her to drop this Zack. Since she told me she had all of her belongings with her, my fingers are crossed this might have already happened."

She gave a frustrated sigh. "I don't understand. What does she see in him?"

Chris chuckled again. "That's because you've got me, the perfect man. There's no comparison between the two of us. Not by a long shot. You don't know how lucky you are, baby."

Carrie closed her eyes, a dreamy smile settling on her face. "I love you. I love you so much."

"I love you, too. I'll see you in a little bit."

Long after they ended the call, they were still smiling.

Livy ended her call with Carrie.

She didn't understand.

Sam?

Nervously running her hand through her hair, she stared down at the phone. Why did it have to be Sam who was coming to get her?

She certainly didn't want to see him. Not now. Not with the emotional state she was in. *My God…* what if she threw herself in his arms and start bawling? Or, going by the way things went the last time they were together, she could very well start yelling at him before he even had a chance to open his mouth. If only because he'd have that nice guy image going on. You know, the one he's just so darn good at.

Remember? That knight in shining armor act of his? He'll come here and sweep you right off your feet. And your imagination will take over, letting you dare to dream again.

She shook her head. There was no way. She wasn't going to let this happen. Remember her vow? She would never rely on a man again. This was her time to shine, her new start in life. And her plan was to do this alone

But right now she needed to freshen up a little bit. She pulled the rearview mirror down to check her appearance.

This turned out to be a bad move.

Could you look any worse? With the dark circles under your eyes, you look like a raccoon. And your hair? It's so shaggy and dull looking. How did you let yourself get to this state?

There was no other way to say it… she was a mess.

She got out of the car and began searching through the trunk for her makeup case. After dragging it out from the bottom of one of the bags, she momentarily considered looking for her contacts.

She hadn't forgotten what Sam said when she told him she was more comfortable wearing her glasses.

"Ah... but by doing this, you're shortchanging the rest of us. You have beautiful eyes."

Where had she packed her contacts?

A quick glance in her packed trunk brought on a resigned sigh. Let's face it... to actually find the contacts would be next to impossible. But this shouldn't stop her from making an effort to improve the rest of her look... making herself somewhat presentable.

You wouldn't be doing this for him, of course. Oh, no... this would only be your way of showing how completely in control and confident you are.

She glanced down at her wrinkled shirt and leggings Not the look she was going for. Searching through one of the suitcases, she finally pulled out one of her better pairs of jeans and the least wrinkled tee-shirt she could find.

Yeah, the shirt was bright purple, not a color she'd normally wear. It also had a big heart with the bold statement—I'm *a book lover... What kind of lover are you?—stamped* across it, most definitely not a statement she'd like to send.

But it would have to do.

Once she returned from the gas station restroom, a harrowing experience and one she wouldn't want to repeat, she settled back in her car, leaning her head back against the headrest.

Her intention to be wide awake and in a cheerful mood when Sam arrived, didn't stand a chance.

She was asleep the instant she closed her eyes.

CHAPTER 6

Sam pulled his SUV into the gas station. After slowly cruising the lot, he finally found a car with New York plates that matched Carrie's description. Parked in the far corner, it looked like someone was sitting in the driver's seat.

He eased his SUV alongside and, cautiously approaching the driver's side, felt relief when he saw it was Livy.

The distant hiss of traffic made the car feel suspended in its own small world. Asleep, her head tipped back against the headrest and mouth slightly open, he watched her breath come slow and even. Whatever journey she'd been on had clearly taken its toll.

Still, he couldn't help the grin that rose at the sight of her—open mouth and all. He wanted to linger in the quiet and savor these few peaceful moments. From experience, he knew everything could shift the instant she woke and realized he was the one who'd come to her rescue.

He tapped on the partially opened window. When she didn't move, he softly called out her name.

"Livy... hey, Livy?"

Her lashes flying open, she woke with a jerk before she turned to face him.

At first, she appeared completely confused. Then, miraculously, she smiled at him. It was a half-asleep and dazed kind of smile, but it was a smile.

Sam liked to think of it as almost a happy smile.

He smiled back at her, his voice soft. "Hey, here I am, remember me? Your knight in shining armor? I had to leave my horse at home, but I brought my SUV. Will this work?"

She didn't answer, only continued to stare at him, the smile still on her face.

Livy was still in that state of half-asleep and half-awake. Which meant she wasn't quite sure where she was, who she was, or what was happening.

Maybe she was dreaming?

Because how could she have forgotten how attractive Sam was, even more than she remembered. Right now, if she were to rate him from one to ten, she'd have to give him a fifty. Heck, maybe even bump it up to a hundred.

His eyes, the same deep navy blue she'd stored away in her memory, were even more mesmerizing than she remembered. And they still had a hold over her, pulling her in. To the point he was all she could see.

This, along with the late afternoon stubble shadowing his face and the disheveled look going on with his hair, ruffled by the late after-noon breeze, gave him an almost devilish look.

Or, maybe more like sexy.

Yes, she'd definitely have to say he looked sexy… or hot. Either one… very much so.

She wanted to stop this moment in time, so she could drink in everything about him for as long as she could. She smiled just thinking about this.

Sam was wondering if he should be concerned. This wasn't the Livy he remembered. At least not the Livy who'd kept him on his toes with her constant barbs and cynical comments. He tapped on the window again. "Livy… are you okay, sweetheart?"

Her smile grew even bigger.

There it was again... sweetheart. It sounded so good coming from him. Especially when it's directed at you.

A sports car roared up to one of the pumps, heavy rap music blaring from the open windows. This was enough to shock Livy completely awake.

Reality pushing its way in, she blinked.

What are you doing?

Yes, what in the world was wrong with her? She had to be out of her mind. Flustered, she turned her face away, and running her hands through her hair, she saw they were shaking.

When he saw her hands trembling, Sam became even more concerned. He opened the car door, sending a blast of hot air right at him.

He stepped back. "Good God, Livy... it's like an oven in here. You're going to get heat stroke." He held out his hand. "Come on, baby, let's get you in my SUV. The air conditioning will make you feel better. Then I'll start loading up your things."

Baby...

Pulled in even more, her heart gave a little leap as her imagination began to take over, just like she'd been so afraid it would.

Her gaze going to his hand, she hesitated. She had the feeling accepting his help would be almost too much to handle. She'd break down and start crying right in front of him, unable to stop.

Sensing her reluctance, he reached over to cup her chin in his hand, gently bringing her to face him. "Livy, come on. It's okay to accept help. You don't have to be strong all of the time."

The corner of his mouth quirked up in a smile. "Come on, give it a try. It's only me."

And here came the tears...

Nervously watching as they began to pool in her eyes, he stepped back, running his hand through his hair. Again, he wasn't good at tears. He also knew, when it came to Livy's tears, how quickly they could disappear, anger taking over.

Shooting a quick glance into the backseat of her car, he was surprised to see it was completely filled. Now, he could be wrong about this, but it looked like she'd packed more than what was needed for the four days Carrie told him she was planning to stay.

So obviously, something had happened. And whatever it was, it had been traumatic enough to have her pack up everything she owned and make the drive by herself.

But he sure as hell knew this wasn't the time to ask her about this. So, to say he was relieved when she finally reached over to take his hand, was an understatement.

Once she was out of the car, he couldn't help but notice her tee-shirt. He studied it for a few moments before he glanced over at her, a smile tugging at the corner of his mouth.

He cleared his throat, nodding over at the shirt. "*Hmm…* interesting. If you're looking for an answer, I don't know if I'm the right person to ask. Though I do vaguely remember discussing something along these lines when we last saw each other. I believe your take on…"

Blushing like crazy, she interrupted him. "Don't be ridiculous. I certainly didn't pick out this shirt with you in mind. I didn't have a choice. I searched for the least wrinkled one, and this was the winner."

She crossed her arms over her chest, unconsciously trying to hide the message printed there. "And, of course I remember our conversation. There's no need for you to remind me. That I even said the things I did, is proof I wasn't thinking clearly at the time."

He nodded. "Ah… I see. So, it wasn't at all a coincidence you chose this particular shirt?"

Now she was beginning to get irritated. It was clear, even though she wouldn't begrudge him his good looks, she'd forgotten how arrogant he could be.

What did he think? She was trying to make some kind of statement? Making a move on him? And she'd do this through a message printed on her shirt?

Seriously?

This completely set her off, her answer coming out fast and furious. "Of course not. Don't flatter yourself. I've better things to do than spend my time thinking about you and your love life."

He merely nodded to this, still smiling. "*Hmm…* if you say so."

Livy didn't know why they were even discussing this, why he was making such a big deal about a silly logo on a tee-shirt. But at the same time, the thought had slowly begun to creep into her head that maybe she did choose the tee shirt with him in mind, hoping he'd comment on it.

This was a very scary thought. Because this wasn't the kind of thing she'd normally do. At least, up until now, she wouldn't have.

She shot a furtive glance over at him to see he was watching her. But he was no longer smiling. If anything, he looked worried.

Very worried.

This made her feel guilty. She was doing exactly what she'd feared. He had come all this way to help her, and here she was, already trying to pick a fight with him.

This is only because you're exhausted. You've been up since 3am. The caffeine has worn off. And that little bag of mini muffins you picked up at your first gas stop? Those wore off hours ago.

He peered more closely at her. "You must have left pretty early this morning. When was the last time you slept? Or had anything to eat?"

At first, she could only stare at him in disbelief. Then her answer came flying out before the words even formed in her head. "How do you do this? Know what I'm thinking? You need to stop, because you're scaring me."

A stricken look on his face, he made a move towards her, almost as if he was going to take her into his arms. Then, with a slight shake of his head, he slowly stepped back.

His voice was soft and very soothing, his expression wary. "Livy, the last thing I want to do is scare you. Because it's obvious you're exhausted . Trust me, things are going to be okay. But for now, let me take over."

She closed her eyes.

And now he's speaking as he would to a crazy person. And that person would be you.

When she went to open her mouth, he quickly put his hand up to stop her. "I know, I know... you don't want my help, but this time I insist."

He took her arm and leading her over to his SUV, he opened the door. He gestured to the passenger seat. "I want you to get in, close your eyes and relax... if only just to humor me."

So, she did.

And for the first time since she'd sat in the human resources office of the J. L. Bagley Publishing Company—listening to George give her the news her life as a book editor was over—she was filled with the tiniest glimmer of hope.

Maybe things weren't going to be that bad after all.

It was when Sam was loading all of Livy's things in his SUV, he found the roll of Lifesavers tucked in the console of her car. He smiled, remembering Carrie telling him about her Aunt Evelyn and the good luck theory she had about the popular roll of candy. For a minute he hesitated, then he stuffed the roll in his pocket.

Who was he to doubt Aunt Evelyn? And the fact Livy had brought them with her? This made him wonder if she was hoping for some luck of her own.

Hell, you could both use some luck at this point. Maybe you, more than her.

He was still smiling as he went over to talk with the station owner to let him know he would send someone to pick up Livy's car.

Once he was back in the driver's seat and saw Livy was sound asleep, he pulled the roll of candy out of his pocket and tossed it in the console.

He gave the roll a stern look.

This is your chance... work that magic you're supposed to possess.

Shaking his head at this craziness taking hold of him, he carefully fastened Livy's seatbelt and started up the SUV.

Livy stirred and opening her eyes, she lazily turned her head to gaze over at him. He reached over, gently tucking her hair behind her ears. This was mostly to satisfy the urge to touch her, something he'd craved since he found her sleeping in her car.

He cleared his throat. "I've got everything under control. Your things are all packed in here and I lined up someone to pick up your car. So, go back to sleep."

Her eyelashes fluttering shut, she did exactly that.

And he was pretty sure, but then again, he could very well be imagining this, she was smiling.

Livy slept her way through what was turning into a much longer drive than usual. As rush hours go, this one was brutal. It was only when a car cut in front of them and Sam had to slam on the brakes, Livy was jerked awake, Sam's arm flung across her chest.

He slowly removed his arm. "Sorry, I didn't have a choice. I can't believe that guy just cut in front of me like he did. I don't know where the hell he thinks he's going. With this traffic, no one's going anywhere."

He checked the rearview mirror before he changed lanes to pull off at the next exit. "Rather than battle this mess, we're getting off at this exit. There's a little Italian restaurant here that's pretty good. I don't know about you, but I'm getting hungry."

He glanced over at the clock on the dashboard. "It's almost seven. You do like Italian food, I presume?"

She nodded, hoping he hadn't heard the loud growl her stomach gave in response to his question. But at the smile that flickered across his face, obviously, he had.

And of course, he had a comment for this.

He chuckled. "I'll take that as a definite yes. A double yes, in fact."

Sam pulled into a parking space in front of what looked like an old farmhouse.

The only indication it was a restaurant was the small sign next to the steps leading up to the large wrap-around porch.

Angie's Place.
Simply Italian

Sam smiled over at her. "Yes, there actually is an Angie. If this happens to be one of the days she's at the restaurant, you're in for a treat. She's been at this location for over thirty years and likes to think of herself as everyone's mother. Or grandmother. She's happiest when people are enjoying her authentic homemade Italian cuisine."

He stepped out, came around, and opened her door. When she took his offered hand, a look of genuine concern crossed his face. "My God—your hands are freezing. You should've told me. I would've turned down the air." She shrugged. "I'm always cold. At least my hands are always cold. Zack said…"

A pained expression came over her face. "What I meant to say is, I should probably check it out. The same with my feet. Sometimes I can't even fall asleep at night because they're so cold. I pity anyone who has to share a bed with me."

As soon as these words came out of her mouth, she closed her eyes, her cheeks flushing with embarrassment.

Oh geeez… did you really need to tell him that?

Another one of those smiles flitted across Sam's face. He cleared his throat. "I'll have to keep this in mind."

What? Keep this in mind? Why?

Afraid she was actually going to come out and ask him this, she pressed her lips together and running her hands through her hair, she feigned a sudden interest in their surroundings.

This was probably for the best, because Sam had absolutely no idea why that comment had come out of his mouth. It just did. To hide his confusion, he began rummaging through the back of his SUV.

He finally pulled out a sweater, one that happened to be his.

"*Ah ha…* here we go." He handed her the sweater. "I remembered seeing this when I was loading all of your stuff. You might as well hold on to it, in case it's cold in the restaurant. You know how they always blast the air-conditioning as soon as the weather starts to get warm."

A grin hitched the corner of his mouth. "Unless you'd rather not. *Hmm…* maybe you'd rather show off that shirt of yours?"

With an angry intake of breath, she grabbed the sweater from him and yanked it on over her head, pulling it down with a jerk. The glare she was sending him was almost enough to wipe the smile off his face... but not quite.

"Again, do I need to remind you it was the best I could find at the time? And for your information, I think this is the first time I've ever even worn the shirt. I got it at a convention a couple of years ago, a romance writer's convention. Believe me, this is not something I'd normally wear."

He raised his eyebrows at this. "A romance writer's convention? *Interesting...* and tell me, did you learn anything worth sharing at this convention?"

She gave an exasperated sigh. "I assure you, attending the convention was not my idea. I was forced to go since I was editing a romance series by one of our most popular authors at the time. I certainly didn't need any additional information when it comes to romance."

She shot him a warning look. "Nor do I need any now." She frowned. "Anyway... everyone knows all of those books are just a glorified version of what really goes on. I can certainly vouch for that."

He merely nodded. And darn if he couldn't stop grinning. With his sweater way too big for her, practically down to her knees and the sleeves completely falling over her hands, it was a little hard to take her seriously.

She, of course, bristled at this. "I don't know what you find so amusing. Because I'm completely serious."

He leaned back against the SUV, his arms crossed over his chest. He studied her for a few moments before he gave a slow nod. *"Hmm...* I see. So, you don't think it's possible for two people to meet, let's say, under unusual circumstances. And maybe, at first, they despise each other. But then for some reason, something keeps drawing them back to each other. I don't know, maybe it's the hint of passion? Desire? Or that instant feeling of being connected? Whatever it is, there's something that feels so right when they're together. And so wrong when they're apart."

He cleared his throat, intently searching her face. "You don't believe this could happen?"

Lips parted in confusion, Livy stared back at him.

Was he talking about them? Because it sure sounded like he was. But surely, she was imagining this.

She wanted to say something, but she couldn't, knowing if she tried, it would come out in some kind of a sputtering mess.

Faced with her bewildered expression, Sam was gripped by the sudden urge to pull her into his arms, throw all caution to the wind and kiss her. If only to find out if she'd react in the same way as when he kissed her on that November night.

A kiss that had not only been a complete surprise to her, but even more so for him.

He wanted to put an end to this uncertainty taking hold of him when thoughts of her took over his mind. Give a try at finding out if they were headed in the same direction, aiming for the same goal. Then he would be able to make his next move.

Aiming for the same goal? Make your next move? You're getting way ahead of yourself here, reverting right back to your football strategy days. But this time, you can't goof up. Because the stakes are so much higher.

His eyes locking with hers, he waited for her answer

She swallowed, before she jerked her head, averting her gaze. "I… I… no, I don't think I do. Maybe it could happen to someone else, but not to me."

Her eyes filled with a sudden sadness. "I'm finding it very hard to believe any of that romance stuff really happens." Then she shrugged. "Not anymore. I think I've run out of luck in that department,"

A sudden smile on his face and holding up his finger, he reached inside the SUV and grabbed the Lifesavers from the console. He took her hand and pressed the roll in her palm. "Here you go."

She stared down at the roll of candy, before she gazed up at him, puzzled. "Where did you get this?"

His smile grew bigger. "From your car. Carrie told me the story about your Aunt Evelyn and her take on these, so I thought you might want to hold on to them." He winked. "Who knows, they may have already started to work their magic."

Stuffing the candy in her pocket, she shrugged. "Again, I don't—"

He cut her short, reaching for her hand. *"Aw Livy…* you need to have a little faith. Come on, let's get something to eat. After some of Angie's good home cooking, I'm sure you'll be in a better frame of mind."

The server had cleared their empty dinner dishes from the table. Thinking Sam was more than eager to get home, Livy had turned down the offer of dessert.

He seemed disappointed. "Are you sure you don't even want to see what's available? Angie always has something new to try."

She fingered the stem of her wine glass, shaking her head "No, really, I don't think I could eat another bite." She smiled. "But thank you so much for dinner. I feel almost human again."

He grinned. "I'm glad you liked it. I know bringing someone with an Italian background to an Italian restaurant was a gamble — but you've got to admit it was un pasto eccellente."

Using an exaggerated accent, he waved off the last three words.

She blinked. "You speak Italian?"

He burst out laughing. "Good Lord, no… I heard someone say that to Angie once. I'm probably not even saying it correctly. If anything, I'm intimidated by other languages. When Carrie and I worked on that project in Quebec, I froze when anyone started speaking French."

She'd forgotten the sound of his laugh. So warm and spontaneous, it matched who he was, mirroring his personality.

Becoming completely lost in the moment, she grinned back at him.

He looked all rumpled. His hair was still all over the place, the stubble on his face, now even more pronounced. The blue and white pinstriped shirt he wore, which at one time had probably been crisp and immaculately pressed, was now limp and wrinkled. With the top three buttons undone and the sleeves rolled up, he had this rakish-like look going on.

A wave of heat hit her for no good reason. She wanted—needed—to reach across, thread her fingers through his hair and pull him close, to beg for the same kiss they'd shared that night in New York.

But this time she'd be ready—and she'd give back every bit of what he gave her.

She blinked.

Oh my God... it has to be your earlier conversation about romance novels that brought on this on.

Sam had noticed all of this. Casually leaning back in his chair, a slow smile spread over his face. "So, I take it you're satisfied?"

"Satisfied? With you?" And yes, she actually blurted this out. Horrified, she wanted to crawl right under the table. Instead she reached for her water glass and taking a big gulp, something she now wondered why she'd even attempted under the circumstances, the water went down the wrong way and she began choking.

A worried look on his face, Sam started to rise out of his chair, only to have her wave him to sit. She held the napkin up to her mouth and closing her eyes, she frantically tried to get herself under control.

Oh my God... could you be even any more embarrassed? Why do you keep letting him get to you like this?

She finally gave him a weak smile.

He gave her a tentative one in return. "You're okay?"

She nodded. When he continued to search her face, a worried look on his, she grew nervous and began making a big production of folding her napkin very neatly and precisely into a triangle. After she placed it on her plate, and gave it one final pat, she looked up to see he was shaking his head.

Something, she realized, he appeared to do quite often when they were together.

After a few moments, he chuckled. "*Hmm...* let's back up a minute here. To what, I believe, started off this coughing fit of yours. I was actually referring to the meal, not to me. But hey, I wouldn't mind knowing the answer to the latter."

He watched as she immediately began to shift into her attack mode, sitting up straighter in her chair, her eyes narrowing. But before she had a chance to say her piece, a silver haired woman came over to their table, putting her hand on Sam's shoulder.

"Sam, how good it is to see you. You haven't been here for quite a while."

Swiftly coming to his feet, Sam gave her a big hug. "Angie! How are you? You're looking particularly beautiful tonight. Everything was great as always, the meal spectacular."

She laughed, giving a dismissive wave. "Oh, go on with you. I look all of my seventy-six years. And as I always tell you, it's just your basic Italian food. Comfort food for the soul, as my kids say."

She glanced curiously over at Livy before she turned back to Sam, a teasing grin on her face. "And who have you brought with you this time? For as long as I've known you, I don't think you've ever brought a woman here to the restaurant." She crossed her arms, her finger going up to tap her mouth. "Hmmm... correct me if I'm wrong, but I believe you once told me the only woman you'd ever bring here, would be the woman you planned to..."

Sam quickly cut her off by giving her another hug, a more enthusiastic one this time. "Angie, Angie... there's no need to share all of our little secrets, is there?"

He gestured toward Livy. "On that note, I'd like you to meet my friend Livy Mazzori. She is from New York and she is here for her sister's wedding this weekend. She actually grew up in Cleveland."

"Mazzori?" Angie's eyes lit up. "Are you in any way related to Chester Mazzori, the baseball player?"

Livy smiled. "Yes, he's my brother."

Angie clasped her hands in front of her, an excited smile on her face. "He's my favorite player. How exciting it must be to have such a talented brother. You must love watching him play."

She sent a sly look over at Sam. "And now you have Sam."

Then she winked at Livy. "He is a keeper. Don't let him get away."

She turned back to Sam. "I see you've finished your dinner. But don't go yet. I'm going to ask your server to bring out a plate of my newest featured dessert, chocolate cannoli. I want the two of you to tell me what you think."

She did a quick scan of their table. "And coffee... you're going to need coffee, too."

After she pulled the server aside to give him the order, she excused herself and made her way over to the next table. It was obvious, for her, one of the most enjoyable parts of running the restaurant was mingling with her customers.

And now it was Sam who had a sudden interest in his napkin. After he'd haphazardly scrunched it up, wiped his face and then plunked it down on the table, he glanced over to see Livy was studying him, a curious expression on her face.

At his raised eyebrow, she smiled. It was a small smile, but for Sam, it was more like a miracle. Her voice was soft. So soft, he almost didn't hear what she said. "I'd have to say, my answer to what you asked would be a yes."

He stilled, his eyes holding hers before they both leaned in. Only to jump back when their server slid a plate with two chocolate cannoli on the table between them.

The color rising in her cheeks, Livy glanced over at Sam.

Darn if he wasn't grinning.

Livy would've been surprised to know, even though he was grinning, he was even more disappointed. Give him another second and his mouth would have been on hers. The missed possibility made him want to groan. Instead, he cleared his throat. *"Ah... here we go. Saved by the cannoli."*

He waited until the server set their coffee down, then shot Livy a sly look. "I dare you to say romance isn't alive and well—sometimes where you least expect it."

Livy was saved from answering due to the cannoli she shoved in her mouth. But if she had been brave enough to answer him?

She would've had to agree.

Carrie and Chris were arguing good-naturedly over the seating arrangements for their wedding reception when her phone rang.

It was Sam.

Carrie put the phone on speaker mode. "Hey, where are you? Did you pick up Livy? How was she? Where is she now? Is she with you?

And, where are you?"

Sam laughed. "*Whoa...* so many questions. Both Livy and all of her possessions are safe and sound with your aunt. I just left there since it took us a while to unload all of her things from my SUV."

"Oh, Sam... thank you. I hope the two of you got along?"

"Yeah, we did. We had a couple of little disagreements, but yeah... it was okay."

After a slight hesitation, his voice softened. "No, I take that back. It was good. I tried to convince her she doesn't have to be so strong all of the time. I didn't ask her what was going on, but just so you know, from the amount of stuff she had jammed in her car, it looks like she's planning to stay for a while."

Carrie gave Chris a high-five before she responded to Sam. "I'm so glad. So, you didn't ask her why she decided to drive? Do you think it has something to do with Zack?"

"Nope, I didn't ask. I could tell she didn't want to talk about it and she seemed completely exhausted. I got the impression this was a middle of the night decision. She'll tell us... I mean, you... when she's ready."

He didn't tell Carrie the real reason he didn't ask Livy about Zack was because, to be truthful, he was afraid of what she'd tell him.

He was content to hold on to the answer she'd given him. This would be her response to his question about whether she was satisfied.

"I'd have to say, my answer to what you asked, would be a yes."

He smiled. That was enough for him.

At least for now, it was.

CHAPTER 7

Coming home... where there's always hope for tomorrow.
~Anonymously Yours

ivy gazed around the small bedroom.

She felt like she'd stepped back in time. It appeared nothing had changed since she and Carrie shared this space while they were growing up.

She had little memory of the time before she, her sisters and Chester had come to live with their Aunt Evelyn. Now thinking back on that time, she couldn't even imagine what it must have been like for her aunt, who'd never married, to suddenly find herself in charge of four young children.

But she'd pulled it off, giving them a safe and loving home.

Since Livy was the middle child, she was more than often alone. Her older sister Carolyn didn't want her hanging around with her and Livy really didn't want to hang around with Carrie, who was younger. And Chester? He was too cool to hang around with a girl. For as long as she could remember, the only thing he wanted to do was play baseball. Coordination not one of her strong points, sports and Livy weren't the best of friends.

But this was okay. As long as she had a stack of books from the library to read, she was more than content. So, it made sense, when she went off to college, she chose to get a double major in journalism and English literature. And after graduation, when she landed an editing job in New York, she thought life couldn't get any better.

But as the years went by, her job settled into what she began to think of as only a job and nothing more. The title of editor had lost its allure.

What she really wanted to do was write. She wanted to write books, she didn't care what kind. Well, she did care... she wanted to write fiction, stories that made people happy. Stories that gave people a way to escape from everyday life and dare to dream a little bit.

Zack had told her she was setting her sights too high. The life of an author was too risky, he'd told her She had a respectable job. She made good money. So, for now, she should be satisfied with what she had. Maybe when she was older and retired, then she could play around with this writing thing. They had rent to pay. And food to buy. And what about their plan to buy a house outside of the city? Start a family? She couldn't forget about that.

But now? None of that mattered anymore.

With a loud groan, she sank down on one of the two twin beds, the bed that had once been hers.

She felt so stupid... so incredibly stupid.

Why had she thought getting back together with Zack would be a good idea? She couldn't believe it had taken her up until now to realize his sudden interest in working out and a healthy diet hadn't been only for his benefit. And he certainly hadn't been doing it for her. No, this new lifestyle was to impress the woman she now suspected he'd been talking to on his phone last night. The same woman he probably went running to, after the special dinner she prepared ended in such a total disaster.

She reached up to run her hands wearily through her hair. This was when she realized she was still wearing Sam's sweater. She brought the sweater up to her face and closing her eyes, she breathed in all of the scents lingering in the fabric. The scents that were him.

She wrapped her arms around herself. If she closed her eyes, she could almost imagine it was him holding her in his arms.

You're starting to confuse fact with fiction again. You know what's going to happen if you don't stop thinking like this.

She'd taken a big chance telling him her answer to his question was a yes. And, what was even more frustrating, she wasn't even sure what he thought about this. He hadn't been able to say anything because of the untimely arrival of Angie.

The little she'd come to know about Sam, he definitely would've had something to say.

Smiling, she thought of the cannoli they'd brought home for Aunt Evelyn. Downstairs, her aunt was no doubt sampling them, already analyzing what Angie might have done differently and whether she could duplicate the recipe. Aunt Evelyn loved a challenge—especially anything involving a cookbook, which to her ranked nearly alongside the Bible.

Well, maybe almost...

She hauled herself off the bed. She'd told her aunt she needed to take a shower. Then she'd come back downstairs so they could talk. Since she was going to stay with her for an undetermined amount of time, she owed her an explanation of why she'd not only descended on her a day early, but also arrived loaded down with all of her belongings.

She needed to tell her what her plans were.

But this was a problem. Because as far as having some kind of plan?

She still had nothing.

Sam sat at his desk, fingers idle over the keyboard, eyes fixed on the blank screen before him. After what felt like several long minutes, he let his gaze wander to the clock — 10:33.

Dragging his hands through his hair, he groaned. Up since the crack of dawn, he was exhausted. And now checking over his itinerary for tomorrow, he saw the day was jam packed with meetings.

What the hell had you been thinking when you put together this schedule?
This meant he should be in bed right now. Sleeping.
Tell your mind that.

When he'd left earlier on his mission to rescue Livy, he hadn't the slightest idea what would happen when he saw her again. He certainly never, and let's put a big emphasis on the word *never* here... nope, he never, *ever* thought he'd be feeling like this.

If you asked him to give his take on their reunion, he'd have to tell you he didn't have one. But this was only because this was all so new to him. This sudden awareness of another person, to the point they were all you could think about, was so overwhelming.

And it was scaring the hell out of him.

He wanted to see her again. Yeah, he knew he would see her at the wedding. And, before that, at the rehearsal and dinner that followed. But this would be in the company of everyone else involved in the wedding.

You want to spend time with just her. Not in a big crowd.

He glanced over at the clock again. It was now 10:47. He looked down at his phone. Along with the location of the gas station. Carrie had also given him Livy's number in case he had to reach her.

Maybe he could call her? If only to ask if she was okay?

Come on, it's late. And why wouldn't she be okay? You can wait until tomorrow. Go to bed before you do something stupid.

He plugged his phone into the charger and turned off the light. Yawning, he made his way to the bathroom.

Ten minutes later he was in bed.

Within five minutes, he was sound asleep.

Out of the shower and in her pajamas, Carrie picked up Sam's sweater from where she'd thrown it on the bed. After she folded it and set it on the dresser, she picked up her phone.

She glanced over at the sweater again. Then she began searching the phone for the message Carrie had sent her when she was at the gas station. It had Sam's number in case she needed to call him.

She hit call and nervously waited for him to answer. But the call went to his voice mail, and for the first few seconds she couldn't come up with a single thing to say. About to end the call, but knowing how lame this would be, she adjusted her glasses and nervously cleared her throat.

Her voice coming out in a squeak, she tried again.

"Hi, it's me, Livy. I still have your sweater and thought you might be looking for it. I guess I'm also calling because I wanted to thank you again... you know, for coming to get me and dinner. And well... just everything. If you ever need me... or want me..."

Oh, for heaven's sake, this wasn't what she'd intended to say. Again shaking her bangs out of her face, she continued.

"What I meant to say, if there's something I can do for you... or you need my help for anything... just ask."

She groaned. She was really making a mess of this. Why did she even call him? She needed to end it. And she needed to do this now.

"Of course, you realize this would all be within reason... So, I guess I'll see you around. Bye... Again, this is Livy."

She ended the call and sank back down on the bed, her eyes closed.

Oh God, you really boggled that up, didn't you? Was it really necessary to add that last remark? Within reason?

The phone still in her hand, she stayed where she was, staring down at it. You know, just in case he called back.

She let at least five minutes pass.... then waited for a few more. But the phone remained silent.

Finally, deciding it really wasn't that big of a deal—though in a way she knew it was—she set the phone on the nightstand and headed downstairs, where her aunt was waiting for her.

She hoped she wasn't going to start asking her questions about Sam. Because again, you guessed it...

She had nothing.

Sam was jerked out of a sound sleep. In a daze, he sat on the edge of the bed.

He had been dreaming.

It was one of those dreams where you had somewhere to go, but couldn't seem to get there, too many obstacles popping up and sending you off in another direction.

He was pretty sure this had been triggered by the busy schedule he had going on tomorrow. What other reason could there be?

Maybe it was because of Livy?

Not wanting to even start thinking about that, because he knew he'd never be able to fall back asleep if he did, he stumbled out of bed to get a drink of water.

As long as you're up, you might as well check your phone for messages.

After gulping down the water, he headed for his office to get his phone. There was a call, followed by a voice mail from Livy.

At the start of the message there was only silence, making him wonder if she'd possibly called him by mistake. Then the sound of her voice flowed through him. He leaned back against his desk and closed his eyes as he listened.

He smiled. That she even thought she had to remind him the call was from her, had him shaking his head. He'd recognize her voice anywhere.

He hit call, only to be forwarded right to her voice mail.

He groaned. This was when he realized how much he'd been counting on her to answer.

After a long and disappointed sigh, he left his message.

"Hey... you're more than welcome. It was a very enlightening experience and I'm glad I was there for you. And don't worry, I'll be sure to take you up on your offer of help. You'll be at the top of my list.

Though I must say, I liked what you said the first time... yeah, that sounded a whole lot better. You know... the within reason option.

In fact, I have a proposition for you. The sweater is yours in exchange for a date. For dinner with me, Thursday night. Let me know. Sweet dreams. And Livy? Just so you know, this is Sam."

He was smiling as he slowly set the phone back on his desk. And he was still smiling when he crawled back into bed. Where he fell right to sleep.

A dreamless sleep this time.

Livy woke to the bright morning sun and the sound of the neighbor mowing his lawn. There was also the delicious aroma of freshly perked coffee and what she was pretty sure were her aunt's home-made cinnamon rolls.

After giving a long, lazy stretch, she threw the covers back and got out of bed. For the first time in she didn't know how long, she was starving.

Then she groaned, closing her eyes. This was a warning she needed to find a place of her own as soon as possible. Otherwise, she was going to wind up eating her way up two dress sizes.

Just as she'd suspected, Aunt Evelyn was already planning a batch of chocolate cannoli. After rifling through her cookbooks, she was fairly certain she'd identified the ingredients Angie had used to create that distinctive flavor. If her first attempt succeeded, she'd make more for the rehearsal dinner—after all, one can never have too many desserts.One could never have too many desserts.

So, it looks like you'll be making cannoli in the very near future... a lot of cannoli. Because you know darn well, Aunt Evelyn is going to nail that recipe.

She was about to go downstairs, when she remembered her phone, still hooked up to the charger. She checked to see she had three calls.

Two were from Zack, along with a voice message.

The third call was from Sam. He'd also left a voice message.

Her heart beating a mile a minute, she sank down on the bed to listen to Sam's message.

Her hands starting to shake, she almost dropped the phone.

She closed her eyes and listened to the message again.

A date? He wants to take you out on a date?

The message from Zack?

She completely forgot about it.

CHAPTER 8

*P*lunk... *plunk... plunk... thump... thump... boink... boink... hisssssssssss...*

Driving Aunt Evelyn's car—fingers crossed—Livy coasted into a parking space in front of Carrie's office and turned off the ignition. The car gave one last dramatic and rattling shake, followed by a loud hissing noise.

To then become completely silent.

She didn't understand.

When was the last time Chester had taken this car in for a tune up? Or better yet, tried to convince their aunt it was time to replace this car with a newer and more reliable model.

She was pretty sure this one could be considered an antique. It definitely seemed to have issues. A lot of issues. It made her car look like a gem.

Well, almost...

She sighed. She could very well imagine her Aunt Evelyn's answer to the suggestion of a new car.

It would be a firm, non-compromising kind of response. The car, she'd say, got the job done. It took her where she wanted to go and this was good enough for her. End of discussion.

Did she mention the car also had no air conditioning? This meant, since she had no choice but to drive with the windows cranked open, her hair was now an unsalvageable and tangled mess.

And yes, proof of how old the car was, cranking open the windows was what she had to do. Evidently, her aunt had considered both air conditioning and power windows as unnecessary luxuries.

So, it was a somewhat disheveled Livy who walked into the reception area outside of Carrie's office.

June, Carrie's assistant, looked up from her computer, a genuine smile on her face when she saw Livy. "Livy! I didn't know you were here already I thought Carrie said you were coming in either tomorrow or Thursday. How are you?"

After she came from around her desk to give Livy a hug and they'd chatted for a few minutes, Livy glanced over at Carrie's office door. "I haven't even had a chance to catch up with Carrie yet. Is she here?"

"Yes, go on in. I'm sure they won't mind." Gesturing for Livy to follow her, she opened the door to Carrie's office and poked her head inside. "Carrie, you have another visitor."

Livy hesitated.

They? Who exactly would that be? You don't think...'

After a tentative smile at June and a few more swipes through her hair in an effort to smooth it into some kind of order, she had no choice but to walk into Carrie's office.

Carrie looked up from her worktable, piled high with all shapes and sizes of designer sample books. A big smile on her face, she dropped the fabric sample she was holding to give Livy a big hug.

"Livy, I'm so glad to see you."

She gestured over to her desk. "Sam and I were wondering when you'd show up." She waved her hand over at the cluttered work table. "We were going over some of the design ideas for the house we are currently working on."

Livy clung to Carrie much longer than necessary before she glanced over to see Sam had risen from his seat at Carrie's desk. His eyes meeting hers, his gaze softened. "So, long time no see, I bet you missed me after I left, huh?"

As soon as these words came out of his mouth, he almost groaned.

You're wondering why she hasn't answered your text yet? Well, with comments like this, what do you expect?

But she completely surprised him. She nodded, a tiny smile flitting across her face. "Believe it or not, I did."

His eyes still holding hers, he smiled. "Good. That's what I'd hoped for."

Again, he was completely mystified as to how he was coming up with these comments. They just came shooting out of his mouth before he even had a chance to think.

For a few, almost breathless, moments, they didn't move, studying each other.

Then Livy turned to Carrie, who had been watching them, a thoughtful expression on her face.

But with Sam watching her so intently, Livy suddenly couldn't remember what she'd meant to say. When the words did come—stumbling over each other in a rush—his grin told her he knew exactly how flustered he had her. And he was enjoying every minute.

"I'm on my way to see Sophie and the twins, but I wanted to stop here first to check the schedule for the next few days—you know, for the wedding and all. Knowing you, everything's organized and ready to go. But I want to help. I really do. I haven't done much so far—if anything, it feels like I've only caused a lot of trouble..."

She flashed an apologetic look at Sam. "Thanks again for your help." He immediately smiled right back at her. "It was no trouble at all. I enjoyed our little outing. And just so you know, I had your car sent over to my trusty mechanic. He's going to check it out."

"Oh... I need to pay you. Tell me how much I owe you so far."

She patted her pockets, a stricken expression coming over her face. "I left my wallet in the car, but I can run out and get it. It will only take a couple..."

He was shaking his head. "Nope... let's not worry about that yet. We'll wait to hear what his verdict is, okay?"

Haltingly, she nodded. And Livy, the same Livy always so quick to let him know she was completely capable of taking care of herself? It appeared that Livy had momentarily disappeared.

"Thank you. That was nice of you to do that." And yes, this was all she had to say. There was no lecture, no sharp comment. She even gave him a big smile.

Unsuccessfully trying to hide his surprise, he nodded. "*Uh, yeah…* anytime."

After another silence, much more awkward this time, they both turned their attention to Carrie who had been curiously following this exchange between them. She was smiling as she grabbed a notepad from her desk and waved it at Livy. "You're in luck, I have my list right here. We all know how I love my lists."

She began reading from the list. "Let's see… the tents, tables and chairs are to be delivered to Chester and Sophie's house later this afternoon and will be set up tomorrow. Our final dress fitting is scheduled for tomorrow at two. It will be me, you, Emily and, of course, Sophie. Chris is picking up his parents, along with Emily and her family, at the airport sometime tomorrow morning and Carolyn is arriving on Friday."

She paused to take a deep breath. "I'm going to need your help on Friday with all the little last-minute details… the place cards for the tables, picking up the cookie favors from Abby and anything else that pops up."

She grinned. "And of course, there's the rehearsal and dinner following on Friday night. But Chris is in charge of that. He told me if I ask him one more time if he has it all under control, he's going to call off the wedding."

She scrunched up her face. "I can't help it. It's killing me, not knowing what he has planned."

She glanced over at Livy. "Which reminds me, tomorrow night, we're going out to dinner with Chris's family. Aunt Evelyn is coming, too. You're more than welcome to join us if you'd like."

She turned to Sam. "You, too. You should both come."

Livy shot a quick glance over at Sam, who was now casually leaning against Carrie's desk, his arms crossed over his chest.

He cleared his throat, his gaze going directly to Livy as he spoke. "Thanks for the invite, but I have to decline. I'm hoping to hear back from someone about a dinner date."

A puzzled look on her face, Carrie glanced from him to Livy. At the telltale color filling Livy's face, she slowly nodded.

"*Ah… so, I see.*" Suddenly galvanized into action, she practically threw the notepad on her desk before she snatched up her phone. As she began backing out of the office, she sent Livy and Sam a smile. "Dinner… that reminds me, the caterer called earlier and left a message for me to call them. Something to do with the appetizers. They weren't sure whether we'd decided on shrimp or scallop kabobs. I know Chris really liked the shrimp…"

She shrugged, pointing to her phone. "But I'm guessing neither of you really care… or maybe even have something more interesting you'd like to talk about. So, I'll go outside to make the call."

Before either Sam or Livy could say a word, she was gone.

After a brief silence, Livy looked over at Sam. He was studying her with an intensity that made her extremely nervous. He tilted his head, a smile touching his lips. "What happened to your glasses?"

The fact he'd noticed she exchanged her glasses for her contacts, Livy became even more flustered, color flooding her cheeks.

This made him smile even more.

She'd made a very determined effort to convince herself she'd made this move as part of her plan to embrace life. What was now standing in front of him was the new and improved Livy. The Livy who was now ready to embrace life, her glasses the first to go. At least this was the plan.

But deep down, she knew it was because of what he'd said on that November night in New York. The comment she found so hard to forget. How she was hiding her beautiful eyes.

And, yes… again, beautiful was the word he'd used.

But there's no way you'll let him know this.

Casually fingering the car keys she was holding, she gave a nonchalant shrug. "It's really no big deal. I guess you could say I decided it was time for a change. And I wanted to get used to them. You know, with the wedding photos and all."

When he only continued to study her, the smile still on his face, she cleared her throat. "I got your text. I didn't see it until this morning since I went to bed not too long after you left."

He nodded, his gaze still holding hers. "I like it... the no glasses look, that is. And, I understand. It was a long day."

Oh boy, he's making this really hard....

And how did she respond to this? By babbling a mile a minute. "I'm sorry if I interrupted what you and Carrie were working on. But I hadn't seen Carrie yet, or even talked to her since her shower. As the maid-of-honor, I know there's certain things I'm responsible for. But I'm not sure what they are, since I've never been a maid-of-honor one before. Since this is a big moment in Carrie's life, I don't want to let her down, I want to do my part to make sure everything goes perfectly."

Why are you telling him all this? No doubt he knows more about this wedding than you do.

He confirmed this with another nod. "Again, I understand. And you weren't interrupting anything. I'm glad you decided to stop by. I know Carrie is, too. She was worried about you."

Unsure of what to say to this, she nodded.

This was followed by another awkward silence followed before she gave him a tentative smile.

He raised an eyebrow. "Back to the text?"

Ah... yes, his text. You need to give him an answer on that.

She reached up to push her glasses more firmly against her nose, only to remember they weren't there. Quickly dropping her hand to her side, she continued fingering the car keys she was holding, nervously swinging then back and forth.

Why was she so nervous? You'd think she'd never been around a man before.

He only asked you out to dinner. He didn't ask you to marry him. Or that you jump into bed with him, for heaven's sake.

At this thought, she became completely undone, the blush rising even higher in her cheeks. When she almost dropped the darn keys, she stuffed them in her jeans pocket.

But now she was faced with the dilemma of what to do with her hands. Fingering the hair tie she had on her wrist, she attempted to pull it off and, after giving it a good yank, sent it flying right at Sam.

He reacted quickly, managing to snag it right out of the air, while ducking at the same time to avoid being hit in the face.

Her hands going to her mouth, she stared at him, horrified. "I'm so sorry. I didn't mean to do that. Honest, I didn't."

He was chuckling as he twirled the hair tie around his finger. "Wow... I didn't see that coming. I'll tell you what... give me your answer to my text and maybe, if you're lucky, you'll get this back."

So, she gave him her answer. And of course, you guessed it—her words all came out entirely wrong. "Yes, I'd like that. Go to dinner with you, that is. Dinner sounds good, no pressure. After all, it's just dinner. We have to eat, I guess."

As soon as these words came out of her mouth, she realized she certainly hadn't given an enthusiastic response to his invitation.

His puzzled expression confirmed this.

And darn if she didn't start rambling again, taking off right from where she'd left off. "What I meant is you shouldn't feel obligated to be with me. It's okay if you'd rather go out to dinner with Carrie and Chris's family. We could both go, I guess..."

She shook her head. "I don't mean we'd have to go together. You know, as a couple. Though Carrie did invite both of us and..."

Her mouth snapping shut, she closed her eyes.

Oh my God... just shut up. You're making this more complicated than it is. If you don't, you'll wind up spending Thursday night alone, eating dinner on a tray table in front of the Aunt Evelyn's TV. With Sam completely out of the picture.

She wasn't even aware he'd pushed away from the desk, close enough to cup her chin in his hand, her face a breath away from his.

Her lashes fluttered open to see he had that quirky smile going on, lurking at the corner of his mouth. The smile telling her he knew exactly what was going on in her mind.

And suddenly… it was all too much.

Way, way too much.

Mesmerized by the warm look in his eyes, along with the feel of his breath brushing across her face as he spoke, she fell right under his spell.

"Livy… I'm sure Chris's family is all very nice, but I don't want to go out to dinner with them. I want to go out to dinner with you. It's you I want to be with, only you. Of course, this all depends on whether you think you can tolerate spending another evening with me and all of my faults."

Tolerate? What faults?

Livy wasn't really capable of anything right now. The fact Sam was so close, his mouth only a whisper away from hers, she was lucky she even knew where she was. Or who she was.

She was aware of only one thing… and this was him.

His lips going on to brush lightly over hers, not quite a kiss, but more than enough to send her heart leaping to her throat, he gently released her chin.

And Sam? He was smiling as he watched the disappointment fill her eyes.

"That was just a beginning, sweetheart. There's no hurry. We've got time. Lots of time."

Livy had no recollection of what happened after that.

In fact, everything was pretty much of a blur until she found herself standing in the middle of the parking lot, trying to remember where she'd parked her aunt's car. Or what it even looked like.

It was only when a truck came barreling down the aisle and she had to jump out of the way to avoid being hit, her brain finally kicked into gear and she managed to locate the car. Sinking into the driver's seat, she dropped her head back against the headrest.

Oh my God... what are you doing?

She was terrified. Yes, terrified would be the only way to describe how she was feeling about what was happening between her and Sam.

She tried to think back to when she first met Zack. Had she'd felt the same? If she had, she certainly couldn't remember. And this kind of behavior was probably something one wouldn't forget, right?

She vaguely remembered pushing Sam away, almost shoving him into the desk, when Carrie came back into her office. The only other thing she remembered after that, was Carrie's reminder of the dress fitting tomorrow. Two o'clock was the time everyone was to meet at the boutique.

Two o'clock... two o'clock. These two words kept repeating over and over in her mind.

At least, she was pretty sure that's what Carrie had said. Yeah, definitely two o'clock.

Or wait... maybe it one?

She shook her head. She'd send her a text later to check on this, just to be sure.

It had been when Carrie invited her to join Sam, Chris and her for lunch, she went into panic mode, mumbling a lame excuse about all the errands she had to run before she went to see Sophie. Then she'd practically sprinted out of the office, nearly tripping over her own feet in the process.

Thank God you didn't hit the floor again. If you recall, this is what started whatever this whole thing is between you and Sam in the first place.

She groaned, closing her eyes. If this wasn't a sign it was definitely too soon for her to even think about getting involved in another relationship, she didn't know what was.

Nope, she wasn't ready. Not by a long shot.

She was too vulnerable right now. She needed some alone time. Time to come up with a plan, get her life in order. This could be the perfect time to take on George's suggestion to start on that book she wanted to write. After editing every different genre of romance imaginable over the past seven years, she, of all people, had a pretty good idea of what to write in order for it to sell.

What was it one of the authors had told her at that romance novel convention she attended?

If you can't live it, you might as well write about it.

Yeah... she could do that. Of course, she could. She'd probably be very good at it.

Feeling much better about life in general, she started up the car and with a great deal of rattling and shaking, she drove out of the parking lot. She hoped a visit with her nephews would be the diversion she needed.

Lord help her, she needed to stop thinking about Sam.

Hands in his pockets, Sam casually meandered over to the window to watch as Livy took off, almost running, to the parking lot.

He continued to watch as she came to a sudden stop to search the area around her for a few moments. From what he could see, it appeared as though she had no idea where she was.

His view momentarily blocked as a big truck lumbered by, he then spotted her briskly making her way over to one of the parked cars.

Hmm... it looked as though he'd been right in thinking she was more than a little flustered when she left.

He was smiling as he returned to sit at Carrie's desk.

He refreshed the screen of his laptop. And this was as far as he got.

Damn...

He had absolutely no recollection of what he'd been working on.

It was killing Carrie that something was going on between Livy and Sam. And she was determined to find out exactly what it was.

Making quick work of checking and signing the orders June handed over for her approval, she waited until after she left before she glanced curiously over at Sam.

He was drumming his fingers on the desk, staring at the screen of his computer.

He appeared confused.

One might say he maybe even looked completely lost.

But as far as Carrie was concerned, he definitely had the look of a man who was falling in love, yet had absolutely no idea this was happening.

She cleared her throat. Loudly.

He ignored this.

She grinned. "Sam, come on. Give. What's up with you and Livy?"

His eyes still riveted to the screen, he began typing something on the keyboard. Little did Carrie know, this was only for effect, because what showed on the computer screen was a line of gibberish.

He loudly cleared his throat, avoiding her gaze. "I have no idea what you're talking about."

Crossing her arms over her chest, she attempted to stare him down. But since he was refusing to even look at her, this failed.

She moved closer. She was trying really hard not to laugh. "Sam, *come on*. I'm not going to let up until you tell me what's going on. You, of all people, should know how relentless I can be. Now, come on… give."

He slowly closed his laptop and leaned back in the chair. All of his concentration was centered on, what looked like to Carrie, a hair tie? She looked more closely. Yes, this was exactly what he was twirling around on his finger.

Still avoiding her gaze, he shrugged. "It's no big deal. I asked her to go out to dinner with me tomorrow night. And be it a miracle, or the stars are aligned or whatever, she said yes."

Carrie did a little happy dance over to sit on the edge of the desk.

"I knew it! I told Chris there was something going on between the two of you. You do like her, don't you?"

She watched as a redness began to spread across his face and down his neck.

What's this? Sam was blushing?

Her smile grew even bigger.

She waited.

After a few moments, he reluctantly met her gaze. "I don't know if 'like' is what I'm feeling. Hell, I don't know what it is. I only know there's something there I can't explain." Still fingering the hair tie, a slow smile came over his face. "She has somehow managed to take over my mind. Almost to the point she's all I can think about. And now... after yesterday and the time we spent together, well... you'd think... gee, I... what I mean is..."

For a few seconds, his thoughts took over his ability to speak. Then, he let out a long groan and throwing down the hair tie, he dragged his hand down over his face. "Good God, Carrie... I've been thinking and saying things I never thought I would, let alone that I should. What the hell is going on here?"

He shook his head, what he'd said to Livy just a few minutes ago replaying in his mind—

"That was just a beginning, sweetheart. There's no hurry. We've got time. Lots of time."

Yes, this was exactly the kind of comments he was coming up with, throwing them out like he knew what he was doing.

Which, of course, he didn't... not by a long shot.

So... where the hell was he getting all this from?

At his bewildered expression, Carrie sighed. "*Ah...* Sam. I don't know how to tell you this, but I think you're falling in love. Or maybe you've already made the plunge. And as mixed up and crazy everything feels to you right now, believe me, it's going to get better. So, so much better. It's going to be wonderful."

She shook her head at him. "This is because, in case you haven't noticed, it's obvious Livy is battling the same emotions as you are. My God, you can feel practically feel the electricity vibrating in the air between the two of you when you're together."

He closed his eyes. "Yeah, but she's got a lot going on in her life now. With Zack at the top of the list. The last thing I want, is to be in competition with him." He frowned. "What am I saying? I don't want to be in competition with anyone."

Carrie shook her head. "And you won't be. Do you want to know what my theory is on the whole situation?"

The look he sent her was wary. "I don't know that I do. But at the same time, I have the feeling you're going to tell me anyway."

She was grinning as she nodded. "I think Livy's been hanging on to Zack only because she was comfortable with their relationship and she really had nothing to compare it to. But then, you come along. And *Bam!* You brought out all of these emotions she's never experienced and this is scaring her to death. I know the feeling. I went through the same thing with Chris."

She stopped to think about how to phrase what she wanted to say. "When Zack came back, she decided to play it safe. But now she's come to realize safe isn't the answer to what she wants. You are."

She watched the slow smile come over his face before he opened his eyes to gaze over at her, a faraway expression on his face.

"I hope you're right. Because if you aren't, I'm in big trouble."

"You'll be fine. Just trust your instincts and go with them."

He raised his eyebrows at this. "A lecture on trust? And this coming from you?" He shook his head. "I don't know…"

She laughed. "I'm getting there. Slowly, but surely. Rome wasn't built in a day, you know."

"*Oh geeez…* now you're comparing yourself to an empire? What next?"

He pushed away from the desk and coming to his feet, he reached for his phone. Scooping up the hair tie at the same time, he stuffed them both in his pocket.

"Come on, let's go get some lunch. When I talked to Chris, he told me he'd have the Newsome contract wrapped up by noon, so decide where you want to go and text him, so he can meet us there. I'll have to cut mine short, because I'm meeting the tile man at the Shaker site at one." He grinned. "All this talk is making me hungry. So, let's get going."

Carrie was already typing. But it was a text to Sophie, not Chris.

> Update: Livy just left for your house. Sam asked her out for dinner tomorrow night. She's in desperate need of a make-over. Can you arrange this? She has no idea I'm telling you this. Let me know.

Within a few seconds, she received an answer.

> Yes, I've been dying to do this ever since I first met her! I'll set something up for tomorrow after the fitting. With my friend, Kelly—she's the best. We'll tell Livy it's part of the whole wedding experience. Mum's the word.

After Carrie sent one last text, this one to Chris on where to meet them for lunch, she smiled over at Sam.

He hadn't asked her why it was taking her so long to message Chris. Instead, he was staring out of the window. He appeared to be deep in thought.

"Sam?"

He turned to her, a distracted smile on his face. "Everything all set?"

She was searching her desk. "Yeah, but what happened to that hair tie you were playing around with a few minutes ago? I want to pull my hair back. It's driving me crazy today."

A faint smile on his face, Sam gave his trouser pocket a searching pat. It was still there.

And it was going to stay there.

He shrugged "Sorry, can't help you out with that."

He knew he was acting like a man who had completely lost his mind, but for some reason, holding on to something of Livy's, even as simple as a hair tie, made him feel like he was holding a part of her.

Carrie stopped her search to gaze over at him. "*Oh, Sam...*"

At the knowing expression on her face, darn if he didn't feel the heat rising in his face again.

And Carrie?

She was grinning like crazy as they left her office.

Sam thought Livy was monopolizing his mind now?

Well... just wait until tomorrow night.

CHAPTER 9

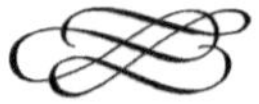

*L*ivy pulled into the driveway with the address Sophie had given her.

For a few moments, she remained in the car, taking in the view.

The rambling three story farmhouse was huge, set back nearly five hundred feet from the main road, the glorious expanse of Lake Erie as its backyard. Today, with the clear blue sky and bright sunshine, the view was breathtaking.

Removing the gifts she'd brought from the backseat of the car—toys for the twins and a bottle of wine for Sophie and Chester—Livy made her way to the front door and rang the doorbell.

Sophie opened the door, holding a baby in each arm. As soon as Livy set the gifts down on the hall table, Sophie handed her one of the babies, along with a bottle.

"You're just in time. Here you go… you're now holding Hunter. He is the more adaptable of the two, least likely to cry even if he doesn't know you."

She pressed a kiss to the top of the head of the baby in her arms. "And then we have Trevor. He's not having a very good day. I'm going to blame it on teething. At this age, it's a very acceptable excuse to use for any baby crankiness."

She grinned. "I was just about to give them their bottle. I hope you don't mind helping out. Once they're finished and down for a nap, we can have lunch."

Hunter was studying Livy very curiously. Then his face began to scrunch up, suggesting he was about to cry. She began bouncing him in her arms and talking softly to him as she followed Sophie upstairs to the nursery. Where, once both babies started on their bottles, a peaceful silence descended on the nursery.

Hunter and Trevor finished their bottles, both fighting a losing battle to keep their eyes open before they were even in their cribs. After Sophie made sure they were all settled in, she led Livy back downstairs to the kitchen, where she turned to give her a big hug.

"It's so good to see you. It's been too long. Well, I guess you were just here for the shower, but it was almost like you were here and gone before we knew it. How long are you planning to stay this time?"

Not quite sure of how to answer this, Livy was silent as she watched Sophie remove a bowl, filled with salad, from the refrigerator and set it on the island. When Sophie glanced over at her, she shrugged.

"I'm not quite sure. I... I've been thinking maybe it's time for a change. To figure things out, change course..." She hesitated, again not sure of how much she wanted to share.

Sophie poured wine into two glasses before she handed one to Livy. "I hope you like white wine. I thought since the salad has chicken in it, white was the best choice. I'm still not all that sure of the rules when it comes to wine. Chester shakes his head, says I'm hopeless." She grinned. "Hey, if that's the least of my faults, he can't complain."

She peered more closely at Livy. "But, go on... as usual, I've interrupted what you were planning to say, a common fault of mine, it seems. You say you've decided you need a change. But what about your job? And Zack… this is his name, right? What does he have to say about all of this?"

After taking a small sip of her wine, Livy took a deep breath. "As of two days ago, I don't have a job anymore. They eliminated my position. And Zack?" She stared down at her hands, her voice suddenly coming out all shaky. "I'm pretty sure he's been seeing someone else. I should've known this was going to happen. After all, he did this once before. And I was enough of a fool to believe his promise that he'd never do it again."

She gave a big sigh. "So, I decided to pack everything I could fit in my car and I left. Without even telling him." She took another sip of her wine. "I left a note, but it was only two words… it's over."

She shrugged. "If only because I really didn't know what else to say."

She picked up her napkin and began smoothing it on her lap in an effort to avoid the concerned expression on Sophie's face. "The only one who knows about this, is Aunt Evelyn. I felt obligated to tell her after I barged in on her with everything I own. But, I made her promise not to say anything. I don't want to ruin Carrie's wedding with all of my problems. My hope is, by the time she and Chris come back from their honeymoon, I'll have everything all figured out."

Her eyes bright, she gave Sophie a big smile. "But, enough about me. It looks like everything is going good for you and Chester. I love the house. And Chester must be ecstatic. He's always wanted to live by the water. I know his condo was on the lake, but it just wasn't the same. This is so much better."

She gazed around the newly remodeled kitchen. "This kitchen is amazing, too. It must be so much fun to cook in a kitchen like this."

The kitchen was huge, the ten-foot ceiling making it seem even larger. It had a very sleek, almost modern look. Not what you'd expect to find in a house of this style. The floors were oak and the cabinets were a soft off-white with clear glass insets. A huge grill took up one end of the large island that could easily fit ten people, with all of the countertops throughout the room, a pale green marble. The wall facing the backyard had four large arched windows, with a double set of French doors centered in the middle. This offered a spectacular view of the large stone patio, with the sparkling blue water of Lake Erie as the backdrop.

Sophie grinned. "Yeah, but the thing is… I don't cook! I'm terrible at it. I always burn everything. But Chester has been getting into it and has made some pretty amazing things. It must be your Aunt Evelyn's influence."

She gave Livy an almost embarrassed smile. "I didn't want such a big house. But, when it went on the market and Carrie brought us here to look at it, both Chester and I knew right away this was the house for us." She rolled her eyes. "Even though it needs a lot of work."

She gazed around the kitchen. "I really like how this turned out. It's the only room we've remodeled since we've moved in. When Carrie asked if she could have her wedding here, it became our first priority, since the original kitchen was pretty much of a disaster. In about two weeks, Chester is throwing a barbecue for the whole team." She smiled over at Livy. "You are more than welcome to attend. This depending on your plans, of course."

Livy could feel her phone vibrating in her jeans pocket. She dug it out, grimacing over at Sophie. "Sorry, I should probably check this out. It might be Carrie." She read the message, a frown coming over her face before she quickly typed out a reply. After she set the phone on the island countertop, she went right back to eating her salad.

Sophie watched all of this while she buttered her roll. She cautiously smiled over at Livy. "Bad news?"

As usual, she wasn't the least bit shy about asking for information. The true romantic she was, she was dying to know if the message wasn't from Carrie at all, but from Sam. And if it was, she had plans to ask Livy what the story was on the two of them. She was intrigued about what Carrie had told her about Sam and Livy's explosive reaction to each other when they met in New York. The fact that Livy had caught Sam's attention when, up until now, no other woman had been able to accomplish this, hinted something serious was going on.

Livy hesitated, not quite sure she wanted to answer. Then she just blurted it out. "It was Sam. Last night he asked me to go out to dinner with him tomorrow night and right before this, when I saw him at Carrie's office, I told him yes." She nodded at her phone. "His message was to let me know he would pick me up around seven. But I said no, I'd meet him at the restaurant. There's no reason he has to come get me."

When this was met with only silence, Livy glanced over to see Sophie was studying her, a thoughtful look on her face. She put her roll down on her plate, before giving Livy a tentative smile. "Can I give you some advice?"

Warily, Livy nodded.

"Sam is one of the nicest guys I've ever met." At Livy's sigh, she nodded. "I know, you've probably heard this from Carrie about a hundred times, but he is. He'd do anything for you. Not only just you, he's this way with everyone. And he hasn't been the least bit attracted to any woman for as long as I've known him. And I know for a fact, the catch that he is, he could go out with anyone he wanted to."

She made a face. "Trust me, a lot of women have tried to grab him up... many times."

She took a sip of her wine. "So, I asked him why he wasn't married yet. He told me this was because he'd never met a woman he could imagine being with for the rest of his life. When he finally did get married, it had to be a marriage that would last forever."

She frowned. "His parents divorced when he was a teenager and it hit him hard. He has a younger sister who also didn't deal well with what happened. She's been in a lot of trouble over the past few years and he's had to bail her out numerous times. Only a couple of months ago, he finally told her no more, she had to start making it on her own. He said this was the hardest thing he ever had to do, and now he's so worried he might have made a mistake."

After a sip of wine, she shook her head. "I used to think he and

Carrie would make a go of it, but the connection just wasn't there." She smiled. "Nothing like how it is between her and Chris."

She shrugged. "And now Sam's suddenly shown this interest in you. I think this says a lot. Carrie told me how the two of you sort of went at each other when you met back in November." She grinned. "She said she'd never seen Sam act like that before."

At Livy's embarrassed expression, she grinned. "Don't worry, it's not like we talk about you all the time. It's just that Carrie and Sam are such close friends she can pick up on what he's thinking. And according to her, a lot of his thinking lately has been about you."

Livy was saved from commenting on this when her phone vibrated on the counter, indicating there was another message.

After she read it, she handed the phone to Sophie. "And this is how Sam responded."

> Nope, I will be picking you up. I asked you out for dinner, and I consider this a date. A real date. Not a meeting between two friends at a restaurant. Bear with me on this, okay? Let's do this right. If you remember, this is the way we knights roll.

Sophie had a puzzled look on her face as she gave Livy back the phone. This made Livy realize she probably shouldn't have shared the last sentence with her.

She cleared her throat. "Umm… that last part… well, that was a silly conversation we had about people who always want to, well, you know, rescue…

Her words trailed off as a big grin lit up Sophie's face. "*Ah ha…* I told you. That's exactly something I would expect from Sam. He wants to be your knight in shining armor… your hero."

She shook her head. "*My gosh,* Livy… do you realize how lucky you are?" Leaning back in her chair, a dreamy smile settled on her face. "Chester is the same way. You probably don't see this because he's your brother. But it's one of the things I love most about him. He has this way of watching over me without becoming overbearing. It's like he really listens to me. He knows what I'm thinking about, what I want. I know I can always count on him for anything. And I'd do anything for him. He's my rock."

She gazed over at Livy, her eyes bright. "And he's the same way with Trevor and Hudson. He's so good with them. It just about kills him when he has to leave for the away games. Each night he calls and wants to face time with them."

She laughed. "They get so excited when they see him on my phone. And confused, trying to figure out where he's coming from and why he won't pick them up. I love watching their faces."

After pouring more wine in Livy's glass, she stood. "Come on, let's go sit on the deck. It's such a beautiful day after all the rain we've had. I'll bring the baby monitor with me."

She grinned over at Livy. "If we're lucky, we'll have another forty-five minutes or so before the little monsters wake up."

Her eyes closed and her head resting against the back of the deck chair, Livy gave a contented sigh. The breeze blowing off the lake and the warmth of the afternoon sun made it the perfect summer day.

Never mind that she had to share her space with Sophie's two dogs, Popcorn and Snowball, who'd jumped up on the chair to settle next to her as soon as she sat down. Whereas, Chester's dog Mr. Pickles, perched on the edge of the deck, scanning the yard for squirrels.

She smiled over at Sophie. "I could get used to this. This alone makes me feel better about leaving New York. Maybe now I can finally take some time to think about what I want to do. "

She frowned. "I need to start making better choices. At least this is what I've been told."

Sophie's smile was hesitant. "You're not mad at what I said, are you? I know it's really none of my business. After all, I don't know what your relationship was with Zack. And I'm certainly not going to say anything bad about him, since I don't know him. But I really hope you give Sam a chance. Because something tells me, beneath that good-guy vibe he has going on? There's a completely different Sam.

And this would be a man who could make a woman very, very happy."

She grinned over at Livy. "If you get my drift."

Livy was quiet.

She wondered what Sophie would think if she shared the conversation she had with Sam about his nice guy versus bad boy image.

You know… how he was biding his time, waiting for that special woman… if only to show her what real passion was all about.

She smiled, closing her eyes.

Sophie thought the sudden color in Livy's cheeks was from the heat of the afternoon sun.

Yeah, the heat was there.

But it was an entirely different kind of heat.

It was late afternoon when Livy finally said goodbye to Sophie, Trevor and Hudson. Fifteen minutes later, she pulled the car into Aunt Evelyn's garage.

She wasn't the least bit surprised by what she found when she walked into her aunt's kitchen. Cooling on the table was a huge batch of just baked cannoli shells.

Chocolate cannoli shells.

There was also a note from her aunt, propped up against the empty flour canister.

I'm pretty sure I figured out the recipe. Went to grocery store to get more ingredients.

Glancing over at the unwashed bowls and utensils piled up in the sink—sweat already rolling down her back—she sighed.

As you've probably already guessed, Aunt Evelyn also didn't believe in dishwashers. There was nothing wrong with a hands-on, good old-fashioned scrubbing, she insisted.

But first, there was something Livy needed to do. She pulled out her phone to respond to Sam's text.

She was smiling as she typed out the message she had been composing, here and there in her mind, since she'd read his last text.

Her response was a combination of Sophie's influence, along wit her own stubbornness.

> Ok, you win. I will be ready and waiting for you tomorrow night. But don't think you're always going to be the one to call the shots. See you at seven.

After she sent the text, she wondered if she'd maybe gone a little too far, suggesting there was a future between them.

Unfortunately, it was already a done deal. So, she could only wait to see how he responded.

It was when she went to take the hair tie from her wrist to pull her hair up in a ponytail, she realized Sam had never given the tie back to her. And for some reason, that he still had it made her feel ridiculously happy.

Which was silly… it was just a hair tie.

A smile on her face, and after tucking her hair behind her ears, she filled the sink with hot water and squirted in some dish washing liquid.

She was still smiling as she began scrubbing the first bowl.

Sam was at his favorite coffee shop, waiting for his order to be filled. Pacing back and forth in front of the counter, he glanced at his watch again.

He had a lot on his mind, most of this concerning Livy and whether or not she was going to come back with an answer to his last text.

This is, if she actually ever did decide to respond.

He glanced down at his watch again. How long had it been since he'd sent the last text? Maybe he'd come across as a little demanding with his choice of words?

But, come on… he'd been so frustrated when she'd informed him she'd meet him at the restaurant. This hadn't gone over well with him at all, as it wasn't something he'd feel comfortable doing. It seemed so impersonal, certainly not what he'd consider proper etiquette for a date. Even more so for a first date.

How would you even know what's right or wrong when it comes to the rules of dating? You've stayed clear of the dating scene for so long, for all you know, this might be completely acceptable now.

When his phone suddenly buzzed in his pocket he whipped it out so fast, he almost sent it shooting across the room.

So, he was more than a little preoccupied when the woman handed him his coffee.

After he dropped a more than generous tip in the tip jar, he sat at one of the tables. He took a fortifying gulp of coffee before he scrolled down his phone and read Livy's text.

For the longest time, he stared down at the phone. Finally, dragging his hand through his hair, he glanced up, a big grin on his face.

Well, this was a pleasant surprise.

She'd agreed to his request. But of course, she hadn't done this without making it very clear he shouldn't expect this was going to be the norm.

You're fine with this. This is the Livy you know. The Livy you expected.

After smiling back down at the phone for a few moments, he started to type out an answer.

Then he stopped and deleted what he'd typed.

Like Livy, Sam didn't like texting.

He also wasn't fond of emails.

If he had something to say to someone, he'd much rather do it in person. Or through a phone call. He believed too much was lost in words written down instead of spoken, especially in this now acceptable abbreviated code everyone went by.

From his past experience, this often resulted in mixed messages and wrong intentions taken. He knew this was an old-fashioned way of thinking. And he knew this was something that bugged both Carrie and Chris, but so be it.

As far as he was concerned, the hands on, personal approach was the way to go.

He found Livy's number, took a long, deep breath and hit call.

. . .

Livy was elbow deep in hot water when her phone rang. She glanced over at the phone to see it was Sam.

After she quickly dried her hands off with a towel, she grabbed the phone right before the call was about to go to voicemail. This explained why her voice came out in a rushed and almost breathless whisper.

"Hi."

Sam closed his eyes.

There was something about her voice that got to him. Every single time he heard it. Like right now, the husky, almost smoky tone of this one simple word traveled through him like fire, all of his senses vying for attention.

To the point he almost couldn't even think.

Livy stilled. Maybe it wasn't him?

"Sam?"

It was when she said his name, he somehow came back to life. He cleared his throat. "Yes, it's me... Sam."

Filled with the sudden urge to let her know what she did to him, he briefly debated whether he should tell her what he was thinking.

But it appeared this had already been decided, his mouth off and running, a hint of a smile in his voice. "I'm sorry. I... well, there's just something about the sound of your voice that does something to me. If everyone answered my calls the way you do, I'd be more than happy to stay on the phone all day."

A smile slowly working its way across Livy's face, she leaned back against the counter. This turned out to be the exact same spot she'd stacked the stainless-steel mixing bowls waiting their turn to be washed.

She watched as they began to topple off the counter.

Uh, oh... not good.

Before she could make a grab for them, they went crashing to the floor, leftover cannoli batter spattering over the ceramic tiles and across the cabinets. This was accompanied by a sound that could only be compared to one you'd expect to hear in an active war zone.

In a panic, Livy dropped her phone. She dove for it and the next thing she knew, her feet went flying out from under her and she landed, hard, on the now slippery floor.

For a few seconds, she didn't move.

"Oh my God..."

Concerned, Sam jumped halfway out of his chair. After he gave a swift glance around the coffee shop, thankful to see no appeared to have noticed, he slowly sank back into the chair,

He waited for Livy to say something. When there was nothing but silence, he became worried. "Sweetheart, are you all right? What happened?"

After a long string of inaudible mumbling, followed by a long drawn out sigh, she finally answered him. "I'm fine. A little bit of a mess, but I'm fine. A few bowls were knocked over, that's all. No big deal. No need to worry."

She certainly wasn't going to let him know she was still on the floor. Sam was grinning. Now that he knew there was no harm done to Livy, he was feeling quite pleased, wondering if what he'd said caused this calamity of sorts. He cleared his throat.

"I hope this wasn't brought on by what I said. Because it certainly wasn't my intention to get you all flustered." His smile came out in his next words. "Do you need me to come to your rescue?"

Of course, Livy became completely undone at this, her answer coming out much sharper than she intended. "Let me assure you, what happened had nothing to do with you. It was an accident. And no, you do not have to come to my rescue. I'm perfectly able..."

He cut her off. *"Ah, ha...* let me make a wild guess at what you were planning to say. That you're perfectly able to take care of yourself. Am I right?" He chuckled. "I don't know... I'm beginning to think there might not be any truth in that claim. Unless these things only happen when I'm around..."

He left the sentence hanging. He knew he wouldn't have to wait long.

Livy was practically sputtering. "Again, the answer to that is a no. I think you need to get over yourself."

Even though she followed this with another long and dramatic sigh, she couldn't hide the smile in her voice. "Now, as you can imagine, I have quite a mess to clean up and I really shouldn't be chit-chatting on the phone. Is there a reason you called?"

"Yes, as a matter of fact, there is. There are actually two reasons. But first, as much as I understand you're not interested in chit chatting, whatever you mean by that, I want to let you know I'm not really a fan of texting. Or emailing. I'm more of a personal approach kind of guy. So, calling you is what I'd much rather do."

When she had nothing to say to this, he continued. "But, the real reason for my call? To be completely honest, I wanted to hear your voice. If only to have it go along with the image of you that's somehow settled in my mind."

Totally floored by what he said, she was silent. Still sitting on the floor, she leaned her head back against the cabinet, another smile working its way across her face.

Then he went on to almost completely ruin the moment. "But I also wanted to tell you how glad I am you came over to my way of thinking, recognizing the logic of me picking you up for our date. But don't worry. In the future, I'll be sure to let you have your way every once in a while."

Her smile was inevitable. "Why, how generous of you. I don't know if I should thank you, or what."

He chuckled. "Though a little half-hearted, your thank you has been accepted."

But now, Livy was frowning. The future? She didn't want to think about the future. Every time she'd attempted this in the past, no good had come from it. And, come on… the likelihood of Sam becoming a part of her future? This was more like a dream than a possibility.

"Livy? Are you still with me?"

She closed her eyes. Yes, she was still with him. This was the problem.

She had been with him ever since she'd opened her eyes to find him gazing down at her as she lay sprawled out on the lobby floor of Carrie's hotel.

She had been with him, if only in her mind, even after she was back with Zack. Always comparing the two of them, to then become so confused and depressed. Always wondering if she may have made the biggest mistake of her life by getting back together with Zack.

And let's not forget about how Sam manages to appear so often in your dreams.

Let's face it, he was always with her.

Everywhere.

At work. At home. Or, even when she was out and about, trying to go about her life.

Somehow, he'd taken over a huge chunk of her mind. Always hovering in the background, he was a reminder it was okay for her to imagine more.

And, though this was almost too dangerous to even admit, he was slowly stealing a piece of her heart, bit by bit.

She sighed. "Yes, I'm still here."

Tell him... go ahead, give him more to go on.

"You make it sort of hard for me to not be, since you keep showing up."

Sam was smiling. "Ah… that's the plan, baby." This was followed by complete silence.

Uh oh...

Fearing he might have gone too far with what he just said, he cleared his throat, this time coming out with more of what he *should've* said.

"But, as you so eloquently put it, enough of this chit chatting. I still have a few more calls to make before I call it a day. And after that fall, you need to get up off the floor and clean up the mess you have going on."

Livy's mouth fell open. "How did you know I fell? And I'm still on the floor?"

He chuckled. "I didn't. But I do now. I'll see you tomorrow night at seven. And one more thing… since this date could be a good opportunity to practice before the wedding, where we're going, there will be dancing."

Livy couldn't help it, she laughed. "Dancing? Are you sure you want to chance it? Haven't I already given you more than enough proof of how uncoordinated I can be?"

Sam chuckled. "This is why I'm suggesting we give it a run through tomorrow night. Since Carrie has partnered us up for the wedding, beautiful or not, I still expect you to be able to dance. After all, I live here, which means my reputation is on the line." He chuckled. "Once again… I'll pick you up tomorrow night at seven. See you then."

She was left staring down at the silent phone.

Carrie had partnered them up for the wedding? And now they were going dancing?

She didn't even want to think about the last time she'd been on a dance floor. If anything, she'd tried to block this embarrassing episode completely out of her mind.

Do you even remember how to dance?

But this wouldn't be just dancing. This would be dancing with Sam. Not only tomorrow night, but at the wedding, as well.

At the thought of being in his arms, she had to close her eyes…

There was no doubt about it. This whole thing with Sam was going to put her right over the edge.

Sam set his phone on the table. He was smiling. He couldn't remember when he'd so thoroughly enjoyed talking to a woman on the phone.

He'd never been able to understand how someone could talk for hours, let alone on the phone. But with Livy? If he hadn't had an obligation to make these few calls, he'd still be on the phone with her. It wouldn't even matter what they talked about. The sound of her voice alone would be enough to keep him hanging on the line.

"Sam?"

He looked up to see the woman who'd filled his coffee order was standing next to him. She was holding a cup in her hand. "I'm sorry to bother you, but I mistakenly gave you the wrong cup of coffee."

She glanced over at his half empty cup, a look of surprise coming over her face. "Wow, I'm surprised you didn't notice. Or at least say something to one of us. You've been drinking a low-fat Caffe Latte, two sugars, instead of your usual Deep Roast, black, no sugar."

She set the cup she was holding down on the table. "Here is the coffee you were supposed to get. Again, I'm so sorry."

Sam looked down at his cup before he glanced back at her. He burst out laughing. "Well, evidently my mind must be on other things, because I didn't even notice. But hey, it's okay. Don't worry about it. Thanks for the new cup."

A relieved look on her face, she gave him a big smile before she hurried back behind the counter.

Still chuckling, Sam picked up his cup and took a big swallow of coffee. An expression of disgust filling his face, he almost spit it out. He looked down to see he'd picked up the wrong cup, the one with the latte.

How the hell didn't you notice what you were drinking? This stuff is awful.

He shook his head. Well, what do you know… it now appeared he had all the proof he needed.

It was official.

He was, without a doubt, in serious trouble.

And going by Libby's flustered state, during what she'd referred to as their "chit-chatting," she was in just as much trouble as he was.

But he honestly felt okay with this. He planned to hang on to what Carrie told him—that it was only going to get better.

Hmm… He'd really like to know how long it was going to take for this to happen.

Livy had been put in charge of baking the last batch of cannoli while her aunt watched the late-night news.

Evidently, this was a nightly ritual not to be missed.

After taking the tray out of the oven, Livy tossed the potholder down on the counter, brushing her bangs back from her damp forehead.

Yep, you guessed it. Aunt Evelyn also didn't think very highly of air conditioning, quick to assure everyone the breeze coming off the lake was enough to keep her house cool.

Never mind that the lake was at least a mile from her house.

A glance around the cluttered kitchen, and giving a big sigh, Lily began clearing up the mess.

Forty-five minutes later, she was sitting on her bed, in her pajamas and her lap top open in front of her. She began typing, the sentences swiftly taking shape in her head. Almost to the point her fingers couldn't keep up, flying over the keys.

Four hours later, exhausted by her efforts, but at the same time, exhilarated, she hit save and closed her laptop.

She turned out the light, drifting off to sleep.

In her dream, Livy was dancing. Amazingly, she was working the floor like a pro. Unfortunately, her dream didn't allow her to see what kind of shoes she was wearing.

Nor was she able to see who her dance partner was.

She was hoping it was Sam.

CHAPTER 10

*L*ivy drove right past the entrance to the parking lot of the Chic Boutique. She didn't even realize this until she had to stop for a red light three blocks down the road.

This was because she really wasn't paying attention.

Something that needed to stop.

Only this morning, she'd put the milk in the cupboard and the cereal in the refrigerator. She'd also spent about ten minutes frantically searching for her phone, to finally find it stuffed in the bottom of one of her suitcases. She had no idea how it got there and she probably never would.

This behavior had begun right after she checked her phone to find she had a voice mail from Sam.

"Hey, beautiful… I just wanted to let you know I'm really looking forward to our date tonight. Have a great day and I'll see you at seven."

She'd listened to it again.

Beautiful?

This immediately sent her into a panic.

Because this was crazy. Downright-out-of-control-crazy.

Seriously? Was there something wrong with the man? She was far from beautiful. If anything, she was a train wreck.

For the next hour and a half, this had her rummaging through every article of clothing she owned, searching for something to wear.

Something suited for dancing.

She'd finally settled on a sleeveless polished cotton sundress. A deep, vibrant shade of rose, she'd bought it on a whim last summer.

She wasn't good at shopping. Especially when it came to clothes. As was the case with most of the things she bought, she'd fallen in love with the dress when she tried it on in the store. But once she'd brought it home, she wondered what she'd been thinking.

The color of the dress was suddenly all too wrong, the deep shade of rose too vibrant and the complete opposite of what she normally wore. She tended to gravitate towards more neutral and safe colors. Or the predictable choice of black, white, gray and tailored—the acceptable attire of young professionals in the city.

Her intention had been to return the dress, but she'd completely forgotten. It was only when she was packing for this trip home, she found it hanging in her closet, the tags still on.

The cut of the dress was simple. Sleeveless, it had a fitted bodice with a v-neckline. The skirt flared out from the waistline, the hemline hitting right at her knees. It would be a perfect dress to wear for a night of dancing.

Her choice of shoes was a much easier decision to make. She was going to wear the same shoes she wore that November night. The same shoes that sent her flying to the floor, the sequence of events following, completely changing her life.

Never would she have believed it would lead to this.

A date with Sam?

Nope... not in a million years.

After Livy finally parked her car, she entered the Chic Boutique to find she was the first to arrive. In fact, no one appeared to be in the small shop, neither customers or sales associates.

She walked over to the sales counter, tentatively peering into the back room. "Hello? Is anyone here?"

After a rustling noise, followed by the sound of boxes falling and a few muttered comments, Sophie's Aunt Louise came bustling out to the counter. She smiled when she saw Livy. "Livy! How are you? I'm sorry, I was trying to stack some of the boxes so we'd at least have room to move around back there. We just got a new shipment in. Sophie warned me she ordered more than usual, but I certainly didn't expect there would be so many boxes."

She shook her head. "But I've learned to trust Sophie's judgment. She hasn't made a bad purchase yet." She grinned, quickly knocking on the counter. "Knock on wood."

Livy smiled, thinking how much alike Sophie and her aunt were. Filled with an endless energy, they both talked a mile a minute, never at a loss for words. "Let me help you. Since no one is here yet, I really don't have anything else to do."

Louise appeared to be horrified at this suggestion. "Absolutely not. Paul has already promised to stop by later this afternoon and he's bringing Sophie's brother, Brian. They are planning to put more shelving along the one wall, which should make it easier to organize everything."

She smiled at Livy. "Let me find your dress. Even though no one else had arrived, there's no reason you can't get a head start on your fitting. Though I'm sure there won't be a problem with the fit. Sophie always takes excellent measurements."

She began searching through the dresses hanging on the rack by the counter. "I'm sure you'll like what Carrie has chosen. The dresses are very pretty and the rose color will be very flattering on everyone." She sent Livy a sly glance. "I'm sure your Sam will approve."

Intent on her search, she didn't see the surprised expression on Livy's face.

I'm sure your Sam will approve?

But before she could comment on this, Louise found what she was looking for, shoving a dress in Livy's hands. "Here you go. The dressing room is right over there. If you need any assistance with the zipper or anything, just yell. I'll come right out to help you."

She gave Livy a gentle push towards the dressing room and she was gone, disappearing into the back room.

A frown on her face, Livy watched her leave. Evidently, she needed to talk to Carrie. Because it was beginning to look like everyone knew more about her and Sam than she did.

But then again?

As Livy would be quick to tell you, she really didn't know much of anything.

About an hour and a half later, Sophie's Aunt Louise was finally satisfied. Everyone's dress fit perfectly and no additional alterations were needed.

After chatting with Sophie and Emily as they packed the dresses in garment bags, Carrie pulled Livy aside. "I wanted to tell you how nice it is to see you're finally wearing your contacts. I was going to tell you this when you came to my office yesterday, but you ran out of there so fast, I didn't get the chance. So, tell me… what was that all about? You taking off like that?"

Livy shrugged. "I had things to do."

Yeah… such as getting away from Sam before you did something stupid. Like ask him to kiss you. Or just grab him and be the one to do the kissing.

It was obvious by the big grin on Carrie's face, she didn't buy this explanation. "Hmm… really? I'll have you know I also managed to get it out of Sam that he asked you out for dinner tonight. And you said yes."

She hesitated for a moment before she dove right in with her next question. "What about Zack? Are you finally over him? Because I don't want to see Sam get hurt if you're still not sure about what you want."

Livy began searching through her purse for her keys in an attempt to avoid Carrie's gaze. "It seems Zack is back to his old tricks. I'm pretty sure he has been seeing someone else. And yes, I know you tried to warn me about this. And double yes, I'm feeling very stupid and extremely upset with myself about how I handled the whole situation. Clearly, I wasn't thinking."

She finally met Carrie's gaze, her voice firm. "Zack and I are over with for good. I don't feel anything for him anymore... absolutely nothing."

She smiled wistfully at Carrie. "And I would never hurt Sam. Never."

Yeah, but he might hurt you. It could happen. You should know.

She took a deep breath. "And as long as I'm at it, I might as well also let you know I no longer have a job. The company made the decision to eliminate my position. So, with no Zack and no job, I had no reason to stay in New York. And right now, I have no desire to ever go back."

As soon this information came shooting out of her mouth, she wished she could take it all back.

Weren't you the one who told Sophie you weren't going to burden Carrie with your problems?

She shook her head. "I wasn't planning to tell you any of this. Not until after the wedding. So, forget I even brought it up. I'm fine with it. I've even managed to convince myself this may be the best thing for me. Maybe it's a blessing in disguise."

Her laugh was shaky. "*Oh geeez...* now I'm starting to sound like Aunt Evelyn. My God, Carrie... I've only been here for a short time and already I don't know how much longer I can stay with her. It's not because of her. No, I love her dearly. But she makes me feel like a little kid again. I'm afraid I'll become completely dependent on her and lose any of the motivation I might have brought home with me. It's bad enough, every time I turn around, she's trying to feed me. She claims I'm too thin. If I ate like she suggested, I'd be as big as a horse."

Carrie was looking at her, a mixture of anger and sadness on her face. "I'm not going to say I warned you about Zack. Even though I can't help thinking this. And you're not going to get as big as a horse. I think you're being a little dramatic. You've only been here for two days. How bad could it be?"

Then her lips parting, her eyes lit up.

This worried Livy. This was an indication she had another one of her ideas. And when this happened with Carrie, there was nothing to do but listen quietly to what she had to say and hope for the best.

"I have a proposition for you, one that will be beneficial to both of us. You can stay at my place while Chris and I are on our honeymoon. Jingles will be in cat heaven if someone is there to keep her company. We'll only be gone about a week, so that should give you enough time to come up with a plan. In fact, you know what? I'm not even going to give you the option of refusing."

She grinned. "Think of it as one of your maid-of-honor duties, okay?"

After Livy finally nodded to this, Carrie sent her a sly glance. "But getting back to Sam and this date. Have you decided what you're going to wear?"

Livy laughed. "Always the big question… what to wear. As a matter of fact, I have. I have this sleeveless rose-colored dress I impulsively bought last summer and never wore. Once I got it home, I thought maybe it was too bright. But since Sam told me where we're going, there will be dancing. I think this dress will be perfect."

Carrie was staring at her so intently, Livy knew she was up to something else. She sighed. "What? Now what are you thinking? Just say it."

Carrie grinned. "Well, don't get mad at me…"

This of course, had Livy beginning to do exactly that. "Carrie…"

Carrie shrugged. "Just hear me out. Sophie's friend Kelly is an amazing hair stylist. She's the same person who will be coming to Chez and Sophie's house to do our hair for the wedding. I asked Sophie if she could get you an appointment and she was able to fit you in this afternoon." She glanced down at her watch. "This would be in about twenty minutes from now."

Livy wouldn't admit this to Carrie, not in a million years, she wouldn't, but she was actually relieved. The more she thought about this date with Sam, the more she wanted to show him she could be just as beautiful as he seemed to think she was. Or at least give him a halfway valid reason for his comments.

She shrugged. "I guess it's about time I updated my look. And I'd like to look my best for your wedding."

So, even though Livy was trying to act as though it was no big deal, Carrie knew she was happy about the appointment.

She was smiling as she called over too Sophie. "Hey, Sophie. Is there anything you need to tell Livy about Kelly? She's leaving for her appointment."

Sophie merely smiled. "Oh good. I know you'll like her, Livy. But seriously, be open to what she suggests. She definitely knows what she's doing."

She grinned.

"Trust me on this. You're going to look amazing."

CHAPTER 11

$\mathcal{A}$unt Evelyn's grandfather clock chimed the three-quarter hour. This meant Sam would be arriving in fifteen minutes.

After Livy zipped up her dress and put on her shoes, she made her way to the bathroom. Her trip there was a bit on the wobbly side, but this was only because she wasn't quite accustomed to walking in the four-inch heels. After all, the only time she had worn these shoes had been that night she was with Carrie and Sam.

She just needed a little time to get used to them again, that's all.

And there was no snow on the ground. No reason to slip and fall. So, she should be all right.

Shouldn't she?

Carefully repeating Kelly's technique for a flawless look, she applied a coat of her new lipstick. According to what was written on the bottom of the tube, Kiss Me Now was the name given to this particular shade. How they came up with a name like this was beyond her. And even though it was definitely not a color she'd choose on her own, it did go really well with her dress.

She was trying not to pay too much attention to the new and improved Livy staring back at her from the mirror. She wasn't quite sure how she felt about this new look. Kelly had cut her hair in soft layers. A lot shorter than she'd worn it, going all the way back to her college days, it now barely brushed her shoulders. She did like how it seemed to almost float back into place, with even a simple move of her head. And with the subtle highlights Kelly had added, her hair now looked so shiny and healthy looking.

It turned out Kelly was also very into make-up. It was her belief, if done correctly, the use of the right products could dramatically change a woman's life. And this could all be achieved in only a few minutes, she'd assured her. With all of the products available, there was no excuse not to make the best of your looks.

It had taken a lot of persuading on Livy's part to get Kelly to tone down some of her ideas. But now, as she gazed into the mirror, she had to admit she did look more sophisticated. And her eyes? They appeared smoky, mysterious. She'd even go on to say they looked almost seductive.

Now, if only she could remember how to duplicate this same look on her own. To at least make use of the numerous products she'd purchased from Kelly. She was pretty sure she spent more on these than she'd spent over the last ten years, total.

After debating on whether or not she needed a purse, she slipped her aunt's house key into her credit card holder. Her plan was to ask Sam if he could put both this and her lipstick in his pocket. Surely, he wouldn't mind doing this?

One more look in the mirror, she smiled. And her reflection smiled back at her.

This was when it hit her. She actually looked pretty. She'd even go as far to say she looked almost beautiful. Filled with a sudden confidence, she turned out the light and made her way downstairs.

With her aunt out to dinner with Carrie, Chris and his family, she was alone in the house. There was no loud drone of laughter and voices coming from the TV. Instead, an almost eerie silence prevailed.

She glanced over at the grandfather clock to see it was now almost seven. Since it was such a beautiful night, she decided to wait for Sam outside.

Seated on the front steps, Livy was taken back to when she was younger. How she had sat on these same steps so many times, waiting for a friend.

She closed her eyes and took a long, deep breath of the warm summer's night air.

This was when she decided, this was exactly how she was going to treat this date with Sam. She wasn't going to consider it a date. No, it would be just another outing with a friend. This way, her expectations would be low.

Because the absolute last thing she wanted to do, was get her hopes up.

At least this was her plan…

Sam was about two minutes away.

As he drove, he was listening to a voice message from Chris. He'd called to let Sam know a friend of his had contacted him about a property that hadn't even hit the market yet. It was a property Chris was pretty sure Sam would want to check out.

Of course, there was a catch. A very big catch.

The house wasn't in the best of shape. In fact, if they didn't move fast on this, there was a chance the house could very well be headed for demolition.

Once the home of a well-known and wealthy family who'd settled in Cleveland close to a hundred and fifty years ago, it was now considered a white elephant. Forgotten and completely neglected for twenty years or so, the only remaining heirs had now decided it was time to sell.

As far as they were concerned, and Chris had to admit he was pretty much in agreement with this, the one and only selling point was the location of the house. Built on an almost two-acre lot bordering Lake Erie, it was considered a prime lakefront property. But, with the state it was in, Chris was confident they could get it for a song.

He had actually gone to check it out only a few hours ago, taking time to walk around and assess the exterior of the property. From the little he could see in through the windows, the architectural details of the interior of the house would probably be more than enough to win Sam over.

But again, Chris was quick to remind him, the house needed a ton of work, and he was talking major reconstruction here. So, Sam's input was needed as soon as possible if they were to even consider making an offer.

Chris ended his message with the promise once his friend got back to him with the combination to the lock box, he'd send it off to Sam.

Sam pulled into the driveway of Livy's aunt's house.

After he turned off the ignition, he debated as to whether he should call Chris. He didn't want to intrude on his family dinner. But for some reason, even though he had nothing to go by except what Chris told him, he was very intrigued about this new opportunity.

It sounded like a no-brainer to him.

Thinking, this one time, a text would be less intrusive than a call, he picked up his phone.

Send me the info and I'll check it out. Maybe tomorrow morning? The last thing we need right now is another property to work on, but you got me hooked on what you said about the interior of the house. So, what the hell? Why not make a go for it?

He grabbed a single red rose from the passenger seat and got out of his SUV.

He was smiling.

Chris had more energy than anyone he knew. He also had this uncanny knack of knowing what real estate purchase would work in their favor. The house they were now working on in Shaker Heights was proof of this. Good at swaying even the most reluctant buyer into making a purchase, he was also able to convince a seller when it was time to accept an offer.

There was no doubt about it, the smartest thing he ever did was agree to Chris's suggestion of a partnership. Right from the beginning, they'd settled into an easy camaraderie, as though they'd worked together for years.

Yes… he had a feeling there were good things ahead for them.

Sam was still thinking about the call from Chris as he made his way to the front door of the house. It was when he came to the steps, he looked up to see Livy.

Right in front of him and her chin propped on her hand, she was curiously watching his progress.

He came to an abrupt halt, almost dropping the rose. Their eyes met, and for the life of him, he couldn't look away, couldn't move. It was as though everything around them had come to a grinding halt, leaving him completely paralyzed.

He didn't say a word. Not that he didn't try… because he did. But it appeared, on top of everything else, his mind had decided to bow out on him, shutting down completely.

The only thing he was aware of… the only thing he could see… was Livy.

The phrase, take your breath away, bounced into his mind. A phrase he'd never quite believed.

But he did now…

All because of the beautiful woman now in front of him.

Seconds, minutes… Sam couldn't even begin to tell you how much time passed before he was finally able to get his act together. He cleared his throat. And then, damn, if he didn't have to clear it again. Moving closer, he cautiously reached out to touch her hair. His fingers slipping through the silky layers, he pushed back an errant strand the breeze had blown in her face.

The only thought in his mind, oddly enough, was Carrie... and how she'd been so right about what she told him.

She said it was only going to get better. And it would be wonderful.

This moment was proof of this.

Livy had watched Sam make his way up the walk, a preoccupied expression on his face. When he finally looked up, and right into her eyes, she gave him a tentative smile.

For, what seemed like a terribly long and tense-filled moment, he didn't move, his gaze slowly traveling over her before coming back to her face. To her relief, he then reached over to gently brush the hair back from her forehead.

His voice came out husky, almost hesitant. "Hey... this... well, I... What I mean to say... this is a surprise."

Having worked herself into a bundle of nerves, worrying about how he was going to react to this new look, Livy wasn't quite sure how to interpret what he said. A surprise? Did he mean this in a good way? Or was he not quite sure if he liked this bold change she'd made to her appearance?

Maybe he was more into the wholesome and natural kind of look? The no make-up kind of woman. Or one who went for the subtle and demure look.

Darn... you should've gone with your instincts and toned down the makeup. And the dress... maybe there's a reason why it still hung in your closet, never worn. The color is too bright... too flashy. What were you thinking?

She avoided his gaze, nervously running her hands over the skirt of the dress, smoothing it down over her knees. Her words were halting, tentative. "It's only a haircut and a few highlights. I also tried out a different make up, if only to freshen up my look a little That's all."

She gave him a hesitant glance, followed with a shrug. "I thought maybe it was time for a change. You know, since everything else in my life is so different now."

When he started to shake his head, her words came out even more swiftly. "I know the color of the dress is sort of bright. I usually don't wear colors like this. But it is summer. And it was the only dress I had that would be good for dancing. You did say, where we were going, there would be dancing."

She sent a quick glance down at her shoes and then back up at him. "And, you probably remember these shoes. I'm pretty sure I've mastered the art of walking in them since you've last seen them. So, there's no need to worry about a repeat of what happened last time. It's not snowing. Or slippery. I thought…"

In the disoriented state Sam found himself in, he'd been slow to realize she had taken his comment entirely the wrong way.

He moved closer, swiftly pressing his fingers to her mouth. "Stop, just stop. *Damn,* I'm so sorry. What I meant to say is it's an absolutely wonderful and amazing surprise. You look beautiful."

His fingers moved in a gentle caress down her cheek. "Everything about you… your hair, your makeup, the dress… they're all perfect. And your dress? You should wear colors like this all the time. It brings out the color of your eyes."

He slowly shook his head. "They look incredible. A man could get lost in your eyes. I should know, since I already have."

Hugging her knees, she let out a long, shaky breath.

His glance went on to skim over her body starting with her face, before traveling down to her shoes, this time in a more leisurely fashion.

This brought a slow blush to her cheeks.

He slowly shook his head.

God, she's gorgeous. How can she not realize this? If she only knew what she does to you… what thoughts she stirs in you.

A smile tugged at his mouth. "And the shoes? You couldn't possibly know how glad I am you wore these shoes that night, to then go and throw yourself right at my feet…"

Just as he expected, she stiffened, her whole body going into her attack mode. She narrowed her eyes at him. "Let me remind you once again. That was an accident. The shoes were new, the floor was slippery. I did not dream up that fall in order to get your attention."

He chuckled. "Ah… and there it is. The only thing about you I never want to change. The Livy I know so well, filled with a passion for everything she believes in. I'm relieved to know, even under this new look, that Livy is still there."

The teasing glint had come back into his eyes. "And come on, let me hold on to that little boost to my ego, leaving me to believe you orchestrated that fall in order to get my attention. This has been the one thing I've been holding on to for all these months. What man doesn't dream of a beautiful woman falling for him?"

His gaze holding hers captive, his look was so tender, she'd swear her heart gave a little flip flop in response.

She slowly smiled back at him. "Okay, I'll let you have that one time. But no more."

It was when he went to take her hands to pull her up from the steps, he realized he was still holding the rose. He handed to her. "This is for you. I wasn't quite sure what kind of flowers you like. The florist assured me this was the best choice."

He didn't tell her, when he'd asked the woman in the flower shop for advice as to what kind of flower he should get for Livy, she'd asked him if he was in love with her or just getting to know her. And damn, if he could do nothing but give her a big grin. Laughing, she told him the look on his face more than answered her question. Even if he didn't know it yet, it looked like he was definitely in love.

Once his purchase had been made and he was back in his SUV, he'd stared at the rose on the passenger seat, grinning the whole

Livy took the rose from him, a shy smile on her face. "Thank you. It's beautiful."

He reached for her hands and helping her to her feet, he pulled her right into his arms. He smiled down at her. "You're more than welcome."

He suddenly started to chuckle.

This, of course, concerned her. "Oh no, now what?"

His hands drifting down her back, he pulled her closer, the sudden need to feel her against him. "I seem to remember we had a wager going on when I was in New York. And I do believe I was the winner in both round one and round two."

He was grinning. "And lo and behold, it looks like I may have won round three."

His grin widened. "Maybe even round four, since I did get you to agree I would pick you up for our date tonight."

Livy was trying really hard to appear angry about what he just said. But she was having a really hard time. Sam watched as she struggled to compose her mouth into a frown, to no avail.

He tilted his head, searching her face. "So, what's this? You have nothing to say? No comeback of any kind?" He shook his head. "My, my, my... I must say I'm a little disappointed at this."

She leaned away from him. Now she was laughing. "You're insufferable. And I don't think you're playing at all fair. When you start to play a game with someone, you're supposed to let them know there's even a game being played. How will I ever catch up? You're already so far ahead of me."

He nodded, very slowly he did this. His arm still around her, he was determined to keep her close for as long as he could. "*Hmm...* well, now you know the score. But I don't believe it's going to matter in the long run. Because, the way I see it, I'm pretty sure we'll both be winners in this game, sweetheart."

He glanced down at his watch. "I see it's now after seven. This means our date has already officially begun. So, we should get going."

As he reached for her hand, she stopped him. "Wait. Can you put these in your pocket for me? Then I won't have to bring a purse." She handed him the credit card holder and her lipstick.

About to put them in his pocket, he flipped the lipstick. "Let's check out what fancy name they gave this lipstick of yours."

Now, Sam would swear he had absolutely no idea why he did this. Honest. Never in his life had he even thought about the name chosen for a lipstick. Or, to be truthful, if he even cared. Red, pink, orange... did it matter?

"*Ah... interesting.*" Slowly lifting his gaze to hers, he was smiling. "Kiss Me Now. H*mm...* this definitely comes across as an invitation, wouldn't you say?"

Before she could answer, this is exactly what he did. It was just enough of a kiss for her to know she wouldn't mind if he kissed her again. Maybe a little bit longer the second time around. When this didn't happen, she opened her eyes to see a smile lurking at the corner of his mouth. "Now, aren't you glad you didn't insist on meeting me at the restaurant? I know I am. Because this moment would've been lost."

And, as what seemed to be happening the more they were together, Livy had nothing to say.

Yep... she was at a complete loss of words.

Instead, she couldn't seem to quit smiling.

CHAPTER 12

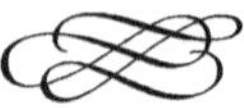

Sam closed the passenger door before he ran around to get into the driver's seat.

As he buckled his seat belt, his glance fell on his phone, tucked in the console. There was a message.

It was from Chris.

> Here's the address and the combination for the lock box. Let me know what you think when you get a chance to check out the property.

Sam sat back in his seat. His expression thoughtful, he gazed over at Livy. For some odd reason, it was suddenly imperative he go check out this house. And, even more importantly, that he take her with him.

And, he wanted to do this now.

Livy hesitantly waved her hand in front of his face. "Sam?"

He blinked. He picked up his phone before he sent her a smile. "Sorry about that, I was thinking. In fact, I have a proposition for you. How do you feel about a slight change in plans? There's something I'd like to look into before we have dinner. It's a property Chris called me about just a short while ago. It hasn't even been put on the market yet.

Since timing is so important in deals like this, I'd like to check it out. And I'd like you to go with me. Are you game?"

The look on his face was so earnest, she nodded.

He set up the call, the connection coming through the car's speaker system. "Ok, let's see if we can change the reservations."

After a loud click, a woman answered. "Good evening and thank you for calling Pier W. This is Brandy speaking. How may I help you?"

Sam sent Livy a quick smile before he answered. "Hello, Brandy. This is Sam Bridges. I have a reservation for tonight at seven-thirty. Is there any way I can move it back, to let's say, eight-thirty?"

"Hi, Mr. Bridges. Of course, we can do that. Same table by the window?"

"Yes, that would be great. Even though it will be almost dark by the time we get there, we'll still be able to enjoy the view of the city skyline. I really appreciate you doing this for us, Brandy. We'll see you at eight-thirty then."

"Anything for you, Mr. Bridges. And just to let you know, your favorite chef is here tonight. We look forward to seeing you and your guest."

At the loud click indicating the call had ended, Sam grinned over at Livy. "Well, that was easy. And now you know where we're going. I hope you'll like it, as it one of my favorite restaurants. The locals consider it as one of the hidden gems in the city. And the chef? He's actually a very good friend of mine, Jake Martin. We go all the way back to high school. Played football together. If we get a chance to talk to him, he'll be sure to bring up how much better he was at the sport than I was." He shrugged, sending her a quick grin. "Which he was... but you'll never catch me admitting this to him."

After he pulled out onto the street, Sam glanced over to see Livy was studying him, a thoughtful expression on her face.

He smiled. "Uh oh, now what are you thinking? Or, should I re-phrase that to, what have I done now?"

She shook her head. "Do you always get what you want? It seems like everything comes so easily to you."

He was silent for a few seconds. Then a small smile played on his lips. "Hmm... I'm not sure if I know quite how to answer. I guess living here ever since I graduated from college, I've gotten to know a lot of people. This had made things a lot easier, you know, having connections and all."

He chuckled. "But as far as always getting what I want? I guess I've always considered myself lucky in that department. But lately, I feel the stakes have become higher, my goals becoming more important. Almost life changing, in a way and not quite yet in my reach."

He sent her a quick glance. "But that's okay, because I love a challenge."

Oh dear...

The look he sent made her think she just might be the challenge he was referring to. So, she needed to change the subject before she came out and said something stupid. Such as, if he was in fact talking about her, there was no challenge as far as she was concerned.

Nope. He's already pretty much won you over to his side.

She searched her mind for something else to talk about... something safe. "What made you decide to live here... in Cleveland, of all places?"

Yes, this is good... not too personal. A very straight forward kind of question you could ask just about anyone. You've got this now...

"Hmm... why did I pick Cleveland..." He took time to think about this before he smiled over at her. "I guess I wanted some stability in my life, something I never had while I was growing up. Even though Cleveland is a pretty big city, it still has that home town feeling. There's also has a wealth of historical properties, which is right up my alley. Like the home we're working on now in Shaker Heights."

He sent her another smile. "To duplicate the same home today, on the same lever of craftsmanship and architectural details, would run anywhere around a few million dollars, maybe even more. I can take you there, if you'd like. It's an amazing property."

She nodded, smiling at his enthusiasm. "I would like that."

Drawn in by her interest, he continued. "But most of all, I knew I didn't want to move somewhere where I'd become just another person in the crowd, another number. I'd already had enough of that kind of life when I was a kid. Both of my parents had high-profile jobs in DC and status was very important to them. Sometimes too important, I'm afraid."

He was silent for a few moments. Then he shrugged. "But that's all over and done with. And now, it's time to move on." There was a slight tone of regret in his voice, along with a hint of sadness.

Remembering the information Sophie shared about his parent's divorce and the situation with his sister, she impulsively reached over and placed her hand on his arm. "I'm sorry. About your parents."

He glanced over at her, surprised to see her sad expression. "You're sorry? You shouldn't be. I'm okay with it now. If anything, I believe it's made me a better person. I know what I want in life and what matters. And even more importantly, I know what I don't want."

He grinned. "Maybe this is why you were so quick to see me as your knight in shining armor. You know the nice guy that I am."

Just to set the record straight, Livy knew she should tell him she didn't think of him as her own personal knight in shining armor. Surely, she'd made it clear she was perfectly capable of taking care of herself.

No, he'd assumed this on his own

But the possibility of this actually happening was comforting.

Too comforting.

But then again, this certainly wasn't something she wanted.

Was it?

And now she was confused. Gently removing her hand from his arm, she placed it in her lap.

Unbeknownst to Livy, Sam was thinking along the same lines. But he had a completely different perspective on what he wanted to happen.

He was more than willing to take on the role of knighthood.

For as long as she'd let you.

Tapping his fingers on the steering wheel, he was filled with the urge to tell her this.

He wanted to tell her everything.

His hopes. His dreams. Even his worries. And all of his fears.

All in the hope she would share the same with him.

He wanted to tell her any confusion clouding his mind had disappeared. And even though he was not quite sure of how she felt, he knew where he stood.

But maybe he was moving too quickly?

You think? Good Lord... if you were to add up the hours you spent together so far, it wouldn't even add up to the hours in a day. That's pretty damn fast.

But this is the way he dealt with everything, be it personal or business. He'd always been one to act when he found what he wanted.

And you want Livy.

It would help if he knew what the story was with Zach. At least then he'd have an idea of what his next move would be.

But obviously, she wasn't ready to share that with him yet.

So, he could do nothing but wait.

A silence fell between them.

In five hundred feet, make a right-hand turn. You will have reached your destination.

This command from the GPS, Sam slowed the SUV to make the turn onto a long gravel driveway. That it could even be considered a driveway was debatable. It was more of a dirt path, overtaken by weeds. They were soon to find out this overgrowth also covered a multitude of deep ruts and potholes, turning the path leading up to the house into an obstacle course.

Sam chuckled, shaking his head. Evidently, Chris hadn't been exaggerating when he said the house was in bad shape. Obviously ignored and left vacant for many years, it now had an almost haunted air about it. Situated about five-hundred feet from the street, it backed up about the same distance from the lake.

At the first huge rut they hit, he stepped on the brakes, bringing them to an abrupt stop. He glanced over to see Livy was leaning forward in her seat, intently studying the two-story brick house in front of them. She briefly glanced over at him, a puzzled look on her face before she returned her attention to the house.

Sam slowly steered the SUV over the uneven ground. "Chris warned me there was a lot of work needed on this property, but I thought he was only referring to the house. I guess I thought wrong. This looks more like a trail than a driveway, so hold on tight." Barely moving above a crawl, they continued to bounce their way over the uneven ground.

He abruptly turned the steering wheel to avoid the next huge hole. "Damn… I hope this isn't a sign of what we can expect of the inside of the house."

This was when Livy, who was gripping the arm rest for dear life, let out a loud gasp.

Sam immediately stepped on the brakes. "God, I'm sorry. Are you okay? I'm beginning to think this wasn't a good idea. Maybe we should just turn around. I can always come back another time."

Livy was shaking her head. "No, no… don't turn around." Excitement filled her face. "I wasn't sure at first, but now I am. Sam, I've been here before. I was at a party at this house when I was in second grade."

She took another long look at the house before she turned back to him. But now she appeared to be almost on the verge of tears. "But it looked nothing like this. Oh, Sam… it was beautiful. I remember telling Carrie I wanted to live here. I told her it was like a fairy tale castle."

She grinned at him. "I remember this made her so mad. She was jealous because she hadn't been invited."

Sam was staring at her, an incredulous expression on his face. "You're serious? Can you remember what it looked like then?"

She slowly nodded. "Oh, Sam… I remember everything… what I wore, what we ate, the cake… everything. It was a birthday party. The theme was an afternoon tea party. It was Darcey Hollister's birthday party and this was her grandmother's house." She frowned. "Since we weren't really friends, I don't think I would've been invited. But she invited all of the girls in the class."

She smiled at him. "I was so excited. They even gave all of us party favors, a gold chain with a ruby pendant. This was because it was Darcey's's birthstone. Of course, it was a fake ruby, but I pretended it was real. I think I still have it, stashed away in my jewelry box."

She sighed. "Darcey never had another party because right after, she moved away. So, I never got the chance to come here again. But I never forgot what a magical day it was."

A dreamy expression came over her face. "The kind of day I'd only read about in books. For months afterwards, I fantasized about living here, planning all these parties in my mind. Fancy parties where the women wore long dresses and the men wore tuxedos. There would be dancing and…"

Her words came to sudden stop.

Embarrassed, she glanced over at him. "I had a very vivid imagination when I was a kid." She shrugged. "I guess I still do."

Silent, Sam studied her for a few moments. Was this why he'd been so compelled to check out this property now? With the need to bring her with him? It had to be. What else could it be? It was too much of a coincidence.

He smiled over at her as he again began to ease the SUV down the bumpy driveway. "Hold those thoughts. Let me try to get as close to the house as I can. Then you can tell me all about it."

He finally maneuvered the SUV up to the side of the house. He stepped out to find, because of the recent rain, the ground was more mud than grass. He pointed over at Livy. "Don't get out. Stay right where you are."

He disappeared to the back of the SUV and opened up the trunk. Livy could hear him moving things around before he came around to open her door. He was holding a pair of beat-up, and what looked like to her, very large and chunky work boots.

"Here… put these on. I always carry extra pairs of boots with me. For times just like this." When she frowned down at the boots, he chuckled. "Come on, baby. Just put them on. No one is going to see you wearing them except me. The ground is all wet and muddy. Trust me, you don't want to ruin your shoes. Look, I have boots on, too."

Yes, she could see this. She also noted the boots he had put on were in much worse shape than what he was offering her.

But it didn't really matter, because she'd already taken the boots from him and was pulling them on. It was the one, simple little word he'd used that more than convinced her to do this.

Baby... when he calls you that? You'll do just about anything for him...

Once Livy had slipped on the boots and he'd grabbed his phone from the console, he took her hand. They cautiously made their way through the overgrown weeds and shrubbery and up the front steps. He was punching in the combination to open the lock box, when he heard her give a long sigh.

He turned. "What is it?"

She sighed again. "Oh Sam, this makes me so sad." She waved her hands at the tangle of greenery, almost overtaking the front steps and what at one time had been decorative flower beds.

"I can remember how this whole area in the front of the house was a sea of flowers. All different kinds of..."

He interrupted her. "Stop, I want to record this. With you describing everything as how you remember it. This will be so more effective than writing it down." He punched out something on his phone and held it towards her. "Here... now say exactly what you were planning to tell me."

She looked down at the phone. She opened her mouth. Then she looked at him. And she started to giggle. Her hand covering her mouth, she shook her head. "I'm sorry, I don't know what came over me. A sudden case of stage fright, I guess?"

The sound of her giggling had Sam grinning. And seriously? He suddenly didn't give a damn about the recording. Impulsively, he leaned over to press a soft kiss to her mouth.

She went completely still, the laugher dying in her throat. It was the questioning smile on his face that finally allowed her to get a hold of herself, almost snatching the phone right out of his hand. "I... *umm,* I think I can do this now. What do I need to push here?"

Sam responded by pressing another kiss to her mouth, this one longer, giving her just enough time to sway towards him, her eyelashes fluttering shut before they slowly opened again to his smile.

He winked. "That's just a little extra assurance you'll take this seriously." He reached over to press the video button on the phone again. "Okay, now go ahead… start talking."

With him watching her so intently, this turned out to be more difficult than it should've been. The challenging glint in his eyes was what finally galvanized her into action.

As she began to describe the entrance way to the house, she decided she was going to go into such detail, he'd wonder later why he'd suggested she record this.

Little did she know, she was way off about this.

Believe it or not, she still had no idea what the sound of her voice did to him.

Once Sam managed to get the combination to work on the lock box, they found themselves in a large, and once very elegant, two-story foyer. After he closed the door to the outside, the silence was almost overwhelming, the sound of their heavy boots against the ornately patterned parquet floor echoing loudly throughout the large space.

The setting sun, still shining in through the windows, picked up the dust particles set free upon their entrance. Floating through the air, they shimmered like glitter, casting a ghostly glow over the room.

Since they'd entered, Livy hadn't uttered a single word.

This had Sam beginning to wonder if he should be worried.

He stood back, watching, as she slowly wandered over to the staircase, or what he'd describe as the piece de resistance of the room. A magnificent display of craftsmanship, the railing and spindles were hand carved mahogany. While the steps, wider than your average staircase, were white Florentine marble. With a thorough cleaning and a coat of varnish, they would both be good as new.

Slowly running her hand over the railing, Livy turned to him.

"Oh, Sam..." She dropped her hand to her side, her mouth open to say something. Instead, she burst into tears.

He was next to her in an instant and taking her into his arms, he held her against him. As you can imagine, he was completely bewildered.

He was also very, *very* nervous. If you recall, Sam wasn't good with tears. And when it came to Livy's tears? This was completely out of his comfort zone, almost too much for him to handle.

He pressed a kiss in her hair. "Livy, what in the world? Tell me, why are you crying?" When she merely shook her head against him, he pressed another kiss in her hair. "My goodness, it's just a house. And so far, from what I can see, I'm more than confident it can be salvaged. I've seen houses in much worse shape than this. You'd be surprised at how, with a lot of hard work and attention to detail, a house like this can be restored to its former glory. You'd never recognize it as the same house."

Her tears coming to a stop, Livy burrowed in even closer to him. She had absolutely no idea why this house had affected her so strongly.

But then again, maybe her reaction wasn't all completely due to the house? Maybe it was a combination of everything that had happened over the past few days, finally hitting her all at once?

She closed her eyes, comforted by the feeling of his arms around her, his voice a soothing rumble in her ear. This was everything she craved. The solid strength of his muscular body against her, the reassuring sound of his heart beat, the scent of his cologne, of him... it all felt so right.

She tried to tell herself this was because, as it stood now, he was the one solid and reassuring force in her life. He was a good friend, someone to lean on, someone who made her feel she wasn't alone. Someone who would be there to pick her up, even at the smallest sign she was beginning to fall.

Deep down in her heart, she knew it was more than this. But at the same time, she was trying so hard not to become swept up in the possibility this relationship slowly building between them could turn into something permanent.

She was in trouble, big trouble. Because the more they were together, the harder she was falling.

And falling fast.

Yes… all this was all going through her mind as he held her.

"Livy?"

She slowly lifted her head, to find he was gazing down at her, concern showing in his eyes. "Hey, baby … are you okay?"

Baby…

Her defenses crumbled and any plans of guarding her heart were blown wide open. Lifting her face up to his, she brushed her lips over his. When his body stilled against her, she did it again, her voice a throaty whisper

"Kiss me… kiss me like you kissed me that night in New York."

His hands came up to frame her face. He did this slowly, as if he wasn't quite sure he'd heard right. Then mimicking her, he brushed his lips just as softly over hers. It was when she pressed even closer against him, a deep groan came from low in his throat as he claimed her mouth in a deep kiss.

This kiss was better than the kiss he gave her back in November. Because this time, she was ready for it, giving back to him with a passion like she hadn't before.

It was a kiss, every bit of the wonderful, Carrie had told Sam it would be.

After a slow brush of his lips over hers, Sam lifted his head. Unable to bring himself to let her go, his hands drifted down over her shoulders, to fall at her waist.

He pressed a kiss in her hair.

"I think this house has worked some kind of magic on us."

At the deep huskiness of his voice, she pressed even more closely against him, her answer muffled against his chest. "I know…"

"Then again… it could very well be you, putting a spell on me." He cleared his throat. "You know what? I do believe you've won this round. Big time."

At the smile in his voice, she lifted her face to his. To then duck her head, totally unprepared for the intensity of his gaze

He was having none of this. "Hey, look at me. You can't come at me like you just did, and then turn away. Unless you're regretting the kiss?"

Her head jerked up. "No, no… of course I'm not."

"Good, because I'm not either, far from it." He chuckled. "I'm beginning to believe there's hope for us after all."

And just like that, Livy came to a decision… if Sam wanted to be her knight in shining armor?

So, be it.

Yes, she was fine with this.

More than fine.

Overcome by these sudden feelings, Livy quickly slipped out of Sam's arms and wandered across the foyer to peer into the dining room.

The room was completely empty, almost gutted empty. Even the ornate crystal chandelier she remembered from the day of the birthday party, had been removed.

She closed her eyes, remembering so clearly how the room had looked like when she'd attended Darcey's birthday party. The elaborately set table with fine china and crystal fit for a princess. The huge centerpiece of brightly colored flowers, along with the gaily wrapped favors at each place setting.

All the girls from her class were all dressed in their pastel party dresses, hers had been pink. And how they giggled and whispered to each other as they drank out of the delicate tea cups and nibbled on the bite sized tea sandwiches and fancy desserts.

She could still see Darcey's grandmother, seated regally at the head of the table as she entertained them with stories of her days as a professional dancer on Broadway. She told them the story of how she'd met Darcey's grandfather. He'd showed up outside of her dressing room after one of her shows and presented her with a single red rose and an invitation for dinner. She claimed she fell in love with him at that very moment, to marry him only a few months later.

As Livy gazed around the room, she remembered everything as if it had happened only yesterday. She didn't see any of the dust or the wear and tear. She only saw the beauty of what took place on that special day.

Sam was right.

The house was magic.

She turned, her plan to tell him this, but he was busy typing something on his phone. Sensing her gaze, he glanced up, a guilty expression coming over his face when he saw she was watching him.

Before she could comment on this, he was by her side to take her hand. "Come on, let's do some exploring. Anytime you think of something you remember, let me know and we'll record it. We're a team here, so I'm counting on your input."

She took the phone from him. "Well, I think we should start right here. With this room, the dining room. Just imagine all the celebrations that must have taken place in this room over the years. Birthdays? And Christmas?"

A dreamy smile on her face, she gazed up at the stairs. "Or maybe even a wedding? With the bride walking down the staircase to a room full of guests."

She sighed. "But of course, her eyes would be searching only for the groom."

She suddenly realized how she was rambling on again. Blushing, she glanced over at Sam, to see he was watching her, a small smile on his lips.

She crossed her arms over her chest. "Oh boy, here I go again. I'm sorry, I don't know what's come over me. I don't know if it's this house or…" She shrugged.

He nodded. "It's okay. I feel it, too. This can happen these old homes, some more than others. It makes everything a little bit more exciting."

He smiled. "Now tell me more about this dining room."

And what had Sam been typing on his phone?

Believe it or not, it was another text to Chris. Yes, once again, he'd forgone his dislike of texts, to send out yet another one. But only out of respect to Chris and his family, of course. And he also found it suddenly very important he send Chris the following message.

> Livy and I checked out the house. I want you to close the deal. If you have to go over what you feel is a fair value, do it. I'll cover the extra. I'll also take complete responsibility for whatever happens from there.

Chris didn't know why he suddenly felt compelled to check his phone. When he saw he had a text from Sam, he excused himself from the table and made his way outside to check it out.

A big grin appeared on his face. Little did Sam know he'd already written up the contract and sent it over to the other realtor and sellers to review.

He knew damn well Sam was going to want this one. Yeah, he'd only known Sam for less than a year, but he'd already figured him out.

He read the text again, finding it interesting Sam had taken Livy with him. He wondered if she had anything to do with Sam's insistence they make an offer.

He sent Sam his answer.

> Thought you'd want this one, so the contract is already in the other realtor's hands. I wrote it up right after I sent you the lock combo. They have until noon tomorrow to get back to us. No clue if there are other offers. Curious, is this business or personal on your part?

Within seconds, he had his answer.

> Both... maybe one more than the other.

When Chris returned to the table, sliding into his seat next to Carrie, she sent him a curious glance. "Sam?"

He nodded. She knew he'd sent Sam the information about the listing. "He and Livy checked it out. Sam wants it at whatever cost."

Carrie's eyes grew wide. "Livy went with him?"

Chris watched as a calculating look came into her eyes. Then she was grinning. "Do you think maybe…"

He stopped her with a kiss. "Carrie, what did I tell you? You need to leave it alone."

But he was smiling.

They were both smiling.

A ball of fire, the sun had sunk low in the sky, hovering over the lake.

The knowledge that in just a matter of minutes, it would drop into the horizon and they'd be left in darkness, Sam shut off his phone and reached for Livy's hand. "Come on, we should leave. It's going to get dark really quick and we won't be able to see where we're going."

It felt so good to have her hand in his again. He hadn't had a chance to do this the entire time they'd explored the house, downstairs and upstairs. He'd been too intent on dictating into his phone all of the different trouble spots and unusual details he'd spotted.

During this time, Livy had been content to tag along with him, listening to his comments and occasionally asking him questions. She loved he was so passionate about what he did, going about his inspection with such seriousness. He checked out even the smallest details, taking the time to explain to her the significance of what he'd discovered. And when he came upon something unusual, unique or not at all what he'd hoped to find, his excitement was contagious.

One of these unique finds was the huge hand carved cherry platform bed in the upstairs master bedroom. Sam had been thrilled about this, even more so because it had been built as a permanent fixture, secured to the floor. This meant it would be included in the sale.

And now, almost after an hour had passed since they first made their way down the bumpy driveway, their inspection of the house was complete.

Except for the basement.

It had taken Livy only one glance at the long and rickety flight of stairs leading into what looked like a black hole, that had her backing away and adamantly refusing to go any further.

But this was okay. Even Sam had been reluctant to check it out.

He was ready to move on. He had all he needed—all the information he collected about the house, along with Livy's testimonials—saved on his phone. Any other little details were now filed away into a corner of his mind.

Now he wanted to devote the rest of the evening to Livy. This had a lot to do with the kiss they'd shared. He couldn't even begin to count the number of times he'd reigned in the urge pull her back against him. If only to experience the feeling of having her in his arms again. With him initiating the kiss this time.

This, of course, was only to return the favor. This was the least he could do.

Abruptly, Livy let go of his hand to bend down and pick up something off the foyer floor.

He moved closer to see what she had in her hand. "Hey, what did you find, baby?"

To his surprise, she pressed a quick kiss to his cheek. She couldn't help it.

Again, when he calls you baby...

She handed him the ring, a thin silver band engraved with a delicate flower pattern. "Oh my, I wonder if this was someone's special ring. Maybe it was a promise ring? And even now, they might be wondering where they lost it."

She gazed around the room before she turned back to him, puzzled. "I wonder how long it's been here... and how it even ended up in the foyer. You'd think someone would have found it by now."

Sam was closely inspecting the ring. "I didn't want to tell you this, but there's probably a lot of little critters who've taken over this house as their own. And since hoarding is one of their favorite pastimes, they've no doubt stashed their finds all over the place. I've run into everything from termites to raccoons. By invading their sanctuary, we may have surprised one of these freeloaders, resulting in a quick drop and run."

He watched as Livy cast a nervous glance at the floor before she sidled closer to him.

He chuckled. "Don't worry, I'm sure they're more scared of you than you are of them. The last thing they're going to do right now, is make an appearance."

He handed her the ring. "You said this is a promise ring? What exactly is a promise ring?"

"It's a promise of love and commitment, with possibly an engagement to follow at a later date? Or, it even could be exchanged between friends, pledging their loyalty to each other."

She shrugged. "I guess it could be a promise of so many different things."

He nodded. "Well, since I can see there's some kind of inscription on the inside of the band, this might be one. I can't read it in this light, so hold on to it and we'll check it out later."

She shook her head as she pressed it in his hand. "No, you keep it. I'll lose it. I'm known to do that."

Or, as of lately, simply forgetting where you put things. Since Sam has taken over your mind.

As he put the ring in his pocket, he chuckled. "I'll have to start referring to this pocket as the Livy Pocket, since everything in it is yours. The ring, your card holder, your lipstick and the…"

His words came to an abrupt halt, bringing Livy to eye him curiously. "The what?"

Sam wasn't going to tell her about the hair tie. Maybe someday he would… soon. But not now.

After all, he'd already let her win a round with that kiss she gave him. And if he were to be truthful, her kiss had them pretty even now.

She may, in fact, have already more than passed him.

He took her hand. "Nothing. Come on, let's get going. I don't know about you, but I'm ready for dinner."

CHAPTER 13

From her seat by the restaurant window, Livy had a perfect view of the city skyline across the lake. Showcased in a blaze of lights, it was a brilliant contrast against the dark, starless sky.

She watched as yet another streak of lightning flashed over the water. "Oh no, it's not supposed to rain, is it?" Concern furrowing her brow, she turned to see Sam was watching her, his mouth curved in a smile.

She smiled tentatively at him in return. He had that look in his eyes again... the one that always had her so flustered, sending a shiver through her. Unaware of what she was doing, she nervously began fingering her wine glass, the wine sloshing precariously near the rim.

In a flash, he reached across the table to gently remove the glass from her hands. After he set it out of her reach, he winked. "Just in case."

Well, she certainly couldn't argue with him about this, could she?

She had already more than proved what a disaster she could be, her clumsiness well established. Merely thinking about the coffee she spilled in his lap when they had dinner together in New York, still made her cringe. Or there was the day he came to her rescue, when she nearly choked to death on her water at Angie's restaurant.

But her most impressive move? Hands down, this would be her epic fall in the hotel lobby… the fall that started it all between them.

He gestured towards the window. "The lightning you see is what they call heat lightning, sweetheart. Nothing to worry about. From what I've heard, the next few days are supposed to be perfect as far as the weather is concerned."

Now that she didn't have her glass to hold onto, and faced with the predicament of what to do with her hands, she clasped them together on the table. "For Carrie's sake, I hope you're right. Because, heaven forbid it rains. Aunt Evelyn would never let her forget how she warned her against an outdoor wedding. I can't even tell you how many times I've had to listen to her go on about this."

Sam nodded. But he really didn't want to talk about the weather. Or about the wedding.

He wanted to talk about her. About him. And even more importantly, about them.

What he really wanted, was to find out if it was possible she, too, was beginning to feel this connection building between them.

The fact that she'd agreed to be with him tonight had to mean something, right?

Wait a minute here... you're getting way ahead of yourself, don't you think? Technically, this is only your first date.

Rubbish… this meant absolutely nothing. As far as he was concerned, they had already experienced their first date awkwardness when they had been thrown together in New York. Through no choice of their own, mind you. That night had started out as close to the all-time catastrophic blind date as one could get.

But tonight?

Tonight was different...

Something was happening… a spark had begun to ignite between them. He liked to think of it as their second chance, their time for a clean start. After he'd messed up that night in New York, he would be a complete fool if he didn't take this opportunity to let her know how he felt.

He cleared his throat, a determined look on his face. "I don't want to talk about the weather. And I don't want to talk about the wedding."

At her surprised expression, he hurried to explain. "It's not that I don't care about the wedding… or Chris and Carrie. Because I do, absolutely. But I know everything will turn out just fine. It will be a wonderful day. No, it's you I want to talk about. You and me… us."

"Us?"

Her heart now beating in a frenzy, she wasn't sure what to say. Clasping her hands even more tightly together, she waited.

Sam hitched his chair closer and placed his hands over hers. Even though this was only to show serious he was about what he planned to say, the thought entered his mind how much he'd like to move even closer. If only to take advantage of the message her lipstick was sending.

What the hell was that name again?

Ah, yes… *Kiss Me Now*

Trying not to think of the possibility of actually doing this, he tilted his head, his gaze slowly traveling over her face. "Tell me… what made you decide to accept this date with me?"

Her lips parting, she stared at him before she dropped her gaze to their hands.

How are you supposed to answer this?

Because to be honest? She wasn't quite sure.

She wondered what he would say if she told him it could have been a moment of insanity on her part?

Or it was because she found it almost impossible to refuse him anything when he even as much as smiled at her.

That might not be a good idea… you can only imagine the response that would bring.

Then there was the most logical explanation… she was merely a glutton for punishment. Since she had already managed to screw up one relationship, why not see what a mess she could make of this one.

She looked up to see he had that quirky little smile lurking at the corner of his mouth as he patiently waited for her answer. Flustered, she pulled her hands from his and, grabbing her napkin from her lap, placed it on the table. When she began smoothing it with her fingers, he took it from her and set it aside.

He reached over to tuck a loose strand of hair behind her ear, his fingers going on to trace the line of her jaw. She could hear the smile in his voice. "So? Come on, tell me. Is it my charming personality? My irresistible good looks? Or maybe… *just maybe*… it was because you wanted a chance to test out that kiss again."

His gaze slowly dipped to her mouth. "Because I know I did."

Their eyes meeting, something she could only describe as magical passed between them—like lightning flashing across the sky. Heat lightning, Sam had called it. A jolt to their senses, it was a confirmation this connection they had was real.

Seduced by the promise in Sam's gaze, it was a feeling unlike anything Livy had ever experienced. There was something there, all right.

And it was scaring her to death.

This is not the way this evening was supposed to go. First, you throw yourself at him while you were at the house by the lake, and now this? Where's the outing-with-a-friend-plan you'd decided on?

Her attempt at a casual shrug fell flat, instead coming out in more of a deep shiver. This obviously had to be in response to his reference to the kiss.

"Livy?" There was that hint of a smile was in his voice again. Her gaze going anywhere except in his direction, her answer came out more as a question. "Maybe I believe in second chances?"

He chuckled. "Ah, Livy…. only you would say this." He reached over to take her hand. When she curled her fingers around his, he smiled.

Ah… this was good… really good.

She glanced down at their hands, then up at him. His smile held a confidence that once would have irritated her; now she found herself leaning toward him, yearning to be closer.

"I guess it would—"

"So, look what we have here... if it isn't my man, Sam."

Livy's words cut off, Sam shot up from his chair. "Jake! I was told you were here tonight. Great to see you."

After sharing a few more words with a man wearing a chef's coat, Sam turned back to Livy. "Baby, this is Jake Martin. After he realized he was never going to win against me at football, he decided to become a chef. A smart choice, as he is one of the best in the business."

He nodded at Jake. "Jake, this is Livy Mazzori."

Jake shook her hand, a teasing glint in his eyes. "It's so nice to meet you, Livy. But, be honest with me... what nonsense did Sam give you so you'd go out with him? As beautiful as you are, you can do better."

He leaned in closer to whisper. "I'll tell you what, when you get tired of all his stories about what a superstar he thought he was, you call me and I'll make you dinner."

He winked at her before he turned to Sam. "I see things haven't changed. You always come out the winner. Or, should I say, the lucky one."

He gazed around the room. "Busy night tonight. But when Brandy told me you were here, I wanted to come out and say hello. In a couple of weeks, I'm heading to Seattle for a month to oversee the opening of a new restaurant." He shrugged. "I decided I needed a change."

After they chatted for a few minutes, Jake nodded over at Livy. "I'll let you in on a little secret, Livy. The best way to win this guy's heart is to make him a big batch of chocolate chip cookies. If you do, he'll follow you anywhere. He was shameless in how he charmed my mom into making them for him."

Livy smiled. "*Hmm...* this is good to know. Thank you for the tip."

Sam shrugged. "What can I say? Except it's true. Her chocolate chip cookies were the best."

Jake nodded. "It was those extra chocolate chips she always added."

He abruptly turned to Sam. "How's Gracie? Have you heard from her?"

A closed look coming over his face, Sam shook his head. "I don't know. And no, I haven't."

For a few seconds, they eyed each other before Jake uncomfortably cleared his throat. "Okay… well, I guess it's time for me to get back to work."

He glanced over at Livy. "You like chocolate, don't you?" When she nodded, he smiled. "Good… I am going to have a special dessert sent out for you. A chocolate lover's dream."

He turned to Sam. "Take good care of her, you big lug. Treat her right." He began walking away, only to turn back to Sam. "Let me know if you hear from Gracie."

At Sam's slow nod, he left.

Sam slowly sat in his chair before he gazed over at Livy. He had a thoughtful look on his face. "Jake's a good guy."

She was hesitant to ask. "Who is Gracie?"

"My sister. For some reason, even after everything she's done and how badly she's treated him, he's still in love with her. Someday I'll tell you the whole story."

As if to clear his thoughts, he shook his head briefly before he reached for her hand, his smile making her heart skip a beat. "But right now, I want to continue where we left off. I believe we were talking about us, weren't we?"

She smiled. "Yes, I told you I'm here because I believe in second chances."

"*Ah…* yes, I remember." A smile tweaked the corner of his mouth. "*So…* you've decided to give me a second chance. I guess I'm okay with this. But what about you… aren't you at all interested in why I asked you out to dinner?"

Her head shot up, her eyes meeting his.

Yes, yes, of course she was.

God… yes.

But wait a minute here… this depended on what kind of explanation it was.

What if he were to tell her this was merely a good deed on his part?

Or this was his way of helping her get over the fact she'd not only lost her job, but also the man who for the past seven years she'd foolishly thought she was going to marry? Or the worst possible reason, now that he knew Carrie was no longer available, he'd decided why not make it easy on himself and settle for her sister?

Well, she didn't want to hear it.

No, you definitely don't want to hear that.

She didn't realize her fingers had tightened their hold on his. But he had. Moving his thumb in a gentle caress over her fingers, he raised an eyebrow. "Well?"

She tucked her hair behind her ear. For some reason, this one strand kept falling in her face and it was driving her crazy. Without even thinking, she blew a big breath up at it. Like she used to do when her bangs always fell in her eyes. Something only a child would do.

Embarrassed and hoping he hadn't noticed, she zeroed in on the third button of his shirt, thinking this would make it easier for her to answer him.

But this turned out to be a mistake... a big mistake. Now the only thing she could think about was how she'd like to undo that button. To then go on and do the same with every other button on his shirt. Just so she'd be able to touch him. To feel, hands on, the strength she knew was hidden beneath the crisp white and navy pin striped button-down shirt he was wearing under his sports coat.

This had her almost groaning aloud.

What is happening to you? You need to get a grip before you throw yourself right at him. Look around you... you're in a restaurant, for heaven's sake...

She swallowed. Hard. "Yes, I'll admit I'd like to know your answer to that. But only if it's a good reason."

He was puzzled by this. "*Hmm...* I'm a little confused. What reason could I possibly have you would consider a bad one?"

For a moment, she hesitated. Then before she could change her mind, she just blurted it out. "I don't want you to tell me the only reason you asked me out was because I was the one who happened to be there when you finally realized Carrie was no longer available. And now I've become her replacement, this made even more appealing because I'm her sister."

There… she'd finally said it aloud. The one concern about Sam she hadn't been able to let go, always lurking in the back of her mind.

For what felt like forever.

These words had been running around in your head since you first met. Waiting for this very moment to be heard.

And now? By the stunned look on Sam's face, she wondered if she may have just made the biggest mistake of her life.

Sam leaned back in his chair.

For a few moments, he could only stare at Livy. completely shocked.

That she would even think this, didn't make sense.

But then again, it did.

After all, a big part of the reason he was even in New York on that November night was because of Carrie. Yes, he had plans to meet up with his cousin and his new girlfriend. And yes, he also had a meeting scheduled with a potential client.

But to be honest, Carrie had been the draw.

At the time, he still hadn't given up hope something might eventually click between them. But now, he could truthfully say this was also when he'd finally realized this was never going to happen.

And to be even more honest? This was something he had no longer wanted. Carrie wasn't the woman for him. Yes, he'd always think of her as a good friend, but this was as far as their relationship would go.

And he was damn sure this was all because of Livy.

Somehow, she had managed to get under his skin, flood his mind. That chemistry thing everyone always talks about? He was now convinced it was real, turning him a true believer in this thing called love.

But unfortunately? He had failed to let Livy know this.

Filled with an overwhelming feeling of remorse, he gazed over at Livy. She was watching him, an almost desperate expression on her face.

He slowly shook his head.

What the hell were you thinking? You've got to fix this.

Livy was trying to prepare herself for what she was so sure Sam was going to say. And the fact he was taking such a long time to do this?

It confirmed what she'd thought all along was true... he still wasn't over Carrie.

Why did you even think this would be different?

And now she wanted to be anywhere else but here with him and in this restaurant.

She reached for her glass.

In one gulp, she drank what remained of her wine.

A hand came down possessively on Sam's shoulder, the fingernails a perfectly manicured shade of glossy, blood red.

This was followed, unfortunately, by a voice he knew too well. Coming from the lips of a tall, lanky blonde, her expertly applied lipstick, a perfect match to her nails.

"Sam, darling... I can't believe you're here. Who would have thought, after spending so much time together this afternoon, we'd run into each other again tonight? At our favorite restaurant, too. Why, we were here only a little over a week ago. And what a great night that was, wasn't it?"

Her gaze slowly traveling over Livy, she began massaging Sam's shoulder, the manner in which she was leaning against him insinuating this was something she had done many times.

Her smile definitely missing the warmth she'd lavishly bestowed on Sam, she extended her hand in a greeting. "I'm Valerie Madison. Sam and I are long-time acquaintances and business partners." She gave an amused little laugh. "I'm assuming this must be a business dinner, no? Are you new in town?"

Not waiting for an answer, her gaze darted back to Sam. "Sam, please don't tell me you and Chris have reeled in another client. I swear, since you two have become partners, I've been forced to work harder than ever. I was just telling Jeff this."

She gestured to the man standing behind her. "This, by the way, is Jeff Ingrams. If he's rolling his eyes, this is because he had to listen to me go on about this only a few minutes ago. Isn't that right, Jeff?"

Jeff, who was busy adjusting his collar, gave a brief nod, his appearance evidently rating higher than the art of conversation. Or maybe it was that Valerie never gave him a chance to talk.

Proof of this was when she turned right back to Sam. "Seriously, Sam… just think what we could do if the three of us worked together. We'd blow the competition right out of Cleveland."

The gentleman he was, Sam had quickly stood to press a quick kiss to Valerie's cheek before he turned to Jeff, shaking his hand. "Sam Bridges here, good to meet you."

The tone of his voice was cool, yet polite in response to Valerie. "Yes, long time no see, Valerie. You're right, we were just here, weren't we?" He shook his head. "And you don't need me or Chris. You're doing fine on your own."

When she sent him an exaggerated pout, Sam quickly turned to Livy, who was wondering if there was any possible way she could make herself invisible. She found Valerie very intimidating, the vibes she gave off almost threatening. It was very obvious she was a woman with a plan, a plan that included Sam.

You can't compete with a woman like this. Nor do you want to.

She gave a frustrated sigh, tightly clasping her hands together. To then watch, almost in fascination, as Sam reached over to cover them with one of his. Almost as if he was offering his reassurance.

She glanced up at him, met with his wink before he made the introductions. "This is my date, Livy Mazzori. You probably recognize the last name, Valerie. She's Carrie's sister, and is in town for the wedding. My partner in crime for the event, as a matter of fact."

He smiled at Livy after he said this, almost as if they shared a secret known to only them.

This didn't go over well with Valerie, her annoyed expression swiftly replaced with an overly bright smile. "Ah, and what is your specialty? Your line of work?"

Again, she didn't wait for Livy to answer. Instead, she moved closer to Sam, placing her hand possessively on his arm. "Just to warn you, if you have any plans of claiming this man for your own while you're in town, you're going to be up against stiff competition."

Sam saw Livy's shoulders tense, anger building in her eyes. That she appeared to be jealous, thrilled him. At the same time, concerned about how she planned to respond, he decided to step in, maybe smooth things over.

He cleared his throat. "Livy is an author. This is alongside her job as an editor at a publishing company in New York. I have a feeling we'll be seeing big things coming from her in the future."

Valerie studied Livy for a few moments. "What kind of books do you specialize in? DIY books? Or, I know... I bet you're into cookbooks."

DIY books? Cookbooks? Nothing against the authors of these genre of books, but seriously? Is this what she came across as to Valerie? The little homemaker? Cupcake in hand and a screwdriver tucked in her apron pocket?

Amazed Sam had even remembered she wanted to write, while at the same time, wishing he hadn't brought it up, she decided... why not have a little fun with this?

She gave Valerie a big smile. "No, I write romance novels."

And sure enough, eyebrows raised, Valerie gave an amused laugh. "Romance novels? How different. Or should I say, most unusual?"

Livy shrugged. "Not really. If anything, they're quite popular. And Sam here," she smiled up at him as she said this, "has so gallantly offered to help me out. You know, with the research part. It's so nice to have a real man's input. Especially when it comes to the main character. And so far, he's been perfect, giving me so many different ideas to work with."

She sent Sam another smile before she turned back to Valerie. "It's very important that a writer experiences first-hand what they intend to write about. Especially when it comes to a romance novel, since they can be so emotionally complicated."

She sighed, shaking her head. "There's always so much going on. Passion, desire, chemistry... I could go on and on. "

And this is what she did... literally.

She rattled off all of the information she could think of about romance novels, including every different genre. In detail, she did this. Most of what she knew Valerie could probably care less about.

Seriously... you even started to bore yourself with all the information you piled on the poor woman.

She glanced again over at Sam, to see he was watching her, a slight smile hugging his lips.

Encouraged by this, she gave Valerie a big smile. "But, do you know what I like best about romance novels? No matter how many rough and bumpy times the main characters struggle through, they always fall madly and completely in love, So, the ending is always a happy one. A fairy tale kind of ending, you'd might say."

She nodded. "So, yes, I write romance novels. This is because I love writing stories that make people happy. And again, I feel so fortunate Sam is so willing to play along with me. It's a bonus he is so good at it, too."

She gave a little giggle before she sent Sam a long, and what she hoped came across as a very loving and intimate glance. Of course, this was only for Valerie's benefit.

This was met with complete silence.

Valerie was seething, struggling to check what she wanted to say. But with the amount of time and energy she'd already invested in her pursuit of Sam, she certainly didn't want to jeopardize her chances by saying something catty.

Jeff wasn't really paying attention. On his phone for the past few minutes, scrolling through his messages, he was trying to ignore how hungry he was. It had been a long day, and right now he was more interested in moving on to their table so they could order dinner.

And Sam?

Throughout Livy's commentary, he had remained completely poker faced, ready to jump in, if necessary. But since it was obvious Livy had the situation completely under control, he was all smiles.

Linking her fingers with his, he gently helped her up from her chair.

He sent Valerie and Jeff a smile. "Now if you'll excuse us, Livy and I were about to take a walk on the pier before we have dessert. I'm sure I'll be seeing you around, Valerie" He nodded over at Jeff. "Again, it was nice meeting you."

Barely lifting his eyes from his phone, Jeff's farewell was brief. But Sam could almost forgive him for this. It could very well be his way of dealing with Valerie.

Valerie called out as Sam began leading Livy towards the door out to the deck. "Sam, one more thing… did you hear an offer has already been accepted for that house on the lake? The property that needs so much work? Can you believe it? It hadn't even been listed yet."

She frowned. "I had a possible buyer, but when I called to set up a showing, I was told it was already a done deal. Do you know anything about this?"

Sam shook his head. And he was being completely truthful. If anything, he was just as surprised with this development as Valerie.

So, the house had already been sold? He wondered if Chris knew this. Or could it have been his offer that was accepted?

Damn… that's impossible. It was only about two hours ago you called Chris to give your thumbs up. It looks like you may have lost out on this deal.

If this was true, it was news he definitely hadn't wanted to hear.

Sam led Livy through the maze of tables and over to the door opening out onto the long pier connected to the restaurant.

Holding her hand, they walked in a companionable silence. The gentle crash of the waves, along with the warm summer night's breeze was a welcome contrast to the bustling atmosphere they'd left inside, their encounter with Valerie slowly becoming a distant memory.

After searching for a more deserted area of the pier, Sam finally brought Livy over to the railing and leaning against it, he pulled her against him. He lifted her chin with his finger to press a soft kiss to her mouth.

"I'm so sorry, baby."

A puzzled look came over her face. "Sorry? Oh, you mean about Valerie?"

She grimaced, her face scrunching up. "I should be the one apologizing to you for the snarly way I acted towards her. I think I may have gone a little overboard, taking off with that long spiel in defense of my choice of writing genre. Then I even went as far as to drag you in."

He chuckled. "No, you were great. With Valerie, you basically have two options. You either ignore her or give it right back to her. She has a tendency to come on too strong, getting on your nerves. Even Chris gets irritated with her and you know how happy-go-lucky he is."

He shrugged. "Me? I think she's basically harmless and actually quite good at what she does." He grinned down at her. "And I certainly didn't mind you naming me as an accomplice to your writing. If you'd like, I'd be more than happy to help you out."

A smile lit up her face. "You would? Even if I were to tell you how wrong you were about me working for a New York publishing company?"

At his puzzled expression, she sighed, her voice muffled against his shoulder. "I was laid off on Monday. I was told the company is going through a restructuring phase, with my position as one of the first to be eliminated. This is part of the reason I decided to come home."

After a short silence, he surprised her with his response. "Having witnessed how passionate you are with everything you do, I find it hard to believe they'd want to lose you. Can't say I'm not happy about this turn of events, since your decision to come back to Cleveland is the end result."

He pulled her closer. "And, yes… I'd be more than happy to help you out with your writing. I'm sure I could learn a thing or two about romance. As a man, I can be pretty clueless at times. "

A faint frown tugged at his mouth. "But, the comment I made

about how sorry I am, wasn't in reference to your conversation with Valerie. It was what you said about me and Carrie."

Her glance shied from his, bringing him to sigh. "Livy, look at me."

Their eyes met, the warm look in his that always made her think only good things were about to happen. It was also the look she was finding so hard not to get caught up in, if only in a desperate attempt to guard her heart.

"Carrie and I will always be friends, nothing more. Any feelings I thought I had for her completely disappeared when I met you. It was then I finally realized how foolish I'd been, trying to force something that wasn't meant to be." He grinned. "Again, this comes from being a man and all."

His gaze slowly traveling over her face, he shook his head. "Now, you… when you came falling into my life, literally, you did this… you shook up my world like never before and I'm embarrassed to say I had no clue of how handle what I was feeling. The one thing I did know… there was definitely something there, be it chemistry or whatever you want to call it."

Brushing away a strand of hair that was blowing in her face, his fingertips went on to trace her jaw. "I'm not sure what the deal is with this Zack, but I'm willing to wait until you figure it out. In the meantime, we'll take it slow, take things as they come. But no matter…"

Livy didn't give him the chance to finish. Her arms wrapping around his neck, she kissed him with an intensity that caught him completely by surprise.

Becoming lost in the feel of her soft curves pressed against him, the intoxicating floral scent of her perfume and the eagerness of her kiss, he responded with a passion he hadn't even known he was saving for a moment like this.

The vague thought registered in the back of his mind, the more they kissed, the more he liked it. But again, maybe 'like' wasn't the correct term he should be using.

He only knew, whatever it was, it felt right.

A long moment later, his forehead pressed against hers, his voice came out so deep, so husky. "I think I may have been wrong."

Concerned, Livy pulled away.

He smiled, his eyes holding hers. "About taking it slow, that is…"

Livy placed her fork on the empty dessert plate before she smiled over at Sam. "That was delicious. I think it may be my new favorite dessert."

At his raised eyebrow, she shrugged. "Ok, maybe I should rephrase that. I think it's one of my newest favorite desserts. You have to admit, you liked it, too. You did eat half."

Again, he raised an eyebrow.

She sighed. "Okay, maybe not half. But you did have a good amount."

He smiled. "Yes, I did. Before we leave, we have to let Jake know how much we enjoyed it. We'll also have to remember to order it again the next time we're here."

There it is again… another reference to the next time…

He stood and held out his hand. "Come on, you've finished your dessert just at the right time. The band is about to play a slow dance."

Once they were on the dance floor, he smiled down at her. "From what you said, it sounds like we have some practicing to do. Even though I have a feeling you're not the terrible dancer you claim you are."

Chuckling at her worried expression, he took her into his arms. "Come on, baby… together, I'm willing to bet we'll rock this dancing thing."

The first time she stepped on his foot, he laughed. The second time, the look he gave her was half amused, half puzzled.

It was the third time he finally came to a stop. He held her slightly away from him, peering down at her. "You weren't kidding when you said you weren't the best of dancers, were you? What's wrong? You're so tense. Did you have a bad experience with someone on the dance floor? It's almost as though you're afraid I'm going to make some kind of surprise move, knock you down, or something."

Her eyes closed, Livy shook her head.

Oh my God... it was high school all over again. What made you think this time would be different? You never should've agreed to go dancing with him, because it's not going to work, no matter what he says.

She eased herself away from him, her plan to walk off the dance floor. Hopefully, once he followed her to their table, any thoughts of dancing would be completely forgotten.

But he was having none of this. He pulled her back and wrapping his arms around her, his cheek resting in her hair, he began moving them slowly across the floor.

"Tell me, sweetheart... what gives?"

When it was obvious he wasn't going to let it go until she gave him an explanation, she shrugged. "Okay. But remember, you asked."

She began with a long dramatic sigh. "When I was a senior in high school, I wanted to go to prom so badly. Both Carolyn and Carrie had gone. Even Chester went, though he went with a big group of his friends. But since I was so shy..."

At this, he came to a halt to gaze down at her, his eyebrow raised. She nodded. "I was. I was terribly shy. I barely talked to anyone, happy to stay to myself. You wouldn't even know I was in the room."

"Hmm..." was all he had to say before he pulled her back against him, moving again to the music.

She was smiling as she slowly began to relax against him. "So, I said yes to the first boy who asked me. He was really big, a wrestler. And for some reason he thought he was a great dancer. Which he wasn't. I don't know if he was trying to impress his friends, or what, but he started swinging me around the dance floor. After I kept begging him to stop, he suddenly let go of my hand and I went crashing into the table where the drinks were set up."

Sam tightened his hold on her. "Oh, boy... not good."

She sighed. "Yes, definitely not good. As you can imagine, this was a complete disaster. Everything went flying and I was covered with every kind of beverage you can imagine. All over my dress and in my hair... everywhere. When I stop to think about it now, I'm surprised I wasn't hurt. But even if I had been, my only goal at the time was to get up off the floor and out of the party center as fast as I could."

A faint smile came over her face. "There was this boy in my class, Marty, who played baseball with Chester. He followed me outside and insisted on taking me home. He even tried to persuade me to stay, but I refused. I wanted to hide away from the world. What was so ironic, I had a huge crush on this boy. But, as embarrassed as I was, I shut him out. I found out later he'd wanted to ask me to the prom but he waited too long. So, he asked another girl in my class. They actually wound up getting married after college."

She sighed. "And there you have it…. the reason for my aversion to dancing."

Suddenly gazing up at him, a horrified expression appeared on her face. "Oh my God, maybe this is why I became so angry at you when I fell in the lobby of Carrie's hotel. I was reliving the whole experience all over again."

Sam pulled her closer, clearing his throat. "Well, if I recall our encounter correctly, I didn't have anything to do with your fall. If anything, I believe I acted in a very courteous manner."

A smile touched his lips. "Even when faced with such anger. So, so, *so* much anger…"

Livy shook her head against him. "Oh Sam, I'm so sorry. I was a little over the top, wasn't I?"

He chuckled. "*Hmm…* a little? Yeah, we'll stick with your take on that. I do have to say I'm glad you didn't stay at the dance. You could be married to that guy right now."

He gazed down at her. "Oh, Livy… I'm sure no one at the dance even remembers what happened. And even if they did, they'd be more apt to remember your date for doing such a stupid thing."

And then he kissed her. This was the only thing he could think of that might help erase this memory she had been carrying inside for so long. It was a kiss to let her know he'd always be there for her. If only to help erase away her fears.

He glanced around the crowded dance floor. A smile on his face, he dipped his head, his lips brushing along her jaw before ending with a whisper in her ear. "Hey, can you feel what's happening here?"

When she shook her head, he smiled. "You're dancing… we're

dancing. And damn, if we're not doing a good job at it. Didn't I tell you this would happen?"

Resting her head against his chest, against the comforting beat of his heart, Livy was smiling.

Remember the dream she had? Where she was dancing?

Maybe it had been with Sam after all.

CHAPTER 14

$\mathcal{L}$ivy dipped both ends of the one remaining cannoli in the melted chocolate and placed it on the tray with the other finished cannoli.

After she put the tray in the refrigerator, she gave a long stretch before she gazed around the cluttered kitchen. Her aunt had made more than triple the amount of cannoli needed for both the rehearsal and the reception. Both the refrigerator in the kitchen and in the basement were filled with trays of cannoli.

But this was to be expected. For her aunt, to run out of food would be unthinkable. How many times had Livy heard the lecture it was always better to have more than enough of everything, than to commit the terrible faux pas of hungry guests facing an empty table. This was her aunt's mantra. She thrived on this motto.

She glanced over at the clock on the stove. She had about an hour before Carrie would be coming by to pick her up. In that time, she needed to clean up the kitchen, take a shower, wash and dry her hair and get dressed.

Their whole afternoon planned out, Carrie told her their first stop would be to pick up the cookie favors from Abby. Then they would take them to Sophie and Chester's house. Hopefully, they'd find the canopy tent set up and the tables arranged to match the layout Carrie had provided.

Their sister Carolyn's flight had been scheduled to arrive this morning, but her flight had been delayed because of bad weather. Since the arrival time had now been bumped back to around three o'clock, Chris had volunteered to pick up both Carolyn and her husband John.

Chris still wouldn't tell Carrie where the rehearsal dinner was going to be held, no matter how hard she'd tried to get the information out of him. She was keeping her fingers crossed he'd set it up at their favorite restaurant, White Oaks.

Glancing at the clock once more, Livy got to work. Once the bowls and utensils were washed and the kitchen clean enough to pass her aunt's expectations, she headed for the shower.

Carrie was talking a mile a minute. She had been chattering away at this pace since Livy first slid into the passenger seat.

But Livy wasn't really tuned into what Carrie had to say. No, her mind was running all over the place. With most of this having to do with Sam.

Aware of a sudden silence, she shot a quick glance over at Carrie to see she was studying her. Or, more like giving her that knowing look. She responded to this with a hesitant smile. "What?"

Carrie raised an eyebrow. "Oh, I don't know… maybe I'm wondering why it doesn't seem as though you've heard a single word I've said?"

Livy gave her an apologetic glance. "I'm sorry. I guess I was thinking about a few things and… you know."

Carrie laughed. "Yeah, believe me, I know. So, I take it by the dreamy expression on your face, dinner went well last night? Just so you know, I talked to Chris just a short while ago and he told me Sam was in an exceptionally good mood this morning. More so than usual."

Even though Livy was happy to hear this, she didn't want to talk about what was going on with her and Sam. Not to Carrie. Not to anyone. She wanted to keep any details about their relationship to herself. Savor it. Maybe even dare to dream bigger.

She also didn't want to take the chance she could jinx them. She wasn't one to be superstitious, but with her track record, she needed to be careful. Why take any chances?

She casually adjusted her sunglasses, her intent to give Carrie a laid back and casual response. "We had a good time. I can't believe we danced until the band played their last song. So, be prepared to be wowed at your wedding." She sent Carrie a tentative glance. "I even told him about what happened to me at prom."

Carrie gave her a puzzled look. "What happened at prom?"

Livy stared at her for a few seconds before she burst out laughing. She shook her head. "I guess Sam was right. He told me I was spending my time worrying about nothing, because probably no one even remembered." She grinned. "And since you're one of those people who doesn't remember, I'm certainly not going to tell you about it now."

Carrie had pulled up in front of a door, one of the many lined up in the long office building. The sign over the door read 'Sweet Abby's'.

She turned off the ignition and grinned back at Livy. "Well, since we're here, you're off the hook. But I plan to get the story out of you eventually. Because now I'm intrigued, wondering what possible disaster befell you at prom."

Still talking, she got out of the car. "Come on, I'm so excited. I can't wait to see what kind of cookies Abby came up with for the favors."

Holding one of the cookies in her hand, Carrie looked like she was about to cry. "Oh my gosh, Abby... I don't even know what to say. They're so perfect. Even the way you packaged them is amazing. And they're exactly what I wanted." These words were muffled in the big hug she gave Abby before she turned to Livy. "Isn't she fantastic?"

Admiring the cookies Abby had set out for Carrie's approval, Livy nodded. Carrie had veered from the traditional wedding themed cookies. Instead, she'd asked Abby to make rose shaped cookies, frosted in shades of white, mauve and pink to compliment the colors of the bridesmaid dresses. The details she put into the cookies were amazing, each cookie a work of art.

Livy smiled over at Abby. "Abby, they're beautiful and they smell absolutely heavenly." She glanced over to where Carrie was looking through the boxes of parchment bagged cookies, all ready to go. "Carrie, you're having a wedding cake, too, aren't you?"

Carrie nodded. "Yes, but I told Abby I don't want to see it until the reception."

Abby laughed. "This is good, since I haven't even started the cake yet. My plan is to make it this afternoon and decorate it tonight."

At Carrie's worried glance, she smiled. "The most time-consuming part of the whole process, the edible decorations, have already been made. Since your guest count is only at ninety, this means the cake isn't humongous and shouldn't take much time to finish."

She pointed over to a large glass covered cake plate. "If either of you want a cookie, feel free to take one of those. There should also be coffee left in the pot. Please help yourself. In fact, I'll join you. I'm ready for a break."

Abby finished the last of her coffee and leaning her chin on her hand, she nodded over at Livy. "So... you and Sam, huh?"

Livy, almost choked on the piece of cookie she'd popped in her mouth. After she took a sip of coffee, she looked up to see Carrie and Abby were eying her expectantly, waiting for her answer.

Shaking her head, she managed a laugh. "Boy, after living in New York for so long, I'd forgotten how it's almost impossible to keep your personal life a secret around here. I guess this is what happens when everyone knows everybody."

Both Carrie and Abby nodded. But, by their expressions, Livy knew her evasive answer wasn't going to do it for them. They knew all of what she just said. What they wanted to know, was all of the details of what was going on between her and Sam.

"I… well, I don't know. Everything is so up in the air right now." She shrugged. "Look at me, I'm a mess. I'm almost thirty years old and living with my aunt, I have no job and no real plan of what I want to do next."

She picked up what was left of her cookie and absentmindedly began crumbling it with her fingers. Brushing the crumbs off her fingers, she sighed. "I like Sam, I like him a lot. But after almost seven years with Zack, only to have it all go for nothing, well… this certainly hasn't made it easy for me to trust anyone. So, even though my heart is all for it, my mind keep butting in, telling me I need to be cautious."

She stared down at her coffee. "Sam told me he's willing to take it slow, but then he seems to be a lot more confident about us than I am. God, I don't know…I wish… I just don't want to get hurt again. And I certainly don't want to lead him on, to then find I'm not ready for this."

Carrie and Abby looked at each other, to then look back at Livy before Carrie leaned back in her chair. She crossed her arms over her chest, nodding over at Abby. "You tell her, Abby. I've already told her what I think when it comes to Sam. But since I'm her younger sister, I guess my opinion doesn't count for anything."

Livy made a face at her, to which Carrie retaliated by sticking out her tongue.

Abby laughed, shaking her head. "I guess this is what I missed by being an only child. This is why I want to have at least two." Absent-mindedly tapping her fingers on her cup, she was silent for a few seconds before she turned to Livy, a slight smile on her face.

"*Hmm…* what can I tell you about Sam? I love Sam. We all love Sam. But lately, we've all been holding our breath because of this new realtor who suddenly showed up, Valerie Madison. Have you met her?"

Livy sighed. "Yes, I have. And to tell you the truth, she scares me. I've run into the likes of her in New York and know how relentless her type can be."

Abby shook her head. "Yeah, no one seems to know where she came from, but boy oh boy… you're right, Livy. She can be pretty scary." She shuddered. "She came waltzing up to me and Kevin at a restaurant, putting on this act like we were the best of friends. Neither of us had any idea who she was. The way she talked about Sam, it was as though he was her own private property. She made it a point to let us know she has big plans for the two of them."

She smiled. "But from what I've been told, from you-know-who," this was said with a nod towards Carrie, "Sam's attention is focused elsewhere, and this is on you. Livy, Sam is not a player. If he chooses to be with you, then he's serious. You're definitely not a passing fling."

Livy glanced over to see Carrie was nodding, a very somber expression on her face. In fact, both Carrie and Abby looked so serious, Livy began to laugh.

"Oh my God, you two… I feel like this is an intervention. Okay, okay, already… I'll give Sam the benefit of the doubt." She ducked her head in an attempt to hide the color filling her cheeks. "It's sort of hard not to, he has this way of making me feel… well, you know. Like he really cares."

Carrie nodded, again very seriously. "Oh Livy, I assure you, he does. He cares a lot."

As she said this, she was thinking of her conversation with Sam after Livy left her office on Wednesday morning. How they talked about his feelings for Livy. Out of respect of her friendship with Sam, she wasn't going to share what he said. Well… maybe she could give Livy a little hint…

She smiled at her.

"Yep, he cares all right. More than you think."

The sound of a door closing had them all turning to see Kevin striding towards them, a big smile on his face.

"Hey ladies…" This was followed by a nod over to Livy and Carrie before he planted a kiss to Abby's cheek. "Hi, sugar."

"So… what's going on here?" Then he chuckled. "Uh oh… what are you three plotting? If you were talking about one of us guys, just to warn you, and not even knowing what it's about, I'm on his side. One hundred percent. I only hope it's not me."

Abby laughed. "Don't worry, you're off the hook this time. We're just discussing things... you know, all kind of things... important women things."

He smiled down at her, his hand dropping to her shoulder. "And you're not going to tell me what these things are. I get it."

He smiled over at Livy. "Livy, it's good to see you. What's this I hear you may be sticking around this time?"

Livy laughed. "What did I just say about nothing is ever a secret in this town?" She smiled over at Kevin. "I'm not sure yet what my plans are. I'll be here for a while, though. At least until I figure out what I'm going to do next."

Abby grinned. "Or someone helps you figure it out, you mean." At Kevin's puzzled expression, they all laughed. But this didn't bother him. He knew Abby would fill him in later.

Carrie stood and giving a long stretch, she looked over at the two big boxes of cookies. Then she looked over at Kevin. "Do you think you can do us a favor and carry these out to my SUV?"

She turned to Abby. "We should get going. We need to get these cookies over to Chester and Sophie's house. And make sure the tent and tables are set. Thanks for the cookies. I guess we'll see you tomorrow? But if you change your mind and decide to come to the rehearsal dinner, please let me know and we'll have someone pick you up. I know Kevin is meeting the guys after the game. I hope it doesn't go into extra innings."

Abby nodded. "I will. But I'll probably be finishing up your cake. If I see I'm going to get done early, I'll let you know. Otherwise, yes... I'll see you tomorrow. I can't wait. I'm so happy for you and Chris."

She was smiling as she gave Carrie a big hug.

"And to think it all started when the two of you met at our wedding..."

Abby watched them leave, eager for Kevin to return. She'd sent him a text, asking him to stop by before he went to the ballpark. She had important news to share with him.

She'd just finished loading the dishwasher when she heard him whistling, even before he opened the door. He came up behind her and after wrapping his arms around her, his voice was a deep rumble in her ear. "Hey, beautiful... I got your message. What's so important you wanted me to stop by before I go to the ballpark?"

Scooting away from him, she picked up a small white bakery box from the counter and handed it to him. It was tied with a pale green ribbon.

Puzzled, he looked down at the box and then back at her. "What's this? A gift for me? A new cookie you want me to check out?" His eyes lit up. "Or a special snack for before the game?"

A big smile on her face, she shook her head. "Just open it."

He untied the ribbon and lifting the lid, he pulled out a cookie in the shape of a sock. At least this is what he was pretty sure it was. But it was a fancy sock. The frosting was a pale green with a white lacy pattern.

Still uncertain, he looked over at Abby, intrigued by the nervous, yet excited expression on her face.

Ah... it must be a sample of a big order she received. Or one of her new designs.

He cleared his throat, to then smile at her. "Very nice. Is this a special order?"

A thoughtful look on her face, she nodded. "Yes, I guess you could say that."

He peered more closely at her. From what he could see, she appeared to be on the verge of tears. Happy tears, he hoped.

Oh, boy...

If he'd learned one thing since he'd known her, any sign of tears could go either way. From ecstatically happy, all the way down to the depths of despair. So, whatever she was trying to tell him, he sure as hell hoped it fell somewhere in the happy range.

He cleared his throat again, giving her a bright smile. "Well, this looks great. If you need my help, you know I'm here for you."

Her gaze fixed on his face, her reply came out in a half giggle, half sob. "I don't think that's necessary. I do believe you've already done more than your part to help out."

And this is when he finally understood what she was trying to tell him. His mouth dropping open, he stared at her in disbelief. He looked down at the cookie he was still holding in his hand, then back at her. He tried to say something, but the words just wouldn't come.

She nodded again.

His eyes never leaving her face, he swallowed. His voice was hoarse. "A baby? We're going to have a baby?"

Now she was nodding like crazy. When he began to laugh, she began to laugh, too. Then, of course, she also started to cry.

In one quick move, he picked her up and holding her tightly against him, he spun them around in circles. They were both breathless from laughing when he finally stilled, giving her a kiss that had her holding on to him for support.

He gazed down at her in complete awe. "A baby... We're going to have a baby. I can't believe it." He tightened his hold as he grinned down at her. "My God, Abby... we're going to be parents." If possible, his grin became even bigger. "I hope it's a little girl. With curly red hair."

Her arms reaching up to wrap around his neck, she smiled. "Are you sure about that? Do you really want another me to put up with? Though I'll admit I wouldn't mind a little carbon copy of you."

A look of pure panic crossed her face. "Oh my God... just as long as it's not twins. Trevor and Hudson are cute and all, but, oh my..."

He chuckled. "I'm sure whatever we have, together we'll be able to handle it. We'll do just fine."

Determination marked his features. This was not only big, this was serious. This meant it was time for him to grow up. He had to make sure, for both Abby and the baby, he would be their rock. He'd make sure everything went smoothly.

Starting right now.

He was suddenly very concerned. "Maybe you should start looking into hiring another assistant? So, you can take it easy." He gave a swift glance around the room. "You don't need to be working so many hours. Or standing on your feet all day."

She reached up to frame his face in her hands. "Kevin, there's no need to be so concerned. Women have babies every day. I don't need another assistant. You're so sweet to worry about me, but I assure you, everything will be just fine."

Kevin nodded. But his mind was already on all of the things he was going to do to make the next nine months easier for her. No matter how much she protested.

He pressed a kiss to the top of her head.

He was going to be a dad.

This brought on another grin… a huge grin.

A baby…

Could life get any better?

CHAPTER 15

Nothing like a family gathering
to remind you why you came back home.
~ Anonymous

Carrie hadn't even pulled out of the parking lot when she grinned over at Livy.

"I bet you fifty bucks Abby is pregnant."

Surprised, Livy glanced over at her. "You think so? Why?"

Carrie laughed. "The first clue was the remark she made about wanting to have two kids. But what clinched it, was the dreamy look on her face when she said it. I wouldn't be the least bit surprised if Kevin shares the news with all of the guys tonight."

She sighed. "I wish they were coming to the rehearsal dinner, but since both he and Chester aren't playing tomorrow night, Kevin decided not to take off tonight, too. Instead, he's planning to join the guys later."

Livy shook her head. "Boy, everybody really does know everything about everyone around here, don't they? In New York, it seems like most people are so worried about what's going on in their own lives, they don't have the time to think about anyone else." She shrugged.

"It's going to take me a little time to get used to this. I guess it's sort of nice in a way."

She sent Carrie a pointed glance. "To a point, that is."

Carrie was laughing as she made the turn into Sophie and Chester's driveway. "Okay, I get it. But it's hard not to be excited about you and Sam. He's such a…"

Livy jumped in to finish her sentence. "Nice guy. I know, I know." She sighed. "I certainly can't argue with that."

As they turned into the driveway of Sophie and Chester's house, it was Carrie who wasn't listening this time, her attention focused on the tent, more than visible behind the house. "Wow… the tent is set up as promised." She laughed. "I guess I didn't realize it was going to be so big."

She was still talking as she and Livy took the boxes of cookies out of her car. "We'll check out the tent and the tables, spend some time with Sophie and the babies and then we'll leave. We need to have enough time to get ready for tonight. I wonder if Chester is here?"

Before Livy could answer, Carrie was off and talking again. "I hope the weather tomorrow is exactly like it is now. But even if it's not, I don't care." She grinned over at Livy. "I'm so excited."

She then went on to describe the dress she was wearing for the rehearsal dinner. She also wanted to know if Livy knew what she was wearing? And was Sam picking her up? She really did hope the dinner was going to be at White Oaks. Since Chris knew it was one of her favorite restaurants, you'd think this is would be his choice. But, then again, it really didn't matter, did it?

Livy let her talk.

The rehearsal went without a hitch. And, as Carrie had been hoping, Chris had reserved White Oaks for the dinner that followed. There had been a lot of good-natured teasing and sincere toasts shared.

Chris's nephew, Connor, had stolen the show at the rehearsal. At five years old, he'd been assigned the position of ring bearer, a job he took very seriously.

He'd also become very attached to Livy, going as far to ask Sam if he was planning to marry her. Because if he wasn't, Connor told him, he would. Very seriously, he had told him this. But Livy would have to wait until he finished school.

Sam had told Connor he wasn't quite sure what was going to happen between him and Livy just yet. But he did give Connor a bit of advice. And this was, it might be better if he were to find someone else. Since he had become quite fond of Livy, chances were he wasn't going to give her up.

But, he'd told Connor…in the end, it all came down to what Livy wanted to do.

And what did Livy have to say about all of this attention coming from two such amazing admirers? She told them, as it stood right now, it would be impossible for her to make a decision.

As Carrie predicted, when Kevin arrived, he made the announcement Abby was pregnant. The moment was made even sweeter because he'd managed to persuade Abby to come with him so they could tell everyone this news together.

Carrie and Livy went home with their Aunt Evelyn. Carolyn and John, went to their hotel.

Sam went out with the guys. It was when he finally left to go home, he almost called Livy. He suddenly wanted to hear her voice. But when he checked the time, he saw it was already after two. He didn't want to wake her.

Too bad he hadn't called.

Because even though Carrie had fallen asleep as soon as her head hit the pillow, Livy was still wide awake.

Thinking about Sam… and wishing he'd call.

If only just to hear his voice.

CHAPTER 16

*a*s predicted, the next day dawned bright and sunny, with only an occasional cloud floating lazily across the brilliant June sky.

Seated on the deck with Carrie and Sophie as they enjoyed their lunch, Livy swiftly reached over to grab Carrie's phone out of her hand, tucking it next to her on the chair. She went on to eat her salad, completely ignoring Carrie's plea.

"Livy, come on… give me my phone. I want to call the florist, just to make sure they'll be here on time."

Rolling her eyes over at Livy, Sophie poured more wine into Carrie's almost empty wine glass. She pushed it over to her. "Here, just drink your wine. The flowers will be here as promised. You've already reminded Kelly she needs to be here at twelve-thirty to start on hair and make-up. And the caterers are already at work in the kitchen. Everything is going to be fine and you need to relax. Or you'll be exhausted by the time the wedding even starts."

Carrie sighed. "Okay, okay. I'll try."

Less than a minute later, she glanced down at her watch. "Carolyn and Emily do know they're supposed to be here by one, don't they?"

"Carrie...come on..."

This warning coming from both Livy and Sophie, almost at the same time, was finally enough to convince Carrie to start eating her lunch.

Carefully making her way down the steps going to the first floor of Sophie and Chester's house, Livy was holding her dress up with one hand, her other hand hanging onto the railing.

She was talking to herself. "You can do this. You're not going to fall. You only have a few more steps to go and you'll be fine."

She'd been sent to see if the photographer had arrived. It was only forty-five minutes before the ceremony was to start and Carrie was wondering where he was.

Finally reaching the bottom step, she let out a long sigh of relief. At the sound of a deep chuckle coming from behind her, she whirled around. Sam was standing by the entrance to the kitchen, his arms crossed over his chest as he watched her. A big grin on his face, he slowly shook his head.

Frozen in place, she could only watch as he casually sauntered over to her, the grin still on his face.

As you can imagine, in a tuxedo, he was total perfection

Let's just say he took her breath away.

He cupped her cheek in his hand and leaned in to press a kiss to her mouth.

"Hey, gorgeous… where are you headed?"

She was having a really hard time, to the point she almost couldn't breathe. The need to touch him came at her so suddenly and so strongly, she reached out to run her hands down the lapels of his jacket, before finally resting them against his shirt front.

He glanced down at her hands, then back at her face, a question in his eyes. "Hey, is something wrong? I thought I did a pretty good job of dressing myself. Had a little bit of trouble with the tie, but it turned out to not be my fault. Somehow, I got Connor's by mistake. But the crisis was averted and all ended well."

It was when she finally got it together enough to shake her head, she saw the twinkle in his eyes. This made her believe he knew exactly what she was thinking, why she was so tongue-tied.

Let's face it, he has you under his spell. You might as well just come out and accept this.

After she made a big deal out of adjusting his tie and smoothing the lapels of his jacket, she stepped back to study the results. "There, now you are perfect. You did a wonderful job. You look absolutely amazing."

A big sigh escaped her. "In fact, I'm afraid you look too good. Every woman at this wedding will want to be with you tonight."

She gave him a sly grin. "Especially when they find out what a good dancer you are."

He pulled her back. He wanted her back in his arms, the thought popping into his mind, even then, she still wouldn't be close enough.

Then he frowned. He didn't like the sound of what she just said. This wasn't what he wanted. "There's only one woman I want to be with tonight, only one woman I plan to dance with. And this is you."

Not only tonight, but every night. You want her as your dance partner for a lifetime.

He blinked at this thought, a smile tugging at his lips as he gazed down at her. "So, again... where are you headed? Are you on some kind of top-secret-maid-of-honor-mission?"

Laughing, she pulled away from him. "No, this is all out in the open. Carrie was getting anxious because the photographer hadn't arrived yet. So, I volunteered to check it out."

Aren't you leaving out one important bit of information here? How you jumped at the chance to be the one to check it out, hoping you might see him?

And lo and behold, she got lucky.

He nodded. *"Hmm...* I'm pretty sure this is because he just finished up with us. I swear he took more photos in the last forty-five minutes or so, than I've taken in a lifetime. From what I remember Carrie telling me, he's new in the business and does great work. He's very thorough, that's for sure."

As he said this, a young man, a frantic look on his face and wielding a camera, went running by them to go charging up the steps.

Before she had any idea of his plans, Sam scooped her up in his arms and began carrying her up the steps. She could only hold on.

"Sam!"

He pressed a quick kiss to her mouth. "Shush… I heard you talking to yourself. This means you know as well as I do, a long dress and steps aren't what you'd call a good combination. And when we add you in to the mix?"

He shook his head. "This could very well lead to disaster. I'd like to have you in one piece for the photos." He pressed another kiss to her mouth. "And definitely for when we wow everyone with our dance moves."

Coming to the top of the stairs, he gently dropped her to the floor. His hand framing the side of her face, he gave her one more kiss before he smiled at her. "See you in a little bit."

Sending her a wink over his shoulder, he went bounding down the stairs.

Thinking her heart couldn't possibly beat any faster, she watched until he was out of sight.

CHAPTER 17

*L*ivy was trying so hard not to cry as she listened to Carrie and Chris exchange their wedding vows. She gazed up at the roof of the tent above them, blinking like crazy in her attempt to hold back the tears.

She'd expected to be a little sentimental. Instead, she was one step away from losing complete control and sobbing like a baby.

Carrie is your sister, so it's natural for you to be a little teary-eyed, right?

The key word here is little... a far cry from the emotional state she'd worked herself into.

She glanced over at Sam. His head bowed, there was the hint of a smile on his lips.

She sighed. No control problem there.

Little did she know, he was as moved by the vows as she was. He had been fine until he handed over the rings and took his place next to Livy. But from that moment on, she was all he could think about.

He glanced over at her at the same time she chanced a glance at him. Neither could tell you what happened afterwards.

At least not until the ceremony was over.

The reception was in full swing,

A plate with a piece of Carrie and Chris's wedding cake in each hand, Livy weaved her way through the maze of tables. Finally arriving at the table where her Aunt Evelyn and her sister Carolyn were seated, she set a plate down in front of each of them.

"Here you go. It's not chocolate like the cake Abby made for Sophie and Chester's wedding, but I'm sure it's just as delicious."

Carolyn grabbed her hand. "Livy, sit with us for a while. I feel like I've hardly had a chance to talk to you since we arrived. But wait… where's your cake?"

Livy sank into one of the chairs. "Sam is going to bring me a piece."

She reached down to massage first one foot, then the other. "Oh my gosh, it feels so good to sit down. I feel like we've been in constant motion since early this morning. My feet are killing me, and I can't even tell you how many times my heels got stuck in the ground and I almost wiped out."

She turned to look back to where the cake was on display. "I told Sam I was bringing you cake and he told me he'd bring me a piece in a few minutes." She smiled. "He was with a group of guys who were definitely having a good time, telling stories and laughing. So, I told him not to worry about me, but he insisted. I see he's at the cake table now."

She wasn't going to tell Carolyn what else Sam said to her. She was still waiting for her heart to calm down in response to that. This had happened when she was waiting for the servers to plate the cake.

Coming up behind her, Sam had wrapped his arms around her. After pressing a slow kiss to the nape of her neck, his lips had trailed up to her ear. "Hey beautiful, what-cha doing?"

She had lifted her face up to his. "I promised my aunt and sister I'd bring them a piece of cake."

"Hmm... I see." His hands pulling her closer, he'd pressed a kiss to her jaw. "Will you promise me something?"

She'd leaned back against him, her breath catching in her throat at the sudden intensity of his gaze. "I... I don't know. It depends on what it is. With you, well... it could be almost anything. So, I need to be careful about the promises I make."

He had smiled, pressing another kiss right below her ear. *"Mmm...* no need to worry, sweetheart. It will always be your call. But right now, I want your promise you'll save the last dance for me. Then we'll leave. Carrie and Chris have already left, so our job here is done."

He'd pressed his mouth to hers, his lips lingering much longer this time. His voice dipped to a husky whisper. "I want to be alone with you. I've wanted this all day."

She'd nodded. So, so slowly, she did this. Her lashes fluttering shut, she'd relaxed against him with a soft sigh.

Then she'd realized what she was doing.

You are at a wedding reception. Standing at the cake table, in full view of everyone. And you're ready to do whatever this man, who is holding you like he's never going to let go, asks of you.

Was she completely out of her mind?

This was proof of what she'd believed all along. Sam Bridges was a man of unbridled passion. And at this very moment, she was being offered a glimpse of what that passion could be like.

You could be that woman.

The one up until now, and in her wildest fantasies, she only imagined she could be.

"Hey, Sam!"

Her lashes had flown open at the same time Sam's sigh brushed across her cheek. Reluctantly lifting his head, he'd turned to look over at the group of guests, from where the voice had come.

"What's this I hear? You played football for Trinity in DC? I played for Lakeside. We annihilated you guys."

He'd laughed, flashing the group a big grin. *"Hmm...* I remember differently. Give me a minute, okay?"

He'd turned back to Livy, who had picked up the two plates of cake, almost dropping one in her flustered state. Grabbing the plate, he'd smiled down at her. "Hey, steady there... your aunt and sister would never forgive you if you dropped their cake."

At his knowing smile, she'd averted her gaze. "That's okay, I've got it now." She had nodded towards the group. "Go and join your friends. As you can see, I need to get this cake delivered before something happens."

Or you do something crazy and entirely out of line... with him.

He'd responded to this by framing the side of her face in his hand, pressing another kiss to her mouth.

Maybe it was the couple of shots he'd toasted with Chris and Kevin at the bar. Or the whole wedding atmosphere playing with his mind. He only knew his thoughts had become completely flooded with Livy, to the extent he'd become intoxicated with everything about her.

He wanted to hold her… kiss her, touch her… or hell… just be able to keep her with him.

Always.

Buoyed by these thoughts, his grin was infectious. "I'll join you in a few minutes. Bearing cake for the both of us."

He'd begun to walk away, glancing back to see she hadn't moved. Her lips parted, she was staring after him, a bemused expression on her face.

Slowly walking backwards, he'd pointed his finger at her. "Don't forget what I said about the last dance." Giving her a wink, he turned to join the group.

Leaving her still staring after him.

So, you can see why Livy was a little preoccupied. In fact, she didn't even hear what Carolyn was chattering about between the forkfuls of cake she was shoveling in her mouth.

That is, until she started talking about Sam.

"Oh my God, Livy… this cake is absolutely heavenly. But, enough about the cake. What I really want to talk about, is you and Sam. Livy, he's a keeper. I was watching him during the ceremony, and I swear he must have glanced over at you at least a dozen or more times. And every time he did, this little smile would come over his face. Why, it was almost as though the two of you shared a special secret between you. I'm sure I wasn't the only one who noticed this. In fact, when we were standing in the receiving line after the ceremony, John asked me if the two of you were engaged. When I told him I didn't think you were, he didn't believe me."

She sighed. "I can't even remember the last time John looked at me the way Sam looks at you. If he did, I'm sure he'd be pleasantly surprised by the way I'd respond." Scrunching up her nose, she shook her head. "Men... sometimes they just don't get it."

She smiled over at Livy. "Except for your Sam. Hang on to him, Livy. If you don't, someone else will grab him up in a second."

Livy cleared her throat. "*Umm...* he's not really mine. I mean, we aren't really serious... at least I don't think he..."

Her voice fading at the amused expression on Carolyn's face, she quickly glanced over to see Sam was still at the cake table, talking to the servers. As if he could sense her gaze, he looked over and right at her.

He winked at her.

Again, she was willing to bet the grin he had on his face was because he knew how flustered he still had her. Swiftly turning back to her sister and aunt, she gave them her full attention. She certainly wasn't going to let Sam get to her.

Yeah, right... like you're going to be able to pull that off.

Aunt Evelyn, who'd been too busy eating her cake to join in the conversation, set her fork on her empty plate and pushed it away. After she patted her mouth with her napkin, she nodded. "I agree with your sister, Livy. I think you should drop this Zack you've hooked up with." At Livy and Carolyn's surprise at her choice of words, she shrugged. "Isn't that how you young people refer to it these days? Well, no matter. Any way you say it, the result is the same."

She nodded over at Livy. "Livy, if a man hasn't popped the question to a woman, going on six years, he has no intention of doing it at all. That's my opinion."

Livy nodded. She wasn't going to admit this out loud, but she completely agreed. She gave her aunt a curious glance. "Did you ever want to get married?"

After appearing to be lost in thought for a few moments, her aunt finally answered. "When I was twenty-two, I did get a marriage proposal. From Tony Palmerrio."

She grinned. "Yep, a good Italian boy. But I turned him down. At the time, I foolishly believed I was in love with another man. A lot older than me, he had no intentions of becoming serious. But by the time I figured this out, Tony had already started dating a friend of mine and they eventually got married. So, I decided I was never going to get married, completely content with my independent life. Then the four of you came along and I realized what I'd been missing."

She laughed. "Having four children suddenly thrown into your life can change your perspective on everything. Don't get me wrong, I loved every minute. The four of you kept me young."

Carolyn leaned her chin on her hand, gazing over at her aunt. "Do you know what happened to this Tony? Is he still married?"

"No, I have no idea where he is. Or, knock on wood, he's even still alive." She sent Carolyn a warning look. "And don't you get any ideas of trying to find him. That's the last thing I want. I certainly don't want him to see how old I've become."

Livy and Carolyn were laughing about this when Sam appeared at their table with the promised cake. He set one down in front of Livy before he sat next to her. To the delight of both Carolyn and Aunt Evelyn, he leaned over to give her a quick kiss. "There you go, baby."

His ever so charming self and with a boyish grin on his face, he nodded over at Aunt Evelyn. "I meant to tell you last night. I believe your cannoli may have surpassed Angie's. But you have to promise you'll never tell her I told you this. It's too bad the two of you don't live closer to each other. I bet you'd have a lot to talk about, both of you with such great culinary skills."

Aunt Evelyn gave a dismissive wave of her hand. "Oh, go on with you... I'm an average cook at best. I'm sure Angie's were better, even though I was quite satisfied with how my version turned out." She shrugged. "I love cooking for people. It makes me happy."

Carolyn smiled at Sam. "Livy has told us so much about you and how impressed she is with what you do, restoring historic homes. What an interesting profession you've chosen. You should seriously think about coming out with a book." She nodded over at Livy. "With her experience, Livy could take over the editing and publishing part of the job. The two of you collaborating on this? I bet the end result would be a work of art."

A smile twitching at the corner of his mouth, Sam tried to act as though he was completely unaware of the frantic head shaking Livy was directing at Carolyn.

He nodded. *"Hmm...* you just might be on to something with that idea. Livy and I will have to talk about it. It's a shame you're leaving tomorrow. Otherwise, I could've taken you to see the house we're working on right now in Shaker Heights. I've already promised Livy a tour. It's such a magnificent piece of history. One of the most interesting homes I've had the experience of working on so far."

"How about the house by the lake?" Livy smiled over at her aunt and sister. "On Thursday, Sam took me with him to look at this house. I got to see him in action, checking everything out."

Sam smiled at her. "Ah, yes. A very interesting piece of property. And grabbed up rather quickly."

He watched Livy very closely as he said this, noting her look of disappointment as she sighed. *"Oh...* I, well I guess that's good, right?"

He was about to respond when the band announced they were about to play their last song of the evening. Rising from his seat, he held out his hand to Livy before he sent Carolyn and Aunt Evelyn a smile. "I hope you'll excuse us. Livy made me promise we'd share the last dance."

He sent a teasing nod towards Livy. "Seems she can't get enough of me."

Livy started to laugh. *"Umm...* I do believe it's the other way around. And this would be for both of those comments."

Sam shook his head over at Carolyn. "Always has to be right, too. Has she always been this way?"

"Always. And stubborn, too." Before Livy could respond to this,

Carolyn continued. "Livy, John and I are leaving in a few minutes to take Aunt Evelyn home. Then we'll head for our hotel. It's been a long day. So, you two enjoy the rest of your night."

She smiled over at Sam. "We'll see you tomorrow at the brunch, I hope?"

"When I fall in love...
It will be completely..."

Sam was humming along with the music as he took Livy into his arms on the dance floor. She stumbled against him as they began to move, his chuckle brushing against her ear before he gazed down at her. "Ah, sweetheart... relax. Think of how good this feels." He smiled. "And it's only me."

Only him?

And therein lies the problem. It wasn't only him, it was *all* him. Did he have any idea of what he did to her? Could he feel her reaction to his touch, her nerves kicking into gear, or the quickening of her heartbeat?

She realized, even if he did, it didn't matter. Her heart had already taken him in and had no intention of letting go.

She sighed against him, this bringing him to pull her even closer, pressing a kiss right below her ear.

"When I give my heart...
It will be forever..."

She reached up to link her fingers behind his neck. "I don't know if you noticed, but my sister is quite taken with you. In fact, it appears both she and my aunt have already decided you're pretty close to perfect."

"Hmm... is that so." This, along with the kiss he pressed in her hair, was his only response.

After a short silence, she glanced up at him. "I thought you'd be happy to hear you received such a glowing review."

He smiled down at her. "I am. It's nice to know they approve of me. But as much as I like hearing this, the opinion I care about most, is yours."

She smiled up at him. "Are you fishing for compliments?"

He pressed a kiss to her mouth, his lips lingering over hers. "Only if you feel comfortable giving them to me. Where, if you were to ask the same of me, I would have no problem naming off everything I love about you. In a heartbeat, I'd be willing to do this."

"And the moment I know...
You feel that way too..."

She stilled, her eyes searching his for an explanation. This would be about the one little, but so very important, word he just used.

If he had really meant for it to be said.

"Love?" This coming at him in a whisper, Sam almost missed it. He chuckled softly before he leaned in close to whisper right back to her. "Yes… love."

Livy wasn't quite sure how to respond to this. After all, he hadn't actually said he loved her, as in, I love you. No, what he *said* was there were things he loved *about* her. Which wasn't the same. No, it was totally different.

Wasn't it?

He twirled her around the dance floor, to then pull her back into his arms. His voice was a husky whisper in her ear. "Yes, that little four-letter word has started to pop into my mind whenever I think of you. And this seems to be happening more and more frequently. To the point it's starting to grow on me, like it's where it belongs."

Well, there you go... there's your answer. Now what are you going to do?

She dipped her head to rest it against his chest. How was it his heart was beating so slow and steady, yet hers was now beating as though it was in a race?

Never had she been so aware of anyone as she was of him at this moment. She wanted to get closer, as close as she could. She wanted to let him take over, fill her mind, body and soul. So she could forget about the rest of the world and everything else.

It was official.

Livy Mazzori had fallen in love.

Completely and madly in love.

And now? She wanted Sam with a passion she never knew she could be capable of feeling.

Yes, this was the same Livy who'd held such pride with the fact she didn't need anyone in her life to make it complete.

Things had definitely changed.

"When I'll fall in love...
All over and over again with you..."

Sam was smiling.

Part of this was because he knew Livy probably hadn't even realized how she was following his lead without losing a beat. Completely relaxed in his arms, he could feel her body slowly giving into this need they'd been dancing around for the past week.

But the biggest reason for his smile was because of the way she'd reacted to his words. He saw this as a sign she was finally allowing her heart to rule over her mind.

There was something, and he'd go as far as to say it was almost magical, happening between them right now. And if he didn't take advantage of this?

You'd be an absolute fool...

He pulled her closer.

"Livy?"

His eyes searching hers, for a long, breathless moment, they barely moved. The music and everything else seemed to have vanished, leaving him only with the woman he was holding in his arms.

The woman he loved.

He dipped his head to kiss her mouth, briefly, softly, before he took a deep breath. His words were a husky whisper against her cheek.

"Come home with me. Stay the night. I want to know what it feels like to wake up in the morning and find you beside me."

They weren't even aware they had come to a complete stop on the dance floor, the words of the song floating over and around them, almost as if this had been the plan all along.

There was no doubt.

No hesitation.

And no need for words.

For it was at this moment, they both realized just how deeply in love they had fallen.

"It will be completely ...
It will be forever...
When I fall in love with you..."

CHAPTER 18

Sam flicked a switch, the recessed lights bordering the ceiling of his condo slowly coming to life. After he tossed his jacket over the arm of the sofa and emptied his pockets of his keys, wallet and cell phone, he glanced over at Livy. Curiously gazing around the great room, she had a surprised look on her face.

He chuckled. "So, I can see by the expression on your face, you didn't expect this kind of décor from me, did you?"

Slowly shaking her head, she began walking around the room, taking it all in.

The décor was the complete opposite of the interior design Sam specialized in. The high and open ceiling, exposed brick wall in the kitchen and the towering windows spanning the one wall, definitely gave off an urban industrial vibe. It was sleek and modern. Yet at the same time, the plush leather sectional arranged in front of the massive river stone front fireplace, extended an invitation of serenity in the most luxurious form.

Her inspection complete, she looked over to where Sam was leaning back against the island countertop, his arms crossed. He was waiting patiently for her opinion.

He smiled. "Well? And what would your verdict be?"

She returned his smile. "I like it. Did you…" She paused, suddenly hesitant. She was almost about to ask if Carrie was responsible for the décor, information she really didn't want to know.

Yes, she was being childish, but she couldn't help it.

He quickly sensed the reason for her hesitation. "An architect friend of mine from college came up with the design. This was shortly after I moved here."

He shot her an almost embarrassed smile. "I was pretty cocky back then. I wanted to come in with this sophisticated and big city look. I was ready to take on the world, convinced I was too good for the cookie cutter kind of condo I thought I'd find here."

He gazed slowly around the room, almost as though he was viewing it for the first time. "But now I feel like I'm ready to move on. I want my home to reflect what I do. The more projects I work on, the more I feel this way."

He sent her a smile. "I don't feel the need to impress anyone anymore, I guess."

Except for Livy. You want to impress her. If only to prove to her how much she means to you.

More relieved by his answer than she should be, Livy quickly changed the subject. "I'm sorry you didn't get the property on the lake. I could see how excited you were about the house when we were there." She sighed. "I only hope whoever bought it, restores it to how it once was."

Worry creased her brow. "What if they bought it just for the land? And they tear it down? How awful this would be."

Sam had moved to stand next to her and taking her into his arms, he held her against him. There was a slight smile on his face as he pressed a kiss in her hair. "Only time will tell, baby. In the meantime, I guess you need to keep the faith. Not all people are hell-bent on demolishing the past, you know."

He slightly pulled away from her. "So… can I get you something to drink? Wine? Or anything else your heart desires?"

Her hands going up to rest against his shirt front, she gazed up at him. "What I'd really like more than anything is to take off these shoes. I don't know what Carrie was thinking of when she picked them out. Between that and worrying about tripping over this long dress, I just want to get out of both of them. I'm about to die."

And again, it appears as if you've implied too much.

They both looked down at her shoes, then back up at each other, with his gaze traveling over her at a much slower pace, taking in the way her dress flowed seductively over her curves. She could only watch, mesmerized, as he lifted her hands to his mouth, pressing a slow and openmouthed kiss to each wrist.

His voice was like velvet. "Well, I'm sure we don't want this to happen, do we? Come with me… I think I know how we can fix this."

He linked his fingers with hers to lead her down the hall and into his bedroom. Gently pushing her to sit on the bed, he went down to one knee at her feet. After he removed first one, then the other shoe, he held her feet in his hands as he gazed up at her. "Your feet are freezing, baby. We need to get them warmed up."

Her imagination immediately becoming caught up in what this might entail, this made even more vivid with the heat of his gaze, her heartbeat soared into high gear.

She swallowed. "I… I warned you. Remember? In the parking lot of Angie's? It's all part of the package."

She almost groaned aloud.

Oh my God… why did you just say that? He's going to think you're trying to get him to make some kind of commitment.

She tried to wiggle her feet free of his hands, but he held tight.

So, she did what she seemed to do a lot of when she was with him, she started babbling. "I don't know why this always happens. It's been like this for as long as I can remember. When I was growing up, I would get so mad at Chester because he would tease me about wearing two pairs of socks at the…"

His hands were suddenly framing her face, a deep groan coming from deep in his throat. "Livy… *please,* just stop talking… let me love you."

His mouth coming down on hers in a deep searching kiss, he eased her back, moving her up with him on to the bed. When his kisses became even more demanding, she arched up against him, responding with a passion that sent a jolt of heat through him, his heart pounding in his chest.

He smoothed the hair back from her face, his lips pressing a slow trail of kisses down to where her pulse was beating wildly in her throat. His eyes holding hers, he put his hand to the back of her dress, his whisper coming against her lips. "Okay, baby?"

Her answer in her nod and the kiss she gave him, he moved, reaching for the zipper. He paused, his hand resting against her back.

"Oh, boy…"

This was followed by a chuckle.

Concerned, because she was pretty sure he shouldn't be finding anything to laugh about right now, Livy's lashes flew open, her eyes searching his face.

Carefully shifting his weight, he leaned on his elbow to gaze down at her, another chuckle coming from him before his lips brushed over hers in a quick kiss. "I think my belt buckle has become caught in your dress. This could turn out to be very interesting."

She groaned, the words leaving her mouth before she could stop them. "Oh my God, just yank it lose. I don't care if you rip it. I just want you to…"

Her mouth snapping shut, she closed her eyes. Now, if this wasn't an embarrassing moment, she didn't know what it could be. After what felt like an unusually long silence, she finally dared to open her eyes, just a crack.

A smile twitching the corner of his mouth, he traced her lips with his finger. "My, my… just as I'd thought, there's a wealth of passion hiding beneath that protective shell you've put up around you." This comment was softened by a kiss.

She squeezed her eyes shut. "*Sam… please…*"

His hand sifting through the silky layers of her hair, he waited for her to open her eyes again. He couldn't hide his smile. "I'm not going to rip your dress. I don't want this first time between us to become a memory of me tearing off your dress. Patience, my love. Trust me, I'm just as eager for this as you are."

With quite a bit of maneuvering and a little bit of laughter, her dress was finally free of the buckle. His mouth swiftly taking over where he last left off, Sam reached again for the zipper, pulling it down to free her from the dress. His hand drifting over the silky softness of her skin, his voice was a husky whisper. *"Damn, Livy... you're beautiful."*

Livy had already gone to work on his clothes, having unbuttoned his shirt and was now pushing it down over his shoulders. She knew she should try to slow down, but she couldn't. She was beyond caring about anything except how much she wanted this with him.

She ached to feel him against her, all barriers removed... the hard wall of his chest, his muscular build, all of which she'd only been able to imagine up until now.

She wanted everything with him.

She wanted to experience the ultimate love between them, of being at one with him, joined by a passion like non other. Only then would they be able to ease this hunger that had been building between them.

It had also been Sam's intention they take it slow. He'd honestly believed he'd be able to do this. He wanted to savor these moments with Livy, take the time to love her with a thoroughness and gentleness she'd always remember.

For him, this would be a promise of his ultimate commitment, a declaration of his love. Again, call him old fashioned, but this was the way he'd always believed the first time should be with the woman he loved.

But this turned out to no longer be an option, the desire that flared between them stronger than he could have ever imagined.

It was a beautiful love... with all of the passion Livy had been longing for. And what had seemed impossible, had now happened.

She was that special woman...

It had started to rain, the wind blowing it against the window.

This, along with the beat of Sam's heart against hers, had lulled

Livy into a state of tranquility, both her mind and body drifting in a half-conscious state.

Sam still hadn't moved, his face pressed in the curve of her neck and his breathing finally slowed. But this was okay. She wanted to prolong the feeling of being in his arms, his body surrounding hers and the feel of his hands against her skin.

She needed this moment, if only to memorize everything about him, everything they shared.

Her hands skimming over the muscles of his back, a long sigh escaped her.

Still coming down from the high brought on by the passion that had raced through them like a storm, Sam slowly raised his head to see Livy's eyes were closed. The tone of his voice was gruff with emotion.

"God, Livy…"

The intensity of their love had rocked him to the core. And now, caught up in this sudden possessiveness that swept through him, he was filled with this need to claim her for his own. He wanted this moment to go on forever, so he could keep her close, keep her safe.

He needed to tell her this. "I think…" In his struggle to come up with the right words, he stopped to press a soft kiss to her mouth. "I don't think I'm ever going to be able to let you go now."

But this wasn't enough, it wasn't what he really wanted to tell her, what she needed to hear. He knew this as soon as he watched her slowly let out a long, trembling breath, her eyes still closed.

Don't cry.

She kept telling herself this, but for some odd reason, she wanted to cry her eyes out. This wasn't making any sense.

A rumble of thunder, much louder this time, shook the building, bringing her to open her eyes again. At his searching look, she lifted her face to his, placing a gentle kiss to his mouth "Thank you."

His gaze searching her face, he was confused. "For what?"

Her fingers stroking his cheek, she took a deep, shaky breath. "For this… loving me like you did. For making me feel almost beautiful."

He slid his hand down her back and, rolling to one side, took her with him so that they were face to face. "Oh Livy… everything about you is beautiful, inside and out. And I'm going to keep telling you this for the rest of your life. If only to convince you how true it is."

She closed her eyes. "Oh God… Sam, what are you doing? Please don't feel you have to make promises to me."

He took a deep breath for his next words "What I'm doing, baby, is trying to tell you how much I love you. I love your eyes. I love your mouth. I love how you feel in my arms. I love absolutely everything about you. Your passion for life, your temper and even your dancing skills. I could go on and on, but just know it all comes down to, if you want me, I'm yours. I will always be yours."

"Oh, Sam…"

And here came the tears… she couldn't stop them for the life of her. Trying to hide this from him, she gave him a kiss that should've been enough to let him know she loved him as much as he loved her.

But he wanted to hear her say it. And for few short seconds after the kiss ended, be began to wonder if this was going to happen.

Propping himself up on his elbow, he edged her bangs back from her face. He regarded her very seriously, his words a little hesitant. "I believe, traditionally, when a person tells another person how much they love them, that other person comes right back to say the same thing. Of course, this is if they, too, are in love.'

And it finally hit her…

He loves you… he really does love you.

To his relief, she wrapped her arms around his neck, pressing kisses all over his face. "Oh Sam, I love you, too. I've loved you since I opened my eyes and saw you looking down at me on the floor of that hotel lobby. I know you might find that hard to believe, but I was so sure you'd never feel the same, so I tried to fight it. Then you gave me that kiss, and I was hooked. From then on, you've never left my mind… or my heart."

He kissed her mouth. "Thank God for that… you had me a little worried there for a minute, I thought the independent Livy, the one who doesn't need anyone, had made a comeback and was ready to make a stand."

He pressed another kiss to her mouth. "Stay right where you are. Don't move."

At her nod, he left the bed and began searching through their clothing scattered on the floor.

Livy peered over at him, mystified. "Sam?"

"Just a minute... *ah, ha...* here we go." He pulled something from one of his trouser pockets to then make his way back to the bed.

Livy watched his progress, taking it all in... every single perfect inch of him.

And she still didn't get it.

How is it, you're with this beautiful man... with him acting as though it was perfectly natural to be standing in front of you, not a stitch of clothing covering him?

It just didn't seem possible. This kind of thing had never happened to her. And she'd already come to accept it probably never would.

"Hey..."

She blinked. She hadn't even realized he was next to her on the bed. A knowing grin on his face, He cupped her face in his hands. "Baby, when you look at me like you are right now, you've got me so I can't even think straight. But first, I have something for you."

He was smiling as he slipped a ring on her finger. A delicate gold band with two interlocking filigree hearts.

Her lips slowly parting in a smile, she gazed up at him. "It's a promise ring."

He nodded. "Yes, my promise to you. I had our names engraved on the inside of the band."

Livy was staring down at the ring. "It's beautiful." She reached up to give him a kiss. "Thank you. I love it, I really do."

"You're more than welcome. I also had the jeweler check out the ring you found. It cleaned up pretty good. Enough to see there is a set of initials engraved in the inside of the band, D. H. and J. B."

An excited look came over Livy's face. "*D. H.* ... Sam, those are Darcey's initials. Darcey Hollister. I wonder if the ring is hers? I'll have to see if I can reach her somehow."

She frowned. "But I don't know the other initials."

"We can check it out. But for now, let's not forget the reason we even came in here." The grin back on his face, his hand traveled down her leg, reaching for her foot. "*Ah... they're warm. But they could be a little warmer, don't you think?*"

Her fingers linking behind his neck, she smiled. "*Umm... definitely.*"

He pulled her against him until his mouth hovered only a breath away from hers.

"But, his time, there's no reason to hurry. We're going to take it slow, baby... real slow."

The sun was just beginning to rise up over the horizon when Livy was awakened by a scattering of soft kisses across her face.

Her eyelashes fluttering open to Sam's smile, she moved closer. "Good morning."

"Good morning, beautiful." His voice was sleepy, gruff. It vibrated along her nerves, sending a shiver through her, everywhere. "I don't know about you, but I think I'm going to want to wake up like this every morning. Having you here is so much better than I could've ever imagined."

She wrapped her arms around his neck. "I know..."

The memory of the night they shared was still with her, the love they shared, so beautiful, so right. And now, as his lips left a slow trail of heat across her skin, anticipation had again taken over her senses.

Craving more, she lifted her face to his, surrendering to his kisses.

For Sam, waking up to find Livy in his bed was everything he had dreamt it would be. No, this wasn't true. It was way beyond what he could've imagined. That this love had happened so quickly and so naturally had blown him away.

If this isn't fate, you don't know what it is.

He moved over her, his hands resting on either side of her head. He gazed down at her, into her beautiful eyes, almost overcome by the love she brought out in him. These were the eyes he wanted to look into every morning and every night, for the rest of their lives.

None other would do.

His whisper brushed across her mouth. "God, I love you."

She sighed into his mouth. "I love you, too."

He then went to show her exactly how much he really did love finding her next to him on this beautiful and perfect June morning.

An unexpected June morning, at that.

Livy woke to the enticing aroma of freshly brewed coffee.

Lazily opening her eyes, she watched as Sam placed two cups on the nightstand before he slipped under the comforter with her.

He smelled wonderful. The combination of shampoo, shaving cream and his cologne coming at her, and all at once, she wanted everything to come to a stop, so she could hold on to this moment forever.

He pressed a kiss in her hair. "*Damn*, Livy… I love your family and all, but I wish we weren't expected at the brunch. I'd rather stay here with you and do nothing all day." He lifted his head, flashing that sexy grin of his. "Or something…"

"I know." She sighed, cuddling even closer to him. "But you only get married once, you know."

He chuckled. "Yeah, I guess you're right."

She burrowed her face in his shoulder, a big sigh coming from her. "I need to shower… and get dressed." She groaned. "Oh geeez… this will be interesting. I certainly can't show up wearing my bridesmaid dress."

He pressed another kiss in her hair. "Well, you can shower here if you want. Or at your aunt's house. It's your call, baby. But whatever you decide, we need to get moving."

He reached for the cups, handing her one. "So, enjoy this moment while you can."

Later that evening, Livy and Sam were camped out on the sofa in his condo, their computers in front of them. Livy was working on her book and Sam was checking on invoices and delivery dates for the Shaker site.

It had been a long day.

What had started out as a brunch, had lingered into the late afternoon hours. After Livy had dropped off what she needed for her stay at Carrie and Chris's house, she and Sam had driven them, along with Carolyn and John, to the airport.

And now they were completely content to enjoy the peace and quiet of the Sunday evening.

Sensing his gaze, Livy looked up to see Sam was studying her, a preoccupied expression on his face.

At her tentative smile, a warm look came into his eyes. It was a look that made her heart race.

It was a look that makes you fall in love with him all over again.

He closed his laptop and after putting it on the coffee table, he held out his hand. "Come here…"

How right this felt, just the two of them, with her in his arms. This was where he wanted her. And this was where she wanted to stay.

So, without a single word exchanged between them, it was decided this is what she would do.

Jingles would be okay for one night. It wouldn't be the first time she spent the night alone. And she didn't need to be fed until the morning.

Yeah, Jingles would be just fine.

CHAPTER 19

Life is full of unexpected surprises.
Yes... it most certainly is.
~ Anonymously Yours

It had now been two days since the wedding, with Sam spending last night with Livy at Carrie and Chris's house.

Her lashes slowly fluttering open to the early morning sun, a smile traveled over Livy's face when she saw the rumpled sheets next to her. Closing her eyes against the brightness, she tried to bring to mind the image of Sam as he'd been only a short time ago. His arms holding her close. His whisper in her ear, telling her he didn't want to leave.

She sighed, and putting her arms over her head, she gave a long stretch.

It came on her so suddenly, the wave of nausea hitting her so intense, she almost didn't make it to the bathroom. Sinking to her knees and leaning over the toilet bowl, she heaved again and again, even when there was nothing left to let go.

Her head finally resting on her arms and her eyes closed, she stayed completely still, hoping this would calm her still lurching stomach.

A warning was flashing in her mind.

A warning that clearly wasn't going to go away.

She wanted to ignore it, but it only became louder and more insistent.

No, no, no, no... please, no... it can't be...

Her heart thundering loudly in her ears, every kind of explanation was running through her mind.

You probably have the flu. Or food poisoning. Yeah, that's what it is. Something wasn't right with the pizza you shared with Sam last night. You should call him, because he might be sick, too.

She carefully leaned back against the wall. Her gaze slowly traveled around the small bathroom before coming to rest on the toothbrush setting on the vanity countertop.

It was Sam's. She had given it to him last night.

She closed her eyes, a chill traveling through her.

It wasn't the flu. Nor was it food poisoning.

And Sam? He wasn't sick.

Of this, she was certain.

Oh, God... what are you going to do?

Livy wouldn't be able to tell you how long she sat on the floor.

The sound of her wildly beating heart echoed through the small bathroom, as she stared almost transfixed, at Sam's toothbrush. Afraid to move, when she finally did attempt to stand, she was thrown by yet another wave of nausea.

But this time, she was able to fight it off.

She turned on the faucet and rinsed out her mouth. It was only after splashing her face with cold water, she lifted her head to face her reflection in the mirror.

Her look of desperation said it all.

She stumbled down the hall and into the bedroom, where she crawled back in bed. Hugging her pillow to her stomach, she closed her eyes.

And this was where she stayed, for the longest time.

She was in shock. And even more in denial.

So much so, she couldn't even think.

Forty-five minutes later, she was back in the bathroom, her gaze anywhere but on the vanity countertop.

In that forty-five minutes, she'd thrown on the first pair of shorts and tank top she could find before she raced downstairs and out to her car. In what had to be the first time in her life, she walked into Target, went straight to the aisle where she picked up the one and only thing she needed to buy, paid at the register and returned right back to her car.

This had all taken place in less than ten of those forty-five minutes, if even that. A record, for sure.

She gave a wry smile. It would probably be a record for every woman who'd ever shopped at Target.

And now she was waiting for the results that could change her life. Not just for now, but forever.

She gazed around the small guest bathroom, her mind taking her back to simpler times, the space almost comforting in its familiarity. The soothing color combination of the pale green and pink ceramic tiles Carrie had chosen, had been popular when the house was built. The towels hanging from the towel bar, their decorative crocheted trim a sign they were for display only and not to be used. To think at one time a whole family would've shared this tiny space, was amazing to her.

The timer on her phone beeped, a stark reminder of reality. Tentatively reaching over to pick up the plastic stick from the counter, she took a deep breath and looked down at the little window.

Two blue lines. And we all know what that means.

Livy was pregnant.

She spent the better part of the morning in denial.

The rest of the time, she cried. She even yelled, maybe screamed out loud. At least a couple of times, she did this.

This had been accompanied by a great deal of pacing and talking to herself, all under the close scrutiny of a wary Jingles.

Thinking back, she knew exactly when this had happened. It was the night she and Zack had been arguing about the fact he was traveling so much. The sex that followed had been their last and desperate attempt to prove nothing was wrong, nothing had changed. But in reality, it had been the end.

But how could she have been so blind to not suspect she was pregnant? There had been plenty of signs… the fatigue, the occasional dizziness. Not to mention she hadn't had, as her Aunt Evelyn had always referred to it, her 'monthly visitor'. But she'd never been one to have a regular cycle.

So, she'd blithely blamed this latest absence on all of the changes taking place in her life.

Stupid… so, so stupid.

How could you have been so blind?

But why was she beating herself up over this? Because right now, it really didn't matter. Nor did it change anything.

She was still going to have a baby.

Just the thought of this had her pacing the floor again.

She stopped in her tracks…

What about Zack? What's going to happen with him?

She began pacing again. She had to tell him. As the father, it was only right he should know. She groaned, thinking of how she'd ignored all of his calls and messages over the past week. It was only yesterday she'd finally listened to his latest voicemail.

It had been a long, drawn out message, one in which he started out by telling her he was not happy and his life was now completely messed up because of her. By the anger in his voice, it was obvious he was trying to turn things around, placing all of the blame on her for this latest glitch in their relationship.

He was irritated that she wasn't answering his calls. They needed to talk and it would be better if they were to do this in person. It wasn't fair she'd left without giving him the chance to explain his actions that night.

He then went on to say he wanted everything back to where it was before. There was too much history between them to have it end this way. Maybe this was a sign they needed to get serious with this marriage thing... jump right in, feet first. They'd find a place outside of the city, to then move on to the next logical step, start a family.

Marriage? Start a family?

Well... the two of you certainly messed up the order of that sequence of events, hadn't you?

She sank down onto the sofa and leaning her head back against the cushions, she closed her eyes.

Oh, God... you shouldn't have listened to his message.

She watched as Jingles left her corner spot on the sofa, leaping down to the floor, where she gave a long stretch. Since Livy wasn't giving any sign she'd be handing out treats in reward for her loyalty, she gave one last mournful meow and headed upstairs to the sanctuary of Carrie and Chris's bedroom.

Livy wasn't too far behind. She needed to take a shower. A long, hot and cleansing shower. Her hands instinctively going to her stomach, she knew she should also try to eat something.

She didn't have much time. She was meeting Sam at the Shaker site around noon.

Now seated at the kitchen island, Livy glanced down at her barely touched bagel and now cold tea. After she pushed them away, her gaze went to the window.

The sky was a brilliant blue, the early afternoon sun shining in through the kitchen window.

It was a gorgeous day, the kind of day most people would see as a promise of good things to come.

A day to be thankful for what you had.

Overcome by a sudden and deep sense of guilt, she rested her head in her hands and closed her eyes. She'd become so caught up in this drastic shake up of her life, she hadn't even taken the time to think about the new life growing inside of her.

This new little person who'd come about through no fault of their own and who was now completely dependent on her.

This little person who, from now on, would have to be her first priority.

But what about Sam?

Yes… what about Sam?

She checked the clock on the microwave. She was to meet him in less than an hour at the Shaker site. He had reminded her of this before he left this morning, something that now felt like it happened a different lifetime ago.

He'd called a few minutes ago, but she hadn't been able to bring herself to answer, instead watching as it went over to voicemail. And now, she couldn't get up the nerve to listen to his message, afraid the sound of his voice would only bring on more tears.

She was so tempted to call him back, but knew he'd sense something was wrong and insist on coming to her rescue.

You know, as your very own knight in shining armor.

But, most of all, she was terrified about what he was going to say… and even more so, what this was going to do to them.

She put her head down on her arms, the tears coming at her again.

Oh, Sam… I'm so, so sorry…

CHAPTER 20

elcome to the City of Shaker Heights…

Old and established, there was a sense of peace and tranquility throughout the neighborhood, the shade from the century old trees providing a welcome relief from the mid-afternoon sun.

Livy pulled up to the curb in front of a majestic Tudor style home. She knew she was at the right place by the large number of cars, pick-up trucks and vans parked in the driveway and lining the street. There was also the whine of a saw and the sound of voices coming out through the open front door and windows.

That she'd made it here in one piece, was a miracle in itself. Twice, she'd almost got lost, her mind finding it a struggle to deal with even the simple directions of her GPS.

She was a mess… a bundle of nerves. It was as though she was set to a timer, ready to go off at any moment. And she was so afraid this was going to happen when she saw Sam.

She checked her phone for the time. She was about ten minutes early, so she decided to wait for a few minutes before she ventured into the house.

She studied the huge house. If someone were to ask her what kind of homes she'd expect to find in the rolling and lush countryside of Europe, this would be the style she'd probably describe. It was almost castle-like. From the diamond paned windows, to the ornate exterior with its elaborate and decorative use of stone and brickwork, this house was an excellent example of homes built by wealthy and successful entrepreneurs over a century ago. Built to impress, these homes remained just as awesome today as they were years ago.

She gazed up at the evenly spaced dormer windows lining the steep gabled roof. She could imagine this might be where the children's bedrooms would've been located, giving them a bird's eye view of the neighborhood. Maybe there was even a window seat to curl up with a good book. Or just to spend the time dreaming.

If you ever have a house, you're going to make sure it has a window seat.

Her mouth curved into a wistful smile. The house by the lake had a window seat in the master bedroom. She'd become so excited when she saw it. Shaking his head, Sam confided he'd never paid that much attention to them. But seeing her excited reaction, he would from now on. He'd even dusted the seat off with his handkerchief so she could sit there while he checked out the rest of the room.

These thoughts sending her almost into a sudden panic, she rested her forehead on the steering wheel.

"Hey, are you all right?" A man, dressed in painter's overalls, was peering in at her. Then he backed up, giving her a tentative smile. "I'm sorry. I didn't mean to scare you. I thought maybe you needed help."

After taking a deep breath, she smiled at him. "That's okay. And no, I'm fine. I'm here to meet Sam Bridges, but I'm a little early. So, I decided to wait a few minutes before I went looking for him."

She smiled. "It's so beautiful here."

He nodded, slowly gazing around. "Yeah, there are some amazing homes here." He chuckled "And it seems like there's always one in need of a new coat of paint. Which is good for me, I guess."

He smiled at her. "But you said you're here to see Sam? Yeah, he's been here since morning. He's probably still in the kitchen." He pointed at the front door. "Go in through the front door and keep going straight down the hall. This will take you right into the kitchen.

I'm pretty sure he's there now, wrapping up a meeting with the carpenters."

He began to back away. "Again, I'm sorry if I scared you. I thought you might be lost. The streets in this neighborhood all run into each other and it can be very confusing. You can end up going around in circles. Take care."

Livy watched as he unloaded paint cans from one of the vans. After he disappeared into the house, she decided she'd waited long enough.

She got out of the car and made her way to the front door.

Her stomach was churning. But this wasn't brought on because of the pregnancy. No, she was nervous. And scared... heart pounding, having trouble breathing, scared. She took a deep breath and walked into the house.

In the state she was in, she didn't even notice the beauty of the interior of the house... the twelve-foot ceilings with the carved mahogany moldings, the arched doorways or the regal staircase.

Her only goal was to find the kitchen, where she was told Sam would be.

She came to the entrance of a room unrecognizable as a kitchen. Completely gutted, it appeared the walls had only recently been dry-walled. The floors were unfinished, waiting for the hardwood to be installed.

His back to her, Sam was in the middle of a discussion with two men, whom she assumed were the carpenters the painter had told her about. He was gesturing to a blueprint spread out on the table in front of them.

She remained by the door. Her excuse was she didn't want to interrupt their conversation.

But this wasn't what she was doing.

No... she was definitely stalling.

Sam would be quick to tell you he knew the exact moment Livy had come into the room. This was without even turning around. To be so attuned to each other, so that he was able to sense her presence... this about blew him away.

It felt good. So good.

A smile on his face, he turned to her.

The moment their eyes met, his smile disappeared. Something was wrong. This was obvious by the way she was standing, her shoulders drawn into her body, as if she'd been handed a heavy burden to carry. An anxious expression on her face, her quivering lip was a warning she was teetering on the verge of tears.

She gave him a shaky smile. If it could even be considered a smile.

Uh oh... could this be why she didn't return your call?

He turned to the carpenters, a sense of urgency in his voice. "Can you excuse us for a few moments? I'm sure we could all use a break."

Livy watched as Sam made his way over to her. It wasn't until he took hold of her arm, she realized she had started to shake.

Without a single word, he steered her into the first room off the hallway. It was the library, the entire room, including the ceiling and the built-in bookshelves lining the walls, paneled in a rich cherry hardwood.

Once they were inside and he'd pushed the door closed, he gathered her in his arms.

His concern had escalated the moment he took her arm, to find she was shaking. He didn't understand. When he'd left her earlier this morning, the memory of holding her in his arms still with him, everything had been fine.

It had been more than fine.

It had been perfect.

"Livy, what's wrong. What happened, baby?"

It was that one word that did it. A word now more fitting than he could possibly know.

Baby...

"I'm pregnant."

She honestly had no intention of blurting this out. And now, she could only hold her breath, so much depending on how he was going to react.

She felt him go still against her. Then he gave a sharp intake of breath, before slowly letting it out, almost in a long *wooosh….*

His voice failing him, he had to clear his throat.

"Pregnant?"

In the span of a single second, his mind had completely emptied, leaving him with nothing. No words, no comprehension… just nothing. He was trying like mad to take in what she'd told him, but how could he? This had been the last thing he'd expected her to say.

The absolute last thing.

Pregnant? How was this possible? They had made sure to take precautions. And how did she find this out so quickly? He wasn't all that sure of how these pregnancy tests worked because, again, he'd never been in this position before, but he didn't think you could get the results this fast.

Could you?

And if this was true? The one part of his brain that had somehow clicked back in, settled into a quick acceptance. Yeah… this was okay. More than okay. It wasn't something they'd anticipated. But they could handle this. It only meant they'd be starting out their life together a little sooner than they'd planned.

A baby? With Livy's eyes and her spirited personality? Yeah, you could get used to this.

Running his hands soothingly over her back, he dropped a kiss in her hair. "Livy, honey… it's okay. We can handle this. We'll work it out."

Then it hit him.

This isn't about you.

For a moment, he froze, searching for something to say. Then he asked the one question he had a feeling he already knew the answer. "I can assume Zack is the father?"

Her nod was barely discernible, but it was enough to let him know her answer was a yes.

And this was when he said the one thing he honestly hadn't meant to say. It was also the last thing he should've said… the very last. He realized this the split second the words left his mouth.

"You're sure Zack is the father? Or could it be some..." Here, for some crazy reason, he put a halt to the rest of what he was going to say. He'd later blame this on his loss of mind.

As you can imagine, in the state Livy was in, what he was trying to say and what she heard were two different things. She thought he was insinuating the father could be just about anyone.

Why she would even think this was ridiculous. She knew better. But once again, she reacted in true Livy style. Everything exploded inside of her. And she lost it, as she'd been so afraid she would.

But, she was scared. And she was feeling vulnerable. Her world had been turned upside down, leaving her in a state of overwhelming uncertainty about what was going to happen next. So, it was understandable even the smallest sign of doubt from Sam was bound to set her off.

Sam was the one person she'd hoped she could rely on, the one who'd be able to help her through this. That he questioned who the father was, planted a seed of doubt in her mind about their relationship.

She pushed her way out of his arms, her expression furious. Knowing he was the cause of her anger, Sam opened his mouth to say something, to promptly close it. He shook his head.

What the hell is wrong with you? What she needs from you right now is your support, not this sudden lack of faith.

Her hands clenched at her sides, her anger took over. "I can't believe you would even ask me this. Of course, Zack is the father. And yes, I'm sure. Is this what you think? That I hop from bed to bed?"

She gave a harsh laugh. Running her hands up and down her arms, her movements were quick and jerky. "Yes, this is what I do. And now that I've been with you, I've already started thinking of moving on. But I guess the joke is on me, isn't it? Yep... it appears this wild life I've been living has finally come to an end."

In one swift move, he took her into his arms, holding her tightly against him.

"My God, Livy... stop it. That's not what I meant. It came out all wrong. Give me a break here. It's just that I... well, this is the last thing I expected to have you tell me right now." Exhaling a deep breath, he rested his cheek in her hair. "I'm sorry... so, so sorry. I think I just need a little time. If only to process everything."

He suddenly pulled back and framing her face in his hands, his expression was almost fierce. "There is one thing I do know, and this is whatever happens, I'll be right by your side, all the way. Tell me you understand this."

She nodded, slowly, her eyes searching his face. "But Zack..."

His answer came out in almost a growl. "I don't give a damn about Zack. I only care about you and the baby."

He sent a quick search around the room. Leading her over to a window seat, piled high with a painter's tarp and paint cans, he shoved these aside so she could sit. Squatting in front of her, he searched her face, his concern elevating. She looked completely drained, the strain in her eyes an indication she was on the verge of breaking down completely.

He reached over to cup her cheek in his hand. "Oh, sweetheart... you should've called me as soon as you found out. I would've dropped everything to be with you"

Leaning into his hand, she slowly let out a long, trembling breath. "I was so afraid of what you were going to say. What you would think..."

He smoothed the hair back from her face, his voice soft, soothing. "*Shh...* Livy, I love you. Nothing you could say or do will ever change this. Not a chance."

He abruptly came to his feet. "We need to get you home. You stay right here. Try to take some deep breaths. I'll be right back."

At the anxious look in her eyes, he leaned in to press a kiss to her forehead, his words a soft brush against her skin. "I'll be back in a few minutes, I promise."

She watched him stride out of the room, to then watch as he turned to come right back to her.

He held out his hand. "Let me have your keys. I'm going to ask one of the guys to drive your car home for you. I think it would be best if I took you home."

She gave him no argument whatsoever, something at any other time Sam would've been quick to tease her about. Handing him the keys, she watched as he again left the room.

Within what seemed like seconds, he was back. Pulling her up from the window seat, he kept a firm grip on her hand as they left the room. When they reached the front door, she stopped him. "Sam, wait... what about your meeting?"

"There's nothing so crucial, it can't wait. It's more important I take you home. You're about ready to collapse."

He almost went on to add she had someone else to think about, the baby she was carrying.

But for some reason, the words wouldn't come. He couldn't get beyond the nagging reminder hovering in the back of his mind, refusing to go away.

Livy is pregnant and Zack is the father.

As much as he wanted to be, he wasn't all right about this.

He briefly closed his eyes.

He would be fine.

Yeah, like he'd told Livy.

Time... he just needed time.

CHAPTER 21

The best place in the world
is in the arms of someone who will not only
hold you at your best, but will pick you up and
hug you tight at your weakest moment.
~ Unknown

Their drive to Carrie and Chris's house was a silent one. This was because, truthfully? Neither Sam nor Livy knew what to say.

For Livy, the reality of what happened had finally set in, leaving her in a state of total exhaustion. Relieved at finally being able to share this news with Sam, the only thing she wanted now, was to go to a place she could close her eyes and go to sleep.

Then she wouldn't have to think.

And Sam? How was he dealing with this sudden roadblock thrown in front of them? Now that he had a little more time to think things through?

Not good.

No… he was having a more difficult time than he knew he should. Still unable to make sense of it all, his mind was racing like a runaway train. He was afraid if he didn't try to slow down every different scenario he could imagine happening next, his frustration was going to take over and he'd come at Livy all at once.

So, for now, he decided it would be best to say nothing at all.

It was only when he pulled his SUV into the driveway and turned off the ignition, Livy finally broke the silence. "You were right. I don't think I could have driven home. Thank you." Her smile was heartbreaking.

The fact she seemed so uncertain, tugged at his heart. This wasn't the Livy he knew.

He groaned. "Livy…"

She swiftly put her fingers to his mouth. "No, don't say anything. Not now, please?"

Don't say something we'll both later regret… or give promises either of us might not be able to keep.

He knew this was what she was trying to say. And he knew she was right. He took her hand, bringing it to his mouth for a kiss.

"Let's get you inside."

The first thing Sam noticed, when they walked inside the house, was the plate with the unfinished bagel on the island countertop.

The practical person that he was, he turned to Livy. "Did you eat? And if you did, was this all you had?" A faint smile came over his face as soon as he said this. He'd asked her almost the exact same thing, when he'd picked her up at the gas station the day she came home.

He shook his head. "It seems like I'm always trying to feed you."

Her tension still obvious, she gave a sharp laugh. "You and my Aunt Evelyn… you both can't seem to accept I'm able to take care…" Her mouth snapping shut, she avoided his gaze. In the silence that followed, she waited. Surely, he had a response to this?

Because it was now more than obvious she wasn't able to take care of herself. If she was, she wouldn't be pregnant.

So, can you blame him? It's clear both he and your aunt have every reason to be concerned.

But he was silent.

Filled with a slight sense of relief, she shrugged. "I can't remember... when I ate, that is. Sometime this morning? But don't worry, I'm not hungry. I'll be fine."

She set her purse on the counter and reaching for the mail still there from yesterday, she began leafing through a catalogue as though she hadn't a care in the world.

Sam watched her for a few seconds before, almost angrily, he turned to throw the uneaten bagel into the trash.

He was frustrated. He knew exactly what she was doing. She was shutting him out, reverting back to the Livy who thought she could handle everything on her own, determined to go it alone. She didn't need help, maybe even more so, if this were to come from him.

This bothered him, this new distance between them. This feeling they were no longer connected.

He needed this. He needed the security of knowing they were still an essential part of each other. Yin and Yang. Peanut butter and jelly. He wanted to know she was there for him, just as he would always be there for her. Even while they were apart, their love would always be enough to keep the connection strong.

He glanced over at the clock on the stove to see it was four-thirty-two. He glanced back over at Livy. She was still turning the pages of the catalogue, but he knew she wouldn't be able to tell him what was in it, were he to ask her.

But right now, this didn't matter. His first priority was to take care of her.

"Livy..." When she reluctantly looked up to meet his gaze, he smiled at her. "Why don't you go upstairs and lie down, try to unwind. You've had a rough morning. Meanwhile, I'll make you something to eat. You need to eat more than half of a bagel."

She closed the catalogue. "I'm really not hungry. And, I don't know if I want to lie down. I... well, I start thinking and..."

Anxiety beginning to cloud her eyes, she looked down at the catalogue. After running her fingers over the cover, she angrily pushed it away.

He gave a big sigh before he moved to put his hands on her shoulders. He peered into her face, waiting for her to finally meet his gaze. "Whether you want to or not, you need to eat. So, please, just do as I ask and go upstairs. I can't promise it will be a gourmet meal, but I'll scrounge up something, hopefully edible, and bring it up to you."

He turned her away from him and gave her a gentle push towards the stairs. "Now, don't argue. Just go."

Twenty minutes later, Sam walked into the bedroom. He was carrying a glass of orange juice and a plate with his attempt at an omelet. This was accompanied by a slightly overdone, but not quite burnt, slice of toast.

Even though he'd be the first to admit his culinary skills weren't anything to brag about, he was feeling pretty proud of what he'd managed to put together.

Livy was curled up on the bed, the quilt pulled over her. Only the top of her head and her eyes were visible, and they were closed. It was as though she'd tried to burrow as far under the covers as she could, to hide from the rest of the world. Thinking she'd fallen asleep, Sam silently crossed the room to set the plate and glass on the nightstand.

He turned to see her eyes were open and she was watching him. He cautiously sat on the bed next to her and gently pulled the quilt away from her face.

"Come on, you need to eat before it gets cold." He smiled. "Like I told you, I don't cook all that often. But when I do, the results aren't all that bad. Certainly not as good as your Aunt Evelyn's, but I think I did okay."

While Livy ate, Sam kept up a running commentary of whatever he could think of.

He talked about what he'd accomplished at the Shaker site before she'd arrived. How there was a mix up on the order for the flooring and they were trying to sort it all out.

He told her, while he'd been preparing her omelet, the mailman dropped off three large packages. This was why the doorbell had rung. He had a feeling the packages were wedding gifts for Carrie and Chris, so he'd put them right inside the front door. This way, they'd be sure to notice them when they came home from their honeymoon.

He also told her about the call he received earlier in the day from the director of the historical committee in Quebec, the same organization he and Carrie worked with last summer. A member of the committee had recently come across old blueprints and photos of the guest house located at the rear of the property. They wanted to know if Sam would be interested in heading the restoration of this. It would involve a much smaller time frame and they'd be willing to work around his schedule. If it were possible, they'd like him to start on this as early as possible. Maybe even within the next few days, if only to get things started.

It was when he finished telling her about the call, Livy put her fork down on her plate and set it on the bed. She was well aware of Sam's frown. This was because she'd barely ate any of the omelet and only a few bites of the toast. She'd spent most of the time pushing the food around on her plate, unable to make herself eat.

He handed her the glass of orange juice. "Here, at least drink this."

After she drank a few swallows of the orange juice, she finally met his gaze. "You should go."

At his startled look, she shook her head. "I'm talking about Quebec. It sounds as if they really liked your work and want you to be the one to finish the job." She shrugged. "So, you should go."

He abruptly came to his feet. Gazing down at her, he jammed his hands in the pockets of his khakis.

He gave, what sounded like to Livy, a very long and exasperated sigh. "Livy, I can't do that. I can't go off and leave you here to face everything on your own. I'd worry about you constantly. The whole time I was gone."

This anger was a side of Sam she'd never experienced before. Suddenly unsure, she saw his irritation aimed more at her than about what happened.

After all, she'd now become a burden to him, the reason for this predicament they were in. But, the conscientious person that he was, he felt it was his responsibility to take care of her.

When she opened her mouth to assure him this wasn't necessary, he cut her off, the frustration in his voice leading her to become even more concerned.

"Livy, no. Whatever you do, please don't tell me you're capable of taking care of yourself. I know you think you are and maybe you can, to an extent. But, this is different. This isn't just about you. You need to swallow your pride and take the help you're offered. Let me be the one to be here for you."

He hesitated, obviously finding it difficult to share what had become his biggest fear. "And please don't tell me you can ask Zack for help." Briefly closing his eyes, a flash of pain crossed his face. "Even the thought of him coming back into your life… well, this is something I don't even want to think about. I'm sorry, but you need to know this is how I feel."

Shocked by both his words and his anger, she watched as he picked up the glass and plate. It was when he started to walk out of the room, she finally found her voice.

"Are you leaving?"

He turned to study her for a few moments.

"Is this what you want me to do?"

She slowly shook her head, her voice barely a whisper. "No… no, I don't."

He shook his head just as slowly. "Then I won't." A faint smile flickered across his face. "I'll be right back. I'm only going to take these down to the kitchen and clean up the mess I made."

When he came back into the room, she hadn't moved, still sitting on the bed. He kicked off his shoes and sliding under the quilt with her, he settled her against him. His fingers gently running through her hair, he could feel her slowly relax against him.

Livy wanted to ask him if they could stay like this forever. The feeling of his arms around her was like magic, the most comforting feeling in the world. This was what she'd been looking for when she first told him about the baby.

He was her safety net against the world.

As if he knew what she was thinking, he cleared his throat, his voice still coming out husky. *"Ah... this is nice, isn't it?"*

At her nod, he smiled. "I never told you what happened that night in New York, did I? After I left you at your apartment?"

She shook her head against him.

He pulled her closer, his voice a deep rumble in her ear. "The taxi driver was just about to pull away from the curb when I saw Zack coming down the sidewalk. He was lugging a huge black garbage bag behind him."

He felt her stiffen in his embrace. After he pressed a slow kiss in her hair, he continued. "When I saw him go into your building, I asked the driver to hold on. Then I waited… and waited. I sat in the backseat of that taxi for probably fifteen minutes, not saying a word. I could tell the driver was starting to get nervous, but I didn't care. I was focused on one thing. This was the door to your building. I was waiting for Zack to come walking back out through that door, still carrying the garbage bag he went in with. Hell, I would've even offered to share the taxi with him. If only to get him as far away from you as I could."

He let out a long sigh. "But that didn't happen. He never came back out. So, I told the taxi driver to take me to my hotel. It was when I was in my room, I wished I had gone back up to your apartment. I would've done this under the pretense I only wanted to make sure you were okay. Maybe even fought for you, if need be."

"Oh, Sam..."

She pressed closer to him, bringing his soft chuckle. "I know, silly, huh? I guess you weren't all that far off with this knight thing. Once a knight, always a knight, I guess."

He pressed another kiss in her hair. "But at the time, I didn't feel like I had the right to make any claim on you. From what I saw, Zack was the man you had chosen."

He pulled her closer. "Ah… Livy. What a fool I was. Everything I'd tried to convince you I was, your knight in shining armor, your hero, or at the time, just your friend… I let it all slip away. Instead, I was so damn focused on how my ego had been shot down. I was confused, nothing making sense to me anymore. Little did I know, I'd already started to fall in love with you."

He gave a soft chuckle. "I certainly wasn't prepared for the way you made me feel. Hell, I didn't have a clue of what falling in love could do to a person. I also didn't know it was possible to fall in love so deeply and that it could happen so damn fast. Again, this was all until I met you…"

His fingers stilled in her hair, a huskiness taking over his voice. "And now it seems Zack is back in the picture, if only because of the baby. If he somehow manages to take you away from me again, I swear I don't know what I'll do. It will break my heart, Livy."

The next thing he knew, her mouth was on his, her hands feverishly moving over him, tugging at his shirt, trying to pull him even closer. And even though he knew this was the last thing they should be doing, he was helpless, only able to follow her lead.

Their only goal to eliminate every barrier between them, clothes went flying everywhere… across the bed and to the floor. Their mouths joining in a non-ending kiss, this sudden passion, this desire, came at them like a fast-moving storm, overtaking them completely.

They were both looking for reassurance, their hope this almost desperate act of love between them would heal their hearts and erase any doubt that had come between them.

For now?

It was what they both needed.

For the longest time, Sam couldn't move, almost hypnotized by the beat of his heart, or maybe it was Livy's, thundering between them.

His breathing finally returning to normal, he lifted his head and smoothed a damp strand of hair from her face. "You belong to me. Tell me you're mine."

"Yes… always." Tracing his lips with her finger, she smiled at him. "Now that I know what it's like to be loved by you, how could I not? You'll never be rid of me. No matter how hard you try."

He tucked her next to him and closing his eyes, he gave a long, satisfied sigh. "Good, I'm going to hold you to that."

Content in each other's arms, it was when Livy stirred against him, Sam finally spoke, his words cutting through the silence. "You don't think we could've…" He hesitated, his voice trailing off.

She stilled, to then slowly shake her head. She knew what he was asking. "No, it will be fine. I'm sure it will."

"I love you." These three little words coming from him were everything to her, what she needed more than anything. Blinking back tears, she closed her eyes.

But he was having none of this. "Hey, baby… look at me." Gazing into her eyes, his whisper was a soft caress against her cheek. "I hope it's a girl. A beautiful little girl, just like her mom. With her mom's gorgeous eyes."

He brushed his fingers through her hair, a smile tugging at the corner of his mouth. "I'll even go as far to say I hope she'll share your spunky personality."

Helplessly shaking her head, this sent the tears flowing. "Oh, Sam… I love you, I do. So, *so* much."

But this moment was tinged with a sadness, reaching deep between them. This was because they both wished there was another way she could've responded. With the words she'd give anything to say.

That she hoped it would be a little boy.

Just like him.

CHAPTER 22

Chester watched as his Aunt Evelyn, and this is the only way he could think of how to describe it, plopped down into the rocking chair. She was holding a squirming Trevor, who was making a valiant effort to grab his bottle out of her hand.

Once she got him settled on her lap and he was working away at the bottle, she glanced up at Chester and grinned. "See? We're going to get along just fine."

Pat, her long-time friend and buddy in crime, smiled over at Chester, nodding in agreement. Already settled comfortably in the other rocking chair, she was feeding Hudson.

Chester sent a quick assessing glance around the nursery. Once he was satisfied everything seemed to be in order, diapers, sleepers and all the other items he'd now learned were absolutely essential in a baby's life, he grinned over at his aunt and her friend.

"So, again… you're sure you can handle this, right?"

A frown appeared on his aunt's face, the warning look she gave him was one he remembered so well. This had him falling right back into his adolescent years and the few times he'd foolishly challenged her authority.

"Chester, you have no reason to worry. We've got this."

He gave her a sheepish grin. "Sorry..."

She waved her hand at him. "Now, go... You told me you wanted to spend some time with your wife, so get on with it. If we need you, we know how to find you."

"Okay, okay. We'll see you sometime tomorrow afternoon. And remember, call me if you have any question or whatever." After one last sweeping glance around the room, just to be sure, he left.

Now he only needed to find Sophie.

He was worried about her. Something just wasn't right between them. Ever since Carrie's wedding, she'd become preoccupied, almost going out of her way to avoid him, something she'd never done before.

Determined to find out what was going on, and even more intent on fixing this, he'd come up with a plan.

Unbeknownst to her and taking advantage of the teams scheduled off day, he'd called his aunt to tell her, with the twins now almost seven months old, he was ready to accept her offer of babysitting.

She'd been asking him about this ever since the boys were born.

More like begging him, he'd have to say.

Since he and Sophie would be gone overnight, his aunt had asked her friend Pat, to come with her. Pat's grandchildren were all out of town and according to his aunt, she'd jumped at the chance to help out.

He'd reserved a room downtown at the Ritz. He also had a couple of restaurants in mind for dinner, but decided to wait and let Sophie make that choice.

He wanted his Sophie back.

He missed her.

Chester found Sophie in their bathroom. Down on her hands and knees, she was scrubbing the bathtub. Coming up behind her, he reached over her shoulder to take the sponge out of her hand.

She jerked away from him, letting out a little scream. "Chester! My

God, what are you doing, sneaking up on me like that? You scared me half to death."

His only answer was to pull her up from the floor and into his arms. When he nuzzled his face under her hair to press a kiss to her neck, she pulled away.

Uh, oh...

Her expression was angry. But, what concerned him even more, she looked uneasy, as if she didn't want his touch.

She confirmed this when she slipped out from under his arms. "Stop it. I need to finish cleaning this bathroom. If anyone saw it right now, they'd think a bunch of animals lived here."

Animals?

A quick glance around the bathroom, to him, it looked pretty spotless. As it always did. Certainly not as if it had been taken over by a herd of animals. He stopped to wonder... what kind of animals would she be referring to?

He shook his head. "Angel, you don't have to do this. Everything looks perfectly fine. The cleaning people will be here in two days. And, come on... who do you think is going to come wandering into our bathroom? No one uses it except us."

"You never know." This was followed by a long sigh.

He watched as she picked up the sponge and began swiping it aimlessly over the rim of the bathtub. Her shoulders slumped, she looked like she was totally exhausted. Even her voice sounded weary. This had him even more convinced this plan he'd come up with, was a good one.

But it was the silence between them, lasting much longer than it should, that was bothering him the most.

He didn't understand. *What was happening here?*

For a second time, he took the sponge from her and threw it in the tub. When this brought an even more worried look from her, he reached for her hand. As he began leading her out of the bathroom, he forced a cheerful tone into his voice.

"I have a surprise for you. I want you to pack your bags. You only need to pack for one night."

She pulled on his hand to stop him. "Chester, what are you talking about? I don't want to go anywhere." She looked like she was about to cry. "Look at me. I haven't washed my hair since Carrie's wedding and I'm in desperate need of a shower. In case you haven't noticed, it's not perfume I'm wearing. It's the intoxicating scent of bathroom cleaner."

He chuckled. "Angel…"

But she wasn't finished yet. "And, seriously? Haven't you forgotten something? What about the boys?" Her mouth dropped open, panic filling her face. "Oh, no… this isn't some crazy idea you thought up for a family vacation and they're coming with us, is it? Do you realize how much work this will involve for just one night? Diapers, bottles, strollers… you know what I'm talking about. Chester, it wouldn't be worth it."

She sent him a guilty look. "Not that I don't love them. I do, but…"

He reached out to stroke her cheek. "I know you do. And no, they aren't coming with us. My Aunt Evelyn has volunteered to watch them."

At Sophie's skeptical look, he began talking fast… real fast. "I swear, she's been asking, more like begging, if she could babysit since the day they were born. She was thrilled when I called her. She's here as I speak, along with her friend, Pat. I found that long and detailed list of instructions you wrote up for your sister when she watched them the night of the rehearsal dinner. I went over the entire list with them and they now know everything they need to know. And probably even more."

That last sentence was added under his breath. He was still shaking his head over some of the things Sophie had on that list. She'd definitely covered every possible scenario, some more crazy than others, when it came to taking care of a baby.

Sophie stared at him, her hands going to her hips. "Chester, first of all, taking care of a baby is a very complicated process, so that list was completely necessary. Second of all… overnight? This will be too much for your aunt and her friend. You know how much work is involved in taking care of the boys. Especially now that they're teething."

She frowned. "And Pat? Who exactly is this Pat? Do I know her?"

"She and my aunt have been friends forever. And, to put your mind at rest, she's a nurse. So, our little guys will be in good hands."

With no more arguments to give him, she was finally quiet as they continued on into the bedroom. After he took her suitcase out of the closet and tossed it on the bed, even going as far to unzip it open for her, he turned to her.

"There you go. You can take a shower, even a long bubble bath if you want, when we get to where we're going." Leaning in to give her a quick kiss, his mouth lingered over hers. "I love you, Angel. And not to sound rushed or anything, but you need to pack quickly. My bag is already in the SUV. So, once you're ready, we'll be on our way."

Sophie watched him leave the room before she sank down on the bed. She didn't want to go anywhere. Truthfully? What she wanted more than anything, was to crawl into bed, pull the covers over her head and take a long, long nap. To be able to do this, sounded like heaven to her.

She just didn't want to be tired anymore.

Between moving into the house, Carrie's wedding, the renovations, taking over the twenty-four-seven care of the twins and helping her aunt run the boutique, it was all becoming too much too handle. She was pretty sure she'd used up any energy she had in her. The fact that Chester was on the road most of the time certainly didn't help matters.

She sighed. She didn't want to make it seem as if she was complaining, but being the wife of a professional baseball player was not all it was cracked up to be. The photos taken at special events and charity benefits, showing all of the smiling and happy faces, only told a part of the story. There was no mention of the times she'd walked the floor at night, all alone and with not one, but two miserable and cranky babies. Because they were teething, or just not in the mood to sleep.

Or how about the time, right after they moved into their house and Chester was out of town, a pipe burst and flooded the entire kitchen? All of this happening at two in the morning.

Chester had told her many times she was trying to do too much. He was all for hiring a nanny. But the thought of someone else taking over the job of raising Trevor and Hudson didn't set right with her. She was their mother. She should be the one to always be there for them.

This was only right.

Chester poked his head around the door to the room. "What? You haven't started packing yet? Come on, get going. And don't worry, if you forget something. We can get it later. Right now, the only thing I care about taking with me is you."

At the warning glance she sent him, he quickly ducked back out of the room. Reluctantly pushing herself off the bed, she began tossing clothes in her suitcase. She didn't even know what to pack, finally deciding she'd pack a little bit of everything.

She pulled on a clean pair of jeans and a tee shirt, ran a brush through her hair and left the bedroom, dragging her suitcase behind her.

Her only hope was, wherever they were going, she'd be able to take a nap.

And of course, she also wanted to be able to check on Trevor and Hudson. Maybe even face time them. If only to make sure they were okay.

No, she wasn't very happy about this.

But to be honest?

Lately she wasn't happy about a lot of things.

Chester pulled his SUV off the exit ramp, coming to a stop at the red light. He glanced over at Sophie to see she was watching him.

But maybe watching wasn't the right word to use. No, it was more like she was giving him that look. You know the look… the one letting him know she wasn't happy about something. The something that usually had a lot to do with him.

He gave her a tentative smile. She frowned at him in return.

Definitely not what you'd say is a good sign.

He cleared his throat. "What's going on, Angel? What are you so upset about?" He sent her his best I-don't-know-what-I-did-but-I'm-really-sorry look. "I thought this surprise would make you happy. At least this is what I was aiming for."

She sighed, running her hand through her hair. "I'm worried about the babies. After all, this is the first time we've left them with someone. I sincerely hope you're right about your aunt. Because you know what a handful they can be."

At the moment, Chester was distracted. Where the hell was the drop off for valet parking? Surely, there would be someone to park his SUV?

After all, this was the Ritz.

He let out a grunt of satisfaction when he saw the sign informing him, that they did indeed, offer valet parking. He smiled over at Sophie. "She raised us with no problems. Look at me, I turned out pretty good, didn't I? So, I'm sure she can handle one night with the boys. She and Pat will do just fine. And if you really feel the need to check on them, you can."

Sophie was still frowning. She knew she was acting childish, but she just couldn't help it. Deciding to make the effort to be nice, she shot him a quick smile. "I'll just have to trust you on this, I guess. But you better send Livy a text to let her know where we are. Just in case."

The smile, even as brief as it was, prompted him to reach over to give her hand a gentle squeeze. "As soon as we get to the room, I will. Then, for twenty-four hours or so, it's going to be just you and me. No kids. No worries. A nice dinner with no interruptions. And whatever else you'd like. It will be your call, Angel."

Although somewhat hesitant, another smile flitted across her face. Again, the thought of that long and uninterrupted nap was what she was envisioning.

Encouraged by this, Chester was smiling as he pulled up to the entrance of the hotel.

Ah... things were definitely looking up.

Little did he know Sophie was on a whole different page.

While he was thinking romance, wine and all the trimmings...

The only thing on her agenda was that bubble bath and long nap he'd promised.

Sophie was gazing out the window of the hotel room. They were on the tenth floor, which gave them a bird's eye view of both the city and of Lake Erie.

Chester had seen the bellboy to the door, sending him off with a generous tip. He was humming as he emptied his wallet, phone and keys from his pocket and set them on the nightstand.

Then he picked up his phone again. He'd told Sophie he'd send Livy a text. He'd better do it now before he forgot.

The message sent, he glanced over at Sophie. Kicking off his shoes, he padded silently across the luxuriously dense carpeting to wrap his arms around

He rested his chin on her head, giving a long sigh. "Just think, angel… for a little over twenty-four hours, it's just you and me. No babies crying, no bottles to fix, diapers to change… just peace and quiet."

When she remained rigid in his arms, only giving a long, drawn out sigh in response, he reached for her hand to lead her over to the bed. He scooted onto the bed, pulling her with him.

His head propped on his hand, he gazed down at her. "It feels like we haven't had any alone time for I don't know how long." He smoothed the hair from her face before he pressed a kiss to her forehead. "I've missed us. I've missed you."

She turned her face, avoiding his gaze. "I know. It's always crazy isn't it? It seems like I spend most of my time thinking about how I'd give just about anything for a night of uninterrupted sleep."

He rolled onto his back, tucking her against him. "Angel, I think we need to get someone to help out. It isn't fair to you, having to take on everything by yourself. The boys, the boutique and overseeing all of the remodeling. Then on top of all that, you had Carrie's wedding to contend with. But at least that's over now."

She gave a slight nod against him, bringing him to pull her even closer. "It's okay to have help, you know. You can still be the one in charge. And everything doesn't have to be perfect. You already have the perfect man, so what more do you need?"

When he didn't receive a response to this, not even a disgruntled one, it came to his attention her body had completely relaxed against him. Lifting his head, he saw she'd fallen sleep. He dropped his head back on the pillow and stared up at the ceiling, a wry smile on his face.

It looks like she was more tired than you thought. So, you might as well close your eyes and take a little nap yourself.

So much for romance, it seems.

At least for now.

CHAPTER 23

The best kind of relationship begins unexpectedly,
when everything happens so suddenly,
and at a time you never thought it would.
~ Unknown

*H*annah Michaels made her way over to what was the only available table in her favorite coffee haunt, Café Latte.

She set her portfolio and muffin bag on the table, sank gratefully into a chair, and took a sip of hazelnut coffee, letting out a long, satisfied sigh.

She glanced around the crowded room.

She couldn't believe how popular the little shop had become. She'd been coming here ever since they first opened a little over two years ago and though she was glad their business was doing so well, she missed the days when it wasn't so crowded and crazy.

She opened the bag and took out the muffin, her stomach giving a long growl of anticipation. She hadn't eaten anything since early morning and she was starving.

She cut the muffin in half, slathering both halves with butter. After the day she had with her latest author client, Laura, she more than deserved the extra butter.

As she'd feared, it had been another difficult meeting. Laura had insisted on making more changes to the illustrations Hannah had given her to review.

Hannah was beginning to think she was never going to be satisfied.

Happily eating the muffin, she took the drawings out of her portfolio and started leafing through them. She didn't understand the latest changes Laura wanted. They couldn't even be considered changes, they were so insignificant. Hannah was beginning to think she was stalling, afraid to let go of the book. This had happened with a few of the authors she worked with in the past, especially the first timers.

Her cup almost empty, she was about to make her way to the counter for a re-fill when a very familiar voice came from behind her. She whirled around and looked right up into the face, for the past seven months, she hadn't been able to forget.

It was Sean Young.

The same Sean Young she met at the hospital the day her nephews, Trevor and Hudson had made their entrance into the world.

Since he was on the baseball team with Chester, she couldn't even begin to tell you how many times she had hoped she'd run into him again.

But she hadn't.

And now, here he was...

Cowboy hat and all.

Sean had spent the day with about fifty young and excited future wannabe-baseball-players and he was completely done in. As he was heading back to his condo, thankful it was an off day for the team, he saw the little coffee shop, Café Latte. The packed parking lot indicating it must be a popular hangout, he turned in and took the first available parking spot he saw.

A cup of coffee might be just what he needed to feel somewhat human again.

As soon as he entered the little shop, he knew it was his kind of place. From what he could see, there were no pretentious people hanging out here. Nope, the crowd looked like a friendly bunch. The kind of people who frequented the place often, to meet with friends over a cup of coffee. Or maybe just to pick out a special treat from the huge glass case by the coffee counter, filled with the largest assortment of baked goods he'd ever seen.

This mouth-watering display, along with the aroma of freshly brewed coffee, made him realize he was starving. A quick glance at the time, he was surprised to see it was almost five.

No wonder you're hungry.

He was smiling as he glanced around the room, checking things out. This was when his gaze fell on the young woman who looked like she was just about to leave her table.

He did a double take.

Dog-gone-it... was this really happening?

At first, completely in shock, he stayed where he was. Then, very cautiously, he moved closer to get a better look.

Yep, it was her.

Hannah Michaels...

His smile grew even bigger.

In fact, it had now turned into a huge grin. If this wasn't fate, he didn't know what was. He couldn't even begin to count the many times he'd gone out, hoping he'd run into her. He'd even seriously considered hanging around the local grocery store, in hopes he'd find her there.

How did he come up with this idea? From what he'd been told, this was a good place to meet women. At least this is what one of the guys on the team told him. The theory was, everyone had to eat.

This came across as pretty sound thinking to him. Who didn't like to eat? He knew he did.

It was only lately he'd begun to grow tired of doing it alone.

He realized it would've been a lot simpler to ask Chester about

Hannah, since she was Sophie's sister. But somehow, he hadn't been able to bring himself to do that. Call it pride. Or maybe it was more like his own plain stubbornness.

And if this got back to the guys on the team… that he had a crush on some woman? They'd be sure to razz the heck out of him.

But what was holding him back the most, was the fear if he finally did get another chance to talk to her, the result would be the same.

She'd walk away from him.

So now, here it was… his second chance. Nervously adjusting the brim of his cowboy hat, he slowly meandered over to her table

He watched as she finished typing something on her phone and slipped it into her pocket before he cleared his throat.

When she turned to look right at him, he tipped his hat in a greeting. While at the same time, he gave her what he hoped was his best smile.

"Hey…"

For what felt like ages, he waited.

Finally, her mouth slowly curved into a faint smile.

"Hey…"

Thank God…

He couldn't believe how relieved he was. Pretty certain his expression mirrored the astonishment on hers, he stood silently as she gazed up at him.

Hannah didn't know what to think. What she did know, she'd forgotten how amazingly good looking he was. It was almost unfair one man could be so perfect.

Maybe it was the hat? Or, could it be his stance… emanating such confidence, yet at the same time coming across so relaxed and effortless… as though he was posing for a photo shoot.

There was also the way his eyes crinkled at the corners when he flashed that devastating grin she remembered so well.

Whatever it was, just one, or all of these things… for her, it worked

Big time.

Dropping her gaze to her hands, she saw they had begun to shake. She set her cup slowly back on the table. Then she nervously picked it up again.

"I… I was going to get a re-fill." Then she couldn't believe she actually did this… she held out her cup. "See, it's empty."

As though it was perfectly natural she should do this, he peered down into the empty cup and nodded before he took it from her. "I was about to get a coffee for myself. So, let me refill your cup while I'm there."

He nodded towards her chair. "Please, sit down. I'd be more than happy to do this for you."

Did she also mention his manners were impeccable?

She slowly sank into her chair. After he gave her another smile, this one accompanied by a wink, he turned to casually saunter over to the counter. And yes, this was the only way to describe his walk. As she watched, she wondered if this was another one of those cowboy things.

And she was off… sailing into her own little dream world. This had her tucked in front of him and his arms holding her close as they rode his horse off into the sunset. Or the sunrise, it really didn't matter. It was only when he set her cup in front of her, she found herself back in the coffee shop, the horse and sun evaporating into thin air.

But he was still here...

"Hannah?"

Almost in a daze she glanced up to see he was standing by the table. A hesitant look on his face and his cup in hand, he was waiting to see if she was going to invite him to share her table. She quickly gathered her drawings into a pile, almost knocking her cup over in the process and gestured towards the table. "Please… sit down."

Her purse was on the chair next to her. Thinking he would take the chair across from her, she watched as he picked up her purse and moved it to the other chair. Again, his impeccable display of manners came through with flying colors. "It's okay if I moved your purse, isn't it? I'd rather sit next to you, instead of all the way across the table."

Resisting the urge to tell him she wouldn't mind in the least, he could sit as close as he wanted, the closer the better, she nodded.

Once he was seated, he stretched out his legs and took a long drink of his coffee. He followed this with a long, contented sigh before he turned to her, an almost bewildered look on his face. "I can't believe I finally ran into you. I was helping out at a baseball camp not far from here and saw this place as I was driving home. So, I decided to stop in for a coffee. I was taking a chance, since I've never been here before."

A smile tugged at the corner of his mouth. "And now I believe it's one of my smarter moves. Who would have thought?"

He sent another one of these devastating smiles right at her. "So, do you come here often?" He shook his head, a deep chuckle rumbling from him. "Sorry, that sounds like some kind of pick-up line doesn't it? At least back home, it would."

Hannah was having a hard time. A really hard time. For some reason, it was as though she'd forgotten just about everything she'd ever learned. Certainly, when it came to the art of carrying on a conversation.

Instead, she could focus on only one thing, and this was how close he was—close enough to be caught in the scent of his cologne. An intoxicating mix of leather and spice, utterly masculine and perfectly suited to him.

It was taking everything she had to keep from leaning in closer so she could breathe it all in.

Flustered, she picked up her cup. She had to do this with both hands, because for some reason, they were still shaking. Hoping he hadn't noticed this, she slowly set the cup back on the table and placed her hands in her lap.

What was wrong with her?

Remember what happened the last time you saw him? You ran away, instead of accepting his offer of friendship. This time, no matter what he says, you need to go along with it.

She sent him a shy smile. "I've been coming here since they first opened. But now it's become the place to hang out and it's so crowded all of the time." She shrugged. "I miss the quieter times."

He was studying her, the intensity of his gaze making her nervous. With the brim of his hat pulled down, shadowing his face, she really had no idea what he was thinking. She wanted so badly to reach over and remove it, so she could at least see his eyes.

As if he could read her thoughts, he removed the offending hat and set it on the table. The corner of his mouth lifted in a smile. "Better?"

She was beside herself.

My God, does he know what you're thinking?

She took a gulp of coffee before she blurted out what she had wanted to tell him all along, going back to the first time she saw him. "You have such an expressive face. It's the kind of face I'd love to draw."

One eyebrow raised, he gave her a big grin. "You want to draw me? Wow… no one has ever said that to me before."

The need to justify why she'd said this, she hurried on to explain "I'm sorry, I do this all the time. I can't help it. It's the artist coming out in me, I guess."

He looked surprised, yet at the same time, pleased. "You're an artist? My mom is an artist. But she leans towards a more contemporary style… pottery and that kind of stuff." He glanced over at the drawings on the table. "Are these some of your work?"

"Yes, I do a lot of book illustrations. Children's books are my specialty. These drawings are for a client who keeps changing her mind." She scrunched up her face in annoyance. "I'm certainly not going to make any money on this job, with all of the work I've put in, trying to please her."

She looked over to see he was grinning, shaking his head.

"What?" She was puzzled. What had she said he found so funny?

"The face you made. Like a little kid."

She could feel the blush creeping into her cheeks. Embarrassed, she began gathering up the drawings.

His hand covered hers. "I'm sorry. I meant it in a good way. If anything, it makes me feel happy." He nodded towards the drawings. "May I?"

Well, then… this is okay. Happy is good, right?

She nodded, an unexpected feeling of disappointment coursing through her when he removed his hand from hers to pick up one of the drawings. She watched as he went through each one, taking the time to study them.

He glanced over at her. "These are great. I can see you're very talented." He grinned. "And if you meant what you said, about doing a drawing of me, I'd be more than happy to oblige. I'd be interested to see how good you could make me look. Maybe add some improvements."

Improvements? Was this even possible? Surely, he must be kidding.

And again, she came out and said exactly what she was thinking. The coffee and muffin had to be responsible for this. Yes, she was high on sugar and caffeine.

Or quite possibly, maybe you could be high on him?

She smiled. "I don't think you need any improvements. You look good. Just the way you are."

A answering smile came over his face. "You think so, huh? Well, this is good to know. Very good, in fact." He sent her a wink. "And you, Hannah Michaels, look good just as you are. More than good, I'd have to say."

He settled back in his chair, watching as she gathered up the drawings and stuffed them in the portfolio, all the while trying to hide the fact she was blushing again.

He set his coffee cup on the table, shifting in his chair so he was closer to her. "Can I ask you something?"

Her heart now beating at an alarming speed with his move, she gave him a cautious look. "Okay, I guess?"

"Why did you run off on me when we were in the hospital? Was it something I said?"

She opened her mouth, to promptly shut it. She certainly couldn't come out and tell him his suggestion they be friends hadn't been what she wanted to hear. This was just as much as letting him know how attracted she was to him.

God, no... what would he think?

Glancing down to see she'd nervously begun to tear her napkin in strips, she swiftly gathered up the pieces and shoved them in the empty muffin bag.

She glanced over at him again. A completely sincere look on his face, he was patiently waiting for her answer.

She sighed.

You might as well tell him the truth. Because, honestly? What do you have to lose at this point?

After another sip of her coffee, her eyes focused on the cup, she gave him her answer. "I guess I wasn't quite sure what you meant when you said you only wanted to be friends. I thought... well, I..." Her words fading, a silence fell between them.

When she finally got up enough nerve to glance over at him, her breath caught in her throat at the huge smile on his face. And before she knew it, she was smiling giddily at him in return.

He cleared his throat. "Hannah Michaels, I do believe we may have wasted a lot of time over a silly misunderstanding. At least, I hope this is the case."

He glanced over at her unfinished muffin and then back at her. "Please don't tell me this is your dinner?"

She laughed. "No, of course not. I hadn't eaten anything all day and I was getting grumpy, so I..."

He was grinning at her again. Something he needed to stop. It was doing strange things to her, sending her heart beating totally out of control. There was also this fluttering sensation in her stomach every time she looked into his eyes. She wondered if this was the butterfly feeling people talked about, the sign you might be falling in love. If it wasn't, she had no idea what else could be making her feel this way.

None of this was making sense. She knew nothing about Sean Young and he knew nothing about her. Why, he hadn't even kissed her yet. She was pretty sure this would be the ultimate test as to whether or not there was something between them. That something they called chemistry, what everyone seemed to think was necessary for true love to blossom.

Sean was shaking his head. "Grumpy... I find it hard to believe you could be grumpy, no matter what the situation."

Ah, there you go… here was the proof she needed. He definitely didn't know her. Of course, she could be grumpy.

"Oh, I assure you, I can be as grumpy as the best of them. I blame this on my creative nature. Ask Sophie. I guarantee she'll be quick to agree."

"Okay, I will. But for now, I'll take my chances." He nodded towards the remainder of her muffin. "I find it troubling all you've had to eat is what looks like," he leaned over to get a closer look at the muffin, "about half a banana muffin?"

At her nod, he shook his head. "In that case, I would very much like to take you out to dinner. Wherever you'd like to go. I don't care where, as long as we don't have to shout at each other to be heard. What do you say?"

Smiling, she nodded. "I say yes." This came out with no hesitation what-so-ever, completely surprising even her.

Just barely managing to reign in his huge sigh of relief, Sean smiled. "Good. And where would you suggest?"

Sean watched as she scrunched up her face again, this time deep in thought. Adorable… this was the only way he could think of to describe her. He had to fight the urge to reach out and run his fingers through her short blonde curls. This hit him so hard, he sat back in his chair, jamming his thumbs in his jean pockets.

But why was he even surprised at this? He'd been fantasizing about doing this ever since he first saw her at Chester and Sophie's wedding. He had the feeling it would be like running his hands through silk.

He needed to squash the possibility of this happening. He certainly wasn't going to take the chance of screwing things up again. As it was, he was still having a hard time dealing with the randomness of running into her like this. And that she'd agreed to go out to dinner with him. If these two things weren't enough to prove they were destined to be together, he didn't know what would be.

She gave him a tentative smile. "Do you like hamburgers?"

"I love hamburgers. I live for hamburgers."

She laughed. "I don't believe you."

"Darlin, I grew up on a cattle ranch. Which means I pretty much lived on hamburgers, steak, ribs and any other bovine related food. It's in my blood."

He snapped his fingers. "I know, what about that little restaurant, truly what-a-ya-call-it, or whatever the name is? One of the guys on the team told me they have good burgers."

"Do you mean Yours Truly?" She laughed again. A sound he was beginning to like the more he heard it. It made him happy. Hell, everything about her made him happy. And for the first time since he'd arrived in Cleveland, he finally felt like this move he made across the world was starting to make sense.

Maybe this town really could become home to him.

"Yours Truly, it is then. Now, since I'm going to assume you also drove, we'll leave your car here. We'll come back to get it later." He was quick to add. "If this is okay with you."

He went to stand, but she stopped him. "Wait..." She reached over for his hat and placed it on his head. It was a little crooked, so she gave it a good tug. Unfortunately, this tipped it forward and down over his eyes.

He chuckled. "Umm... this is not how I usually wear it, but if you think..."

She carefully tugged it back off his head, impulsively reaching over to brush his hair back out of his eyes. His surprised expression made her jerk her hand back, as she gave a nervous laugh. "Sorry... I didn't mean..."

"No, it's fine. Unfortunately, this is one of the drawbacks of wearing a hat. But I'm not ready to give it up." He winked at her. "Old habits die hard, I guess."

She swiftly shook her head. "I like the hat. It's you. The more I see you wearing it, the more I like it. It's very sexy."

Then she made it even worse. "I'm sure I can find you... I mean the hat, easy to love."

As soon as this came out of her mouth, she made a big deal out of checking the contents of her portfolio and zipping it up. She had no idea why she kept blurting out everything she shouldn't even be thinking.

Yes, he'd asked her to go out to dinner. But this didn't mean anything. With his outgoing personality and everything else he had going for him, she'd be willing to bet her entire collection of expensive French illustration markers, he was never in need of companionship. He could probably have a different woman for every night of the week, if he so desired.

Nothing lasts forever. So, just enjoy this while you can.

He cleared his throat. She turned to see there was a teasing glint in his eyes. "Hey, you take as long as you want. I'm willing to wait."

She looked so startled, he wondered if once again he'd said too much. After he gathered up their empty cups and her half-eaten muffin, throwing them in the trash, he turned to smile at her. "Ready to go?"

And then he couldn't stop himself. He reached over to tuck her hair behind her ear, his fingers slowly slipping through her curls.

Just as he'd thought...

Silk.

CHAPTER 24

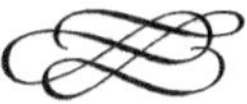

*L*ivy picked up her phone from the coffee table in Carrie and Chris's living room.

There was a text from Chester.

> FYI, Sophie and I are spending the night at the Ritz. Aunt Evelyn and her friend Pat are watching the boys. I have a game tomorrow night, so we'll be back sometime tomorrow afternoon.

As she set the phone down, she was smiling. Evidently Chester had decided to take advantage of the team's off day before the start of the three-game series with Detroit tomorrow.

She'd be willing to bet the only reason he'd sent her this text was because Sophie made him. This would be the first time they'd be gone overnight since the twins were born. So, it was understandable Sophie would be worried about how Trevor and Hunter would react. After all, they were still only babies.

She reached for her laptop, another one of those sharp pains traveling across her lower back. This was the third time this had happened over the course of the day and she was beginning to wonder if she should be concerned. Her hands going protectively to her stomach, she was hit by a moment of panic.

Even though this is something you're not ready for, at the same time, you don't want anything bad to happen.

Unfortunately, after the first pain had come at her, she'd made the mistake of looking up the possible complications of pregnancies on the internet. She'd quickly learned, not only was there a lot she didn't know about the whole process of having a baby, it also appeared there was even more that could go wrong along the way.

It certainly hadn't taken you very long to realize this was a bad move to look up this information. What were you thinking?

That she was going to have a baby, and she was planning to do this on her own, was still so overwhelming to her. Just thinking about the responsibility of raising a child was enough to send her into a panic, her mind becoming clouded with doubt she'd be able to pull it off.

What if she wasn't a good mother? She'd had very little experience with children. Even less with babies. Becoming an aunt to Trevor and Hunter had been a whole new experience... she was still learning.

She rested her head back against the cushions of the sofa and closed her eyes. There was one thing holding her together, and this was the promise Sam made to her. His assurance he'd be right by her side throughout the whole experience, was a promise she knew he wouldn't break.

At least you don't think he will... after all, you thought that with Zack and look what happened there.

But, she didn't want to start thinking about this. Instead, looking down at what she'd typed on her laptop, she was feeling quite proud of herself. After spending most of the morning and afternoon writing, she was finally beginning to make progress. If she kept up at this rate, she'd be finished with her first attempt at writing a novel in no time.

She was reading over what she'd recently written, when she heard a car door slam. Thinking it was Sam, she closed her laptop and went into the kitchen.

Another streak of pain shot through her, this one sharper and stopping her in her tracks. She made a mental note the next time this happened, she would tell Sam.

She peered out through the screen door. It wasn't Sam's SUV that was in the driveway.

And the person who just shut the car door and was now walking towards her? This wasn't Sam, either.

In disbelief, she closed her eyes. Only to open them again to see that, yes… it was Zack.

Her heart beating furiously in her chest, she nervously watched as he made his way to the door, where he hesitated, one foot on the bottom step as he peered through the screen door.

She was shocked by his appearance. He looked as if he'd just rolled out of bed. He was unshaven, his shirt all wrinkled.

Then there was his hair… it was sticking straight up, as if he'd been running his hands through it. She knew this look. This is what happened when he was either really tired or angry about something.

For a few tense moments, there was only silence. He was the first to finally speak, the tone of his voice dry, and most decidedly, sarcastic.

"Surprised?"

Her answer was barely a whisper. "What are you doing here?"

Slowly making his way up the steps, his annoyance at her question was evident in the long penetrating stare he gave her.

"I came to see you, of course." His hand went to the door handle. "So, are you going to invite me in? After all, I did come all this way."

She could only nod.

He yanked open the door and walked right past her into the kitchen. After a quick glance around the room, he gave a slight nod.

His gaze zeroed in on her again. "So, this is where you decided to hide out. I can't say I blame you. It's a nice place."

He reached into his pocket and tossed a small address book on the island. "In case you're wondering how I knew where to find you, this handy little book is what gave me a head start on where to look."

He ran his hand through his hair, making it stick up even more. "Believe it or not, this was the first place I decided to check. With the way my life has been going lately, I didn't expect it would be this easy. I guess for once, luck was on my side."

Livy didn't know what to say, her gaze on the address book. She had searched all over for the little book when she'd packed up all of her belongings, to finally give up. She could just as easily find the same information on her phone or computer. It didn't matter if she left it behind.

Well, it looks like you were wrong about that. The fact Zack is now standing in front of you is proof of this.

He leaned against the kitchen counter, his arms across his chest. He shook his head. "I assume from the expression on your face, I'm the last person you expected to see. But since you never returned any of my calls, I had no choice but to get on a plane to come here."

He gave an irritated frown. "Which, by the way, wasn't cheap. The airlines are getting away with murder with what they charge for such a short flight."

Dragging his hand over his jaw, he gave a long sigh.

"But I didn't come here to talk about the damn airlines. I'm here to talk about us."

Livy's mind was running all over the place.

The baby... you need to tell him about the baby.

This would be the only right and logical thing to do. But with so much anger radiating from him, she didn't think this would be the best time. From her past experience with an angry Zack, she knew how quickly things could deteriorate. His explosive temper wasn't something to be taken lightly.

News like this would be more than enough to set him off.

She closed her eyes, massaging her temples. She couldn't do this. She wanted him to go away. His absence had made it easy for her to block his part in all of this out of her mind. The insane thought had even crossed her mind, maybe by some miracle, he wasn't the father after all.

No, Sam was.

She knew this was crazy. And it was wrong. But it was the only thing, up until now, that was helping her cope.

But now, with Zack here and in person, things had become real.

Too real.

Zack opened the refrigerator and after an impatient search, he pulled out a bottle of beer. He opened it, and leaning against the counter, he took a long drink. "God, I needed that." He took another drink before he looked over at Livy. "So, tell me, why did you leave? If it was because of how I reacted because of the cake, I'm sorry. But, you have to admit, that turned into a real mess."

She stared at him, incredulous. How could he be so blind? Did he think she was that much of an idiot to not know, when he left that night, he'd gone right into the arms of another woman? Her intention to confront him about this, she opened her mouth. To then promptly close it. She didn't want to fight with him. The only thing she wanted, was for him to be gone.

According to the clock on the microwave, it was six-thirty-six. This meant that Sam could be arriving any minute. The possibility of a confrontation between the two of them, here in a house that wasn't even hers, was something she didn't want to even think about.

Especially since Sam had made it very clear how he felt about Zack.

Zack cleared his throat. "So? Are you going to tell me?"

Another sharp pain radiated across her back, this one even stronger. She slowly sat down onto the arm of the sofa, trying to hide the pain as she spoke.

"You know very well why I left. It was obvious you went to meet someone else, because when I left in the morning, you still hadn't returned. Which meant you spent the night with someone. But whoever it was, is not important. You promised you'd never do anything like this again. But you did. You've done nothing but make promises you never intend to keep."

Angry, he plunked the bottle down on the counter. "It was just a friend, that's all. And I was mad. It had been a horrible day and I was surprised to see you when I walked in. Admit it... you always come home after I do. You practically live at that damn life-sucking job of yours." He sent her a puzzled look. "By the way, what did you tell them? You needed a vacation?"

Livy sighed. "No, I didn't tell them I was going on vacation. I came home early because I got laid off from that damn life-sucking job, as you so eloquently put it. They eliminated my position, told me my services were no longer needed. So, you weren't the only one who had a bad day."

He groaned, rubbing the back of his neck. "Oh geeeez, Livy. You lost your job? This is the last thing we need right now. How are we supposed to cover the rent without your salary coming in?" He narrowed his eyes. "Was this part of your plan? By leaving, you'll get out of paying your half?"

Now Livy was mad. Burning mad. This was all he had to say? He was worried she wouldn't be able to pay her half of the rent? She could only imagine what he was going to say when she told him she was pregnant with his child. This would definitely send him over the edge. Not only would he be left paying all of the rent, he'd have the added expense of child support as well.

And this was when she decided it didn't matter.

You want him out of your life for good. And you're not going to take a dime from him.

At the sound of a car coming up the driveway, followed by the slam of a car door, Zack gave her a sharp look. "Who would that be? Your sister?"

"No, Carrie and Chris are on their honeymoon." She sighed. "Remember? They got married this past weekend. I asked you to come to the wedding with me, but you refused."

Giving an irritated swipe through his hair, he frowned. "You know the heavy schedule I have. I can't take off for every little thing that comes along. And when I do get the rare chance for some free time, I'm certainly not going to waste it on some small-town wedding, God knows where."

Hr attention focused on the door, Livy was only half listening. "Don't worry, because from now on, you won't have to. At least not with me."

The door opened and Sam walked into the room. His gaze traveling from Zack to Livy, his eyes met hers in a question.

She gave a slight shake of her head.

He crossed the room, and pressing a kiss to her cheek, his inquiry was barely audible. "You okay, baby?"

Only after she nodded, he acknowledged Zack. "Hey, long time no see. What brought you to Cleveland?"

Of course, Sam knew exactly why Zack was here. To take Livy back to New York. But this wasn't going to happen. As far as he was concerned, Livy was no longer his to have.

Let's just say Sam had learned his lesson. And now that he was on his home turf, he wasn't going to stand back and let Zack win this time.

Recognition flooded Zack's face. "Hey, you're the guy with Livy in Gracie Ann's back in November." He turned to Livy, his voice sarcastic. "And you have the nerve to accuse me of playing around? Just how long have the two of you been seeing each other?"

Livy could feel the tension emanating from Sam. Moving closer, she laid her hand on his arm before she responded. "After that night at Gracie Ann's, the next time I saw Sam was when I was stranded at a gas station on my way home. My car died and he was kind enough to come and pick me up."

Zack gave a short laugh. "What did you expect? I'm surprised you made it as far as you did. You should've never attempted such a long trip with that car. I don't know why you didn't listen to me when I told you to get rid of it."

Sam slowly shook his head. "I don't think the state of Livy's car, or the decision she made, is the issue here. The fact she was alone and stranded was what concerned me the most."

Zack frowned. "Livy was fine with my decision not to attend the wedding. She knows what a demanding schedule I have. And if I'd known she was planning to drive, I never would've approved. Hell, I'd assumed she booked a flight like she did the weekend of her sister's shower."

He set his beer bottle down sharply on the counter and turned to Livy. "We're wasting time. I didn't come here to talk about your car. Or why I didn't come with you for the wedding. I came here to talk about us. Is there somewhere we can speak in private"

Again, it was Sam who spoke. "Unless Livy asks me to leave, anything you have to say, you can say to the both of us."

Livy tightened her grip on Sam's arm as she turned to Zack. "As far as I'm concerned, we have nothing to talk about. I left New York, and as it stands right now, I have no plans of returning. I also have no desire to get back together with you. But you can only blame yourself for this. I tried, but you didn't. You promised to be faithful and you weren't. Again, let me remind you… not once, but twice you did this."

She took a deep breath. "I'm sorry you felt like you needed to make the trip here. And I'm sorry it was so expensive. But the only thing I want right now, is for you to leave."

She'd no sooner said this, when she gave a sharp gasp. An expression of pain flashing across her face, she slumped against Sam, her hands going to her stomach. Concerned, he looked down at her just as she gave a soft moan and closed her eyes.

He put his arm around her, his voice deep with concern. "Livy, sweetheart… what's wrong? Is it the baby?"

No sooner had these words left his mouth, Zack reacted. Running his hands through his hair and his expression one of shock, his voice came out almost an octave higher than usual. "Baby? What do you mean, baby?"

He glared at Livy. "You're pregnant? My God, Livy… how could you have let this happen?" Adamantly shaking his head, his gaze swung over to Sam. "You have my word I knew nothing about this. If it's even mine, that is…"

Fortunately, Sam didn't hear any of this. If he had, Lord knows what he might've done. His attention was on Livy, who had now doubled over in pain, her words coming out between short gasps of breath. "Oh my God… Sam… what's happening?"

He scooped her up in his arms before he jerked his head over at Zack.

"Open the door for me. I'm going to take her to the hospital, to the ER. You're welcome to come if you'd like."

After he opened the door, Zack followed Sam to his SUV, where he watched as Sam carefully settled Livy in the front seat. Nervously running his hand over his chin, he began backing away. "I'll follow behind you."

His focus still on Livy, Sam didn't hear what Zack said. Nor did he see him go to his car.

When he found her hands were ice cold, he grabbed a blanket from the trunk and tucked it around her before he jumped into the driver's seat and started to back out of the driveway. He reached over to take her hand when she let out another moan, relief filling him when her fingers curled around his to hold on.

He pressed a kiss to her forehead. "Hold on baby, you're going to be fine. I'll get you to the hospital as fast as I can, so we can find out what's wrong."

Livy had no idea he followed this with a prayer.

Sam would be quick to tell you he continued to pray, all the way to the hospital. He also kept hold of her hand.

Never once did he look in his rearview mirror to see if Zack was following them.

When Sam pulled up to the entrance of the emergency room and began to help Livy out of the SUV, she put her hand to his cheek.

"Sam?"

"What, baby?"

"Promise me you won't call Chester or my aunt? I haven't told either of them about…"

She gave a sharp intake of breath. He waited, to finally have her whisper. "Promise?"

"Sure, sweetheart… I promise. Though I'm pretty sure, the only thing either of them are going to care about, is that you're okay."

She shook her head. "No, Chester and Sophie took a night off from the boys and I don't want to..." Another sharp pain overtaking her, her voice caught, her lashes fluttering shut. "Oh God, Sam... what's happening? It hurts so bad ... and the baby..."

His worry accelerating, he swiftly picked her up, pressing a soft kiss to her cheek. "I won't tell Chester or your aunt. I promise. Now, let's get you inside. Where they can fix what's wrong."

And yes, he was still praying.

Like he'd never before prayed in his life.

CHAPTER 25

On the other side of town, the familiar sound of a baseball game on TV filtered into Sophie's consciousness.

Still half asleep, a faint smile traveled over her face as she burrowed deeper into the luxurious warmth of the down comforter. The vague thought briefly invaded her mind that she didn't remember it ever being this quiet.

Her lashes flew open.

Wait a minute, it was too quiet.

The babies...

Oh my God... what happened to the babies?

Why weren't they crying?

Throwing off the comforter, she sat straight up and gazed wildly around the room to finally focus on Chester. Next to her on the bed, a mountain of pillows propped up behind him, he was watching TV.

She let out a long, relieved sigh.

Remember? You're in a hotel room at the Ritz with Chester. The babies are at home.

Chester turned off the TV, and scooting closer, he brushed her hair from her face. "Well... hello there, sleepyhead. I was wondering when you were finally going to wake up."

"Still in a daze, she dragged her hands through her hair. "I'm sorry. I guess I fell asleep. What time is it?"

He glanced over at the clock on the nightstand. "It's a little past seven. I was just contemplating whether I should order room service. But, now that you're up, if you'd like, we can go out somewhere for dinner. We can even eat in the hotel restaurant. I'm sure it's good. Whatever you'd like, I'm game."

The realization he hadn't eaten, instead waited for her to wake up, tugged at her heart. She scooted next to him, his arms pulling her close suddenly the most wonderful and comforting feeling in the world.

"Oh Chester, I'm so sorry. Here you planned this weekend so we could be together and what do I do? I go and fall asleep on you. I... I didn't mean... I..."

She burrowed into his chest, shaking her head.

He pressed a kiss to the top of her head. "Hey, it's all right. Obviously, you were exhausted, because you were out like a light. I was talking away when I looked down to see you'd conked out."

He chuckled. "I guess I've lost my touch. But, it's okay. I got in a good nap, too. Evidently, we both needed some shuteye. And I was perfectly happy, being here with you."

His stomach begged to differ with this, letting out a loud and rumbling growl. He grinned. "Though, as you can hear, I'm pretty hungry."

Half laughing, half crying, Sophie lifted her head. "I'm hungry, too. As a matter of fact, I'm starving. But can I take a quick shower first? You can pick the restaurant."

He smiled, swiping at her tears with his thumb. "Sounds like a plan. Take your time. I'm not going anywhere."

Chester poured the remaining wine from the bottle into their glasses.

He smiled up at the server as she cleared their dinner dishes. "If you can bring us the dessert menu, that would be great."

Once the server had left, Sophie primly placed her hands in her lap. She shook her head. "I don't want dessert."

He sat back, a surprised look on his face. "You don't want dessert? Come on, this is a special night, our special night. You can't tell me you're going to pass on dessert."

She was shaking her head. Avoiding his gaze, she fingered the fork she picked up from the table. "No, dessert is the last thing I need."

Puzzled, he reached across the table and taking the fork from her, he set it aside. He reached for her hands. "Angel, what's going on? In all the time I've known you, I don't think I've ever seen you pass up dessert. In fact, I've come to enjoy that we share it together. It's become sort of like our own little tradition."

He could see her eyes were starting to pool with tears.

Again, he was at a loss. These tears had to be due to more than tiredness. And certainly not just because she didn't want dessert.

What the hell was going on? Was it something he did? Something he said?

She pulled her hands away to take a sip of her wine. Gripping the stem of the glass in her hands, she stared down at it, completely silent.

He sighed. "Angel, come on, look at me. Tell me what's going on, what's wrong. You know you can tell me anything."

One look at the concerned expression on his face and everything came pouring out. She started talking, her words coming out in a rush, Sophie style.

"Oh, Chester… how can you not see what's wrong? Look at me. I'm a mess. My hair is a disaster, one big mass of frizz. I haven't had it done in I don't know how long. None of my clothes fit anymore and I'm so damn tired all of the time. I can't even imagine what customers think when they come into the boutique. I wouldn't be surprised if they thought I was a homeless person, looking for a handout."

She pushed her wine glass away and staring up at the ceiling, she began blinking to keep back the tears. "I thought I was going to pass out during Carrie and Chris's wedding because I could hardly breathe, my dress was so tight. And I know it didn't fit like that the last time I tried it on. So, this tells me, not only am I becoming rundown and old, I'm getting fatter by the minute. In a nutshell, I look like hell."

Whoa...

Chester slowly sat back in his chair. Running his hand through his hair, at first, he could only stare at her. He didn't know if this was because he was in complete disbelief over what she said, or more in shock by the fact she swore. Twice she'd done this.

This wasn't your typical Sophie behavior. She never swore. If anything, as of late, she'd been on this campaign to get him to stop swearing, cold turkey.

This was all because of Trevor and Hudson.

Not that he was one to swear with every other word, but according to her, the little he did, was uncalled for and completely unnecessary. More than once she'd told him this. Children were like little sponges, soaking up everything they could whenever they had the chance, she'd gone on to tell him. Did he want their children to be kicked out of preschool because they had the vocabulary of a truck driver?

She didn't think he did. She knew she didn't.

Chester was pretty sure she was a little over the top with this, but he was making a sincere effort to change. Not that this was an easy thing to do.

Come on, you hang out with a bunch of guys all of the time... baseball players. There's no mincing of words with these guys. The majority of them have a much stronger vocabulary than you do.

He leaned forward, reaching for her hands, but she swiftly put them in her lap.

Ah... another warning sign, you're afraid.

He cleared his throat. "Angel, you're imagining all of this. You're beautiful. You always have been and you always will be. I've seen the way people look at us when were together. Wondering how I got so lucky." The corner of his mouth twitched in a wry smile. "No doubt thinking it was my money and fame that attracted you to me."

This had her glaring at him, ready with a retort. But he beat her to it. "I'm kidding, I'm kidding." He shook his head. "If anything, you're more gorgeous now than you were before you had the babies."

This was true. He was more attracted to her now than he'd ever been. And since he'd been crazy about her since the very first moment he saw her, this was saying something. After giving birth, there was a new softness about her... a sexiness that stirred his senses, sending that ever so familiar jolt of heat right through him. And this happened whether he was with her or just thinking about her.

His claim she'd put a spell on him, sprinkling that ever-so-potent fairy dust of hers over him, now stood truer than ever.

Well, maybe not now, not with the way she's glaring at you. Suggesting if there's any blame to be handed out for the way she's feeling, it would go to you, hands down.

She gave a sharp laugh. "Oh Chester, come on. How can you even say that with a straight face?" She saw his mouth twitch as he tried not to laugh. "See, you're trying not to laugh right now as I speak."

"Yes, I'm trying not to laugh, but this is only because what you're saying is so ridiculous. Come on... you have to know this."

This time when he reached for her hands, she didn't pull them away. Relieved at this, the expression on his face became completely serious.

"Angel, I love you. I love everything about you. You are my life, you and the boys. Everything I do, I do for the three of you. I think all of this self-doubt you're carrying around is because of the stress you're under So, we need to change this. We're going to bring in some help. At least while the season is going on. My God, it's not like we can't afford it."

She dropped her gaze to their hands before she looked back up at him. "I don't want you to think I'm not doing my part. "

He studied her, the show of anxiety in her eyes and the way her shoulders were slumped, you'd think it was the end of the world. He wanted to get out of his chair, take her into his arms and kiss her until she couldn't think anymore. Or at least until she stopped thinking the way she was. Right in the middle of the damn restaurant, he'd do this.

Ooops... at least you didn't say that out loud.

How she could even think she wasn't doing her part, was beyond his comprehension'

He tightened his hold on her hands. "Angel, look at me."

The face she lifted to his was filled with such sadness, it tore at his gut. "You are the one who keeps us all together. You do more than your part. In fact, I think we've all taken advantage of all that you do for us. I love you, angel. Trevor and Hudson love you. I know this by the way their eyes light up when they see you."

A smile tweaked the corner of his mouth. "In fact, when we get home, I'm going to sit them down in those crazy bubble seat things you got for them and give then a serious lecture about the changes that need to be made. It's about time they started doing their part to help out. Heck, they're already seven months old, close to going on eight. It's time they started to toe the line."

She gazed up at him, and even with the tears spilling down her cheeks, she was unable to stop the laughter that bubbled up inside of her. She shook her head. "No, they're already growing up too fast as it is. I think this is a big part of my problem. I'm so afraid I'm going to miss something, so I try to spend as much time with them as I can."

His smile was still there, a spark of something deeper appearing in his eyes. "You do know it's not a done deal. It doesn't have to end with them. We can always have more babies. Look at the amazing job we've done with Trevor and Hudson. Imagine what we could do with the next one. Or the one after that. Or…"

Now she was laughing. "Chester, stop. I don't know how to tell you this, but that baseball team you've envisioned is probably not going to happen." She grinned. "What am I saying? Of course, there's no chance of that. It's a little bit too much to ask, don't you think?"

He grinned right back at her. "*Ah…* I seem to remember this breathtakingly beautiful bride, telling her infatuated and newly wedded, adoring husband, when it came to kids, the number ten sounded like a good number to her. I also remember how eager she was at the time to make that happen."

Color filled her cheeks. "I was very vulnerable at the time. When it comes to things like that, you can be very persuasive."

Like right now. The look in his eyes is sending a shiver right through you. Whatever he's thinking, if you weren't in this restaurant, you'd agree to it in a heartbeat.

"Come here…" His whisper inviting her closer, his breath brushed across her jaw an instant before his mouth did, covering hers in a kiss that went soul deep.

When he eventually pulled away from her, the huskiness of his voice traveled through every inch of her, bringing her to lean in even closer, her eyes drifting shut. "The more I'm with you, the more I want you, angel. And this will always hold true. I love you with everything I have."

Then, as though nothing unusual had happened, he sat back in his chair and sent a casual glance around the restaurant. "I wonder where our server went. It's taking her a long time to get back to us with the dessert menu, isn't it? I'm eager to see what they have." He turned back to her, his eyebrow raised.

Her lips still parted from his kiss, she slowly opened her eyes. She shook her head in resignation at the teasing glint in his eyes.

But she had to admit… she really did want dessert.

A big part of this was because, like him, she loved it was something they shared.

Like he'd said, it was their own special tradition.

Sophie put the last spoonful of chocolate mousse in her mouth, her eyes closed as she savored it. After licking every bit of mousse from the spoon, she looked over at Chester. Watching her, the burning intensity in his gaze almost made her drop the spoon. In an attempt to hide the blush tinting her cheeks, she grabbed her napkin and daintily patted her mouth.

After she'd set the napkin back on the table, right next to her phone, she saw she had a call. She sent Chester a quick glance. She knew he hadn't been very happy when she insisted on having the phone out on the table. But she'd held firm, reminding him of his promise she could check up on the babies if she felt the need.

"It's Sam. Why would he be calling me?" Puzzled, she took the call.

Chester listened to the seriousness of Sophie's brief answers, worry beginning to kick in. Whatever Sam was telling her, it wasn't looking good.

After Sophie ended the call, she slowly set the phone on the table before she looked over at Chester. "That was Sam."

His nod was impatient. "Yes, you told me that. What happened?" It wasn't his intention to be abrupt, but while he'd waited for Sophie to end the call, every possible scenario had come at him and all at once. Livy or Sam had received a call because something happened to the twins. Or something happened to his aunt. Or something had happened to Carrie and Chris. It could be any number of things.

Sophie reached for his hand. "He's at the hospital. He said he was with Livy when she suddenly doubled over in pain, so he took her to the emergency room. I'm not quite sure why, but he said Livy made him promise not to tell you or your aunt. But he felt uncomfortable about this and made the decision to call me instead. He said he didn't have any information yet on Livy's condition, but he'd call as soon as he heard something."

Chester had already come to his feet and taking out his wallet, he threw some bills on the table. "We have to go… what hospital?"

As Sophie quickly rose from her chair, the look in his eyes softened, imploring her to understand. "Angel, I'm so sorry. This certainly isn't turning out to be the evening I'd planned. But I'd never forgive myself if it turned out to be something serious and I wasn't there for Livy."

"Oh, Chester… I know that. I'd be disappointed if you didn't go. Sam said they're at University."

"Okay, let's go." Planting a quick kiss to her mouth and taking her hand, they almost ran out of the restaurant.

CHAPTER 26

$\mathcal{S}$am was finding it hard to sit still. Hospitals made him nervous, emergency rooms even more so. The few times he'd spent in one with Gracie, was something he wanted to forget.

Hands in his pockets, he wandered over to the windows, staring mindlessly at the busy parking lot. After a few minutes of this, he turned to send another irritated glance over at Zack.

His mouth tight with anger, he dragged his hand through his hair before his gaze shifted once more to the parking lot.

He'd about reached his limit as far as Zack was concerned. Having barely spoken a word to each other since they arrived at the hospital, his continuous pacing had Sam on the verge of suggesting it might be better if he left.

Or more to the point, get the hell out of the hospital. Maybe even go as far as to tell him to get the hell out of their lives.

He knew he was being unreasonable, but he blamed Zack for the reason they were now in an emergency waiting room, faced with the unknown.

Yeah, even though Zack is responsible for the fact Livy is pregnant, he isn't the cause of what's going on right now. But you want to blame someone, so it might as well be him.

Turning from the window, he shoved his hands back in his pockets and watched as Zack went striding over to the coffee station to pour out yet another cup of coffee. Sam was pretty sure this was his sixth or seventh cup since they had arrived, this more than explaining his agitated state.

He had also been on his phone the majority of the time, which certainly wasn't boosting the opinion Sam had of him so far. Who he could possibly be talking to all this time, Sam couldn't imagine.

Nor did he care.

He looked over to see the door leading to the emergency room swing open again. He held his breath, hoping against all hope the name they'd call out this time would be his, coming from a doctor ready to give them a report on what was happening with Livy.

But this didn't happen.

He sank down into the first available chair and checked the time on his watch. They had been waiting for over three hours and as far as he was concerned, this was way too long. This was why he'd finally decided to call Sophie and let her know this was where he had to bring Livy.

Yeah, he'd promised Livy he wouldn't call Chester. Or their Aunt Evelyn. But he never promised he wouldn't call Sophie. If Livy got mad at him for this, well... he was willing to take that chance. To not let someone in her family know what was going on, this wasn't something he felt comfortable with.

He glanced down at his watch again. Too much time had passed and he was worried.

The door to the emergency room swung open. Again, it wasn't his name they called.

He leaned his head back and closed his eyes.

He could do nothing but wait.

"Sam..."

His head coming up with a jerk, Sam opened his eyes to find Chester and Sophie standing in front of him.

After he struggled to his feet to greet them, Chester began firing questions at him. "What's going on? What happened to Livy? Do you know anything yet?"

"Mr. Bridges?"

At the sound of his name, Sam glanced over towards the emergency room to see a doctor standing at the door, his gaze searching the room. Swiftly making his way over to him, with Sophie and Chester following right behind, Sam scanned the doctor's name badge before he reached out to shake his hand. "Dr. Evans, I'm Sam Bridges, a very good friend of Livy's."

He gestured to Chester and Sophie. "This is Livy's brother and sister-in-law, Chester and Sophie. I hope you've come to give us good news?"

Dr. Evans smiled at Sam, shaking his hand. "Your friend is going to be okay. You did know she was pregnant, didn't you?"

Chester gave a sharp intake of breath, but before he could say anything, Sophie put her hand on his arm, shaking her head.

Noting this, there was a moment of hesitation on the doctor's part, but at Sam's nod, he directed his next remarks to him. "Livy had an ectopic pregnancy, or what is commonly called a tubal pregnancy. This is a pregnancy that occurs outside of the womb. Fortunately for Livy, the pregnancy terminated on its own, this the cause of the pain she had. But this also means she lost the baby."

He smiled at Sam. "It's a good thing you acted quickly, bringing her in as soon as you did. As odd as this may sound, Livy was very lucky, her body taking on the job of putting an end to the pregnancy on its own. In some of the cases I've dealt with, this doesn't always happen. Complications can arise, leading to a more serious outcome."

He gave them all an encouraging smile. "But right now, things are looking good. It might help if you all think of this as nature's way of weeding out, what may have been the beginning of a bad pregnancy."

Chester, who was still trying to take in the fact Livy had been pregnant, finally spoke. "Will she be okay? There won't be any lasting side effects, will there?"

Dr. Evans shook his head. "Livy will be fine. And no, she shouldn't have any problem getting pregnant again."

Briefly closing his eyes, Sam could feel the relief flow through him, some of the tension draining from his body. He cleared his throat, his voice gruff with emotion. "Thank God for that. Not about the baby, of course. But, I'm so relieved to know Livy is going to be all right. When can we see her?"

Already pushing open the door to the emergency room, Dr. Evans stopped to check the chart he was holding. "She's being moved to a room as we speak. Give us about a half hour to get her settled. Then, we'll send someone out to take you to her room. We'll plan on keeping her overnight, just as a precaution."

He sent them a nod "She will probably be pretty out of it, with the pain medication we've given her, so it might be best if you kept visitors to a minimum."

He smiled. "A good, healing sleep is what she needs right now." His smile deepening, he nodded over at Sam. "You're more than welcome to stay with her, if you'd like."

Sam watched the door shut behind the doctor before he turned to Chester and Sophie.

He could see the muscle working in Chester's jaw, anger blazing in his eyes. A worried Sophie was patting his arm.

Chester finally spoke, his questions coming out fast and curt. "Livy was pregnant? Did you know about this? I'm assuming Zack is the father? Does he even know about this?"

He briefly closed his eyes. *"Damn...* I'm sorry, I don't mean to be so abrupt, but I'm still trying to understand. Did she tell you if this is why she left New York?"

This is when Sam remembered Zack.

To be honest, he'd completely forgotten all about him. His gaze traveling around the waiting room, he finally spotted him over by the windows, still on his phone. This, no doubt, was probably because the reception was better in that area.

Sam wouldn't even be able to describe how furious this made him. *Why was he even here?*

He reached up to massage the back of his neck before he turned to Chester, nodding towards Zack. "That's him over there. Somehow, he found out Livy was staying at Carrie and Chris's house and he showed up there this afternoon. I think his intention was to talk Livy into returning to New York with him, but she told him no."

He shook his head. "It was after I arrived, she began experiencing the pain. When I asked her if it could be because of the baby, Zack heard this and by his reaction, I don't think he had any idea she was pregnant. He definitely appeared to be shocked at the news, deciding to follow us to the hospital."

He glanced over at Zack again. "We've barely talked since we've been here. He's been on that damn phone of his almost the entire time."

As if he knew he was the topic of their conversation, Zack looked up from his phone and after ending his call, he sauntered over to them.

"He held out his hand to Chester. "Zack Morris. You must be Livy's brother Chester." At Chester's brief shake, his steely gaze enough to make any man become cautious, he merely nodded over at Sophie."

He turned to Sam. "So, what did they say? What happened?"

Sam briefly nodded. "She's going to be okay. They want to keep her overnight, just to be on the safe side. The doctor told me we'll be able to see her shortly."

He waited for Zack to ask for more information. Specifically, if her pain was due to her pregnancy. Or, even more importantly, what happened with the baby.

But he didn't.

Sam finally cleared his throat. "Unfortunately, she lost the baby." He then went on to tell him what the doctor had told them.

Zack took some time to think about this before he frowned. "Well, this definitely changes things, doesn't it? But, I can't even think about any of this right now. I'm beat and I need to find somewhere to crash.

I also need to book the first flight I can back to New York. I can't afford to take any more time off."

He grimaced, running his hand through his hair. "You know how it is. You can't slack off. You either stay on top of things, or you lose out."

The tight set of Sam's jaw was the only indication of how angry he was. His expression unreadable, his voice was calm. "So, you're leaving? Just like that? You don't even want to see Livy, if only to see for yourself she's okay?"

Completely oblivious to Sam's anger, Zack shook his head. "I'll take your word for it. Because, let's face it, she's already made it perfectly clear she wants nothing to do with me. It looks like I could've saved myself a lot of money if I had known this before I made the trip."

He scratched his head. "I have no idea where I'm going to go now, though."

For a few moments, Sam studied him. He was struggling with what he wanted to say and what he knew he should say. He wasn't one to become physical, but he was seriously wondering if a good boot in the pants might be the very thing Zack needed right now.

Don't even waste your time or your energy on him. He's not worth it.

He pulled his keys out of his pocket and unhooked the key to his condo.

He handed it to Zack. "Here, you can stay at my place. You should be able to find something to eat in the fridge. Leave the key on the kitchen island and lock the door when you leave. I have another key."

In an attempt to control his anger, he jammed his hands in the pockets of his khakis. "Do me a favor and be out sometime in the morning. Because I've got to level with you… I really don't relish the thought of seeing you again."

At the puzzled expression on Zack's face, Sam shook his head. "I'm sorry, but right now, I'm having a really hard time trying to understand what Livy ever saw in you."

He waited.

He could see Zack was torn, one part of him angry about what he'd said. While the bigger part of him liked the idea of a free night's stay.

For a moment they stared at each other. Zack's face, an angry glare... Sam's, one of a barely controlled indifference.

The free accommodations won out.

Zack sent a curt nod to Chester and Sophie. "Nice meeting you. Too bad it couldn't have been under different circumstances."

When Chester made a move towards him, his hands clenched at his sides, he quickly stepped back and turned once more to Sam. "Can you tell Livy something for me?"

At Sam's nod, he cleared his throat. "Tell her I'm glad she's okay. And, tell her... tell her I'm sorry about the baby. But maybe it's for the best. Because it appears you two are better suited for each other than Livy and I ever were." His laugh was bitter. "It looks like you won this one. Take good care of her."

He gave them all a mock salute before he turned to leave.

Sam watched until he was out of sight. This was only because he wanted to make sure he was really gone.

This time, for good.

Sam turned to Chester and Sophie. "Don't be mad at Livy. She was planning to tell you about the baby as soon as she went to the doctor to confirm the pregnancy. She had an appointment scheduled for tomorrow."

A sad smile touched his lips. "I'd planned to go with her. If only for emotional support, I guess." Running his hand through his hair, he slowly shook his head. "I think everything coming at her all at once was too much, this unexpected pregnancy the last straw. I told her whatever happened, I'd be there for her."

He shrugged. "But now, I don't know what this is going to do to her. Because as much as she was upset about the connection between the pregnancy and Zack, I think she was beginning to get excited about the baby." He paused, his expression wistful. "For that matter, so was I."

Sophie completely surprised him by launching herself at him to give him a big hug. "Oh, Sam… I'm so sorry. For both of you. But Livy will get over this, I know she will. Especially since she has you. You'll just need to give her time."

And Chester? He was still fuming. He knew he needed to calm down, but right now he was having a really hard time trying to wrap his mind around what happened. He wasn't angry at Livy, it was Zack he had a problem with.

A brief smile crossed his lips. If it hadn't been for Sophie's tight grip on his arm, who knew what he might have done. If only to let Zack know exactly how he felt about the way he'd treated Livy.

He cleared his throat. "Sam, I don't know how to thank you for being there for Livy. I think the first thing I need to do, when she's recovered from this, is shake some sense into her. If only to make her realize what a gem she has in you. As far as I'm concerned, you're already a part of the family. I just hope to God, Livy has enough sense to realize the same." This was followed by a hug. Though a bit more brief than Sophie's, it was just as heartfelt.

After a short silence, Sam sent Sophie and Chester a smile. "Hey, you two need to get out of here. Livy told me this is your special night out, no babies allowed. So, you should go. I'll stay here with her until they release her." He grinned. "This may be easier said than done, knowing Livy and her I-can-go-it-alone mindset. But either way, we'll be fine."

Chester gazed down at Sophie, who was leaning against him. When she gave him a big smile, he turned back to Sam. "That would be nice. Promise you'll call if anything changes. In the meantime, I'll figure out what to tell my aunt. Or, if I should tell her anything at all right now."

Sam nodded. "I promise. And I'll let Livy know you were here."

He grinned. "Now go… get out of here."

Sophie watched Chester run the keycard through the lock to open the door to their hotel room.

He did this almost angrily, as if the door hadn't opened fast enough.

She was worried about him.

He had been very quiet on their drive from the hospital. His response to almost everything she'd said had been mostly a curt yes or no. His tight grip on the steering wheel, along with the hard set of his jaw, was an indication he was still having a hard time dealing with what happened.

Once they were in the room, he sat on the edge of the bed and kicked off his shoes. Where he didn't move, staring into space.

Finally, to her relief, he glanced over at her. He shook his head.

She moved to sit on the bed and leaning against him, she rested her head on his shoulder. "Are you okay? You're not mad at Livy, are you?"

He put his arm around her, pressing a kiss to the top of her head. "*Ah, angel...* no, I'm not mad at Livy. If anything, I'm mad at myself."

She didn't understand. "Why are you mad at yourself?"

"I feel like I let her down." He sighed. "I'm afraid Livy has always been the forgotten one in our family. But this is because she's always been so independent. I'd even go as far to say she's also probably the most stubborn of all of us."

At Sophie's skeptical look, he chuckled. "Yeah, I know I can be pretty stubborn at times. But, she has me beat. She's always been quiet, to the point of being painfully shy, but when she's passionate about something, watch out."

He pressed another kiss in her hair. "Growing up, she was always happiest when she had a pile of books to read. So, after she graduated from college and landed the job at the publishers in New York, we all thought she had finally found her niche. She had a great job and what we thought was a steady boyfriend. She never led us to believe things were any different."

He shook his head. "It bothers me that she didn't think she could come to one of us for help. This isn't right. We're a family. We should be there for each other."

Sophie reached up to kiss his cheek. "I don't think you should beat yourself up like this. She's going to be fine. And she has Sam." She smiled up at him. "My goodness, it's so obvious he's in love with her. Did you see his face when the doctor told us she was going to be okay? He looked like he'd just received the best news in the world." She began to frown. "Or when Zack..."

Chester interrupted her, his anger obvious. "Angel, I can't even tell you how much I wanted to lay into the guy." He suddenly began to chuckle. "The only thing that stopped me was the grip you had on my arm. I was afraid if I did go after him, you wouldn't let go, maybe even be the one to throw the first punch."

Sophie settled closer, nodding against him. "I was so mad. I was also impressed with how Sam reacted, even going as far to offer Zack his condo for the night. Though I'll admit, for a minute there, I was worried Zack was going to come out and say something that would set one of you off. My only reassuring thought was we were in a hospital in case someone got hurt."

Chester had slowly begun to move them to the middle of the bed and propping himself on his elbow, his gaze traveled over her face. "God, I love you, angel. You ground me. I always know everything is going to be all right when I'm with you."

Framing her face in his hand he pressed a soft kiss to her brow before his lips trailed down to her mouth. He kissed her, slowly, tenderly, as though he was trying to savor the moment.

His fingers going on to trace along the neckline of her dress, he pulled down the shoulder strap and pressed a slow, hot kiss to her collarbone. "You're beautiful, angel." His whisper fanned her cheek. "So, *so* beautiful."

His mouth hovering over hers, he waited. He needed to know she wanted this, too. Just as much as he did.

A heat had begun to travel through Sophie, his hands moving over her, caressing her, so familiar. Mesmerized, she could only gaze wordlessly at him before she lifted her mouth to his, completely surrendering to his kiss.

When he finally lifted his head, the love and tenderness in his gaze reached deep into her soul, his words the ultimate promise.

"I love you. I will always love you."

Right before he captured her mouth in another kiss, her answer came in a whisper across his lips.

"I love you, too. *Always.*"

His Sophie was back…

CHAPTER 27

Sometimes a certain darkness is needed
to finally see the stars.
~ Anonymous

Slowly opening her eyes, Livy gazed around the dimly lit hospital room.

She had no idea what kind of medication they gave her, but whatever it was, it was strong. And it was starting to work, her body beginning to settle into that soft, relaxed feeling. As though she was becoming completely weightless.

The nurse had told her it would help her sleep through the night. This way, she said, tomorrow Livy would feel almost as good as new.

Livy didn't think there was much of a chance she'd ever feel as good as new again. And if she did? She seriously doubted it would last. This was the pattern her life seemed to be following lately, a few promising ups, only to be followed by way too many downs.

She had little recollection of what happened after Sam brought her to the emergency room. The same nurse told her this was when she'd passed out from the pain.

The next time she opened her eyes, she was here and in this bed.

She burrowed even deeper under the blankets. Even though the promise of a long and uninterrupted sleep was so tempting, she was desperately fighting the urge to close her eyes, her gaze glued to the entrance to the room.

She couldn't fall asleep. Not yet.

She was waiting for Sam

She shivered. She couldn't seem to get warm. Tugging at the blanket, she pulled it even higher over her shoulders.

Where was Sam? Did he leave?

Her eyelids growing heavier by the minute, she finally gave in and closed her eyes.

She promised herself this would be only for a minute.

Because Sam would be here soon...

She knew he would.

Sam nodded his thanks to the nurse and cautiously pushing open the door, he walked into the dimly lit room assigned to Livy. At first glance, he thought the nurse might have made a mistake, bringing him to the wrong room. A room that still needed to be readied for the next patient. It was when he heard the faint, steady beep of the heart monitor machine, he realized what he thought was a pile of blankets on the bed, was actually Livy, hidden beneath them.

He gently pulled the blanket back from her face. When she gave a faint moan, huddling even deeper into herself, he tucked the blanket back around her. Pulling a chair close to the bed, he sank into it, exhaling a long, drawn out breath.

He closed his eyes and bowing his head, he slowly let go of what was left of the tension and worry still crippling his body and his mind.

The last few hours had been a living hell.

He'd never been so scared in his life. He was still scared. The possibility of losing Livy had completely taken over his mind, exhausting him to the point that he still couldn't think straight.

Faced with the sudden knowledge of how swiftly things could change, he'd taken this time to re-evaluate what he wanted in life. And this was when he realized everything he wanted, always came back to Livy.

She grounded him.

She was his lifeline.

She was the other half of this mysterious thing called love that had staked a claim on him, body, heart and soul. And now that his mind was made up, he was going to tell her this as soon as he could. He no longer saw any reason to wait.

Yes, they had told each other, I love you. But he wanted more. A ring on their finger and a for better or worse kind of more. A permanent, until death do us part, more.

He gazed over at Livy, a down-to-the-bone-weariness coming over him. He gave a huge yawn and stretching out his legs, he settled in the chair as comfortably as he could, closing his eyes.

But he couldn't sit still.

Pushing out of the chair and leaning closer to the bed, he drew comfort in the sound of Livy's soft, even breathing. After rearranging the blankets once more, tucking them even more securely around her, he pressed the softest of kisses to her cheek

"You're going to be fine, baby." This was barely a whisper. "Sleep. I'll be right here if you need me. I love you."

Dropping back into the chair, he gazed around the room, the continuous beep of the heart monitor machine a comforting reminder everything was under control. He pulled out his phone and after turning it to mute, he once again tried to find a comfortable position in the small chair.

After another big yawn, he closed his eyes.

It was going to be a long night. But this was okay.

There was no other place he'd rather be.

Sam had no idea how long he'd been asleep when he became aware someone was knocking softly on the door to the room. Groggily blinking down at his watch, he saw it was almost midnight.

Eleven-fifty-one, to be exact.

He watched the door slowly open, the same nurse who had earlier escorted him to Livy's room, entering the room. She was holding a tray with a covered dish and a container of coffee.

She smiled as she set it on the bedside table. "Hi, I remember you told me you hadn't eaten since lunchtime, so I brought you something from the cafeteria." She spoke in whisper. "You're lucky, the cook on duty is our favorite and his chicken pot pie is to die for."

She glanced over at Livy. "I also wanted to check on Livy." She nodded over at the tray. "Go ahead and start eating while it's still hot."

Sam lifted the cover, the tantalizing aroma of the pot pie making him realize how hungry he was. He began scooping the savory mixture of chicken and vegetables into his mouth as he watched the nurse take Livy's pulse.

She turned to smile at him. "I think that's about all I'm going to do for now. I don't want to wake her. Even though I don't think I could, even if I tried. She's out. I'll come back later. In the meantime, I'll have someone on the housekeeping staff bring you a blanket and a pillow."

When he started to thank her, she shook her head. "One of you needs to stay strong. And I'm thinking that job falls to you."

She smiled. "I could also see you aren't planning on going anywhere. So, go ahead and eat. Enjoy."

After Sam finished off the chicken pot pie, he settled once more into the chair. With the blanket and pillow the housekeeping staff had delivered, he felt like he was in heaven

After one more glance over at Livy, to see she was still sound asleep, he closed his eyes.

He was out like a light.

Someone was calling his name.

Slowly opening his eyes, in his half-conscious state, it took Sam a few moments to realize it was Livy.

Livy was dreaming. In her dream, she could see Sam. Very clearly, she was able to do this. He was waving, motioning for her to follow him. But every time she got almost close enough to reach out and touch him, he would slip from her fingers and disappear. Only to reappear off in the distance, waving at her once again. Afraid she was going to lose him for good, she called out for him to stop.

She called out again.

Struggling his way out from under the blankets he had become tangled in, Sam finally made his way over to Livy. Still huddled deep under the blankets, her face was completely hidden. Smoothing the damp tendrils of hair back from her flushed face, he kept his voice soft, so as not to startle her. "Hey, baby... I'm right here."

Her lashes flying open, for a few seconds she stared wide-eyed at him.

"C-c-c-cold... so c-c-c-cold..." She whispered this while she tried to pull the covers more tightly around her.

He grabbed the blanket they had brought him and tucked it around her.

She shook her head. "St-t-t-ill c-c-c-cold..."

He didn't even hesitate, kicking off his shoes to slide next to her under the blanket.

Confronted with the violent chills running through her, he pulled her against him and tucking her head under his chin, he briskly began running his hands over her, trying to warm her. When her shivering finally began to taper off, his hands stilled to hold her against him.

He could hear the hurried footsteps and muted voices coming from outside in the hallway, signaling the night shift was almost at an end. But in the room he and Livy occupied, there was only silence. Wrapped up in each other's arms, for them, it became a comforting, almost healing kind of silence.

Something they both desperately needed.

He pressed a kiss in her hair. "Hey, are you warmer now?"

"Yes, thank you." Her whisper was muffled against his chest, "I thought you left."

A smile touching his lips, his fingers drifted through her hair.

"Nah… I couldn't do that. You, of all people, should know I'd never pass up the chance to aid a damsel in distress."

Her response wasn't what he expected. "The baby?"

He stilled, his stomach muscles clenching in response to her question. She didn't know? He'd assumed they would've told her. "The doctor didn't talk to you?"

Aware of the sudden tension in his body, she raised her head, her eyes anxiously searching his face. "No, I was waiting for you. I wanted to talk to you. I tried to stay awake, but whatever they gave me, it was too strong and it knocked me out."

His fingers sifting through her hair, his gaze was filled with such tenderness. "Oh, sweetheart… they couldn't save the baby. Your body had already given it up. The doctor said it was probably a blessing in disguise. He explained it as nature's way of terminating a pregnancy that had gone wrong. He also said you should in no way blame yourself for what happened."

She dropped her head on his chest and was silent. This was when he realized she'd begun to cry, her tears soaking through his shirt.

He hugged her close. "*Ah… Livy…*"

She took a big, gulping breath. "I'm sorry. I know how you hate when a woman cries."

He sighed. "That's not completely true. Lately, I've found it doesn't bother me all that much when other women cry. It's only when you cry, I have such a hard time. This is because I want to fix what's wrong. But, I think this is one time I need to let you cry."

So, she did.

It's safe to say he shed a tear or two right along with her.

It was almost noon the next day when Sam drove his SUV up the driveway of Carrie and Chris's house. Once he'd turned off the ignition, he slowly turned to see Livy was watching him.

At the sadness he could see in her eyes, he reached over to run his knuckles gently down the side of her face.

He cleared his throat. "Hey…"

Her gaze slowly traveling over his face, she opened her mouth, only to shut it again. She shook her head, her gaze going down to her hands, clenched in her lap.

Sam was worried.

Since they left the hospital, she hadn't said a word, her head against the head rest and her eyes closed. So, he decided to let her be.

But now?

His concern had escalated. Everything suddenly felt so wrong between them. Somehow, from the time he'd held her in his arms while she cried about the loss of the baby and up until now, things had changed.

A distance had come between them, one he couldn't bridge.

A barrier brought on by Livy alone. Leaving him struggling.

Before they left the hospital, the nurse had pulled him aside. She warned him, even though Livy seemed to be taking the loss quite well right now, this could change when she got home and in familiar surroundings. She might become depressed, prone to tears and maybe even angry.

But, she'd assured him, this should only last for a few days, the symptoms eventually easing off. If, for some reason, she didn't start feeling better, they should call her doctor.

Well... from what he now saw, she was definitely feeling differently. And though he knew this was to be expected, he didn't like it one bit.

"Livy?"

She slowly turned to face him, her expression unreadable.

He reached over to hold her hand. "Why don't you come stay with me today? I'll take the day off and we can just chill. Or do whatever you'd like. I'm game for anything."

She slowly shook her head. "No, I think it would be better if I stay here. Maybe spend some time alone." She reached over to stroke his cheek with her fingertips. "It's not that I don't want to be with you, but I'd feel guilty, keeping you from your work. I know you have a lot of things going on and people who are counting on you."

Her eyes suddenly bright with a new threat of tears, she averted her gaze. "I'll be fine. I just need time to sort everything out. Time… isn't this is what everyone keeps telling me?"

Sam was torn.

He didn't want to leave her. But, she was right. The emails and texts were piling up on his phone.

There were problems at the Shaker site. He had contractors lined up and waiting for his okay to start work at the lake house. He should be on hand to oversee both of these projects. If Chris and Carrie were here, there wouldn't be a problem. But they weren't due back for another five days.

Livy saw the conflict in his features. As she reached for the door handle, she turned to give him a bright smile.

"Sam, honest, I'll be fine. Really, I will. I promise to take it easy. The only thing I have planned right now is to maybe work on a couple more chapters of my book. And maybe update my resume." She shrugged. "After all, I do need to find a job of some kind. I don't want to deplete all of my savings. Or take advantage of my aunt."

She reached out to stroke his cheek. "I'm not planning on going anywhere."

Then come stay with me. You can write all you want. We can even work on making another baby, if this is what you want. Let me take care of you. Forever I'll do this.

No, he didn't say any of this out loud. This is what he was think-ing, what he wanted to say. But he didn't think Livy was ready to hear this right now. Certainly not with the pain of losing the baby still so raw.

But if he could, he would tell her this in a second.

Instead, he got out of the SUV and coming around to the passenger side, he opened the door for her.

He walked her to the door and watched as she unlocked it. He even followed her inside. Where he took her into his arms and held her until she gently pulled away.

She gazed up at him, her voice dropping to a whisper. "I love you. I don't know what I'd do without you. I wish I…" She shook her head.

He smoothed the hair back from her face. "You wish what?"

She slowly shook her head. "I'm scared. I wish this hadn't happened… the baby, everything. I feel like every…"

Her words fading, he pulled her back against him, closing his eyes. He knew he should reassure her, but nothing he could think of sounded right. He also didn't trust himself to not say the wrong thing. So, he held her, hoping this would be enough.

She stirred in his arms, thinking his silence was a confirmation he was feeling the same. Gently pushing away from him, she gave him a shaky smile. "You should go. I'll be fine, I promise."

After he had her promise she would call if she needed anything, and he meant *anything,* he left.

It turned out to be a pretty useless day for both of them.

He didn't really get any work done and everything she wrote, she ended up deleting.

And her resume?

Again… she had nothing.

CHAPTER 28

*S*eated at the kitchen island, Livy looked up from her computer. On this early afternoon, her view out the window was of a cloudless blue sky, the leaves of the big oak tree right outside the window, dancing in the light breeze.

Her attention drifting back to her computer, she brought up the email she'd received earlier. It was from a long established and prominent publishing company in Chicago.

According to what was written, her name had been submitted to them as a possible candidate for the position of head editor of women's fiction, starting immediately. If she were to take on this position, it could eventually lead to the title of head editor of romance as well, as plans were now in the works to combine the two into one department.

She had come very highly recommended and because of her experience and qualifications, the starting salary for this position would be in the six-figure range.

If she was interested, she was to contact the head of human resources as soon as possible. An interview would be set up and travel arrangements would be arranged through the company. The name of the person to contact was listed, along with their direct phone line, at the bottom of the email. There was also an attachment of the current handbook for all employees, outlining the company's policies, benefits and bonus programs.

Hopefully, this position might be something she'd seriously consider. If so, she should contact them as soon as possible.

Livy gaze again went to the window. She wondered if George had been the person to recommend her for this position.

She suddenly reached over and turned off her computer. She didn't want to deal with this now.

She *couldn't* deal with it now.

Her life, as she had known it, had come to a halt. Her priorities were no longer the same… they were different. She was different.

How could something, so little and so uncertain, completely shake up your life like this?

For the last two days, she'd been walking around in a fog, her mind refusing to let go of what happened. She was trying, she really was. But she still couldn't get the nagging thought out of her mind, that somehow, it was her fault she'd lost the baby.

Her only contact with Sam during this time had been through phone calls. He hadn't pressured her, he'd only listened. Last night they'd talked on the phone until the early morning hours, sharing everything… their thoughts and even their most private dreams.

He'd made her laugh. And he'd made her cry… but it was a good cry, a cleansing cry. For the first time in her life, she finally felt like she'd found the person she could lean on, the one person she could trust completely.

The person she wanted to be with for the rest of her life.

And now, their phone conversations were no longer enough. She missed his smile. She missed his kisses. She even missed his teasing comments. But most of all, she missed the feeling of his arms around her, his heart beating next to hers.

She needed this.

More than she'd ever needed anything.

She smiled, visualizing the look he would give her if he was with her right now. It would be the look she'd come to love, the one that told her he knew exactly what she was thinking. And that she'd never have to worry… he would always be there for her.

And you'd fall in love with him all over again.

She was smiling as she glanced over at the clock. She had promised her Aunt Evelyn she'd run some errands for her. Down with a bad cold, she claimed she was too sick to leave the house.

So, Livy had a plan. Since one of the stops she had to make for her aunt was the grocery store, she would call Sam to tell him she wanted to come over to make him dinner. Or they could prepare it together. Whatever he'd like to do. This would be her small way of thanking him.

Yes, she knew it wasn't enough. But it was a beginning.

Or, as you like to think, the real beginning of you and Sam.

Filled with a sudden purpose, she started up the stairs to check out her wardrobe.

She wanted to look good for the man she loved.

Then she turned to run back down the stairs and grabbed her phone.

First things first… she needed to call Sam and let him know what she was planning.

CHAPTER 29

In every relationship, there will be challenges.
it's how you face them together that matters.
~ Unknown

Valerie Madison made sure to sashay as provocatively as she could out of Sam's office. Unfortunately for her, he wasn't paying the least bit of attention. He was more interested in who was calling him on his phone. It was Livy.

He was smiling as he answered.

"Hey…"

Livy could hear the smile in his voice. Sinking down on the bed, she closed her eyes, an answering smile curving her lips.

"I hope I'm not bothering you."

The sound of her voice flowed through him, everything in his world falling into place. Leaning back in his chair, he closed his eyes.

"Baby, you never bother me. And if you do, it's in a good way. What's up?"

"I have a proposition for you."

His smile grew.

He was so damn happy to hear the change in her voice. He hoped this was a sign she was beginning to come to terms with everything that happened.

He picked up the hair tie from his desk, twirling it around his finger. "You do? And tell me, will I like this proposition of yours?"

"I am going to take a wild guess here and say yes. Because it involves food. From what I've heard, the way to a man's heart is through his stomach. At least I think this is what they say."

He chuckled. "Sweetheart, I can think of a few other ways you can capture my heart, all very pleasurable and none of them involving food. But I guess this theory of yours could also hold true. With a ready back-up plan."

When this was greeted by silence, his smile grew even bigger. "*Uh oh...* are you still there?"

Livy's mind had gone off on a whole new train of thought, almost as pleasurable as Sam's, and now she was trying to think back to why she'd even called him in the first place.

Ah... the dinner. Yes, this was what she wanted to talk to him about... dinner.

Her voice came out all breathless. "I thought I'd come over and make you dinner. Or, it could be fun if we prepared it together. I want to do something to show you how much I appreciate everything you've done for me over the past few days. I owe you. I know I couldn't have done it without you."

A memory popped into Sam's mind. It was of their conversation when they were at dinner that night in New York. She'd told him how she envied the hosts on the cooking shows because it looked like they were having so much fun cooking together.

Maybe someday, she'd wistfully said.

Damn.... Why didn't you remember this? You could've surprised her, arranged something like this before now.

"I would love to get all domestic with you in the kitchen. And you owe me nothing. You never will."

She was laughing, the sound carrying over in her voice. "*Hmm...* domestic, huh? I don't know about that. Just a warning here... like dancing, kitchen skills tend to elude me. So, you need to be prepared."

He chuckled. "Okay. But I'm not worried. If it doesn't turn out, which I'm sure it will, I know we'll be able to find something else to keep us occupied. As long as I'm with you, I'll be happy."

She gave a long sigh. "Oh Sam, what would I do without you? I really do love you. So much, I do."

Sam closed his eyes, all of the worry clouding his mind over the past few day? Poof! It was gone, just like that. The Livy he knew and loved was back in his life.

Momentarily overcome, he had to clear his throat. Even then, his voice came out gruff and a little shaky.

"I love you, too. So, what time should I expect you?"

"I'll be there around seven."

He smiled. "Okay, seven it is. And Livy?"

"Yes?"

"Wear something for dancing. Even though we're not planning to go out, doesn't mean we can't dance. Until seven, then."

Livy was left staring down at her blank phone.

Wear something for dancing?

She definitely needed to text Carrie. To ask her if she could borrow something to wear.

Something sexy...

She was humming as she headed for the shower.

It felt like maybe, just maybe, her world was finally starting to settle into place.

A good place....

Hardly daring to breathe, Valerie was leaning against the wall outside of Sam's office and hidden out of sight. This had enabled her to hear his entire phone call with Livy.

Thank God his secretary was out of the office.

From what she could make out from Sam's side of the conversation, Livy was coming over to his condo tonight to make dinner for him.

She frowned. She didn't do dinner. This is what restaurants were for. Her theory on this? By having someone else prepare the meals, she was helping them out, providing them with a job.

Makes sense, right?

But... *domestic?* He wanted to get domestic with her? What was all this about? To her, this sounded like a sign that whatever was going on between Sam and Livy? It was getting serious.

Too serious...

This was irritating the hell out of her. It was also completely screwing up her plans. As far as she was concerned, she was the woman for Sam. The two of them would be perfect together.

He only had one fault that she knew of, and this was he was too nice. Way too nice. He needed to tone down this nice guy act he had going on and become more aggressive. More sure of himself. If he didn't, he was never going to reach the level of success she envisioned for him.

But even with this one defect, she still believed they could be the ideal couple. But in order for this to happen, he needed to drop this Livy.

She glanced down at the contract she held in her hand. The closing of the sale had been contingent on Sam taking on the restoration work of the existing house. And now that she had Sam's approval on the work orders this entailed, she only had to get the buyer's signature.

And... *Voila...* it would be a done deal.

She had big expectations for this particular sale. She'd already managed to obtain the promise of the local newspaper to feature her and Sam in their Sunday home and garden section. If they were lucky, it would garner the attention of the associated press, throwing them right into the limelight. Something that was well deserved, she'd have to say.

This would then lead to the next obvious step. They'd become partners, this snowballing on to even bigger and better things. Maybe even their own TV show.

Yes, she had it all planned out in her mind. Now she only had to get it going in real life.

She tilted her head, listening. There was only silence. That meant Sam must have ended the call. At any minute, he could walk out of his office to find her still here.

And, she had absolutely no idea how she'd be able to explain this.

Silently tiptoeing her way over to the door, she opened it as quietly as she could and slipped outside. Knowing her time was limited, she almost ran to her car. Not an easy thing to do in her four-inch heels.

She sent a determined smile at herself in the rearview mirror.

There would be no dancing for Sam and Livy tonight.

Not if she had her way.

Sam neither heard, or saw Valerie leave. Still sitting at his desk, he was fingering Livy's hair tie. Silly as this may seem, he'd begun to think of the tie as his good luck charm. Always in his pocket, it had become his own special version of a rabbit's foot.

He was thinking about Livy... about the next step he'd already begun to take in their relationship.

The permanent step.

And for the first time, he was confident his plan was a good one.

A *really* good one.

He gave a long stretch. A big smile on his face he went back to studying the computer layout of the Shaker house.

Understandably, he was having a hard time concentrating.

CHAPTER 30

After coming to an almost screeching halt in front of Sam's condo, Valerie put her Land Rover in park and shut off the ignition. A quick glance in the rearview mirror showed her lipstick was still intact.

She glanced down at her Cartier watch to see it was six-forty-one. She peered more closely at the watch. Carefully wiping at a smudge on the face, she was relieved to see it wasn't a scratch. She had treated herself, buying the watch after she reached her first quarter sales goal. Even now, gazing down at the watch, there was a satisfied smile on her face.

The loud roar of a motorcycle passing through the parking lot made her jump, her head jerking up. She groaned.

What are you doing? Stop fussing over the watch. You need to hurry.

Becoming flustered, not at a reaction she was familiar with, she took a deep breath. First things first... she needed to get out of her car.

In order to do this, she had to slide across the seat while holding onto the car door. This was because the skirt she chose to wear was so tight, even a simple movement such as this was almost impossible to pull off.

She had deliberated very carefully about what to wear, finally settling on the short faux snakeskin skirt and an almost transparent, low-cut ruffled v neck silk blouse. She had picked this particular outfit because the ruffles hinted at her feminine side, while the snakeskin print gave off a sexy vibe, showing off the voluptuous curves she worked at so hard to maintain. Her hope was, these two things, along with her black peep-toe stilettos, would make Sam realize just how desirable she was.

After she grabbed the bottle of wine and two wine glasses from the front seat, she made her way to the front door of his condo.

A quick glance down at her watch showed it was now six-forty-four.

She was frowning as she hit the doorbell. She knew she needed to pace herself very carefully. As she impatiently waited for Sam to open the door, she tossed her head to give her hair a fuller, sexier look.

She cleared her throat and pasted a bright smile on her face.

She was ready.

Valerie was the last person Sam expected to see when he opened the door.

Let's just say he was surprised, disappointed and irritated. All rolled into one.

What the hell is she doing here? Did she tell you she'd be stopping by?

Dragging his hand slowly through his hair, he eyed her warily..

Flashing a huge smile and catching him completely by surprise, she reached up to plant a firm kiss to the corner of his mouth. Satisfied with the vivid lipstick smear she'd left behind, she waved the wine bottle at him as she slipped past him and into his condo.

"It's time to celebrate, darling!"

Sam didn't move. Finally shaking his head, he closed the door. His hands jammed in his pockets, he nervously watched as she walked over to the kitchen and began searching through the cabinet drawers.

She sent him another big smile. "My goodness, Sam... there's no order whatsoever to these drawers. Just as I've suspected all along...

you need a woman to bring some order into your life. Where do you keep your corkscrew?"

Without thinking, he pointed to one of the drawers. He watched as she pulled out the corkscrew, to then flash another big smile at him.

Then he groaned.

Damn... you should've told her you didn't have one.

Now mad at himself and becoming even more confused as to why she was in his condo, he ran his hand over his jaw. "Can I ask what you're doing here? And what's with the wine?"

She sent him a coy look. "Like I said, we have a lot to celebrate."

She yanked the cork out of bottle and tossed it over to him. "Here you go, darling, a souvenir. For what I'd like to think of as the beginning of us."

Darling? Beginning of us?

This is when a flicker of unease started up inside of him.

He nervously watched as she poured out the wine and made her way over to him, handing him one of the glasses. Her smile was huge as she tipped her glass to his in a toast. "To us, Sam. The buyers accepted the terms of the contract. Admit it... together, we make a great team. In more ways than one."

He'd had enough.

You want her the hell out of your condo.

Even though he was growing more irritated by the second, he very slowly set his glass down on the table. He cleared his throat. "That's great they agreed to the contract. It should be an interesting project, But, what exactly are you trying to say with this beginning of us? I'm confused."

And yes, he truly was baffled. Otherwise, he would've already escorted her out the door.

Instead, he watched as she moved closer, still holding her wine glass. "Sam, you have to see what a great team we are, not only in business, but also on the personal level. We complement each other. Together, we could be the new upcoming and most admired power couple to ever hit the city of Cleveland."

She took a sip of her wine, sending him a flirty glance over the rim of her glass. "In fact, I've got exciting news. I've already been able to arrange for the local news to put together a story on us. This could be the beginning of our move to the top." Moving closer, she was now only inches away.

Between the cloying scent of her perfume and the fact she was standing so close to him, Sam began to feel claustrophobic. He stepped back, impulsively throwing up his hand to ward her off.

Not a good move.

His hand hit her wine glass, sending wine splashing down the front of her blouse.

She shrieked. "Oh my God, what did you do? I just bought this blouse."

She set her wine glass next to his and frantically began wiping at her blouse with her hands. "What the hell was I thinking, bringing red wine?" She glared at him."Where is your bathroom? I need to get this out before it stains."

He pointed to the bathroom. He thought of apologizing, but her furious expression had him vetoing that possibility.

After she stormed off, leaving him to cringe at the loud slam of the bathroom door, he glanced at his watch to see it was almost seven.

Damn... you need to get her out of here before Livy comes. You need to get her out of here... period.

Grabbing the wine glasses, he headed for the kitchen.

As if on cue, the doorbell rang.

Double damn... this was not good... not good at all.

Even though Sam's mechanic had done the best he could with Livy's car, he'd been quick to inform her there was no promise something else wouldn't go wrong.

The car was old, he'd reminded her. So, she couldn't expect it to last forever.

And proof of this, it was now making a strange noise. She'd noticed this when backing out of her Aunt Evelyn's driveway after delivering her groceries.

For a brief moment, she'd considered taking her aunt's car, but decided against this. She certainly couldn't leave her with a car that might not start. Not when she wasn't feeling well.

She had spent more time with her aunt than she'd planned. Aunt Evelyn wasn't one to handle illness very well and she'd been in a very sour mood. After being forced to listen to a long lecture on the lack of responsibility of the current generation, Livy almost ran to her car when she was finally able to make her getaway.

The further she drove, the louder the noise. At least there wasn't any smoke coming from under the hood like the day she drove home from New York. At least, not yet, there wasn't.

She finally pulled into the parking lot of Sam's condo. Since there was a Land Rover parked in his guest parking space, she had to park a good distance away. Vaguely wondering whose it was, she grabbed the grocery bag from the back seat of the car and headed for Sam's condo.

Little did she know what was waiting for her when she rang the doorbell. If she had, she could have turned around and left.

This would have saved her and Sam a lot of heartache.

Sam looked down at the wine glasses in his hand.

Then he glanced over at the door. Finally setting the glasses back on the table, he went over to answer the door.

If there was such a thing as a flustered Sam, this was definitely what was happening at the moment. A woman hidden in his bathroom and another woman at his front door? He didn't even know where to begin.

Livy was gazing back at her car when he opened the car. She shook her head. "I have a feeling my car died for good this time."

She turned to Sam, the start of a smile on her face. "You may be stuck with…" Her smile had disappeared, her words coming to a halt.

Sam leaned in, his intention to give her a kiss, but she ducked, backing away from him. He had no clue this was because of the telltale lipstick smear Valerie had left on his face.

Serious warning bells were going off in Livy's head as she pushed past Sam to enter his condo. After she placed the grocery bag on the island countertop, she gazed slowly around the room. This is when she saw the wine glasses, one with a lipstick print, the same color as the print on Sam's face.

Visibly upset, she turned to him. "Sam, what's going on? Who's here?"

Sam made the mistake of glancing over at the bathroom, to then look back at Livy, an expression of complete panic on his face. Again, his reaction was because he'd never been in this kind of situation before. Things like this just didn't happen to him.

The only thing he knew to do, was tell Livy the truth.

He nervously cleared his throat. "It's Valerie. She came over because she wanted to celebrate a sale we worked on together. She brought wine and well, things..."

And this was when Valerie made her dramatic entrance into the room.

Valerie was aware that Livy had arrived.

Smiling at her reflection in the mirror, she made one last dab at her blouse. Not only had she been able to wipe away the stain, it looked as if everything was moving along just as she'd planned.

She unbuttoned the top three buttons of her blouse and after pulling half of it from the waistband of her skirt, she ran her hands through her hair, roughing it up. She blurred her lipstick with her finger, gave one last look in the mirror and walked out of the bathroom.

Livy and Sam watched, almost in fascination, as she came into the room. She didn't look up as she began to talk, her fingers working at the buttons on her blouse. "*Wow*, Sam... I wanted to celebrate, but never did I think this would happen. You've more than met my expectations, darling."

This is when she finally glanced up, a look of surprise on her face. Her hand going to her mouth, her glance slid over to Livy, then to Sam. "Oh, my goodness. I had no idea you were expecting someone."

She smiled gaily over at Livy. "Are you and Sam working on a project of some kind? If so, don't worry. I was just leaving. I've already got more than I bargained for, as it is ."

This was accompanied by a wink over at Sam.

Grabbing her keys from the counter, she blew Sam a kiss. "Bye, darling… I'll call you later so we can discuss our next move."

She paused to give him a long assessing look after she opened the door. "You really are amazing. Little did I realize what you have going on behind that nice guy image of yours."

She blew him one last kiss and with a wave to Livy, she was gone.

For what felt like an eternity, neither Sam or Livy spoke.

When Sam thought about it later, he realized he'd made a huge mistake. He should've jumped in to reassure Livy that what she'd seen wasn't at all what she thought. But he hadn't. So, in Livy's eyes, this made him look guilty.

It was only when Livy turned and started for the door, he came to life and took off after her.

He groaned. "Livy… wait. Let me explain."

She whirled around, her face livid with anger. "No, I don't want to hear it. There is nothing to explain. I never should've have listened to everyone when they said you were such a nice guy."

Her hand went to her mouth. "Oh my God… it's just like Valerie said. I don't need any more proof than that, do I?"

Tears pooling in her eyes, she kept shaking her head. "They were all wrong, weren't they? And I was a fool to believe them. Or even more of a fool to believe you. And to think I trusted you."

And the tears flowed. "*Oh my God*, Sam… how could you?"

He began to move closer, only to stop when she backed away. He groaned, running his hand through his hair. "Livy, don't say something you don't believe. Please listen to me… nothing happened with Valerie. *Nothing.* I had no idea she was coming here. And if I had, I never would've answered the door."

He shrugged. " I thought it was you."

"Evidently, you must think I'm stupid if you expect me to believe that. I saw how she looked." Her fists clenched to her sides, she closed her eyes, a sob rising in her throat. "I can't believe you said all the things you said to me, to then turn around to be with her. This is Zack all over again. I thought with you, it would be different. But now I see I was wrong. Maybe everything happened too fast. Or maybe I wasn't ready. But now? None of this matters anymore, because for you, it appears I'm not enough."

Her hand suddenly went to her mouth. "*Oh, no*... the baby. What about all those things you said about the baby? Please don't tell me that those were all lies, too?"

He had no idea why the next words came out of his mouth. This was something he shouldn't have been thinking, let alone say out loud. But he did, making everything worse.

A lot worse.

"What happened here has nothing to do with the baby. But if you must know, that you were pregnant with Zack's baby was not the easiest thing for me to accept. *My God*, Livy... I felt like I was suddenly living some kind of country music song, sleeping with a woman who was pregnant by her ex-boyfriend. I didn't know how the hell to react."

This, of course, made her furious. "You think it was hard for you? What about me? I still can't stop thinking it was something we did that caused me to lose the baby."

His gave he a sharp glance. "What do you mean by we?"

"Like you just so eloquently stated, we slept together."

His look was one of disbelief. "You think we're the ones at fault... you truly think this?" He shook his head. "I don't know what to say. Don't you remember what the doctor said? The loss of the baby was through no fault of yours."

This was when he suddenly understood what she was trying to say. "*Ah...* so I see. You're going to put all the blame on me."

She shrugged, refusing to meet his gaze. "I don't know what to think. Or what to believe anymore."

He groaned. "Livy, I really don't know what to say, except you're wrong. But if you want to blame me for what happened... fine, do that. But don't even think I didn't care, because I did. I'd already begun to think of us as a family, if only because the child was a part of you. I don't know what else I can say to prove this to you."

Both breathing hard, a charged silence stretched between them.

The first to speak, Livy's voice was barely audible. "I got a job offer from a publishing company in Chicago. It's a good job. I think it might be best if I accept. Because I can't stay. I can't do this again. I can't."

This was when Sam lost it. Only because he couldn't believe she was giving up on them so easily. He didn't understand. Wasn't this what love was all about? Working things out? Weathering the storm? If so, this had to mean Livy couldn't love him as much as he loved her. And this made him angry

Massaging the back of his neck, he gave a frustrated sigh. "Fine. If this is the way you feel, then go ahead, take the job. Because I'm at a loss here. Evidently there is nothing I can say to persuade you to change your mind. But if you think running away to Chicago is going to make everything better, you're wrong."

Her hands clenching at her sides, she glared at him. "I am *not* running away."

He shook his head. "That's exactly what you're doing. When things get tough you run. You ran from Zack and New York. And now you're going to run, not only from me, but all of the family and friends who love you. I only hope to God you find what you're looking for."

He nodded, as if to reassure himself. "Where I can at least live with myself, knowing I tried to make this work." Turning to pick up the wine glasses and the half empty bottle of wine, he emptied the wine into the sink. Little did Livy know how hard it was for him to turn his back on her.

But he was mad.

He also hoped she'd think about what he said. Enough to come back with enough of a response that would make him want to turn back to her.

Preferably, this would be along the lines that she still loved him. She didn't even have to say those exact words. Or in that order.

Right now?

He'd take just about anything.

Unfortunately, Livy wasn't thinking at all. By turning his back to her, Livy was convinced Sam had written her off. And this was the one fear she'd been carrying around with her ever since the beginning.

She yanked open the front door. But then she turned to him. There was one more thing she needed to say. She knew it was childish, but at the moment, it was all she had.

"A knight in shining armor? *Ha*, I guess that was all fake, too. And now that I know this, I never want to see you again. Not in a million years."

She left, slamming the door behind her.

Livy shut the door to her car... hard. So hard, it made the whole car shake.

Shaking to the point she almost couldn't put the key in the ignition, she finally managed to start up the car. Only to have it quit on her. After three times of this, it refused to start at all.

She dropped her forehead to the steering wheel and began to cry—great big, gulping sobs.

So, when the car door opened, she didn't even look up.

Please, please don't let it be Sam...

Unfortunately, that's who it was, the sound of his voice making her cry even harder. "Livy, come on. You can't stay here. I won't let you."

She shook her head.

He sighed. "Baby, come on..."

Her head shot up. "Don't call me that. I'm not your baby."

Once more he sighed, gently taking hold of her arm. "I'm not going to let you sit out here in your car all night. And I'm not going to let you drive. Not in the state you're in. Come on, let me take you home. You won't have to talk or even look at me if you don't want to."

After a long, tense moment, she finally nodded.

Since she really didn't have much of a choice, did she?

Once they were in Sam's SUV, the tension between them was almost suffocating.

Livy couldn't stop crying. While Sam was reluctant to say anything, afraid if he did, it would escalate into another argument. Too many things had already been said that he wished could be forgotten.

When he pulled into the driveway of Carrie's house, Livy opened her door to get out almost before they came to a stop.

He reached out to grab her arm. "*Whoa...* are you in so much of a hurry to get away from me, you'd jump from a moving vehicle?"

When she merely shook her head, he groaned. "Livy, *come on.* You're overreacting. Why can't you try to be logical about this?"

Oh boy.... Bad move here. Really not the best thing to say.

So he tried to smooth things over. "What I meant is…

Livy shook off his arm, cutting him off. "I'm not overreacting. And there is nothing logical about what happened. I found you with Valerie and it was quite obvious what went on between the two of you. So, there's nothing more to say, except we're done, it's over."

In her agitated state, she couldn't even unclasp her seatbelt, he had to unbuckle it for her. This is when she finally glanced over at him. "Remember when you asked me why I agreed to go to dinner with you and I told you it was because I believed in second chances? Well, you've had your second chance. And you goofed it up. Big time."

She stepped out of the SUV, only to turn back to him, tugging at the promise ring on her finger. Resisting the urge to throw it, she slapped it down on the passenger seat. "Here, this no longer holds true for us, does it? But once I'm gone, you can give it to Valerie."

Dragging his hand through his hair, he stared at her in disbelief. "You can't mean you're planning to go through with this Chicago offer? You really plan to leave?"

"I guess that's something else you don't remember." She watched as he closed his eyes at this. "You said she could expect big things from me in the future. At the time, I didn't think it would be in Chicago, but maybe this is a sign."

She slipped out of the SUV and without another glance, she left, leaving him staring after her.

Sam sat in his SUV for a long time, holding the ring in his hand. It was only when he saw the lights go off, all of the windows finally going completely dark, he slipped the ring into his pocket.

His fingers coming in contact with Livy's hair tie, he leaned his head back against the headrest, closing his eyes.

So... just like that, it's over?

Wearily starting up his SUV, he drove to the main road. For a long moment, he couldn't remember which way to turn. Because, honestly? He was still in shock.

And to think he had believed what he and Livy had was for real.

When Sam walked into to his condo, the first thing that caught his eye was the bag of groceries Livy left on the counter. For one insane moment, he actually thought of getting back in his car and delivering them to her. If only to have one more chance to explain… to make things right.

He sighed, rubbing the back of his neck. There was no way she would even answer the door.

He picked up the bag, his intention to put it in the refrigerator, bag and all. It was when he was trying to fit it on the shelf, he recognized the box tucked on top.

It was one of Abby's, the Sweet Abby's logo on the box. There was a note tucked under the string tied around the box.

Sam, since this was so spur of the moment, I didn't have time to make you chocolate chip cookies—these are from Sweet Abby's. Next time I'll make them from scratch to show you how much I love you. Love, Livy

His hands gripped the edge of the counter, the kitchen blurring around him. Never had he felt such misery—it was as if the world he'd trusted was slipping through his fingers.

He also hadn't bargained for this heartache; every plan he'd made had been meant to be shared with her.

But now he stood alone.

CHAPTER 31

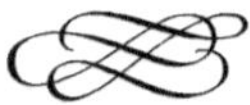

*B*lurry-eyed, Livy was sitting at the kitchen island, her mood matching the dreary view she had outside the window.

It had stormed all night and now it was still raining, the wind whipping up the leaves in a frenzy, plastering them up against the window.

Even though her hands were wrapped around her cup of hot coffee, she was cold... so cold. She felt physically and mentally exhausted. If she didn't know any better, she'd swear she was hungover.

In a way, you are. Hungover from another failed relationship.

She'd spent a miserable night, trying to avoid the empty space next to her. If she'd even slept an hour, she'd be surprised. Most of the night was spent staring wide-eyed into the darkness, her mind going over... and then over again, what happened.

And it still didn't make sense. Nothing made sense to her anymore.

How could Sam have done something like this?

She picked up her phone to see Sophie hadn't responded to the text she'd sent only minutes ago. This had been in response to Sophie's earlier text, reminding her about the barbecue she and Chester were throwing for their friends and the baseball team. This would be three days from now. Sophie had ended the email with the reminder Sam was also invited.

Livy had spent a lot of time thinking about how she should answer this, finally deciding on the truth. She re-read what she'd sent.

> Thanks for the invite. Maybe I'll stop by for a bit, if only to visit with my favorite nephews. Sam and I have decided to call it quits. So, I can't answer for him.

It hurt to even read the words.

Much more than it should.

She glanced over at her computer and the newest email she'd received from Elliot... Elliot Green. She'd begun to think of him as her new friend.

Elliot was the person in charge of arranging her interview with the publishing company in Chicago. He'd called her this morning, only minutes after she sent an email to let him know she was interested in learning more about the position.

She only had to say the word and they would get the ball rolling. They'd arrange everything... her flight, hotel and interview. If possible, they'd like to do this within the next couple of days.

It was when he asked if she'd like him to set up an appointment with a local realtor to check out her housing options, she found she suddenly couldn't breathe, her heart responding by beating in a panic.

Feigning another call, she'd told him she'd call him back later. After she ended the call, she hadn't moved for the longest time, waiting for her heartbeat to return to normal.

Everything was moving so fast... too fast.

Is this what you really want? Are you sure?

She only knew if she stayed in Cleveland, she wouldn't be able to face anyone. Not after they'd all welcomed her so warmly. They'd expect an explanation of what happened between her and Sam. An explanation that could possibly hurt the close friendships they all shared.

See? You're not running away like Sam said you are... you're only trying to make things easier for everyone.

She closed her computer and curled up in the corner of the sofa with Jingles. She was going to close her eyes for a few minutes, maybe even take a nap. Then she wouldn't be able to think. Later, she would visit her aunt to see if she was feeling better. Or if she needed anything.

This was when she remembered she didn't have her car.

She sighed. She'd worry about that later.

After Sophie finished loading the dishwasher, she picked up her phone from the kitchen counter to see there was a text from Livy.

She smiled. Hopefully it would be a yes to the barbecue on Sunday night.

She read the text... then she read it again, her brow furrowing in concern.

Livy and Sam had called it quits? This didn't make any sense. Absolutely no sense at all.

She wondered what Chester would have to say about this.

She went upstairs to the nursery, where she found Chester sitting on the rug with Trevor and Hudson. For a few seconds, she watched them, smiling at the antics of the babies, who were crawling all over Chester, trying to get at the foam baseball he kept tossing up into the air.

Chester was laughing when he glanced over to see her watching them. Pulling both babies onto his lap, he pointed over at her. "Look, guys... mommy's here."

As Trevor and Hudson began crawling towards her, she scooped them up and sat next to Chester. She handed him the phone. "Read this text from Livy and tell me what you think. It was in answer to the text I sent as a reminder about the barbecue."

After reading the text, he gave her a puzzled look. "What? They broke up? What the hell?"

Sophie clamped her hand over his mouth. "Chester! Seriously? Have you been listening at all to what I've been telling you? You know how I..."

Her words were swallowed up in the kiss he gave her. When she finally opened her eyes, it was to his grin. "Sorry, it was the only way I could get you to stop yelling at me."

She frowned. "I wasn't yelling. I was merely giving you another reminder."

He was reading Livy's text again. He shrugged. "*Hmm...* if you say so. But getting back to this thing about Livy and Sam, I'd have to say I'm clueless. Absolutely clueless."

This was when he saw the determined look on her face.

Uh, oh... He knew that look. Squeezing his eyes shut, he waited...

"You have to go talk to them, both of them. Now, before they do something stupid."

Slowly opening his eyes, Chester stared at her. "You want me to talk to them? Me? You think I can straighten them out?"

He was shaking his head as he grabbed Trevor, who was trying to crawl off the rug. "I don't think I'm the right person to do this."

Sophie didn't agree. "Chester, you have to do this. Remember what happened to us? How we almost broke up because of something stupid? We can't let this happen to Sam and Livy."

When he saw she was on the verge of tears about this, he glanced down at his watch. Then he looked at her tragic expression.

He sighed. "Okay, I have a couple of hours before I have to get to the ballpark. I guess I'll trek on over to Sam's office. Then, depending on what happens there, I'll stop in to see Livy. I've been planning to go see her, if only to make sure she's okay after what happened."

At her raised eyebrow, a guilty look came over his face. "I was, honest. I wanted to give her time to recover."

When she continued to give him that look, he finally gave her a sheepish grin. "Okay, I was putting it off. You know how I hate all of this emotional stuff. So, I guess now would be just as good a time as any."

Sophie leaned over to give him a big kiss, Hudson squirming between them. "You're the best. And since you're being so good about this, I'll return the favor. Whatever your heart desires."

The gleam in his eyes, letting her know he was already thinking about her promise, sent a shiver through her.

He gave her another kiss. "Angel, you've got a deal."

Chester pulled into a parking space in front of Sam's office building. He entered to the sound of Sam talking on his phone. Tentatively poking his head around the corner of the door to his office, he was just in time to see Sam throw the phone down on the desk. After leaning back in his chair, he closed his eyes, giving a long groan.

"Damn... damn... damn..."

Not quite sure what to do, Chester gave a tentative knock.

Sam's head shot up, his gaze zeroing in on Chester. He groaned again. "If you came here to confront me about Valerie, it's not true. Nothing happened. Nothing ever will. No matter what Livy told you."

Chester had no idea what he was talking about, why he brought up Valerie. What he did know, Sam was a mess. Everything about him... his hair, his clothes and his face... they all looked like they belonged to a man who'd gone through a major storm of some kind.

Chester knew this look. He'd been there, done that. And now it was up to him to figure out why Sam was in the same boat.

He pulled a chair up to Sam's desk and looked him directly in the eye. "Before you say anything, I want you to know I'm not here to judge you or Livy. Sophie sent me. She received a text from Livy that said the two of you decided to call it quits."

Closing his eyes, Sam nodded. "Yep, that about says it all. At least as far as Livy is concerned. Believe me, this wasn't something I wanted to happen."

Clasping his hands behind his neck, Chester leaned back in his chair. "So, tell me why it did. I've got time."

For a few moments, Sam didn't say anything, concentrating on something he was twisting in his hand.

Chester peered more closely… what the hell was it? It looked like one of those rubber-band-thingies Sophie was always hunting for to pull her hair back in a ponytail. When Sam threw it down on the desk, Chester saw that's exactly what it was.

He sent Sam a puzzled look.

Sam shook his head. "Long story." He grimaced. "A long, sad story."

He then proceeded to tell Chester what happened. How Livy had walked into his apartment just in time to witness, what was probably the greatest act Valerie had ever put on in her life.

After he finished with a brief summary of the exchange of words he and Livy exchanged, all the way up until he drove her home, he slowly shook his head.

"I'm trying really hard to understand how she could actually think this is something I'd do to her. With Valerie, of all people? The whole situation is just so damn unbelievable."

He picked up the hair tie, twisting it around his finger. "I keep trying to put myself in her place to see if I can understand her point of view. But, I can't even go there, because like I said, it's just so damn crazy."

He threw the hair tie down on the desk again.

"Then, I started thinking maybe her reaction might be more in response to what happened with the baby. Since she's decided to blame both of us for the loss, in her mind, it would be better if we weren't together."

He gazed over at Chester, his expression bleak. "She told me she received a job offer from a publishing company in Chicago and if all goes well with the interview, she's planning to accept the job. So, as of right now, I don't know what more I can do."

A silence stretched out between them.

Since Chester wasn't saying anything, this made Sam think he didn't give Livy and him much of a chance

While Chester was wondering why in the hell he'd let Sophie talk him into having this conversation with Sam. Because, for some odd reason, he wasn't worried. Sam and Livy didn't need his help.

He wondered… maybe this was some of that woman's intuition Sophie was always talking about, rubbing off on him? Because he was totally confident everything was going to be fine.

Finally, Sam cleared his throat. "So, looks pretty hopeless, huh? I'm sorry. I know this must be difficult for you since Livy is your sister. So, go ahead, call me names or whatever. You can even punch me out if you want. I'm beginning to think this is what I deserve."

Chester shook his head. "No, can't do that. Don't want to do that. And do you know why? Because I have a feeling everything is going to work out between the two of you. But in order to have this happen, you need to talk to each other."

He shook his head. "Damn, I never thought these words would come out of my mouth, but here goes. The two of you need to share what you're feeling. Get everything out in the open."

He grinned. "God, you have no idea how proud Sophie would be to know I said this."

Sam actually chuckled. "I hope you're right. I'll do whatever it takes."

Chester nodded. "But for now, let things cool off a bit. Give yourself some time to calm down, think things through. After all, remember what they say? Absence makes the heart grow fonder."

Sam glanced down at his watch. "Well, since I have a flight I need to be on in a couple of hours, that will be easy to do."

At Chester's raised eyebrow, he nodded. "I am off to Quebec. They want an my recommendation on the newest project involving the property Carrie and I worked on last summer. This time it's the guesthouse."

He rubbed his forehead, a rueful smile on his face. "I impulsively made the flight reservations only a while ago. I felt like I needed to get away, think things through. I'm not sure how long I'll be there."

Chester stood, holding out his hand. "Well, don't be too long. In the meantime, I'll let Livy know where you are."

Their hands joined in a firm grasp, an unspoken message passed between them.

They had each other's back.

The insistent knocking is what woke Livy.

She hadn't intended to fall asleep for so long. Slowly sitting up, she gazed around the room. When the knocking started again, she stumbled over to the front door and peered through the peephole.

His hands shoved in his pockets, Chester was pacing back and forth on the porch, a serious look on his face.

Her eyes closed, she rested her forehead against the door.

Oh God, no... you don't want to talk to him. He's probably here to lecture you about the baby. You know you should've called him. And now, things are even more of a mess.

After combing her fingers through her hair, she opened the door.

Chester knew he didn't do a very good job of hiding his shock when Livy opened the door.

But come on, she was looking pretty ragged.

He thought Sam had looked pretty pitiful, but now confronted with Livy's deplorable state, he decided, if nothing else, they deserved each other.

For better or for worse, they would both definitely fall under the worse category.

Putting it mildly, Livy looked like hell. And he was being very generous with this assessment. Her hair was uncombed and tangled. There were huge dark circles under her eyes, this magnified by the glasses she was wearing. And the old tattered chenille bathrobe she was wearing looked like it had seen better days.

And this would be the better days of long, long ago.

His plan of how he was going to approach her no longer seemed feasible. This had been to come right out and tell her from now on, no matter what kind of situation she found herself in, she was to come to him for help. He'd planned to include Sam in on this, but after the last hour or so he'd spent with him, and what he now knew, he didn't think this would be a good idea.

Casually making his way over to the sofa, he patted the cushion next to him, indicating she should join him. Instead, she sat all the way at the other end of the sofa, perched almost on the edge of the cushion. Wrapping her arms around herself, she refused to look at him.

He cleared his throat. "So, how are you feeling? Are you okay?"

She merely shrugged, staring into the fireplace.

He sighed. "Livy, look at me." When she did, the expression on her face was so sad, he scooted closer. "Livy, I'm not here to lecture you. If anything, what happened has made me realize I need to apologize to you for being such a poor excuse for a brother. You should have been able to come to me for help... or for any reason at all. Like I told Sophie, we're family. We need to be there for each other. This is what families do."

Livy shook her head, her gaze returning to the fireplace. This was really all she could manage. She was afraid if she opened her mouth, she'd start to wail. There was no doubt in her mind this would scare Chester to death, possibly sending him running right out the front door.

Chester was starting to become frustrated. Couldn't she at least look at him? "I went to see Sam before I came here."

Her head jerking up, she stared over at him. "Sam? You were with Sam?"

Watching as a tear slowly began to trickle down her cheek, he reached over to hand her the tissue box setting on the coffee table. She'd been carrying this box around with her all morning. It was easier that way, with all the crying she did.

"Yes, Sam. He was on his way to the airport. I believe he said he was going to Quebec? Something related to the job he and Carrie worked on last summer?"

Livy closed her eyes, her words coming out in a moan. "Oh God... I forgot all about Quebec."

Well, that makes it easy, doesn't it? He'll be there. You're here. And there's nothing to be done. And maybe by the time he returns, you'll be gone.

Chester nodded. "Yeah, he said he didn't know how long he'd be gone. It all depended on how things go."

Livy stared down at the tissue box.

So, just like that, it could be over.

Chester cleared his throat. He didn't feel like he was getting anywhere with her. But he wasn't ready to give up yet, still determined to knock some sense into her. He came here on a mission and he wasn't going to leave until he finished the job.

"Can I ask you something?"

Pulling a tissue out of the box and blowing her nose, she nodded.

"Sam told me what happened. I don't understand. How could you even believe he'd do something like this? With this Valerie, of all people? Good God, Livy... the guy is in love with you. He looked like death when I saw him. He even started rambling on about the possibility of moving to Canada. Said he no longer had any reason to stay here." He shook his head. "He was making absolutely no sense at all."

She was shaking her head again.

She took out another tissue, only to wad it up in her hand. "I don't know what he told you, but all of the evidence was right there in the open." She briefly closed her eyes, a clear vision of a disheveled and what looked like, a thoroughly loved Valerie, flooding her mind.

A bitter smile touched her lips. "I know by now what the signs are when a man is cheating on you. Even though, after what I went through with Zack, you'd think I would've picked up on this before now."

Chester held her gaze. "Sam also said you blame both him and yourself for what happened, that you somehow caused the loss of the baby. I don't know your reasoning, but you have to put this completely out of your mind. Because it isn't true. I was there when the doctor told us this. These things happen for a reason, not because of something you did."

He'd moved until he was right next to her. He put his arm around her. "Livy, I can't tell you how sorry I am about the baby. I'm so thankful Sam was there with you. And don't even start thinking he's not upset about what happened. Because he is. He would have been a far better father than Zack would ever be. He would've loved the child as his own."

She remembered what Sam had told her… that he hoped the baby would be a girl. Just like her. Leaning her head against Chester's shoulder, darn if the tears didn't start up again.

She was barely able to get out what she wanted to say, what was breaking her heart the most. "But it doesn't matter anymore. The baby is gone. And now I've lost Sam, too. I've lost both of them."

Relieved they finally seemed to be making progress, Chester let her cry. When she finally grew quiet, he put his finger under her chin and lifted her face to his.

"I want you to look me in the eye and tell me you believe Sam cheated on you. Because I don't think you can. I don't know, maybe you were looking for some kind of flaw, unconsciously comparing him to Zack? Whatever it was, I know deep down inside, you know Sam loves you too much to ever want to hurt you."

She closed her eyes, shaking her head. "I don't know. I don't know what to think anymore."

Chester chuckled.

At Livy's puzzled expression, he smiled. "I'm thinking about how Sophie and I went through something similar, almost breaking up. Somehow, she got it in her head I was going to leave her and move on to someone else."

He shook his head. "Yeah, like that was going to happen. Women certainly weren't standing in line, vying for my attention. At least, not the kind of women I'd want to spend the rest of my life with. It took a hard hit ball, slamming into the side of my face and rendering me unconscious to finally knock some sense into the both of us."

He grinned. "After that, I married her as fast as I could. I didn't want to take the chance of losing her again."

Livy's smile was wistful. "I envy what you and Sophie have. I wanted so much to believe I'd found the same with Sam."

"From what I've witnessed when the two of you are together, I'm pretty sure you already have." Chester patted her knee before he hauled himself to his feet.

He was feeling quite satisfied with the way things had turned out, confident his job was finished. At least he'd sent Livy's thoughts heading in the right direction.

Sophie would be proud of the way he'd handled things. Maybe she'd been right after all, sending him to talk to Sam and Livy.

He smiled. "Yeah, the best thing that ever happened, was the day Sophie ran out into the middle of the road to rescue that puppy. Since then, she's gone on to rescue me many times."

He clasped his hands over his head in a long stretch before he dug his keys out of his pocket.

He looked over at Livy. "I guess what I'm trying to say, don't let your pride take over. Talk to Sam. Let him tell you exactly what happened. *Really* listen to what he has to say. I'm sure, between the two of you, a lot of heated words were exchanged. It happens… trust me, I know."

At her tentative nod, his smile was one of relief. "But now, I need to get going. I'm running late as it is. I wasn't sure if there'd be a game tonight. But the rain seems to have stopped."

She followed him to the door, where he turned to her. "Promise you'll think about what I said, okay?"

She nodded, her try at a smile, almost working. After he enveloped her in a big hug, she watched as he ran down the steps and out to his SUV.

As she made herself a cup of tea, she thought about what Chester said. And now, the only thing she wanted, was to talk to Sam. But in person, not over the phone. She wanted to be able to look into his eyes when he told her nothing happened between him and Valerie. She needed this. If only for her own sanity.

She opened her computer.

There was a new email from Elliot. He wanted to know if she was ready to finalize the arrangements for the interview and had she given any more thought to his suggestion of meeting with a realtor? If she could let him know as soon as possible, this would be great.

She couldn't do this.

Not now.

Not when everything was such a mess.

She dropped her head down on her arms and closed her eyes.

It was much later she finally got up the nerve to pick up her phone and hit Sam's number. It rang once before she received the message his number was unavailable.

So, even though she knew how he felt about texting, she typed her message.

> I wonder if we can talk. I tried to call you, but got the unavailable message. Call or text me. Any time.

When this also refused to send, a horrible thought crossed her mind.

Did he block you?

This made her mad. So mad, she tossed her phone on the counter and crossing her arms over her chest, she glared at it.

Fine. If this is the way he's going to act, then you don't need him.

With this lie echoing in her head, she headed for the stairs. This is when the roll of Lifesavers caught her eye. On the counter, she knew darn well, Chester had left it there. After warily eyeing the roll of candy for a few seconds, she picked it up and dropped it in her robe pocket.

Hey, she could use all the help she could get

But now she was going to go to bed.

She'd figure it all out tomorrow.

Sam tossed his bag on the bed. He would be the first to tell you there was nothing fun about traveling out of the country.

After a rocky flight, a long and stressful series of delays in customs and fighting for what seemed to be one of the few taxis available, he was now almost finding it hard to care about the deplorable state of his hotel room.

He cringed as yet another loud crack of thunder shook the building. Brought on by the long line of thunderstorms passing through the city, this also explained why he was soaked to the skin.

He was exhausted. And he was in a very bad mood.

The last place he wanted to be, was in this God forsaken hotel room. In what he now found was considered a less desirable part of Quebec.

Yes, he knew since his trip had been unplanned and unannounced, he was lucky to have even found a room. But how the hell was he to know it was the week of their annual film festival?

You could have checked this out before you left. Instead of jumping on the first flight you could get. You did exactly what you accused Livy of... you ran away.

To make things even worse, he was now minus his phone. It was only when he went to check into the hotel, he realized he'd left it behind when he went through customs. With the help of the hotel personnel, he'd contacted the border security department, only to be told the earliest they'd be able to get back to him would be tomorrow morning.

So, it was a disgruntled Sam who was sitting on the bed in his hotel room, flipping through what appeared to be a very limited number of TV stations. Five, to be exact.

It was also a Sam who was feeling very sorry for himself... still reeling from everything that happened with Livy. But at the same time, he was so damn tired, he was finding it even hard to care anymore.

He needed to get some sleep. After stripping out of his wet clothes, he called down to the front desk for a wake-up call. Without even pulling down the blankets, he stretched out on the bed and closed his eyes.

Thunderstorm and all... he was asleep within seconds.

CHAPTER 32

*S*am tried to pay attention to Lucy. For the past ten minutes she'd been rattling off far more detail than he wanted about the elaborate, faded drapes in the guest house bedroom. But she spoke so fast, hardly pausing to take a breath, that he was finding it hard to follow along.

Lucy was the only daughter of Eliza VanDoran, the outspoken and very opinionated head of the Friends of Quebec Historical Society. He hadn't known what to think when Eliza arrived at the guesthouse that morning, introduced him to Lucy, and informed him, with unmistakable authority that they would be working together on the project.

As a team, she'd said.

Lucky, lucky you...

Since then, Lucy hadn't shut up. Like her mother, she had a very vocal and commanding personality. Topped off with a very loud and annoying laugh. Already he could feel a headache looming, and he hadn't even spent more than an hour with her.

Was it his imagination, or did she keep inching closer to him as she talked? For what had to be the fourth time, he found he had to step back. When she quickly eliminated the space between them, he decided, no... he definitely wasn't imagining this.

What the hell? Is she putting the moves on you? This is the last thing you need right now. God knows, you're not in the mood.

The way he was feeling, about women in general, he was ready to write them off forever.

Every damn single one of them.

That is, except for Livy.

"Sam?"

He blinked. Lucy was searching his face, an expectant expression on hers. "So, what do you think? Should we go with the elegance of heavy silk or the versatility of the cotton duck?"

Elegance? Versatility?

Resisting the urge to say he really didn't give a damn, he wearily ran his hand through his hair before he flipped through the book of fabric samples set out on the table.

He paused, pointing to a sample. "This is a good fit. It was a very common option during the time this guest house was in use. In fact, we used something very similar to this in the main house."

He closed the book with a flourish and gave Lucy a bright smile. "Now that we've reached a decision on that, I think it's time we took a break. We can't do anything more until the paint expert gets here and that won't be until later this afternoon."

He glanced at his watch before exhaling a long breath. "In the meantime, I have a lot of emails I have to answer. And I'm sure you have some work to catch up with, too. So, let's plan on meeting back here at 2:30. I'll see you then."

Without waiting for an answer and trying not to feel guilty at the bewildered expression on Lucy's face, he headed for the door and slipped outside.

He *didn't* want to be here.

He *shouldn't* be here.

You want to go home.

When Sam arrived back at the hotel, he checked at the front desk to find his phone had been delivered to the hotel while he was out.

After going through what he thought was a lot of unnecessary proof of who he was, the phone was finally in his hand and he was on the way to his room

Once he was in his room, he decided to check out any messages he might have missed, only to find the phone was completely dead. Mumbling under his breath, he plugged it into the charger and taking out the sandwich he'd picked up on his way from the site, he plopped down into the chair to eat his solitary lunch.

Since your only other alternative would have been lunch with Lucy, you shouldn't be complaining.

It wasn't that Sam was full of himself, or unsocial. Again, he just wasn't in the mood. And after the restless night he had, or make that restless *nights*, he was in desperate need of a nap. Even a short one would do it for him.

He didn't even want to think of how little sleep he'd had since he last saw Livy.

The clock on the nightstand read one-forty-eight when Sam finally opened his eyes. Now feeling a little more awake, he decided to check his now charged phone. The first thing that popped out at him, were the four texts, two calls and just as many voicemails from Carrie. He did a quick run through of the texts.

> 10:56pm I just talked to Sophie. What's going on? Call me.

> 7:20am I tried to call Livy, but she's not answering. WHAT HAPPENED? Again, call me.

> 8:46am Livy still isn't answering. I'm getting worried.

> 11:22am What the hell did you do?

He stared down at the phone.

He didn't want to even think of what Carrie had to say in the voice mails.

You don't want to think at all. What you'd rather do, is go right back to sleep.

As he went to toss the phone down on the bed, it rang. Startled, he almost dropped it. He looked down to see it was Carrie.

Debating as to whether he really wanted to answer it, his conscience kicked in and he hit answer.

"Hey…"

"Sam? Thank God you finally answered. I had no idea what I'd do next if you didn't. What's going on? What happened? And why in the world are you in Quebec?"

"I wasn't answering because I didn't have my phone. Long story short, I left it at customs and just got it back."

He closed his eyes, giving a long sigh. "I really don't feel like talking about what happened. Let's just say it looks like Livy and I made a mistake and we're done. She thinks I'm someone I'm not and I can't get her to believe my side of the story. And why am I in Quebec? I guess because they wanted me here."

A bitter laugh came from him, almost like a bark. "At least someone wants me."

This was met by silence.

Thinking he may have been a little dramatic, Sam was the first to speak. "Are you still there?"

He could hear Carrie's long sigh. "Yes, I'm here. Sophie told me what happened with Valerie. Sam, come on… you know Zack hasn't done much for Livy's confidence, so how did you expect her to react to something like this? He cheated on her. Twice, he did this. So, she's not really big on the trust issue. But this doesn't mean you should give up on her. You need to talk this out."

Irritation setting in, Sam tried not to show his anger. "I know, talk, talk, talk… that seems to be the answer to everything, doesn't it? Chester already drilled that into me. You don't think I tried? Trust me when I say Livy wanted no part of talking, no matter if I did it until I was blue in the face. Her mind was already made up."

He could hear Carrie sigh. "Then it's up to you to stand firm, make the next move. But first, you need to come home. Forget about hiding away in Quebec. If you promise me you'll come home in time for Sophie and Chester's barbecue, I'll get Livy there so the two of you can talk."

What? Hiding away?

This made him a little mad. Coming to his feet, he started pacing the room. "I am not 'hiding away' as you just insinuated. I came here to work. And maybe do some thinking."

When she didn't respond to this, the memory of how he'd accused Livy of doing the same exact thing, was right there to remind him.

Face it… you're both running away. What does this say about the way you're handling this?

He sighed. "Okay, so maybe I am hiding… a little. But this is because I don't know what else to do."

Carrie sighed again, her voice softening. "Oh, Sam… it's going to be all right. Just promise me you'll come home."

Tension building in the back of his neck, he sank down on the edge of the bed.

Great, now you'll probably come down with a pounding headache. This is all you need.

He rubbed the back of his neck. "I'll try. After I get a feel of what needs to be done here. Fortunately, they don't seem to be in much of a hurry with this project. But I've run into a little problem with Eleanor. I think she's trying to push her daughter on me. Suddenly this Lucy and I are a team. She just graduated from college and I think Eleanor decided this would be a good starting job for her. There's two problems… she has a tendency to stand way too close and she never… never… shuts up."

Carrie started to laugh. "Wow, you seem to be the man every woman wants all of a sudden. What's your secret?"

He growled out his answer. "Believe me, there is no secret. There's only one woman I want in my life. How ironic is it, she turns out to be the one woman who doesn't want me?"

Carrie was still laughing. "I don't believe that for a second. About

Livy not wanting you, that is. I'll call her again. If she keeps refusing to answer, I'll talk to her when we get home on Saturday."

For the first time in the last twenty-four or so hours, Sam felt a sliver of hope. An actual smile on his face, he glanced over at the clock. "I need to get going. And you need to enjoy your honeymoon. You shouldn't be spending your time trying to fix the mess I made of my life. I'll let you know if I book an earlier flight. And Carrie? Thanks."

Carrie was smiling, too. "You're welcome. Let's just say this is my way of keeping you close. Maybe even as part of the family. I could very easily see you as my favorite brother-in-law."

Sam couldn't answer at first. When he finally did, Carrie could hear the emotion in his voice.

"Carrie, I can only hope…"

CHAPTER 33

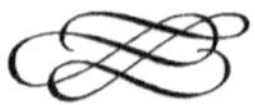

It's funny how someone can break your heart
and you still love them with all you have.
~ Anonymous

Livy glanced once more around Carrie and Chris's clean house. She had wanted to make sure it was as spotless as when she'd first arrived. The refrigerator was stocked with groceries and the pantry filled with treats. On the island countertop she'd left a bottle of wine and a box of Abby's assorted cookies.

She paused, wondering if Sam had found the chocolate-chip cookies and the note she'd slipped into the grocery bag she left at his condo—but then just as quickly, brushed the thought away.

And it really didn't matter anymore, did it?

Jingles came over to rub against her leg, giving a long meow. She picked up the fluffy cat, hugging her close.

"Oh Jingles, I'm going to miss you. I want to thank you for being such a good friend and listening to all of my problems." Setting the cat back on the floor, she watched as she went shooting up the stairs. Where Livy knew she would curl up right in the middle of Carrie and Chris's bed.

She picked up her keys and was about to leave when she heard a car door slam, followed by a second one.

Unable to do anything but wait, Livy watched Carrie walk into the kitchen.

She didn't look happy.

If anything, she looked mad.

Livy sent her a tentative smile.

"Hi… you're home early."

Carrie wasn't mad. Well, maybe she was… a little. But now, faced with Livy's forlorn and hopeless expression, she didn't know how she felt. The fact Livy had gone back to wearing her glasses wasn't helping matters.

She set her purse on the counter and picked up Jingles, who had come running back downstairs. Hugging the cat close, she nodded over at Livy. "Yeah… we were able to get an earlier flight."

She glanced around the room. "It looks so neat and clean." Her gaze falling on the bottle of wine and box of cookies, she sent Livy an inquiring glance.

Livy shrugged. "Those are from me. Sort of a welcome home treat."

Carrie smiled. "Thanks. I never even had a cookie at the reception. So, I can't wait to have one of these. But, I'll do that later. Right now, you and I need to talk."

Briefly closing her eyes, Livy sighed. "Carrie, *please*. You just got home. We can talk some other time."

Before Carrie could answer, Chris came in, loaded down with suitcases. After he set them next to the steps to the second floor, he made his way over to Livy and gave her a big hug. "Hey, if it isn't my favorite sister-in-law."

When Carrie rolled her eyes at this, he grinned "Carolyn's not here, so I can say this." After he glanced down at his watch, he gave Carrie a quick kiss on her cheek before heading for the door. "I know you two probably have a lot to talk about, so I'm going to make a quick trip to the office. Just to make sure all is well, since Sam's not around to take care of things."

As soon as he was gone, Carrie motioned for Livy to join her on the sofa. "Okay, tell me what happened."

So, Livy did. It was when she finished, she sighed. "I feel like everything changed after what happened with the baby."

Carrie reached over to hug her. "Chester told me about the baby. I'm so sorry. I can't even imagine how hard it was for you. He also told me Sam stayed with you the whole time."

"I don't know what I would've done without him." Livy swallowed, trying not to cry. "I... I tried to send him a text and a voicemail, asking if we could talk, but neither went through." She shrugged. "I don't know, maybe he blocked me."

Her bottom lip starting to tremble, she averted her gaze to stare at the fireplace.

You are not going to start crying again. You've cried way too much already. Stop talking about Sam... change the subject.

She took a deep breath. "I received a job offer from a great publishing company in Chicago. They want to set up an interview, but I don't know... I'm finding it really hard to make any kind of commitment right now."

Jingles had jumped into Carrie's lap. As she ran her hand through the cat's silky fur, she shook her head. "I don't think you are in the right frame of mind to start thinking of moving away and taking on a new job. You need to wait on the interview for a few days."

She shook her head, a wry smile on her face. "I'm beginning to think you and Sam deserve each other. You're both running away instead of trying to work things out."

She abruptly changed the subject. Because, who was she to talk? She ran away from Chris not only once, but twice. That they were now married, was a miracle in itself.

She sent Livy a bright smile. "You're planning on going to Sophie and Chester's barbecue tomorrow night, aren't you?"

"After everything that's happened, I don't really want to, but I promised Sophie I would. If only to help out with the babies."

"Good." Carrie nodded. "We'll pick you up at seven."

Livy began to protest, but Carrie, who was already on her way over to where the packages were stacked by the front door, pointed a finger at her. "Nope, no arguments. Seven it is."

She was smiling as she picked up one of the boxes, shaking it as she held it up to her ear.

She made a face at Livy. "Darn, I guess I should wait until Chris comes back to open these."

She grinned. "I love weddings. I can't wait until the next one. Even if it's not mine."

"How about you?"

CHAPTER 34

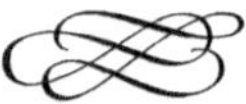

*E*ven though she'd arrived early, preparation for the barbecue was in high gear when Hannah walked into Sophie and Chester's kitchen.

Skirting around the two women chopping ingredients for the huge salad they were making, she made her way over to the refrigerator and retrieved the two baby bottles of milk Sophie had told her to get.

According to Sophie, the plan was to have both Trevor and Hudson fed and sound asleep in their cribs by seven-thirty. This would give them a few minutes to relax before everyone showed up for the barbecue around eight-ish.

Already this plan was way behind schedule. It was pushing eight, people were starting to arrive and both Trevor and Hudson were still wide awake.

Hannah had been busy since she arrived. But this hadn't stopped her from searching the guests gathered on the deck and around the backyard, hoping to see a certain guy wearing a black cowboy hat.

Yes… this would be Sean.

And, yes… she knew it was a risk on her part, but she couldn't help it… she was crazy about him.

She hadn't been able to stop thinking about him since they ran into each other at Café Latte and he'd asked her out to dinner. Reluctant to end the evening, they'd lingered at the restaurant until it closed. Sean had driven her back to the little coffee shop to pick up her car and ignoring her protests, he had insisted on following her home.

He was going to see her right to her door, he told her. This was just the way he did things.

After he'd walked her to her front door, he'd asked if she was going to be at the barbecue, casually throwing out the suggestion they go together. But she had to tell him, no, she'd already promised Sophie she'd come early to help with the babies. Undeterred, he persisted, asking if she'd at least consider spending time with him during the evening.

Consider?

Of course, she had said yes. How could she look into those eyes, with those to-die-for-eyelashes, and say no?

But she hadn't heard from him since. She hoped this didn't mean he wasn't going to show up.

Nah... it was still early yet. He'd be here, right?

As she started up the steps to the nursery, she was smiling.

In fact, she hadn't stopped smiling since she first saw him in Cafe Latte. This is what he did to her.

Now if only she could get him to kiss her.

Trevor and Hudson had been fed, rocked and were in their cribs, hopefully settled for the night

Hannah came back downstairs, relieved to see Sean had come as promised and was in the kitchen talking to Abby. And as with every other time she saw him, her heart did a little flip flop, a smile automatically spreading across her face.

Smoothing her hands down over the skirt of her blue flowered sundress, she slowly made her way over to them. From Abby's *ooohs* and *aaahs*, Hannah knew the photos he was showing her on his phone had to be those of his two-year old niece, Carly.

Lifting his head, Sean saw Hannah. Both his niece and Abby completely forgotten, he turned to her, a slow smile coming over his face. Slipping his phone in his pocket, he put his hand to the brim of his hat and tipped it to her.

Now granted, this wasn't something he'd normally do. But the smile she gave him when he did, made him decide he was going to do it from this moment on.

There was something about her smile that got to him. Every single time. It sent his mind running all over the place, leaving him unable to think of anything but her.

This was why he hadn't called her. With four games in the last three days, two of these part of a double header yesterday, all of his concentration needed to be focused on his pitching skills.

But now? He was ready to devote all of his attention to her. She had been the only thing on his mind since he'd left the ballpark.

For a few moments they studied each other, unaware that Abby, sensing this attraction between them, had silently slipped away.

It was Sean who made the first move. Impulsively, he reached over to run his fingers through her hair, to then tuck it behind her ear.

Again... it was like silk. This sent his imagination soaring, wondering what it would feel like to bury his hands in the shining curls before he tipped her face up to his for a kiss. A kiss exactly like he'd envisioned in his dreams.

He blinked.

Whoa...

This had his greeting coming out much huskier than he intended. "Hey darlin'... how are you?"

Completely flustered by his touch and the rough, almost sexy tone of his voice, she impulsively reached up to give him a quick kiss to his cheek. For some reason, this felt like the right thing to do.

"Hi... I wasn't sure if you were still going to come."

He groaned, grabbing her hands. "I'm sorry. The last three days have..."

Again, she did what any other woman would do in this situation.

At least, any woman who was lucky enough to have a man like

Sean Young gazing into their eyes. She reached up to give him another kiss, if only to stop his apology, this one hitting the corner of his mouth.

"It's okay. The only thing that matters, is that you're here."

For a moment, just as shocked as he was by her move, they stared at each other.

She was the first to speak. "So, are you hungry?"

Hungry? For her, yes.

Fortunately, this wasn't what he said.

Instead, he laughed, his hand going to the small of her back to pull her closer. "Yes, I'd have to say I am. There's nothing I like better than a good old-fashioned barbecue."

His gaze sweeping over her face, he gave her a slow smile. "But there's something I want to do first… or I swear, I'll go crazy."

He took her hand and pulling her into the small sitting room next to the kitchen, he slowly slid his hands through her hair, tipping her head back.

His gaze pulling her in, the huskiness of his voice had her breath hitching in her throat, her heart racing out of control. "I've been thinking about doing this ever since I first saw you at Chez and Sophie's wedding."

His head came down, his hat blocking her view of everything but him. Covering her mouth with his, the kiss he gave her traveled straight to her soul, taking her to a place she'd never been before. She found she was leaning into him, tightening her grip on his arms, in hope of prolonging the kiss.

She wanted it to go on… and on… and on.

Was there chemistry at work here?

Oh, yes… definitely.

He was the first to move, his hands drifting down her arms to link his fingers with hers.

He cleared his throat, his voice coming out even more seductively husky. "Sorry about my manners there. I really should've removed my hat for a kiss like that. This is what a true gentleman would do."

She surprised herself on how fast she answered, shaking her head as she pressed her fingers to his mouth. "No, I liked it. It felt like it was only you and me, with no one else around. It felt… well, it felt right."

Her smile slowly spread, reaching all the way to her eyes. "It was nice… good."

Pretty sure his smile now mirrored hers, he placed a soft kiss to her forehead. *"Ah…* Hannah Michaels, where have you been all of my life?"

He took her hand and began leading her out of the room.

"Just so you know, Darlin', I felt it, too. Now, let's go get something to eat.

He grinned. "When I'm happy, I'm hungry. And right now?"

He pulled her close in a hug. "I'm *really* hungry."

CHAPTER 35

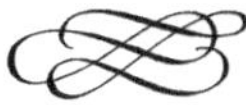

Sam would be the first to agree it was the perfect June evening.

The skies were clear, the temperature a perfect seventy-two degrees and there was only a slight breeze blowing off the lake.

This had to be a good omen, right?

Evidently everyone, who knew anyone, had been invited to the first annual summer barbecue at Sophie and Chester's new home. This explained why almost every inch of their front yard was occupied by parked cars.

After he pulled into what was probably the last available space, Sam remained where he was. He was trying to drum up the courage to get out of his SUV and make his way to the backyard of the house, where everyone was gathered.

He scrubbed his hand over his jaw. It had been a long week and he was exhausted.

His usual good mood was suffering from a lack of sleep. Add to this, the long delay before his flight even got off the ground and another slow-moving line through customs… and you can understand the current state of mind he was in.

When his flight had landed in Cleveland a little over an hour ago, he'd hoped a quick shower would revive him. And it had… for a while.

But now? He seriously didn't know if he had it in him to do this.

Well, you promised Carrie you'd be here, so don't even think about leaving.

He couldn't shake this nagging uncertainty he'd been carrying around with him the past few days, every possible scenario playing in his mind of what could happen when he finally did see Livy again. And now he couldn't stop thinking about what he was going to do if this evening didn't turn out like he hoped.

Hope is a mild word here. You need more of a prayer for something like this.

He thought of this as his last chance, a do or die situation. Sort of like one of his old high school football plays… fourth down and goal to go, with only seconds left in the game.

Yep… winner takes all. This is what you're going for… you want it all.

It was only when a man and woman strolled past his SUV, giving him a curious glance, he decided he'd stalled long enough.

He began the long walk towards the house.

Maybe it was because he was barely hanging on and in an almost a dream-like state. Or maybe it was because his mind was working overtime, but he suddenly felt like he was stepping right into the start of a film set.

Behind the house, the sky was a blaze of oranges and pinks, the sun, now a huge ball of fire, slowly sinking into the lake. Carried along with the breeze, the sound of laughter and music floated through the air around him.

For a few moments, he stopped to take it all in.

A smile hovered on his lips. Yeah, this would be the perfect setting for a movie. A love story of sorts. The part of the story where the plot could go either way. Depending on what kind of ending one chose.

Everything could suddenly go all wrong. Or so wonderfully right.

A wry smile on his face, he shook his head.

Now you're imagining you're one of the main characters in a love story? Man, you really are crazy.

What was it Livy had told him about romance novels?

Ah, yes… a small smile coming to his lips, the memory of how seriously she went about explaining this, coming to him so clearly.

According to her, the focus of a romance novel was on the relationship and romantic love between two people, always with an emotionally satisfying and optimistic ending.

In other words, all flowery words aside, no matter what obstacles come their way, the main characters always end up falling in love. To then go on to live happily ever after.

But what about him and Livy? What if this wasn't their kind of story?

He frowned.

Come on, you've always been the optimistic-just-take-a-deep-breath-and-be-patient kind of guy. You can't start thinking like this now.

Nope… this wasn't going to happen.

He was going to fix this.

He walked around to the back of the house, his gaze traveling over the large crowd.

There were people everywhere, in groups scattered here and there, on the lawn and up on the deck.

But there was no Livy.

No… Livy was nowhere to be seen.

He was sure of this. If she had been, he would've known right away. He could still remember the exact moment and how it had come almost as a shock to him, when he realized he could always sense when she was near.

Shaking his head, he smiled. This is what she'd done to him. She'd managed to become a significant part of him. As necessary to him as his next breath.

Unfortunately, this had also been the day she came to the Shaker site, looking for him.

To tell him the news that would rock their world.

"Sam!"

He glanced over to see this was coming from Carrie. Waving frantically, she was making her way towards him, dragging a willing Chris with her.

He grinned. "Well, if it isn't the new Mr. and Mrs. Gardner. How was the honeymoon?"

Carrie gave him a big hug. "It was wonderful." She sent a teasing grin over at Chris. "I do believe I picked the perfect husband."

After he gave Sam a quick hug, Chris returned Carrie's grin. "Something I've been trying to convince you of all along. Let's hope you'll still be saying the same thing fifty years from now."

This earned Chris a kiss on his cheek.

A pang of jealousy flitted through Sam, to just as quickly disappear, replaced with a sudden longing for the same. He wanted a love like they had.

No... with Livy it would be even better.

He sent another casual glance over at the deck. Just to be sure.

Carrie picked up on this right away. She grinned. "She's not there." At the quick look of disappointment on his face, her grin became even bigger.

Chris took pity on him. "What Carrie is trying to say, Livy's not outside. She's in the house. According to the baby monitor, one of the babies, I believe it was Trevor, was awake and fussing. Livy volunteered to go check it out."

Fighting the urge to take off running into the house, Sam jammed his hands in his pockets. But the smile coming over his face? He couldn't stop that for the life of him. If only because he was so damn relieved. This was the one thing he'd been the most worried about, that Livy may have left. That she might not even be in Cleveland anymore.

He cleared his throat. "Ah… that's good to know." He looked over to see both Chris and Carrie were grinning at him. He sighed. "It's that obvious, huh?"

They both nodded before Carrie gestured towards the house. "This is your chance to be alone with her. Go. Go talk to her. Or kiss her like you never want to let her go. Or whatever. Just do something. It's driving all of us nuts, watching the two of you suffer like this."

Chris laughed, pulling Carrie against him. "I guarantee this woman is never going to let us live this one down. She called it from the beginning." He shook his head. "I'm slowly learning there's nothing worse than a woman who knows she's right."

"Which, as we all know, is ninety-nine-point-nine percent of the time." Carrie softened this remark with another kiss to his cheek.

Nonchalantly, or so he thought, Sam started to back away, sending both of them a smile. "Okay then, I'll let you two talk that out. I'll catch up with you later. Wish me luck."

Fighting the urge to take off in a sprint, Sam settled for a brisk stride across the yard before running up the steps to the deck. Once there, he was forced to stop a few times to acknowledge people who wanted to say hello.

Finally slipping into the house, the echo of his footsteps hitting the hardwood floors was the only sound beside that of the caterers, who had taken over the kitchen.

Taking the stairs, two at a time, he made his way to the nursery. He came to a stop right inside the doorway.

Livy was standing by the window, her back to him.

Completely unaware Sam had come into the room, she was rocking Trevor in her arms, talking softly to him. Even as young as he was, Trevor seemed to be mesmerized by the huskiness of her voice, his eyes trained on her face.

Sam smiled. He could understand this.

Already he could feel the tension beginning to roll off his body at the familiar and soothing huskiness of her voice. He inched a little closer, closing his eyes as he listened.

"I know… you want to go outside and party like everyone else. And do you know what? If either you or your brother were to do this? You'd be a hit. How could you not, as cute as you both are?"

She sighed. "But it's late. Two late for a little one like you to be up and so wide awake. You need your sleep."

She pressed a kiss to the top of Trevor's head, a sadness creeping into her voice. "Unfortunately, you'll soon learn, you can't always get your way. Or get what you want. Some things just aren't meant to be, even if it turns out to be the one thing you want more than anything else in the world." She pressed her cheek against his. "Oh Trevor, what have I done? What will I do if I've lost Sam for good?"

The emotion in her voice hit Sam hard, her pain becoming his. He had to clear his throat, his voice coming out deep and unsteady in the silence.

"I'm pretty sure you haven't lost him."

She spun around to face him.

"Sam…"

Even in the dim lighting of the room, he could see the tears brimming in her eyes. She opened her mouth as though she was going to speak. Then she shut it, slowly shaking her head.

His voice came out husky with longing. It pulled at her, all the way across the room. "And what you just said… that's not completely true, you know."

Livy found she couldn't remember a single word of what she'd said, her words coming out in a whisper. "What's not true?"

He began to move closer. "You just told Trevor that some things aren't meant to be. That you can't always get what you want."

She swallowed. But the words wouldn't come. The most she could manage was a nod.

He was now standing right next to her. Close enough to reach out and brush his fingers down the side of her face.

He almost sighed with relief.

It felt like heaven to finally be next to her, to be able to touch her.

Encouraged by her stillness and that she hadn't backed away, he moved even closer. "No, if you want something badly enough and the other person wants it just as much, there's always a way. At least, this is what I believe."

It was so hard for her to believe he was so close, his touch having sent her heart beating so hard and fast, she was afraid it was going to burst. Unable to take it all in, she dropped her gaze to the baby she was holding in her arms.

When he took Trevor from her arms, she gazed up at him. He was smiling. "Let me put him in his crib. Since it appears he's finally given up the fight and has fallen asleep."

He gently laid the sleeping baby in his crib, waiting until he was settled. Only then did he turn back to Livy.

Her arms wrapped around herself in an attempt to keep from falling apart completely, she was watching him. Stuffing his hand in his pockets, he followed her lead, his gaze traveling over her, drinking in every detail.

God, how he'd missed her.

Remaining completely silent under his close scrutiny, she was wondering how it was he was even here. After all, she had told him she never wanted to see him again.

She briefly closed her eyes, the memory of that time almost as painful now, as it was then. So many times over the past few days, she'd gone over in her head what she would say to him if she got the chance. But now, given the opportunity, her mind had gone blank. There were only three words running through her mind, over and over again.

I'm so sorry...

Hesitantly running her hand over the railing of Trevor's crib, she finally spoke. "I thought you were in Quebec."

He cleared his throat. "I was. But once I was there, the only thing I could think about was how much I wanted to come home. So, I worked twenty-four-seven to get everything all set up so I could book an earlier flight. I told them I'd be back, but first, there was something I needed to work out."

Yes... and if you can't? Then it doesn't matter what happens. Hell, maybe you'll even move to Quebec.

When she remained silent, he sighed, running his hand through his hair. "It's been a long week. A long and lonely week. With way too much time to think, way too much time to myself."

A faint smile touched his lips. "I guess you could say I've changed, I no longer like being alone."

He jammed his hands back in his pockets, when what he wanted to do was pull her into his arms. If only to get back that feeling he got when he was with her. The feeling he was where he was supposed to be.

Where you belong.

He took a deep breath, the roughness of his voice pulling at her, drawing her closer. "The only thing I could think about was you. Everything else... the jobs, the awards, the money... God, Livy, none of these would mean anything if you weren't with me to share them."

He moved closer, the longing in his voice more intense in the silence that surrounded them. "I love you... and I need you, Livy. More than I've ever loved or needed anyone."

Livy had gone completely still, her fingers going to her face in an attempt to wipe away the tears spilling down her cheeks. She couldn't seem to stop shaking her head, her words coming out even more unsteady than his.

"I... I... *oh, Sam...* I'm so, so sorry. For everything. I didn't mean any of what I said. Honest, I didn't." She started to reach out to him, uncertainty bringing her to drop her hands to her sides. "How can you even want to be with me after what I put you through? I've turned you away... again and again. And then the baby... You should just run. Leave. Now. Before you..."

"Oh, Livy... no..." This came almost in a growl as he swept her into his arms, his mouth coming down on hers in a deep, hungry kiss.

It was a kiss that traveled deep, spreading through her, through him, to consume them both. At her faint moan, her arms reaching up to wrap around his neck, he drew her even harder against him, intensifying the kiss.

Even after his mouth finally left hers, he refused to let her go. He couldn't. Not when he was finally holding her in his arms, something he'd been so afraid he'd never be able to do again. He wasn't going take the chance he could lose her, by letting go.

He rested his forehead against hers, his eyes searching hers. "This is what I came home for. You... it's always you. You're on my mind and you're in my heart. And this is never, ever going to change. Even if you cry. Or challenge every word that comes out of my mouth."

He paused, a hint of a smile coming through in his words. "Or if you're a terrible dancer."

Her head came up, her eyes narrowing. "I am not a..."

Before she could finish, he pressed a kiss to her mouth. He was grinning. "Ah... there's the Livy I love. The Livy I missed. I don't care how you dance, as long as it's with me and in my arms."

His gaze was intense, his eyes darkening as his hands followed the curves of her body to press her against him. His intentions were clear of what he wanted, what he needed.

Remember... it was that hidden passion they'd come to know so well. Waiting to surface. It was there. They could both feel it.

He reached into his pocket. "But first, you're missing something..." He slipped the promise ring he'd given her on her finger, bringing her hand up to his lips for a kiss. "Back where it belongs. After all, a promise is a promise... forever."

His hands drifted down to hold hers. "Come on, I want to take you away from here, to where we can be alone. We have a lot of time to make up and I want to start by holding you in my arms. So, I can love you the way I've been dreaming of all week." A smile flashed across his face. "Possibly even give you some material for the novel you're writing."

His lips drifting to her ear, the husky drop in his voice, sent a shiver through her. "I'm willing to do whatever it takes to help you out with that."

Seriously? She'd let him take her right here in the nursery, right on the floor, after what he just said. As it was, she was already clinging to him for support, as though she hadn't a single bone in her body.

A slow, satisfied smile had come to his face when he felt her lean into him, her hands gripping his arms. He pulled her more tightly against him, his words a deep murmur against her mouth. "I want you, Livy. I live and I breathe for you."

He followed this with another kiss, one that had her melting into him.

So, as you can imagine… that about did it. She was completely and totally gone. She'd follow him anywhere.

She let him lead her across the room before, somehow, she remembered the reason she'd been in the nursery in the first place. She turned to send one last look over at the babies.

Trevor and Hudson were sitting in their cribs, their eyes wide open.

"Oh, no..."

At her cry, Sam turned just in time to watch as Hudson pulled at the railing of the crib in an effort to stand.

Sam's laughter filled the room. He glanced down at Livy. "It looks like we haven't done a very good job, does it? A sign we'll need a lot more practice before we think of having one of our own."

At her quick glance, he grinned. "It going to happen, you know. Probably much sooner than we expect."

He sighed. "I believe there's only one thing we can do."

Her hand still in his, they made their way back to the babies. After Sam handed Trevor over to Libby and he'd tucked Hudson securely against him, he reached for Livy's hand.

"Come on, these guys are going to join the party." He shrugged. "Even though we may have failed here, I believe our job is done. We're going to turn these little guys over to their rightful owners. Like I just told you, there's only one thing I want right now."

He planted a quick kiss to her mouth.

"And this is you."

Each holding a wide-eyed baby in their arms, Sam and Livy were immediately surrounded when they walked out onto the deck. Livy's earlier prediction to Trevor, that he and his brother would be the hit of the party, was confirmed within seconds.

Chester casually strolled over to them, both Hudson and Trevor eagerly reaching for him. After he'd settled a baby in each arm, he shook his head at Livy and Sam. He was laughing. "You guys are easy pushovers, I see. But it's okay. I'm just as bad. I can never get enough of these little buddies of mine. Sophie accuses me of spoiling them." He smiled at the babies, getting two toothless grins in return "But I ask you, how can you possibly spoil a seven-month old?"

He glanced from Sam to Livy, immediately sensing the change between them. There was a new possessiveness in the way Sam was holding Livy against him. While she was leaning into him, as though she couldn't get close enough.

He smiled. It looked like they needed an excuse to make an early exit. "You guys taking off? Because you look like you have a lot to talk about. Or just need some time alone." His wink over at Livy sent a slow blush across her face.

If it was possible, Sam pulled Livy even closer. His eyes meeting Chester's, he grinned. "Yeah... a yes to both of those."

His message to Chester was clear in his eyes, he had no reason to worry. He cleared his throat. "Like I told Livy, we've got time... a lifetime..."

At Chester's nod, Sam reached over to give Hudson and Trevor's little hands a gentle squeeze. "Enjoy the party, guys."

Chester watched as they walked away. When Sophie came to stand next to him, he smiled down at her. "It looks like they finally figured it out." As she took Hudson from him, he shook his head. "But as far as kids go? They're definitely not ready yet for that part of their life."

Sophie gazed up at him.

Then she started to laugh.

"Seriously, Chester? Who is?"

CHAPTER 36

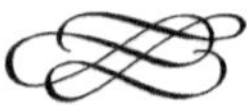

*S*am knew he should slow down and mind the speed limit. But every time he glanced at Livy the heat in his gut tightened and he wanted to press the pedal—hard. Never had a drive felt so endless.

Every look, every brush of her hand stretched minutes into miles, and all he could think about was how badly he wanted her—first in his arms, then even more in his bed.

He hadn't told her where he was taking her, but he had a feeling she already knew. Like him, she didn't care where they'd end up—all that mattered was that they were finally together.

They needed to be alone.

They needed this more than air.

The cars ahead slamming to a stop, Sam hit the brakes, his arm shooting out instinctively to shield her.

He smiled over at her, recalling how the same thing had happened when he picked her up from the gas station—the day she came home and everything was so new and uncertain between them.

And now look how far they'd come.

He stole a glance at her.

A faint smile played at the corners of her mouth—the kind of smile that told him she was right back inside that wild, unforgettable moment with him.

He cleared his throat. "That was some crazy day, wasn't it?"

Her breath hitched as she turned to him, eyes wide.

She still didn't understand how he could read her so perfectly every single time.

Keeping one hand on the wheel, he eased the SUV into the next lane and let out a low, amused sound. "Your face gives you away every time, sweetheart. "Not with anyone else. Just me."

"I'll have to remember that so I don't get myself in trouble." She laughed softly. "And yes—I hope I never have to live through a day like that again. I was miserable, probably terrible company. In all fairness, I felt like my whole world was falling apart."

She paused, voice dropping. "I felt like such a failure. I didn't know what to do or where to turn."

Reaching for her hand, he threaded their fingers together. "You'll never have to feel that way again. I'll be here. Always."

He leaned over and kissed her—long and slow, the kind of kiss that made the world beyond the windshield disappear. When they finally broke apart, his whisper brushed her lips. "Ah, Livy... I missed you."

"I missed you, too."

The traffic now at a complete standstill, he groaned. "Come on, already. What the hell is going on?"

Livy's hand tightened in his. He looked down at their joined fingers, then back at her. Her smile was small and sure. "Remember what you said? We have time... a lifetime. I'm not going anywhere. Not unless you're right there with me." Her voice held the quiet certainty of someone who meant every word.

She was right. As long as they were together, nothing else mattered—not even the clock. Maybe these stupid delays weren't so terrible after all.

He leaned in and pressed another gentle kiss to her mouth. "That's all I needed, baby. To hear you say it."

Since it looked like they weren't moving anytime soon, he put the

SUV in park. "Talk to me," he said, smiling. "Tell me everything you did while I was away. All the little details of what went on in your life. Did you do any more writing? And if you did, are you going to let me read what you have so far? This, of course, would be only to give you a man's point of view."

He squeezed her hand. "And then there's the most important thing of all… tell me again how much you missed me."

Twenty minutes later Sam set the SUV in park and cut the engine. He hurried around, opened the passenger door for Livy, and pressed a quick kiss to her mouth before taking her hand and leading her to his front door.

Once they were inside, he watched conflicting emotions flicker across her face as she slowly took in the room. Her gaze drifted toward the hallway that led to his bedroom, then skittered away.

He wasn't surprised. There was still too much left unsaid between them. The last time they had been here, it had ended in an argument that exploded into hurtful accusations and a slammed door—her parting words a furious, "Never in a million years."

Everything after that had spiraled, widening the rift between them.

If only he could gather up every one of those ugly words and throw them so far they could never be found again. He wanted to hold her, to kiss away every hurt he'd caused. He wanted the way she melted into him, the soft surrender of her body against his, the passionate, loving Livy he knew so well.

God, how much he craved all of this.

But he knew she needed time.

So, that's what he would give her.

He rubbed his hands together and cleared his throat. "Would you like a glass of wine? Toast to a new beginning?"

Some of the tension eased from her shoulders at the warmth in his voice. She nodded and walked over to the island, leaning on the counter across from him.

"Okay," he said, smiling. "While I take care of the wine, you can be in charge of the music." He tapped his phone and slid it across the counter to her. "There—choose whatever you want. I set it to play through the speakers, so just hit play when you're ready."

He reached for the wine bottle and glasses, and was about to pull the cork, when a jarring blast of bass and electric guitar exploded through the condo. The bottle nearly slipped from his hands.

He lunged for the phone, and after turning down the volume, he looked at her, brows raised.

Horrified, but at the same time, she started to laugh. "Oh my God, I'm so sorry. I must have hit the wrong thing. You know how terrible I am with anything tech related."

She watched him type, mesmerized by the movement of his fingers. The memory of those same fingers on her skin—and how they'd traced every curve of her body—she drew in a steadying breath and lifted her eyes to his.

The air between them thickened, charged with everything they hadn't yet dared to say. She watched as he set the phone down with slow, deliberate care, his eyes never leaving hers.

"Livy..." The sound that left him was low and rough, almost pained as he leaned across the counter. His fingers sliding gently beneath her chin, he drew her even closer as he brushed the softest, most tender kiss across her mouth.

A shiver raced through her, so full of longing it made her heart ache. For one endless heartbeat neither of them moved, lips barely parted, breaths mingling. Then he kissed her again, still gentle, but deeper this time, sealing a promise that went far beyond words.

As if on cue, Josh Groban's rich voice filled the room. Sam's mouth hovered over hers before he pulled back, clearing his throat with a laugh. "I certainly hope you're making a mental note of that for your writing. If that wasn't perfectly timed, I don't know what would be."

He leaned in again, kissing her gently, lingering a beat longer this time. "This music is more like you," he murmured against her lips. "Classical-rock. Much better than whatever you just blasted at full volume."

His glance turned teasing. "But could it be your preferences have changed? You still do like romantic music, don't you?"

He grinned. "Don't worry, I haven't forgotten the few things you're not fond of… such as unnecessary endearments, or someone to lean on. No matter how much that person wishes you would."

Filled with the urge to touch him, she reached over and ran her fingers slowly through his hair, brushing it back from his face. "You know that wasn't what I intended to happen. And you know I like romantic music. How could I not? I write romance novels, remember?"

He caught her hand and brought it to his mouth for a kiss. "*Hmm…* and what about the endearments? Or someone to lean on? Could you learn to like those, too?"

She smiled, soft and shy. "I think… well, I'm sure I could learn to like those, too. But only with the right person."

He cleared his throat. "So… just to be clear, am I that person?"

Tracing the marbled granite with her fingertip, her eyes searched his. "I don't know… you tell me."

He went completely still, suddenly unsure where to start, what to say.

God, there was so much he wanted to tell her.

Starting with how much he'd missed her—so damn much. He never knew it was possible to miss someone the way he'd missed her.

He wanted to explain that he hadn't meant what he'd said about the baby. He'd been so frustrated, so terrified of what she might do, the decisions she might make that didn't include him.

But most of all, he wanted to tell her again how much he loved her. That hadn't changed. It never would.

He reached over and gently lifted her chin with one finger. "*Aw, Livy…* let me be that person. Give us another chance."

The longing in his voice mirrored everything she was feeling. *Her answer in the way she leaned into his kiss, giving herself to him completely.*

Without another word, he picked up the glasses and bottle of wine. Linking their fingers, he led her down the hall to his bedroom.

He set the bottle and glasses on the nightstand and turned to her. She was watching him, eyes luminous in the low light.

A groan rising from deep in his throat, he reached for her. "Aw, baby... come here."

Baby... yeah, she was definitely getting used to that.

She walked straight into his arms. This was where she belonged. It didn't matter what had happened in the past. It didn't matter what tomorrow might bring. What mattered was right now—this moment, this man...

And how much she loved him.

Reaching up to link her fingers behind his neck, she gazed into his eyes. Her voice came out husky, the perfect form of seduction. "Just so you know, you're that person. You always have been."

She rose on her toes and kissed him softly. "And if you're really sure you want to take me on, you always will be."

Burying his hands in her hair, he brought her mouth to his. The moment their lips touched, the memory of the love they'd shared before ignited again—hotter, deeper, more certain than ever.

He poured everything he had into the kiss.

He was sure.

He had never been more sure of anything in his life.

There was a deep sense of healing in the love that followed.

This union wasn't just about desire or need. Each kiss, each touch, and each whispered word was a vow between two people who had found in each other their other half, their soul mate, their lover, and their best friend.

It was a love that ran deep.

A forever kind of love.

The kind of love Livy had always wanted to write about.

Much, much later...

The bedsheets in disarray around them, Livy sighed with pure contentment as she trailed a fingertip along Sam's lower lip. "I'm sorry I didn't believe you."

He opened his mouth to answer, but she silenced him with a gentle press of fingers to his lips, shaking her head. "Please, let me finish. I think… when I saw you and her… Valerie… I had already convinced myself it was going to happen. Maybe not with her, but with someone. I should have trusted you. I should have listened instead of assuming the worst. But instead I went crazy. I feel so ashamed, and I don't know how I can ever make it up to you."

He gathered her close, his arms wrapping around her like a promise. "Baby, we both said things we shouldn't have. The pregnancy, then the loss… it put us both on guard."

He chuckled. "Some of the things that came out of my mouth sure as hell weren't what I wanted to say."

She lifted her head, eyes questioning. "Like what?"

He was shaking his head, "The comment I made about the country-western song. I don't know where that came from."

She smiled against his chest. "I don't know… it sort of fit the whole situation, if you stop to think about it. We couldn't have scripted it any better if we'd tried."

"The problem was I didn't want to be part of any song. It was only you I wanted. I had already started falling in love with the idea of the baby coming into our lives, and I wasn't going to let you push me away, no matter what."

He pressed a kiss into her hair. "I would've loved that baby as my own, Livy. If only because it was a part of you."

Livy wrapped her arms tighter around his neck. "Oh, Sam… I know. Having that to hold on to was what kept me sane. I can't even begin to tell you how many times I wished the baby could have been ours. I know I was wrong to think that, but I did. You'd make such a wonderful father."

He kissed her mouth, slow and tender. "If it was wrong, then I'm just as guilty. Because I felt the same. Someday… remember? We have a lifetime ahead of us."

Livy closed her eyes. All the tension and uncertainty of the past few days had finally drained away. Sheltered in Sam's arms—the only place she ever wanted to be—she was at peace.

Sam pressed another kiss to her hair. "Right now, I think what we both need is sleep. You told me earlier you weren't planning on going anywhere. Well, neither am I. I love you, baby."

Already drifting off, her answer came in a whisper. "I love you, too."

CHAPTER 37

*L*ivy opened her eyes to a loud rumble of thunder.

It traveled through the building complex housing Sam's condo, before ending in a big boom.

Squinting at the clock on the nightstand, she was surprised to see it was almost nine-thirty, the dark and overcast sky making it feel much earlier in the morning.

She burrowed deeper under the comforter and closed her eyes. She wasn't quite ready to get up yet.

After all, it was Saturday.

She heard the front door slam, the sound of Sam's whistling bringing a smile to her face.

"Hey, sleepyhead..."

She opened her eyes. He was sitting on the bed and smiling as he nodded over at the two take-out cups on the nightstand. "I brought you coffee. I also picked up croissants from that little bakery down the street. I was told they just came out of the oven. But you'll have to get out of bed and go to the kitchen for one of those."

He pulled his shirt up and over his head, his words muffled. "Not a good morning to go running. I got caught up in this torrential downpour and now everything's soaked."

His shorts were the next to hit the floor. Pushing aside the comforter to settle next to her, he pulled her against him. He gave a long, satisfied sigh. "*Mmm...* you feel so good. You're so nice and warm."

His foot, traveling down her leg, nudged hers. He chuckled. "Well, this is a first. Even your feet are warm."

She snuggled closer, the hard length of him against her already sending her pulse skittering, her heart echoing in response. "Do you want me to warm you up? It might be a smart move on your part to accept my offer, because who knows when this could happen again?"

He lifted his head to look down at her, a sudden spark in his gaze. "Well, then... in that case, I'm all yours. But how about I help you get started?"

Lifting the hair away from her neck, he pressed a slow kiss to the base of her throat. And being the nice guy that he was, always ready to please, he didn't stop there.

Which was more than fine with her.

His fingers trailing through Livy's hair, Sam gave a deep, contented sigh. "I don't know how I lived without you."

Her eyes closed, she gave a long, lazy sigh. "I don't know. Doesn't seem possible, does it?"

"No, it doesn't." He chuckled before placing a kiss in her hair. "What are your plans for tonight?"

She gazed up at him. "My plans? I haven't really thought about it. Do you have something in mind?"

He edged the hair back from her forehead, an earnest look on his face. "I want to take you out to dinner. I made reservations at Jake's Place. I want to celebrate us."

"I would very much like to go out to dinner with you. And I would love to celebrate us." She smiled. "We really do have a lot to celebrate, don't we?" She sighed, a sudden sadness in her features. "Starting with how I completely shook up your life."

"No worries. I have a feeling, with you, life will be full of shake-ups." He chuckled. "But I'm looking forward to it… I think…"

She laughed. "Hey, I've sent out plenty of warning signs. And you should've realized what you were getting into from the beginning, back to when we first met. If you still thought there was a chance of something happening between us after that crazy night, well… what can I say?"

He gazed down at her, a tenderness in his eyes. "Baby, I love you. And I always will." He shook his head. "Even though you can't dance worth a darn."

He was laughing as he threw the comforter aside, diving out of the bed to dodge the pillow she threw at him. After he pulled on a dry pair of shorts and a tee shirt, he picked up the two take-out cups. He sent her a teasing smile as he headed for the door.

"If you want your croissant, you better hurry. Otherwise, I could very well eat both of them. With some of that homemade strawberry jam your aunt gave me. It seems I've worked up quite an appetite."

Scrambling out of the bed, she wasn't too far behind him.

CHAPTER 38

*S*am was nervous.

He'd be the first to tell you, he'd never before been this worked up over something.

Nope, never....

Standing in front of the bathroom mirror, he ran the brush through his hair one last time, trying to ignore the piece of tissue stuck to his cheek.

He tossed the brush down on the vanity, a wry smile on his face.

When is the last time you cut yourself shaving? The night of the football awards banquet in high school? Come on... get your act together.

He slipped into his sports coat and after double checking the pockets and satisfied with the contents, he headed for the kitchen.

His mouth felt dry, like he couldn't swallow. Thinking he must be having a panic attack, he grabbed a bottle of water out of the refrigerator.

He then proceeded to miss his mouth completely when he took a drink, dribbling a good portion of the water down his shirtfront. Muttering to himself, he was mopping up the water with a paper towel when Livy walked into the kitchen.

The dress she was wearing was Carrie's.

Livy hadn't asked to borrow the dress. It was only when she told Carrie she was planning to wear the same dress she wore for the rehearsal dinner, Carrie insisted on dropping off this new dress. It would be perfect, she said.

For some reason, she had been horrified by Livy's choice of outfit. She needed to wear something new and different, she told her.

Something sexy...

The dress was definitely sexy. And certainly more revealing than what Livy usually wore. It was a deep cobalt blue, sleeveless and dipped low in the back. It was also form fitting and a heck of a lot shorter than she would have chosen.

When Sam turned to see her standing in front of him, he halted in his tracks. His first instinct was to fling the paper towel over his shoulder, take her into his arms and kiss the living daylights out of her. But at the same time, he was almost afraid to touch her.

Crossing his arms and leaning back against the counter, a bemused smile tugged at the corner of his mouth

She was perfect.

Everything... the sexy, pewter high-heeled sandals, the flawless fit of her dress and her hair, falling in shiny waves to her shoulders.

Then there were her eyes, her beautiful eyes. Like he'd told her, he became lost in them—every single time.

When he saw the blush filling her cheeks, he pushed away from the counter and slowly sauntered his way over to her. "Baby... you look absolutely gorgeous. I'm one lucky guy."

He pressed a quick kiss to her mouth, to then became all business-like, taking hold of her arm. "But we better get hopping... we don't want to be late for our reservation."

Before she could even utter a single word, he whisked her out the door.

Livy was a little worried about Sam.

He seemed preoccupied.

He also seemed to be a bit on the nervous side.

No sooner had they been seated at the restaurant, he knocked over his glass of water. He'd also shoveled his dinner down so fast, she wondered if he even knew what he ate. When he saw she was watching him, he'd quickly assured her this was only because he was really hungry.

She hadn't been convinced, but he'd seemed so anxious she believe him, she'd only nodded.

She'd also caught him staring at her during dinner, a preoccupied expression on his face. On at least four different occasions, this had happened. Two of these times, she had to wave her hand in front of his face to get his attention.

This was when she finally decided to say something. "Are you sure you're okay?"

His answer was bright—more like overly cheerful, she'd have to say. "Yes, of course I am. And why shouldn't I be? I'm with the most beautiful woman in this restaurant tonight."

She shook her head at this. "Sam, you're scaring me. Tell me what's going on? Are you worried about Jake?"

When they'd first arrived, Sam had asked their server if Jake was the chef of the evening. A worried look coming over her face, she told him Jake had called in to say because of a personal matter, if he came in at all, it would be late. Since he was leaving within the next couple of days for the set-up of the new restaurant, they were concerned. It had to be something pretty serious to keep him away. He never missed his shift at the restaurant.

Sam rubbed his jaw, still unsettled by the server's words, then stood and held out his hand. He couldn't seem to sit still. "No, I'm sure he's fine. Come on, let's go for a walk on the pier."

Hand in hand, they casually strolled down the pier. Leaning against the railing, they watched as a large yacht went through the slow process of docking at the next pier over.

Again, Sam glanced at his watch.

This had Livy wondering if now she should be more angry than concerned. It was almost as though something more important had pushed their date into second place.

She didn't understand... what was going on with him?

Wasn't it Sam who had suggested this dinner? "To celebrate us" he'd said. Those had been his exact words.

Just as she was about to remind him of this, he glanced once more at his watch. Unbeknownst to Livy, this was the message he saw.

Fifteen minutes and you're ready to go. Good luck!

A big smile on his face, he grabbed her hand and began leading her back into the restaurant. "We need to leave... there's someplace I want to take you."

As Sam pulled his SUV out onto the main road, he didn't even notice Jake go flying pass them when he turned into the Jake's Place parking lot.

CHAPTER 39

How am I supposed to find the strength
to keep believing, when you always leave,
taking another piece of my heart with you.
~ Anonymously Yours

As Jake Martin pulled into Jake's parking lot was as unaware of Livy and Sam as they had been of him.

His mind was filled with Gracie.

After he parked his Jeep, he strode into the restaurant, a storm of anger and confusion etched across his face. It was enough to warn his co-workers he had zero intention of explaining why he was late.

He made it very obvious he'd only shown up because he had to. He'd promised to teach his temporary replacement every little detail of his signature dishes before he left to oversee the new restaurant—and that was exactly what he would do.

The minute he was finished, he was gone. They could manage without him.

All he wanted was to be back in his condo. Where he could check on her. If only to make sure she hadn't left again.

He sighed, dragging a hand through his hair. The last thing he'd expected when he'd returned home earlier from the gym was to find someone sitting on his front steps.

At first he hadn't even wanted to get out of the Jeep. Because even though he was almost certain it was her, he didn't think he could handle the crushing disappointment if it wasn't.

God, not again.

It was only when he stood right in front of her that she finally lifted her face and looked straight into his eyes.

Gracie...

It had been six months since he'd last stared into those eyes and let himself believe nothing had changed. They still pulled him under, still made him hope—against every scrap of evidence—that this time things between them could actually work.

Unfortunately, hope had never been enough. Not last time. Or the time before that. Or any of the times before that.

Nope. Every single time he started to believe, he only had to turn around for a second and she was gone.

Again.

He averted his gaze and stuffed his hands deep into his pockets—anything to stop himself from reaching out and hauling her into his arms. He still had a little pride left. What little there was.

He cleared his throat. "Hey, Peaches... what are you doing here?" Peaches was the nickname he'd given her the day they met. Why he'd chosen it, he couldn't remember anymore, but it had stuck.

She'd only been thirteen then, and he—eighteen and far too cool—had seen her as nothing more than his best friend's kid sister. He and Sam had even argued when Sam warned him Gracie had a crush on him and told him not to encourage her. It wasn't until after culinary school, when he ran into her at a friend's party, that something had shifted. That night he finally saw her differently.

And you've been hooked ever since.

Yeah. And if you think back to that night, you'll remember how she got totally drunk and passed out on you. Maybe that's part of the problem—you always block out the bad times.

Blinking away the memories, he looked down at her. She was still gazing up at him, arms wrapped tightly around her knees like she was trying to disappear inside herself. The clothes she wore were too big, her tennis shoes scuffed and worn. He wondered if they'd once belonged to someone else.

She looked like she'd lost weight again. He didn't even want to think about what that meant.

When she finally spoke, her voice was barely a whisper. "I need your help, Jake."

Trying not to drown in her eyes, he let out a weary sigh. "If it's money you want again, I can't do it. You know what I told you last time. I'll do anything but that. I'm not going to support the life you've chosen. You mean too much to me for that."

She shook her head quickly. "No. I don't want money. I just… I need help. I can't do this anymore." Her voice cracked on a sob. "But I don't know where to start."

When he stayed silent, she pushed to her feet. "Okay, I get it. I've worn out my welcome. I'll leave."

"You'll never wear out your welcome with me. You know that." The words were barely out before he caught her arm and pulled her against him. "I'll help you. But you have to promise you'll stick with it this time. I'll be here for you. If I see you slipping again… I'm done for good."

When she nodded against his chest, he slid a finger under her chin and lifted her face to his. Fighting the fierce urge to kiss her until they both forgot everything else, he cleared his throat instead. "When's the last time you slept? Or ate?"

Resting her head against his chest, she sighed. "I don't know… maybe yesterday? But what I really want right now, more than anything, is a long, hot shower."

Still holding her close, he slid the key into the lock and pushed open the door to his condo. "Okay. Go take your shower. You know where everything is. While you're in there, I'll make you something to eat."

So completely wrapped up in the solid warmth of his arms, it took real effort for her to answer. She sighed again. "I feel like I've been dreaming about your cooking for months. Like that omelet with caramelized onions and spinach…"

He chuckled softly. "I'll see what I can do. Go on."

Leaning against the counter, Jake took another slow drink of his coffee.

He felt both frustrated and heartbroken as he watched Gracie eat, shoveling the food in like she hadn't seen a real meal in days.

Sensing his gaze, she glanced up, color flooding her cheeks. She laid her fork down slowly. "I… I'm sorry. It's just that I'm so hungry. And this is so good. I'll try to—"

He groaned. "Honey, don't apologize. Eat as fast and as much as you want."

He set his cup down and ran a hand through his hair on a heavy sigh. "It's just… I'm so damn relieved to see you. To know you're still alive. It's been hell not knowing where you were, what you were doing, if you were even safe."

Or even alive.

But he wouldn't let himself finish that thought.

He closed his eyes briefly, shaking his head. "So right now I just want to take it all in. Get my fill of you." The smile he gave her was wistful. "If only as proof you're really here."

Her eyes filled with tears. She toyed with her fork. "I know… I'm sorry. I've been so much trouble to everyone. I don't want to be. Honest, I don't."

He slid onto the stool beside her and gently tucked a strand of hair behind her ear. Once again he tried to avoid her eyes—the longing in them was almost more than he could stand.

"Peaches, we're going to beat this. Together. For starters, you're going to stop blaming yourself. You have so much to offer once you believe it. And I'm going to do everything I can to help you see that."

"Promise?" Her eyes—still that deep, crystal blue that reminded him of a cloudless winter sky—searched his.

"I promise." This time he met her gaze. A promise wasn't a promise if you couldn't look the person in the eye. But Gracie was the one who looked away, her fingers creeping up to her neck before she dropped her hand into her lap.

He noticed immediately.

Back on the front steps, the first thing he'd checked was whether she was still wearing the necklace he'd given her—the thin silver chain with the tiny peach pendant, a symbol of the faith and trust they'd once promised each other. She'd sworn she'd never take it off.

Now it was gone.

He wasn't going to ask. Truthfully, he wasn't sure he wanted to know where it had gone—or why.

He picked up her fork and handed it back to her. "Here. Finish everything on your plate, or I'll be insulted. You know how big my ego gets when it comes to my cooking."

Her faint smile encouraged him, and he smiled back. "Then you can sleep for as long as you need. I have to go into the restaurant, but I won't leave until you're settled."

Jake tucked the quilt around Gracie with careful hands. "There you go. If you need anything, you have my number. I shouldn't be back too late."

He was almost out the door when her soft plea stopped him cold. "Will you stay with me until I fall asleep? Lately... I've been having such bad dreams."

She held her breath, terrified he would ask what kind of dreams. She didn't think she could bear telling him the ugly details that haunted her now.

Relief washed through her when he said nothing. He simply settled beside her on the bed.

He couldn't refuse the wistful catch in her voice. And he was almost certain, in her exhausted state, she'd be out in seconds. He made sure not to touch her when he lay down. He didn't trust himself.

"Thank you," she murmured, the words followed by a long, shaky sigh.

He nodded, even though her eyes were already closed. He didn't trust himself to speak, either. Everything he was holding inside could come spilling out, and he wouldn't be able to stop it.

All that can wait—now is not the time.

He didn't know if he was more tired than he realized or simply because she was finally next to him again, but when her breathing evened out in sleep, he drifted off too.

It was only when she cried out—sharp and frightened—that he jolted awake. She'd shoved the quilt aside and grabbed onto him, clinging tight, those tiny whimpering sounds tearing at his heart. He knew she was trapped in one of the nightmares she'd mentioned.

He wrapped his arms around her, murmuring soft, soothing words until the struggling stopped. When her breathing finally slowed and deepened again, he eased himself off the bed, tucked the quilt back around her, and slipped from the room.

After leaving a note on the counter, he headed for the restaurant.

He was so damn afraid that when he came back, she'd be gone again.

Which is precisely why the restaurant was the last place on earth he wanted to be right now.

CHAPTER 40

*L*ivy leaned her head against the headrest of Sam's SUV. The warm summer night air, blowing in from the open windows, ruffled through her hair.

She glanced over at Sam. "Are you going to tell me where we're going and what you're so excited about?"

He smiled as he reached for her hand. "You'll just have to wait and see."

He shot her a teasing glance. "I'll give you one clue... I need your opinion on something I've been working on."

Sam slowed his car to turn down a driveway. Puzzled, Livy glanced over at him. "The house by the lake? Why are we here?" Peering out at the house and surprised to see lights in the windows, she glanced over at him again. "Oh... I think I understand. You've been helping the new owners with the renovation and they've asked you to check out the latest progress." She grew quiet as she studied the house again. "But why do they want you to do this now? Did the house need to be rewired for new lighting and they wanted to see it at night?"

Sam shook his head, a faint smile on his face. "My, my… so curious, so many questions. Why don't you wait until we get inside? Maybe then you'll get some answers."

He pulled the car up to the side of the house. Before he got out, he leaned over and cupping her chin in his hand, he gave her a long, sweet kiss.

Her lashes fluttered open to find his eyes shining into hers, his voice low and husky. "I love you."

Before she could respond, he was out of the car and around to open her door. Taking her hand, he led her up the walk to the front door.

Busily commenting on the improved state of the newly cleared flower beds, Livy was completely unprepared for what greeted her when they walked inside.

All of the dust was gone, leaving the large foyer almost sparkling. The marble and mahogany of the staircase had been buffed and polished to look brand new. From where they were standing, she could see there was now an ornate crystal chandelier hanging in the dining room.

To say Livy was in shock, would be an understatement. She gazed slowly around the room before she finally looked over at Sam. "Oh, Sam… you were right when you said this house could be brought back to life. The owners must be thrilled with the renovations so far. Who wouldn't love to live in a house like this?"

He sent her that quirky look he always had when he was slightly amused by what she said. "*Hmm…* so you approve, do you?"

"Oh yes, it's almost exactly how I remember it, minus the furniture, of course."

She abruptly stilled, and tilting her head, she gazed up towards the second floor. "Is that music?"

It was.

And it sounded very familiar.

"When I fall in love...
It will be forever..."

At her puzzled expression, Sam placed his finger against her lips and taking her hand, he began leading her up the stairs. "Come on, I think we should check it out."

She held back, worry creasing her brow. "I don't know... maybe we shouldn't. I feel like we're trespassing."

He merely smiled. "I think it will be fine. Come on, don't you want to see what's been done with the master bedroom? I'd really like to get your opinion."

"Or I'll never fall in love..."

It was when he brought her into the master bedroom, she began to shake, her hands going to her mouth.

The room looked like a scene out of a fairy tale. There was a trail of rose petals leading to the bed, with more rose petals scattered across the plush cream-colored bedding. Candles were everywhere, flickering in the breeze blowing in from the open windows, the long sheer curtains billowing in the warm night air.

The tears had already begun to slip down her face before she turned to Sam.

He was down on one knee and in his hand, he was holding a small black velvet box. It was open to show a beautiful round cut diamond ring.

An engagement ring.

At first, she could only stare at him, her lips parted in shock. But then, she saw how nervous he was. That he would even feel this way, made her love him even more.

Her hands clasped over her heart, she moved closer.

He cleared his throat.

"Livy, I love you. You've become my life, the reason for everything I do. I want to share all of your dreams, all of your hopes and be there for you when you need me the most. I want to wake up next to you every morning, if only to know you're mine for another day. And I want to make babies with you… beautiful babies. But most of all, I want you… only you."

He paused, his gaze so intense, she could barely breathe.

"Baby, will you marry me?"

She was in his arms even before his last words had left his mouth, hers covering his in a kiss that seemed to go on forever.

It was when she felt him start to smile against her lips, she leaned back to look at him.

He cleared his throat. "Even though, by that kiss, I'm pretty sure your answer is a yes, I'd still like to hear you say it aloud."

Half crying, half laughing, she framed his face in her hands and gazing into the eyes of the only man she would ever love, her words were a vow against his lips.

"*Yes*, Sam Bridges… a thousand times, yes. I love you. I will always love you."

"And the moment I know…
That you feel this way, too…"

But hold on a minute… this was Livy. The same Livy who had that independent streak, along with a little bit of self-doubt, still hanging around in the back of her mind.

Obviously, this was a Mazzori trait.

She searched his face. "Are you sure you want to do this?"

Sam had removed the promise ring she was wearing, to slip it on the finger of her other hand. Once he was satisfied the engagement ring was now on her finger and right where it should be, he nodded. "Oh, baby… I'm sure. I've never been so sure of anything in my life."

A sudden twinkle appeared in his eyes. "There's also the fact I had the ring engraved, so it probably can't be returned."

Surprisingly, her answer to this was only to give him another kiss before she gazed down at her hands, smiling at the two rings. "I do believe this could be considered a double promise."

Then her expression became serious as she reached up to give him another kiss. "I promise you'll never have to return either of these. Never."

He kissed her right back. "And my promise to you is I'm going to hold you to that."

He'd taken her hand, leading her over to the bed. She hesitated, pulling back. "Sam, what if the people who own this house come up here?"

She sent a nervous glance towards the door to the room. "Do you know if they're even here?"

He merely smiled as he gently pushed her back on the bed, to settle next to her. The slow kisses he began pressing along her jaw sent shivers through her. To the point she almost forgot what she had asked him.

The owners... remember?

"Sam..."

He gazed down at her "I don't think we need to worry. Yes, they're here, but I know for a fact, one of them more than approves of us being here."

His lips went on to trail across her cheeks before ending at her mouth. "And from what I know of the other one, I'm pretty sure they can be easily persuaded to agree."

Trying to ignore his kisses, which at the moment, was becoming almost impossible, she pushed her hands against his chest. "Sam, please... I don't want them to..."

Her words were swallowed up in another kiss before he whispered in her ear. "Baby, we're the owners. I bought this house. I bought it for you."

At the stunned expression on her face, he smiled as he moved so she was beneath him. Lifting himself to his elbows, he buried his hands in her hair, his eyes smiling into hers. "Livy, I want to spend the rest of my life making all of your dreams come true. Starting with you walking down the stairs of this house... *our house...* on our wedding day. Your eyes searching for only me."

A teasing smile tweaked the corner of his mouth.

"Well, maybe... I might insist on walking down those steps with you. A wedding dress, stairs and you? *Hmm…* this seems a little risky, wouldn't you agree?"

She started to smile as he pressed another kiss to the pulse beating in her neck, his lips lingering a little longer. "I want to celebrate all of the birthdays, anniversaries and holidays with our family and friends, gathered around the table in the dining room."

His eyes holding hers captive, his lips teased hers. "And finally, I want this room to be our own little oasis, our hideaway. Where together, we can shut out the rest of the world. Where you can curl up on the window seat, writing or doing whatever your heart desires… maybe even dream of me."

"Sam… but I… you… *Oh, Sam…*" She threw her arms around him, shaking her head. It appeared, once again, Livy was speechless.

He kissed away the new tears falling down her face.

"*Aw, Livy…* will you please let me love you? I want to find out what it feels like to make love to the only woman I'll ever love, the woman who just accepted my proposal of marriage. I have a feeling it's going to be even more than wonderful."

A smile on his lips, his mouth hovered over hers.

"Baby… it's going to be amazing."

"It's when I'll fall in love, over and over again…
with you…"

~

Aunt Evelyn's Chocolate Cannoli Recipe

Sam gives these a thumbs up! Aunt Evelyn swears, on her hand mixer, it's the mascarpone cheese and toasted almonds that makes them so good. She already has plans of making a big batch of them when Sam and Livy get married.

(By the way, she and Angie have become Facebook friends and Angie has already offered to help her make them.)

Filling Ingredients:
    2 cartons (8 ounce each) mascarpone cheese
    1/3 cup powdered sugar
    4 teaspoons unsweetened cocoa powder
    1 teaspoon vanilla
    1/2 teaspoon finely shredded orange peel
    1/4 cup mini semi-sweet chocolate chips
    1/4 cup toasted and finely chopped almonds

Cannoli Shell Ingredients:
    2 cups all-purpose flour
    1/2 cup sugar
    1/2 cup unsweetened cocoa powder
    1/8 teaspoon salt
    1/4 cup shortening
    2 eggs, slightly beaten
    1/4 cup milk
    2 tablespoons honey
    1 egg white
    Oil for deep frying
    1 cup mini semi-sweet chocolate chips, melted
    1/2 cup toasted and finely chopped almonds
    Powdered sugar, optional

Directions for Filling: In a medium bowl stir together mascarpone cheese, powdered sugar, cocoa powder, vanilla, and orange peel until almost smooth. Stir in 1/4 cup chocolate chips and 1/4 cup chopped almonds. Cover and chill.

Directions for Cannoli Shells:

1. In medium bowl, stir together all-purpose flour, sugar, cocoa powder, and salt. Using a pastry blender, cut in shortening into flour mixture until mixture resembles coarse crumbs.
2. In small bowl, stir together beaten eggs, milk, and honey. Add egg mixture to flour mixture. Stir just until mixture forms a ball. Divide dough in half.
3. On a lightly floured surface, roll each dough portion into a 16-inch square. Cut each square into sixteen 4-inch squares. Wrap each square lightly around a cannoli mold.
4. In a small bowl, lightly beat 1 egg white. Moisten overlapping edges of the dough with the egg white; pressing gently to seal.
5. Fry cannoli shells, a few at a time, in deep, hot vegetable oil (360°F) about 1 to 3 minutes or until golden brown. Remove from hot oil and carefully slide shells from the molds and drain on paper towels. Cool. Repeat with remaining squares and other half of dough.
6. Dip ends of cooled cannoli shells in the melted chocolate, then in chopped almonds. Chill until shells are ready to be filled.
7. To assemble, spoon filling into a pastry bag fitted with a large open star or round tip. Pipe filling into cannoli shells. If desired, cover and chill for up to 1 hour.
8. Before serving, sprinkle cannoli with powdered sugar, if desired.

10 to 12 Servings

ABOUT THE AUTHOR

~

L. B. Joyce lives in Chagrin Falls, Ohio. A freelance artist by day, with designing Christmas ornaments her specialty, she's also a writer by night. She loves getting lost in a good book, has redecorated almost every room in her house more times than she'd like to admit, loves baking up a storm in her kitchen, hates housework with a passion and will drive just about anywhere because of her fear of flying.

To keep up with news of the first eight books of the Twelve Months, Twelve Love Stories series - *A Million Decembers, For the Love of July, February's Angel, Promise Me November, An Unexpected June, A January to Remember, September's Moonlight Serenade, and Goodbye Heartbreak, Hello May, and March, a Song and a Dance* - along with the first book of the new *Holidays in White Oaks Valley* series, *A Grand Slam Kind of Christmas,* be sure to check out:

Website/blog at: lbjoyceauthor.com

Or if you're on Facebook at: @ LBJoyceAuthor

Then take a minute to check out the latest L. B. Bear Christmas Ornament designs and just about everything you ever wanted to know about Christmas on Facebook at: @LBGlitterGirl.

Email: lbjoyce12@gmail.com - questions and comments welcome!

ACKNOWLEDGMENTS

When I Fall in Love
Songwriters: Edward Heyman, Victor Young

Cover by *Soxsational Covers*